FINDING DAN

FINDING DAN

MARK QUINN

Copyright © 2016 by Mark Quinn.

Library of Congress Control Number: 2016918102
ISBN: Hardcover   978-1-5144-9970-2
        Softcover   978-1-5144-9969-6
        eBook   978-1-5144-9968-9

All rights reserved. No part of this book may be reproduced or transmitted in any form or by any means, electronic or mechanical, including photocopying, recording, or by any information storage and retrieval system, without permission in writing from the copyright owner.

This is a work of fiction. Names, characters, places and incidents either are the product of the author's imagination or are used fictitiously, and any resemblance to any actual persons, living or dead, events, or locales is entirely coincidental.

Any people depicted in stock imagery provided by Thinkstock are models, and such images are being used for illustrative purposes only.
Certain stock imagery © Thinkstock.

Print information available on the last page.

Rev. date: 11/08/2016

To order additional copies of this book, contact:
Xlibris
800-056-3182
www.Xlibrispublishing.co.uk
Orders@Xlibrispublishing.co.uk
742243

Contents

Thursday, 2 November 1967 1
   Coalisland

March 1974 3
   Edendork

July 1998 7
   Phelim

Buckshot, 7 December 1922 13
   by Malachy Quinn

5 August 1998 28
   Ballymena

28 March 1922 35
   On the Run

10 August 1998 47
   Winnie

An Irishman in an English Gaol, 25 November 1925 61
   By Malachy Quinn

1922-1924 68
   Argenta

Spot Dance, October–November 1923 90
    By Malachy Quinn

13 August 1998 146
    McConaghy

11 September 1932 151
    Bob Stack

Sunday, 10 April 1966 158
    Thirty-Seven Seconds

Finding Dan O'Rourke, October 1961 176
    By Malachy Quinn

17 May 1938 213
    Creenagh

15 August 1998 246
    Laming

17 August 1998 262
    Patsy

Finding Dan, Thursday, 2 November 1967 272
    By Malachy Quinn

For my Dad, who showed me how to find Dan.

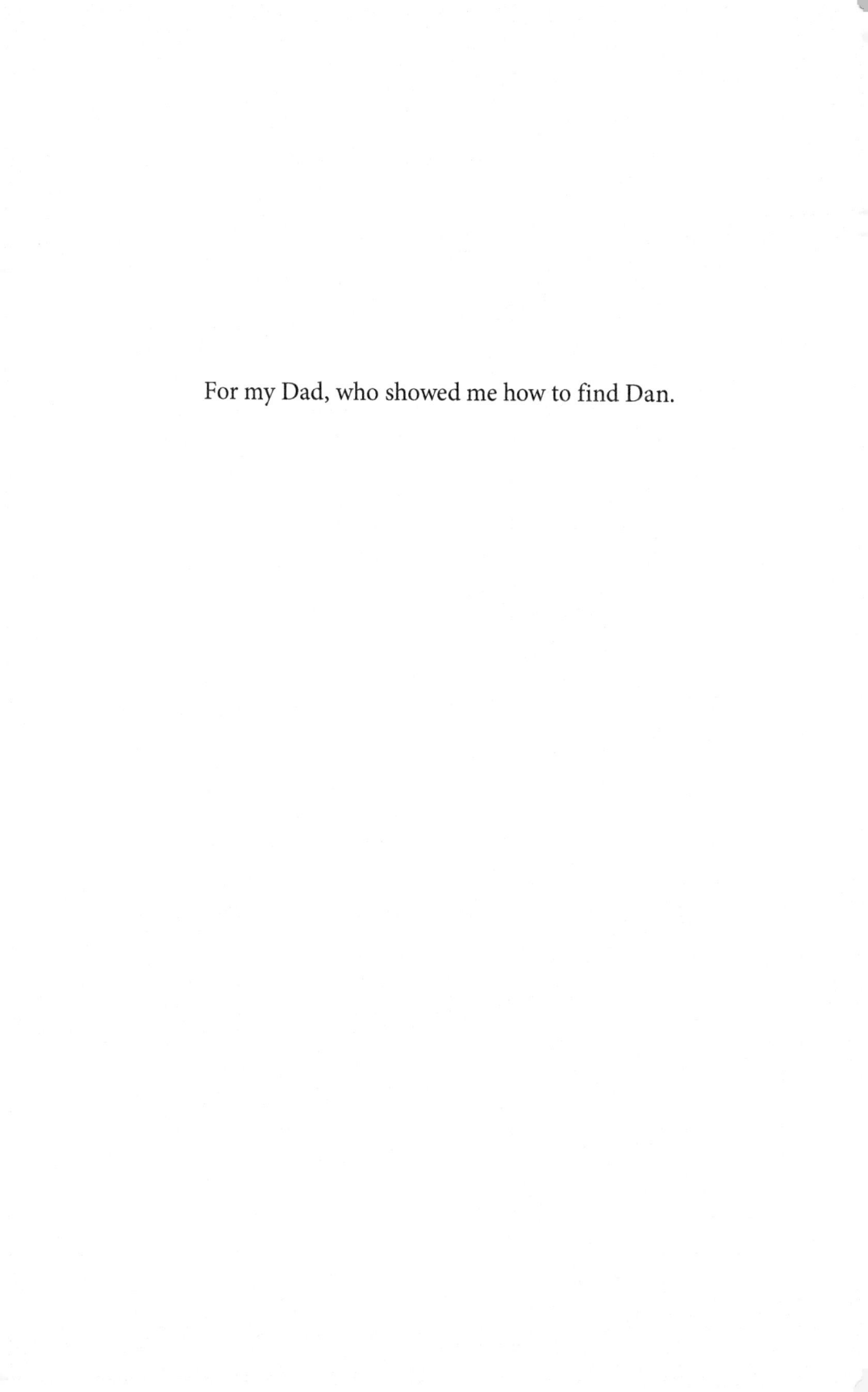

SCALE 1:10 000   1967

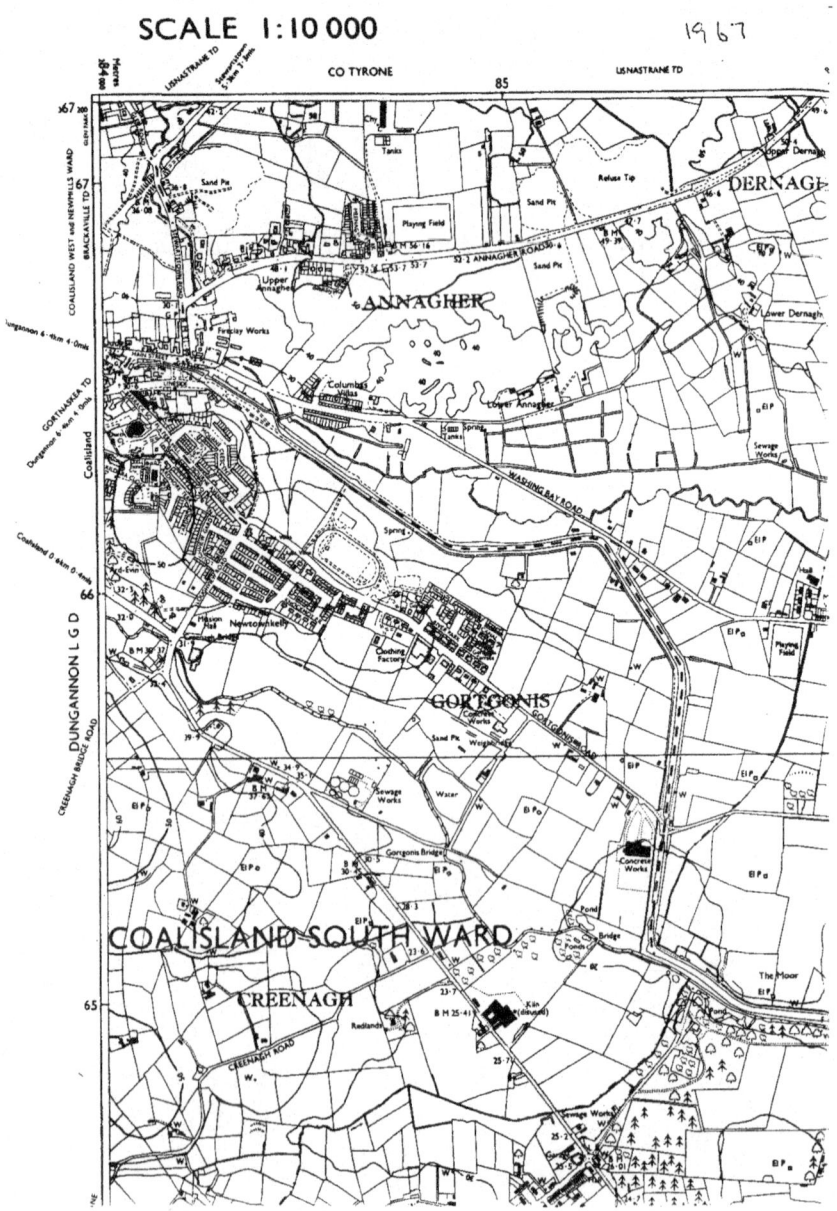

FOX, MARY ALICE (NÉE O'ROURKE)

Mary Alice Fox (née O'Rourke) of Yonkers, NY at home on 25 October 1999. Born and married in Ireland, direct descendant of the O'Rourkes of Breifne, the remains of the castle can be found in Leitrim, Ireland. Mother of Capt John Fox, Ronald, and Brian Fox. Grandmother of Kathleen Fox, Maura Stangohn, Patricia Fox, great-grandmother of Megan Stangohn. Calling hours at the Fred H. McGrath & Son Funeral Home, Bronxville between the hours of 2 to 4 and 7 to 9 p.m., Tuesday. Mass of Christian Burial St Eugene's Church, Yonkers on Wednesday, 27 October at 10.30 a.m. Internment Mt Hope Cemetery.

Thursday, 2 November 1967

Coalisland

On the day the moon covered the sun, there were people who were not in Coalisland who later said they had been. They said Dan had looked fine to them, handing out sweets on Main Street. Some recalled him with a handful of winter flowers. If he had stolen the flowers, that could be overlooked, for they all thought of him as a good man. A man who had spent his life as Dan had could be forgiven a lot, and what could not be forgiven did not have to be spoken about.

There were others who claimed to have seen him before that, up at St Malachy's chapel in Edendork, his knees on a bag, tugging at weeds around his parents' grave. The turf, sodden every day of the year, slid away from the church above it, pulling its well-preserved bodies to the ditch at the bottom. He would have been glad of his boots. Dan was not the only one that All Souls' Day offering two prayers: one for the dead to be rested; the other pledging not to join them, dear God, not in this bog. To make sure, he lit candles for Margaret and for Joe, his ma and da.

The ride into Coalisland is easier than the ride out of it. He called on Kathleen with the flowers. He didn't call on his other sister Winnie as she would have been busy in her shop. He must have pushed his bicycle up Plater's Hill: it was a poor place to house an old man with a bad leg. The sun still shone, the birds still sang. The kids outside his house, gazing up at the sky and waiting for the eclipse, said they saw him take his key from his jacket pocket, turn the key, and let himself in. He left his bike outside.

March 1974

Edendork

'Mum! I'm going to the shed!'

'Well, mind your hands, Mal.'

The boy leaned into the dog-damp coats at the back door and stepped his feet into someone's work boots: he was heading for the woodshed at the back of the cottage, where he spent most of his free days, when he wasn't running wild. The shed was dominated by a seven-foot workbench with a cast-iron gripping vice on the end, and a sleek steel rule along one edge, measured out in inches. A rusted circular saw blade, fit to cut your head off, rested against one wall ready to roll, and a pair of heavy-duty gloves lay dismembered beside it, palms up. Pins, tacks, nuts, flatheads, bolts, hooks and washers, arranged like specimens in jam jars, screwed into their lids, nailed to the underside of shelves. The old people who owned this were in Canada. The boy had overheard plans about them moving too, but for now Mal lived here with his parents. It was cold, and the woodshed was damp. Mal liked the earthy smell, and sometimes he felt as if the cut wood could take root again and lose itself among the trees that jostled the cottage. He made things with the wood, like ships to sail away in. He sawed, he hammered, he painted; from an old carpenter's bag, he pulled more exotic tools, and he drilled, he filed, he planed. He discovered that wood has a grain, and that his plane bucked and jammed if he tried to work against it. His father, Frank, found him a tin of gold paint and told him wood was in the family. 'Let me see those hands,' his dad had said. 'You'll be cutting timber with them one of these days, you'll see.'

The boy was six. Today, he had had enough of woodwork. He'd cut his thumb. The dog that sometimes called at the house had not called today, so he was alone. At the back door, he changed into a pair of plimsolls, called to his mum (thumb in mouth), and ran off into the craggy wilderness of Edendork. Like he did most days, he ran first for the mossy rise at the back of their cottage, and allowed his momentum to tip him rolling over the other side. He was a fugitive—like one described on the news—returning to a weapons cache, or seeking refuge in the scrubby forest. The B-Men would be after him, hunting him down. Or the Brits would. In the school playground the Brits were like the Indians, and so always the enemy. Mal didn't know what a Brit was, but he had learned that he did not want to be one.

His escape took him around the back of the church and out onto the road that went to Dungannon, or Coalisland, depending on which way you faced. Mum's family going one way, or Dad's the other. By Uncle Phelim's watch, he was five minutes from home, ten minutes if he was carrying an injury. Mal could see the magnificent dance hall, domed like the Taj Mahal. Mal himself had never been allowed in. Sometimes, on Fridays, his dad took his mum dancing, and Mal stayed nearby with his aunt. At closing time, the revellers carried on their dancing and arguing in the vast, glass-gritted car park. Now he saw a car there, not parked but abandoned, by the corner of the hall.

Mal cupped his hand to his mouth, calling in the suspect car to Command, and waited for instructions. He knew the words of the game. He circled the vehicle first, satisfying himself there was no one about, that this was not an ambush. The passenger door was open, and stuff had been pulled from the glove compartment into the footwell. The rear seat had been entirely ripped out, leaving some wires exposed. Mal sat. He tried the horn. It didn't work. If it

FINDING DAN

had, the blare would have bounced off the walls and the concrete of the car park. There was no one about, so Mal banged the horn again and made the noise himself. In the silence that followed, he could hear the tick of an engine cooling. Who left this here? Command would want answers. He might also need to tell his dad. Then he remembered that his dad would give him a hiding if he found out. Amongst the stuff on the floor were receipts for a garage and an AA manual, but nothing with a name on. Someone—the police—must have reached the scene before him. Like he had seen his father do, he pulled down the flap of the driver's sun visor, hoping maybe for a licence. A key fell on to the seat beside him. He picked it up; now not a game. Mal tried to rehearse the warnings his parents had filled his head with. He knew what he shouldn't do. The cooling engine ticked louder in his head. The stray dog that came to their house had not been for two days. He placed the key in the ignition. Voices called, high-pitched, and so very distant. The key jammed, so he pulled on the steering wheel to unlock it. The boy glanced over his shoulder again. In the space behind him, where there should have been a seat, there was only a mess of wires. From somewhere far away, he heard steps dancing and skidding in the gravel of the car park, and screams joined the other voices in muffled argument. Mal had changed out of the old work boots because these plimsolls were better for running in. He scrambled to get out of the car. He slipped on the papers in the footwell, and hurt his cut thumb on the loose stones. He ran, but was lost for which way to run. So he just ran for the road, holding his ears against the blast.

Eilis called her son out of his room for his dinner. He allowed her to spoon gravy over his bacon and cabbage. They were making their plans for the evening. The TV was on, some variety show with men singing and girls dancing and the audience clapping, without a care.

'Where's that, Frank? Is that Blackpool?'

'Southend this week. Blackpool was last week, wasn't it?'

'Those poor girls will catch their death, standing like that. Someone give them a coat!'

MARK QUINN

'It's warmer in England than here, Eilis.'

Then the sound was muted, and the screen went blue. Quiet, quiet! Frank hushed them all for the *NEWS FLASH*. Mal looked away from the television, tried setting his face to show he was blameless. There was a suspect device in Edendork. The RUC had cordoned off the area. Keyholders were to return to their premises. The police would be carrying out a controlled explosion. He was only six, but Mal knew all of these words.

The laughter and dancing and colour returned to the screen. Mal held his hands to his ears.

July 1998

Phelim

From where he sat with the letter, Mal could see the tops of the trees that grew in the open space opposite his flat. No birds there today. A plant he could not name wilted on the windowsill. On the street below, Mrs Gaston the Tramp would be chasing the papers in the breeze, gathering them for her bed. Tim, who sold reconditioned fridges by the corner with the Wetherspoon's pub, would be standing amongst his henge of white goods, drinking tea. The traffic, bullied by the lorries with their names rippling on their sides, crept eternally towards the concrete and metal core of London.

The letter was from Frank.

> *'Dear Mal,*
>
> *Got a plan for when you two come over at the end of the month. Been digging into some family history, my Uncle Dan mostly. Amazing what they let you look at in the public records office! Molly, in New York, put me on to it. Think she might be losing it. She called me, said she knew secrets about Dan even her father didn't know, and she wrote a sort of memoir, but Bram (her son) destroyed it. She is still at it though—says*

she'll send over another copy if she can smuggle it past Bram! Maybe you could cast your eye over it with me?

*Your mother is well,
Love, Dad'*

Mal picked up his dinner things and the cutlery opposite him. He folded the letter into its envelope, and put it in the box with the others he kept from his parents. He saw them rarely these days. They didn't like travelling, and he had found easy excuses not to travel to Northern Ireland. *I've got a great story for you to write up*, Frank would say—and it often was—but Mal preferred to write it from his flat in London. *You're like our foreign correspondent*, Frank liked to say.

'Are you going to indulge the old man?' Phelim asked. Frank's brother, Phelim, lived three Tube stops away from Mal in Stratford. With his wife, Diane, they had assembled the remnants of lives spent together on the road with the world's greatest bands. Like gardeners, Phelim and Diane gathered their collections in drifts of rock-chick jewellery and bonsai settlements of Japanese hi-fi; their LPs, hedged in perfect shelves, slotted in well-tended sleeves.

Mal thumbed through the records. 'Yes, I'll have to. I might get something out of it.'

'Another of your wee Irish stories?' Phelim smiled at his nephew's discomfort. 'Be careful if you want to write about Dan: there'll be people wanting to read it.'

It was the evening; they all sat at the small wooden table in the kitchen. They drank red wine, they tore at hunks of homemade bread, and they cut tiny pyramids of English cheese. Phelim was a short, handsome man. He wore a misshapen T-shirt, jeans, which were fraying at their ankles, and tennis shoes that had been recently whitened.

'Or Molly, I could make something of her. She seems like an impressive woman.'

FINDING DAN

'Do you think?' Sometimes Phelim just let a question swing on its hook, and would nod its point back.

'How well do you know Molly?' Mal asked. Phelim was chewing on some bread, but was ready to take up his share of the conversation.

'She was my mother's sister, that's how I saw her. She looked like Mummy. All the sisters had the same large build and sparkling black eyes and big coif of hair, straight from a salon. The only nonsense she would let be heard was that coming from her own mouth. I would be saying something innocent about the weather or the clothes people wore, and if she didn't agree, she would stare at you with those eyes. She'd drill them into you until you'd stopped. I was a cocky wee so-and-so back then, and maybe I'd swear a little in front of her just for effect, and she'd shoot back, "No one fucking curses in my house. This is a godly home, and I'd be gratified if you would remember that." And you'd be so stunned she'd said it, you'd almost believe she couldn't have.

'That was in the Seventies and early Eighties. I'd be in New York a lot then, doing the lighting rig for the bands. I'd tease her about coming along to a gig, and she used to say, "When you have Old Blue Eyes, then I'll come along and you can impress your auntie." She had a good set of Sinatra LPs, and others as well. She called them her "pack rats". She'd known them from her "hotelling days", as she put it. "They might be living the high life upstairs", she said, "but they always sent down beautiful clean sheets to me. Never a mark. You noticed such things," she said. Those were her best days, Mal, but none of us ever saw them. She'd be a worthy subject for a story, you're right.'

'She didn't care much for me,' Diane interjected, pouring another glass, and stretching her legs the length of the sofa. 'I was the wrong sort of woman, leading her little nephew astray!'

'Not good enough for Phelim? I can't believe that.' Mal couldn't.

'It's hard for any woman to be good enough for an O'Rourke man. But an Englishwoman never is.' Diane stroked the air between them as if it were Mal's cheek. 'Sorry, dear, I didn't mean you.'

'Well, I did get to do the lights for Sinatra,' Phelim persisted. 'She wasn't well enough to come. I felt so sorry for her. I knew she would have been in heaven. I called round on her the next day with flowers. When I got there, she was already surrounded by neighbours, drinking iced tea, and eating cake. She was telling them all about her nephew, straight over from Ireland, and how Mr Sinatra had called me especially because only I knew how to light him. "Isn't that the way it happened, Phelim?" she demanded, already nodding my answer for me. I agreed. "Almost exactly like that, Aunt Molly. Get me Molly's nephew, is what he said." "And were they all there, Phelim?" she asked. "All of them, Molly. Sammy Davis Jr., Dean Martin, all of them, Molly. Even Warren Beatty put in an appearance." "Oh, I like him!" she cackled, and all her mates cackled too. She could make you blush, Mal, she could.'

'What were her politics? Did she still see herself as Irish?' Mal asked.

'Oh, Christ, yes. She spoke Yankee, but always got more Irish when she spoke of home,' said Diane. 'Like you now, Phelim, your politics heading one way while your accent goes the opposite. The Irish are all the same.'

Mal reddened again. The fact that his accent had slid since he had moved to London made him doubt himself: a writer was supposed to be secure with voices, including his own. Phelim had his Irish consonants and American vowels, which was fine because his was an accent in permanent transit, like the man himself. Mal sat in his flat all day, travelling only in his head. He had no excuse.

Phelim went on. 'Ours would have been a pretty Republican family all along. Dan was imprisoned in the Twenties for being in the old IRA. Did you hear that? But I never heard any of us, not even Dan, talk the way Molly would about the English. "About time too," she said when the IRA started their bombing in England in the Seventies. I'd try to tell her that innocent men and women had been killed, but she just talked about our people, and how we had lost good men ourselves.'

'You were embarrassed?'

FINDING DAN

'Yes, Mal, it was embarrassing. I'd say that's why Bram burned her book. She was a better woman when she wasn't going on about that sort of thing.'

The kitchen floor shuddered as Diane pushed out her chair to get up. She collected several plates deftly in one hand and reached them without looking into the dishwasher. She kissed her husband goodnight and left, forgetting Mal. The kitchen was now colder. Mal folded his arms into his body to stop a shiver. His red wine was as cold as abandoned tea, but he drank it anyway, warming it in his mouth before swallowing. His uncle seemed unaffected. His limbs had been browned and his skin had been thickened from a life touring the world, a roadmap etched in relief on the muscles and veins and scars of his arms. Yet his hands were an electrician's: hard and nimble and capable of magic.

'I was sitting across from her in her dim New York flat with its oversized furniture and ridiculous gilt-framed reproductions, and the last of the grey winter sun was poking out from behind the curtains on her balcony window. Just the two of us, and she pushed a plate of fruit cake over to me, leaned in. I thought she was about to whisper, but then in quite a normal voice, she said, "It's not true what they said about Dan, you know, but he died rather than admit what they had done to him." She then shifted her silhouette before the balcony window, so all I saw of her was a blot against the light, and the pearl of a tear resting below her eye. I waited for a second for her to continue. Then, when she was still silent, I wanted to avoid words that would either upset her too much, or launch her on another lecture on the dirty British.' Phelim paused then sagged back in his chair, apparently finished.

Mal opened his mouth to speak, trusting that the right words were there ready for use. He studied his uncle and imagined Phelim studying his aunt. 'Did you ask her what she meant?'

'No.'

'Did you guess what she meant?'

'I guessed.'

'What do you think she meant?'

Phelim didn't speak. Frank had reported something similar in his letter. Whatever it was, others must have some idea.

'There's Winnie and Patsy,' said Phelim finally. 'Dan's sister and brother still in Coalisland. But, Mal, I reckon you should tread softly with Dan.' Phelim's right hand reached for his left arm, and Mal noticed a rash of goosebumps along his scar there. His smile had sunk back into his face. 'Within every family, there are people with secrets. You are charming enough, so they will start talking to you, and before you know it, they have told you more than they wanted to. Are you sure you know what to do with the things people tell you?'

'You don't think I should write about Dan?'

'I'm not sure they always treated Dan well. Like they moved him out of the home, and put him in the shed. You might watch what you ask Patsy even though he's a decent, upstanding man.'

Later, Phelim sat alone in the kitchen, barely awake. His nephew had left. He wasn't sure when, but maybe hours before. He had wanted to say more, but was afraid he might say too much, and now he was on his own again. There was something more that only he knew, and he could remember it as plain as day. There was the big table in the hall, or rather the table in the front sitting room by the window in Mummy's house on Main Street. You'd go into the wee hall, go up the two steps to the kitchen where the big range was. I was at home all day the day Dan died; I must have been suffering for something. No, not that. Dan had made me promise to call in on him at this house on the Ardmore Road. He had something planned, I never found out what. And I swear on my mother's grave that this is true. There was a bunch of flowers from someone in the middle of the table, and they died. Just like that, they turned their heads down and died. On my mother's grave, I swear to God. It was the day he died, whether it was the time he died or not, I don't know. My mother near beat me for those flowers dying.

Buckshot, 7 December 1922

by Malachy Quinn

Under the terms of the Anglo-Irish Treaty of 1921, which brought an end to the Irish War of Independence, a Dáil was elected as a provisional parliament in September 1922. It ratified a new constitution, and established the Irish Free State in December. Northern Ireland, comprising the six counties of the north-east of the island, remained within the United Kingdom. Those opposed to the Treaty refused to recognise the new parliament, plunging the country into civil war. Friends, who had fought together in the IRA, were now pitched against each other as enemies.

'Just one letter for you today, Mr Hales.'

'Thank you, Tim. Are you working tonight? I may be calling for a bottle of your dark stuff later this evening for me and my friend here.'

'I am sorry, Mr O'Maille, I never saw you there. Your key, sir. Perhaps you won't be needing to stay with us for too much longer?'

'Now, now, Tim, let's not be complacent. We will have to watch our backs for some while yet, I'd say.'

'Oh, but Mr O'Maille, the evening papers are all about President Cosgrave's speech in the Dáil. "Open your eyes and realise that freedom is in your hands" is the headline. He's a peacemaker, I think. Would you say? Was it like they say?' Tim, normally deferential as his post demanded, was too excited to stop. He held the newspapers up for the guests to see, as artefacts of the moment.

'Just as they have it, Tim,' said O'Maille. 'Though they appear to have left before I got up to speak.' Tim scanned the columns, desperate to prove him wrong.

'Now, Padraig, what interest would the good men of the press have in what a mere Deputy Speaker of the Dáil had to say?'

O'Maille had grabbed a corner of the paper from the doorman. 'We agree a new constitution, and our Dublin press is still more interested in that man Craig in the North,' he complained.

'I'm sure I saw you in here somewhere, sir,' said the doorman shyly. 'I might need to look more closely.'

Hales nodded. 'Under the circumstances, Tim, I suggest you give up your search for us in your papers. And I fear we may have need of your discreet hotel for some time to come.'

Padraig O'Maille and Sean Hales retired to the lounge to await their evening meal. Mr Goulding, an occasional guest, was already dining with another gentleman. The room, despite the early hour, was dim and cold. Mina, without asking, brought them each a whiskey and a small jug of water. She turned on an electric lamp in the corner, the light amplifying her golden hair and the roundness of her breasts. A man's voice was singing in the background. Padraig noticed how his friend's hand trembled, as he brought the glass to his lips.

'Sean, will you ever hold that glass still? Tim might be right. The President spoke well today, and he carried the House behind him. They are even saying de Valera is on his way to Dublin and will have to talk peace. The worst is over. We'll be able to sleep in our own beds soon enough.'

'The worst is not over, Padraig, when Lynch can order the shooting on site of any judge or newspaperman who doesn't toe his anti-Treaty line. When he can have killed any TD and every senator who signed the Public Safety Bill. Padraig, I think that may include you and me. The "murder bill", he's called it. And sure, isn't he right?

FINDING DAN

Haven't we just executed Erskine bloody Childers? Tell me, Padraig, if that wasn't bloody murder!'

'Liam Lynch can issue all the orders he likes,' answered O'Maille. 'The IRA is not what it was when the Chief of Staff can make his threats and nothing happens. Haven't you noticed? There have been no killings in over a week. Cosgrave was right. If they kill one of our men on the street, then we execute one of their men in prison. These were our friends before now, and execution is a bloody business. But if it's what we need to end civil war, then I'm for it.'

'But Childers? He negotiated the friggin' treaty for us with Michael. How did we end up executing him?'

'Sean, he had a pistol that he had no business having.'

'Didn't Mick give it to him!'

The two men had shocked each other into brief silence at mention of the name of their dead leader. Just three and a half months had passed since the assassination in Cork of Michael Collins. Sean had been one of the last men to see him alive. The Hales boys had all, at one time, been Collins men. In Dunmanway, Michael had made Tom Hales Commanding Officer of the 3rd Cork Brigade of the IRB, with Sean his Vice OC. When the British captured and tortured Tom in Bandon Barracks, Sean took over. His younger brothers, William and Bob, were also under his command. So was Dick Barrett. Altogether, they had caused merry hell throughout the West, burning loyalist farms, and ambushing RIC patrols. 'Give 'em the buckshot!' Sean would order his men, as the Black and Tans came prowling around Woodfield, the Collins' home. And 'Buckshot' is what his men would thereafter call him. They helped drive the king's imperial forces to the negotiating table. Sean didn't like the Treaty any more than his brothers did, but he loved Mick and trusted him. Tom hadn't seen it that way, and nor had Bob or William or most of the rest. Dev walked out of the Dáil, taking much of Sinn Fein with him, and the course was set for civil war. When the anti-Treaty boys occupied the Four Courts in Dublin in April, Dick Barrett was there with them, and Collins had to use cannon borrowed from Churchill to blast them out. Now, Dick was languishing in Mountjoy Prison. Because he had stuck with Mick, Sean was brigadier general of the Free State Army in Cork, and elected to the Dáil as TD and now Speaker. His brother, Tom, meanwhile, was in a Free State gaol.

Tim, the doorman at the Ormond Hotel, brought dinner to the distinguished guests. They had never tried to disguise their identity from him even though other members of the government were sleeping in their offices for fear of being seen by Lynch's men. Indeed, this was more safe house than hotel: these guests did not pay in the customary way. Though Mina and Lydia cooked the meals, and a girl came in each morning to make the beds, Tim performed all other roles. Most importantly, he kept an eye on the door, questioned everyone he did not know, and conveyed messages to his guests when called upon. Though only a boy still, and from Glasnevin at that, he would tell himself to be vigilant, for his country depended on it.

The two TDs continued their talking throughout their meal, and then carried on in O'Maille's room. They smoked and drank bottles of porter. O'Maille recognised the mood of his younger friend. He was haunted. Twelve years before Sean had been held for nine months by the British in Cork. He had fought through the whole Easter week in Dublin in 1916, and spent the rest of that year interned, while greater men than he had been executed in Kilmainham. Sean Hales was a simple man, a strong man, a champion weight-thrower in Munster, better even than O'Maille himself. It was his association with Michael Collins, however, that had turned him into the scourge of the British in Cork. Buckshot. For all these past years, Sean Hales had been running, hitting and running, living on his nerves. The Treaty was meant to put an end to that for him. O'Maille saw before him a major general in the army of the Free State, and a revered member of the new country's parliament; but he was a man who appeared to have been diminished by his official titles. O'Maille had known enough fear in his own life to recognise it in another's. He would allow Hales, the Speaker, to speak all night, for talking meant you were still alive.

FINDING DAN

'How did we come to this, Padraig?' O'Maille had come back into his room, having used the lavatory in the corridor. He had found Hales sitting on the end of the cot bed.

'It's where we go from here that matters now, Sean. It's to the likes of you and me that the country is looking now.'

'Well, God help them then.' Sean shifted his weight on the bed to tip the ash of his cigarette into an empty stout bottle. 'Mick would have known what to do.' Sean lay back on the bed, his cigarette pointing up to the ceiling high above. For a moment, he was distracted by the smoke folding over the plaster rosette from which hung the single naked light bulb. He thought of other rooms he'd hid out in—in farmhouses and guesthouses—running and hiding, but never in fear. Back then, his only concern was that he should not die now and miss out on all the fun. The smoke curled and became lost. 'The first thing Collins did when he arrived at the GPO at the start of the Rising was to throw out the two tierces of stout they had stored there. "I'm not havin' insobriety in the ranks," he said. "It did for Wolfe Tone's men in '98, but it's not doin' for mine!" I'd say he got down the name and address of every man fighting there that week. What do you think he did that for? Mick knew Easter was a bloody disaster. He was planning already for the next push, and he was leaving nothing to chance. I'd say Mick kept everyone going that week right to the very end. Only when it was over did he find a bottle of whiskey from somewhere, and he and Jim Ryan, the big doctor, got drunk on it. For maybe two hours, he had given up. Then he was himself again.'

O'Maille handed Hales another bottle of stout, his fourth. 'Wasn't Jim Ryan with Collins in Stafford?'

'He was, though Mick himself was lucky to be there. He could, by rights, have been killed with the others in Kilmainham Gaol. Four hundred and eighty-eight of us were marched through the city to the North Wall in Dublin Port. You know, the people hurled some abuse at us that day, they might have lynched us themselves if the Brits had let them. Instead, they herded us on to a boat made for cattle and sent us to Holyhead in Wales. The smell of shit is what

I remember, and not all of it from the cows. There, in Wales, they split us up. Two hundred to Knutford and the rest to Stafford. Mick counted every one. That was the way of him, always organising ahead.'

From outside, the sound of a barge knocking against the Liffey wall, a dog barking pointlessly at it. The men were quiet for a while.

'Jesus, Padraig, I wish he was here now.' Hales looked for another cigarette. 'He would deal with de Valera, and get him to call off Lynch's dogs. None of us is safe, O'Maille…' His friend lit his cigarette. 'I'm not safe. Better than me have gone already. Padraig, you shouldn't be around me, you know.' Hales stood up, as if to put a safe distance between them.

'Settle down, will you, for Christ's sake. Neither the two of us is going anywhere. You just keep drinking and talking, and I've paid so I'm staying. Sure, there's no other company to keep.' O'Maille wanted to rest a hand on the younger man's shoulder, but for whose reassurance, he didn't know for sure. He opted to keep his friend talking of his hero, although he knew where that would lead. 'So you were with Collins in Stafford too?'

Hales nodded. 'Mick hated it there. Like several others, he spent the first few weeks in solitary with no contact with any of the other detainees. But the guards made sure we knew about the executions in Kilmainham. They tried to make us feel guilty about surviving when Clarke and Connolly and Pearse and the rest had been shot. We were traitors in their eyes, anyway, for fighting the British when the War was still on. "So why aren't you fighting the Germans, then, you bloody lousers, instead of babysitting us wee paddies?" That was Mick. He knew how to wind them up when he wanted to.

'But he was on a short fuse himself even after they allowed us to communicate with the outside. We would play wild horses where you have to leap over the other team's backs, and they, over yours. Mick was always put in the lighter team on purpose, and so would have the heavy men. Jim Ryan was one, and Denis Daly and Mort O' Connell climb all over him and break him. He hated losing. He'd bite. He'd wrestle them and claim his bit of ear.'

FINDING DAN

'Then they moved us to Wales,' O'Maille prompted.

'To a bog, to make us feel at home, I'm sure. Frongoch had been a German prisoner of war camp. We called it *Francach,* after the rats.'

'Gaelic. Is that where Mick got his interest in the language?'

'It may have been,' said Hales before correcting himself. 'No, I remember in Stafford he insisted for a while that we call him Miceal O'Coileain. If we thought in Irish, we would shake off our English. But Mick was mad for languages in general. He even took up Welsh: he paid the kitchen boy (Robins... Roberts) to teach him Welsh on his day off. He gave the boy a gift of a Connemara tie-pin, and pretended it was from his mother. And his mother had been dead for years!"'

'There were many smart men there,' said O'Maille. 'The Republican University, they called it.'

'Desmond Ryan was there, the writer,' agreed Hales. 'And Mick went up to him one day, and he was reading this book, and Mick, Mick from West Cork, says, "Is that Chesterton you are reading?" And Ryan nods, and they go on talking with Mick saying things like, "And only Sunday was not turned by the police", and Ryan, citing the bible and the *Book of Job*. One thing I do remember was Mick quoted, "If you don't seem to be hiding, nobody hunts you out." He said that more than once, otherwise I'd not remember it now.'

'Wise words, Sean, it would maybe do us no harm to read that book. Desmond Ryan was in the GPO too, was he not?'

'I don't recall the name of it. Chesterton, definitely.' Hales closed his eyes and was drifting to sleep. But from his semi-conscious state, he conjured images of the camp, in detail only a trained paramilitary would recall. 'It was little more than a bog. Even after they made us lay cinder paths, we would sink in the mud above our boots. Mick, better dressed than the guards even with no collar and tie, could not keep his boots clean. It had been a distillery, converted at the start of the War to house interned Germans and prisoners of war. There was a high brick chimney, a railway siding, a hospital wing, a cookhouse. They had taken a number of buildings—oat houses, tun sheds, and the like—and adapted them to keep us busy. So there was a barber's shop and an artist's shed, and workshops for engineers and shoemakers and tailors and carpenters. Every bloody thing. Then there was the censor's office. We could write only one letter per week, and that had to go through the censor. We argued that it was a contravention of our rights as politicals, but they would hear nothing of it. All surrounded by barbed wire. You could try to escape, but you were bound to get caught, and in the meantime, they made the rest suffer.

'The guards tried constantly to get the names and addresses of all the men. They said it was to buy us our tickets home, but Mick refused, and instead we gave them our own lists. They were trying to conscript us, especially those like Mick who had lived in England. If they conscripted us, they could court martial us, and then they could shoot us for desertion. Or worse, send us to fight their war in France. Failing that, they tried treating us as common criminals and not prisoners of war. When they forced us out on route marches across the moors, we bested them, and of course, it was always Mick who was back first, hardly out of breath. He was The Big Fellow all right. The guards were reduced to sending some away, to more 'criminal' prisons, such as Reading and Wandsworth.'

Hales appeared to run out of things to say, or the energy to say them. O'Maille, too, had started to dream, but roused himself.

'We know you were his favourite, but do you remember who else was there with you?' O'Maille felt compelled to keep Hales talking, to make him reckon for the man he had become.

'"Dick Mulcahy. Richard McKie. Gearóid O'Sullivan. Thomas McCurtain. Padraig O'Caoimh. Seamus Robinson. Terence Mac Swiney."'

'You remember....' O'Maille was becoming transported by the litany of names, but Hales was continuing.

'Patrick O'Malley, who escaped and was caught again. That was a time! Thomas Malone. Joe O'Reilly, who went carousing with Mick and Gearóid in Dublin on Christmas Eve after they let us out.

FINDING DAN

Denis McCullough—he set up the New Ireland Insurance Company with Mick and O'Reilly. O'Reilly, the one whom Mick beat in the 100 yards dash on the sports day we had when I beat Mick in the weight-throwing. Henry Dixon, the old solicitor, who was librarian in the camp. Batt O'Connor. And poor Eamonn Tierney, who went mad because of the hunger strike.'

'Good men, some of them,' tried O'Maille.

'Good men, them all, and some of them dead now. And some others not dead, but against us, and the reason we are hiding in this hotel. Mick counted eighteen hundred Irishmen, most from Dublin and Cork, and some from every county. Sinn Féin sympathisers, the hundreds of us from the Rising in Dublin, and the rest men who had risen with Liam Mellows in Galway. Liam, who's now in Mountjoy with my mate, Dick Barrett.'

'Liam was my man, Sean.' O'Maille knew it was his task to keep Hales talking, but he had his pride too. 'After I helped set up the Volunteers in Connemara, I would have been happy enough staying on my farm. But Liam Mellows was a persuasive man, and all those like me who were active in the Gaelic League, or the IRB—he had work for us in Galway in 1916. We fought too, Sean, not in Dublin I grant you, but we answered the call.'

There was knocking at the bedroom door, tapped out like Morse code. Hales lay where he was, now over the edge of sleep.

'It'll be Tim,' O'Maille reassured him needlessly, and it was. In his arms, he was carrying several more brown bottles.

'You'll have us dead, Tim.'

'Not me, Mr O'Maille, I'm for the Free State, and the right to drink as much as you like when you like.'

'Right you are, Tim. You'll be off now, I take it? Glasnevin?'

'You are a gentleman for remembering, Mr O'Maille. I'll be back in the morning though. Goodnight. Good night, Mr Hales. Can I get you anything, Mr Hales, before I go?'

'Mr Hales just wants another of those bottles of yours, Tim, then he'll be right. I'll let him sleep for a while now. Goodnight, Tim.'

Tim lingered at the door. For a moment, he felt he was his guests' equal. 'You must miss your young wife, Mr O'Maille. You were married recently, is that right?'

'It is, Tim, only last year. Eileen from Claddaghduff. Now, doesn't that sound as pretty as a poem? It does to me, let me tell you. I'm 44 years old, Tim. A man of my age oughtn't to be stopping away from home with such a pretty wife alone in her own bed.'

'Not long now, Mr O'Malley, I'm sure of it.'

Tim left O'Maille to himself. O'Maille stood at the window. Below, the dark River Liffey could be made out only by the rippled reflections of the moon. He watched its flow: eastwards out of Dublin, out of Ireland itself, out to the sea. A journey he had taken himself when he and Mellows' men were sent to that prisoner of war camp in a Welsh bog. O'Maille had been unable to stand it there. It was partly the loss of freedom and the imposition of petty regulations. He found intolerable the accusing stares of the guards. These were soldiers, men he felt he would have no qualms befriending in normal circumstances, but who looked upon him now with venom. But the isolation O'Maille felt most keenly was that from his fellow prisoners. He could not reach them. He found them rough and uncouth when he, himself, had been educated beyond National School standard. He could have been a scholar at University College Galway like his brothers; or, like his cousins, entered the medical profession. Unlike Hales, he had not found the men discussing literature or questing for self-improvement. He realised now that that had been his own blindness. At the time, he had been driven half-mad by his separation from his countrymen about him, from comradeship, from his home, Muintireoin.

Then he'd seen Gwen. He never asked her her age, but she could have been no more than twenty. Every Sunday, she and the priest came in with the van that delivered food to the hungry and religion to the faithful. At first, she would look at him with the same loathing she did the numberless others, with the same fear or disgust at the state of his clothes. O'Maille was ashamed at having provoked these feelings in another person, but found himself

FINDING DAN

counting the hours to her next visit. And he was encouraged that, over time, she showed less contempt, and her glances seemed only for him and not the other detainees. When he was allowed the privilege of working in the kitchen, alongside the local boy, Roberts, he had excuse to talk to her and found that this was not forbidden. That's when she told him her name. She refused to hear his, and he admired her for her nous. She was resourceful too. She brought him extra beans and pickled herrings. And then, almost casually, she had said she could get him out of Frongoch. Padraig had known instantly that he would accept her help to escape, whatever the risks to himself, the other prisoners, or even to her. They discussed no plans, but the following Sunday, she arrived with a large bundle, which they opened together in the privacy of the kitchen storeroom. It was a priest's cassock. Either she had stolen it, or coaxed it out of her priest friend. No one would find it strange if two priests left in the van that morning, she said. And, incredibly, no one did.

Out in the peaty Welsh wilderness there was a shepherd's hovel, and they stayed there. In it, she had already gathered food, and water, and blankets, and candles. They feasted, and they made a sort of salving love. In the morning, she was gone—back, he assumed, to her own life. He was not surprised, and he put up no resistance when he heard the guards with their dogs. They marched him roughly, hands tied behind his back, over the moors and back through the high fencing into the camp. Ten of his fellows, in reprisal, had been placed in solitary confinement on starvation rations. He would join them. But he saw the looks on the faces of the other prisoners, lined up as an unintentional guard of honour for his return. They were showing him respect. As they stood there, he thought they stood taller, and he realised that they had drawn dignity from his act of selfish rebellion. Thereafter, the detainees increased their campaign of non-cooperation even after he, himself, was transferred to Wandsworth.

'Then there was the hunger strike, isn't that right, Padraig?' Hours had passed. Both men had slept some and both were now awake.

'It is, Sean. It lasted three days. Colonel Heygate-Lambert refused to allow the camp doctors to attend to any who would not give their real names. But three days was enough,' continued O'Maille. 'Michael was able to get statements out to the *Manchester Guardian* and the *Cork Free Press*, and these were picked up in America. We had friends then in America. It was probably that, as much as anything, that got us the amnesty in December.'

'But Padraig, it was enough too to drive good men mad. Nothing good came of Frongoch.'

'Sean, I can't agree. We resisted. It taught others, like us who have and will come after us, how they should behave when incarcerated for their beliefs. And don't you think it gave us time to consider what went wrong at Easter? Never again would we allow ourselves to be holed up in a building with them raining merry hell down upon us. You learned that, Sean, you better than almost anybody. We learned the ambush, the hit-and-run, striking them, and offering only a shadow for them to strike back at. Nobody did that better than you, Sean.'

'Unless you include Tom.'

A winter sun was now rising low over the Liffey. O'Maille, looking left out of the bedroom window, saw the red morning sun reflected in the river, so that there were two suns, gently separating. 'You should tell me about your brother, Tom.'

'He's in a Free State gaol, that's enough to be telling you.'

'No, Sean, it is not.' O'Maille would insist now on a full disclosure. 'It's a new day, the seventh of December. Soon, we will be back in the College of Science for the second day for our new country, so for me, this is a day of history. You have been talking all night, Sean, and I have let you because you are working out what has brought you to this historic day. Sean, talk about Tom. Talk about your brother, tell me what happened to Mick in August.'

'Why have you to hear what you already well know?'

'I knew the rest too, Sean, but you saw fit to tell me it. Where did Mick go that day?'

FINDING DAN

After some time, Hales surrendered. 'He toured the towns, well, the public houses of West Cork. Bandon, Clonakilty, Sam's Cross, Rosscarbery, Skibbereen, Crookstown. Rosscarbery and Bandon more than once. I saw him in Bandon. They, all Mick's men, were drinking. Mick loved being home, even now. He knew, see, that he wasn't only among friends. After the Treaty. Even Mick couldn't convince Cork to agree to partition, and Cork loved Mick as much as he loved it back. Tom saw Mick as a brother, but over the Treaty, he would not be reconciled. I warned Mick to be careful. I promise I did, Padraig. Not that I knew anything exactly, but it was no secret that they were laying an ambush for him. "Sure, they'd never attack me, Sean." That was the last I heard him say. He did not have the look of a man who knew he was about to die. He was as confident as ever he had been, and that affected the rest of us too. They might try to attack him, but here he was invincible. We all thought it.

'There was a lot of them at Beal na mBláth, not just Tom. I will never believe that my brother shot dead Michael Collins. But he was there, and he maybe even planned it. And may he rot in prison for it. We owe it to Mick to hold a full inquiry whatever that means for ending this war.'

By now, Sean Hales was weeping. He stepped to the mirror and basin, splashed water on his face, and looked upon his reflection. 'Do you know who I am, Padraig?'

'I know well enough, Sean. I think we are ready.'

It was time to go. The two men were due to speak at the morning session of the Dáil. The new Government Buildings, requisitioned from the old College of Science, was perhaps a ten-minute walk from the hotel, over the river and south-east. When they reached the hotel lobby, Tim was already there at the desk. He was straining to see through the hotel door, out to the street. There was a man, a boy really, no more than five feet seven in height and with fair, almost feminine, hair. Tim was sure he recognised him.

'Good morning, Tim,' called O'Maille. 'Will it be the usual breakfast?'

'It will, sir. Lydia will bring it to you there in the lounge.'

'I intend to thank you for last night, Tim,' said Hales.

'That's kind of you as always, Mr Hales, but I expect no special thanks for just doing my job.'

'It seems your job has become to keep people like me sane. I do have something for you here....' He rummaged through all four pockets of his suit jacket. 'It may have no value, but it is special in its own way. And I would be gratified if you had it.'

Hales handed to the doorman a coin—an old penny. He explained that it dated from 1826, the last year an Irish coin was minted within the British Empire. 'That penny is from the time of Daniel O'Connell. He never would have thought it would take us another hundred years before we won our freedom. But here we have it, as fragile and precarious as it is. But we'll be safe, so long as there are fine Irishmen such as yourself still here, Tim.

'Is everything all right out there, Tim?'

'Yes, Mr Hales. And I'm touched by your kindness again. It's just someone I recognise from Glasnevin.'

The men sat in the lounge at one of the higher tables, and Lydia, the barmaid, brought them their breakfast of bacon and eggs. Their mood had improved since they had come downstairs. Hales' gesture, and the sight of the girl with the food, made them forget their sleeplessness and drunkenness. They turned their conversation to the debates they would hold that day, which would, no doubt, focus on events in the North.

They finished, grabbed their coats and hats, and headed for the lobby.

'Shall we walk, Sean?'

'The walk will do us good, Padraig.'

Tim was still staring out of the lobby door. He remembered now the name of the boy he had seen, Owen Donnelly. He knew the boy's father worked at the Custom House, but he could not think why Donnelly himself was in this part of Dublin at this time of the morning.

'Gentlemen', Tim insisted, 'it is cold. Let me hail you a cab.' The three men stepped out on to the pavement. Tim could no longer

FINDING DAN

see Donnelly. He raised his right arm, and a jaunting car pulled up. Though the morning air was cold, the low sun was already promising a warmer day. At the quay, three men were unloading casks from a brewer's barge. Their metal was smacking on the hard ground, echoing in the crisp air. Tim saw O'Maille on to the seat beside the driver; and, as he opened the door of the cab to let Hales climb in, he just saw from his left a man emerge from Capel Street. He heard a man's shout, 'O'Maille, this is for you!' Then the ringing of repeated rounds of bullets bouncing off the pavement and the walls, skittering through the air, puncturing the car, and embedding at last in the flesh of the two men. Tim saw the body of Mr Hales slumped and lifeless across the seat of the cab. The driver had lost the reins to the horse and was sitting dazed as the animal reared up in fright. Mr O'Maille, though badly wounded, reached for and held the reins. 'Get us to the hospital, in Jervis Street!' he screamed to no one in particular. The jaunting car stuttered forward then ran right across the road before correcting itself, and heading in the direction of the nearby hospital. Tim was left standing by the door of the hotel. The gunman had run off back up Capel Street. The brewer's men had disappeared, the beer caskets rocking gently against each other in the gutter. Two pools of blood, a yard apart, had started to mingle and become one with the dust of the road. The sun rose higher over Dublin.

On 7 December 1922, Dáil Deputy Speaker, Padraig O'Maille, and Speaker Sean Hales were shot by anti-Treaty IRA gunmen, as they were leaving the Ormond Hotel in Dublin on their way to parliament. O'Maille suffered serious injury; Hales died instantly.

On 8 December, four members of the IRA Army Council, who were being held in Mountjoy Prison for their occupation of the Four Courts in Dublin in April, were executed in reprisal. One for each province of Ireland, they were Rory O'Connor, Liam Mellows, Richard Barrett, and Joe McKelvey.

5 August 1998

Ballymena

The Irish Sea is a north-west Mediterranean. Its waters curl up in a meniscus around its rim of Brittany, Ireland, Britain; binding together, as well as separating, the lands it touches. Ireland might begin at the ferry terminal at Holyhead: the accent starts there. The Irish Sea laps at the edges of Britain with waves of Hibernian sibilants. To be sure. To be sure. Standing on the deck of the ferry as it unzipped the water, composing these songs in his head, Mal watched Britain recede. With Anglesey out of sight, he resorted to an all-day breakfast, and tried to think above the white noise of the engines. Children ran the length of the boat, enjoying its churning heave as if on a fairground ride.

The ro-ro docked and burped its passengers out. Portside roads are laid out so idiots cannot get lost. All traffic this way. Dún Laoghaire, Dublin, Drogheda, Dundalk: it sounded like the start of a tale featuring Paddy Irishman. Paddy Englishman, Paddy Irishman and Paddy Scotsman walk into a bar. The barman turns around and says, 'What is this, some kind of joke?' Mal laughed. He focused on not getting lost. He had never driven in the South before, though he preferred not to think of himself as a total foreigner there. A ring road allowed him to miss Dublin, and he only found Drogheda by accident. Out of Dundalk, he started noticing the

FINDING DAN

signs for 'Punts for Pounds', and 'Cheap Southern Fuel'. He knew he was over the border when the Mourne Mountains appeared like a watercolour, gently defined against the clear sky. Essing through the chicane of concrete barriers outside Newry, Mal spotted the British Army observation post high in the hills above, built like a Neolithic fort surrounded by a barbed wire palisade.

Mal had packed his car with road maps of Northern Ireland and a *Lonely Planet* guide. Although he had lived there most of his life, he did not live there now. On his visits back, it was common for him to be asked where he was from. No one suspected he was from Ballymena. In his car now, with its English number plates, he was in disguise.

He was nearly there when he saw Slemish. If he could not love the town, he was always drawn to the mountain. From whichever angle he viewed it, its semicircularity never altered, rendering it mysterious and useless as a landmark. From the south, Slemish was on his right, and he entered the town through the conjoined village of Harryville. He drove as cautiously as a stranger. Over there were the remains of a motte and bailey castle, now with the scar of winter snow sledding down its face; the derelict linen mill; joyless, loyalist bunting. Everything blended with the colours of the kerbs. A council estate, white with pebble-dash. Red glares of fast-food chains and petrol stations. People shirted in Rangers blue. By recent custom, every Saturday night, gusting around the nearby Catholic church, the very air would be constituted like the union flag: streaks of sharp white oxygen; red surges of rage, beating their drums and throbbing in their veins; blue shards of profanity. The church itself, its stained glass like a million shattered curses, was shaped like one of those folded paper fortune tellers where you lift the flaps. They hate you, they hate you lots. On Saturday nights and Sunday mornings, Ballymena Catholics sidled into this wholly Protestant part of town to pray in their chatterbox. The church's location, Casement Street, was an absurdity or a provocation. Now, after the peace agreement at Easter, it was where suppressed hatred was vented. There were many there. There were the tribal braves with their B&Q pots of warpaint and stone throwers attracted by the rubble. The scion of a native preacher-politician, treading his father's path; the mad dogs with Glasgow tattoos and gallowglass biceps. 'Where are you from?' 'I'm from here.' Like it or not.

When he arrived, his parents noted he was alone (No Rosa?) and offered him tea.

In the evening, Frank told his son about the research he had already managed to start at the Public Records Office in Belfast. He had discovered Dan's police file. Dan had been on the run, evading arrest until 1922. Letters on him named him as a terrorist, too dangerous to release, so he was transferred for internment. Frank remembered being told, probably by his mother, that he was interned on the prison ship, *SS Argenta*, moored off Larne. He served in the region of four years in all in gaol. Frank found letters received by Dan in prison, one from his mother, apparently alluding to an incident where she and her sisters had their heads shaven by the Black and Tans as they searched for Dan. There was another letter from a woman whom Frank took to be Dan's girlfriend.

'I can't recall the name now. I ought to have written it down. Tinnelly or Finnelly. Is that a name? It was a queer wee letter. I think it may have been in code or something. What she would try to do for him, that sort of thing. I recognised the name (though I can't find it here now). Dan never married, but he was a good-looking man, and I am sure there would have been no shortage of lassies after him in his younger days. Findlay, maybe. Sorry, I am veering away there.'

'Why didn't he ever marry, do you think, Frank?' Eilis sat between her son and her husband. 'Did you ever think there was maybe something wrong with him?'

'God, would you just listen to yourself, Eilis!' Frank protested.

'No, that's a fair question,' insisted Mal. 'I'm not embarrassed.'

'I'm not talking about your shame. Unless you think there is something wrong with you?'

Mal shook his head. He *was* embarrassed.

'These days', Frank continued, 'you can ask anybody anything. But it's not something you could have asked someone at the time, at

FINDING DAN

least not to their face. Funny, Jim never married, and Bassie didn't either. As I say, he would have been a catch, being handsome in his younger days, and a footballer, and famous about those parts on account of his being on the run. Maybe he didn't see himself married.'

'Not all men do,' said Eilis. Whatever she was thinking, she offered a knowing wink to Mal, as if that were something only mothers could be expected to understand.

Mal tried to set what his father had found out, alongside what Phelim had said. Phelim thought Dan was born in about 1906. If Dan was first imprisoned in 1922, after some time on the run, that now seemed unlikely. His dad now reckoned that Dan was older than Molly who was born in 1904.

'But I'm only guessing,' Frank admitted. He had looked through every record, but could find no Daniel O'Rourke born any time around then anywhere in County Tyrone. Elsewhere, Daniel O'Rourke was born in Dunmanway in 1900. Daniel O'Rorke was born in Manorhamilton in 1901, and in the same year, Daniel O'Rourke popped out in Kilmallock. Manorhamilton bore another Daniel O'Rorke in 1902. Bandon saw the arrival of Daniel O'Rourke at the same time. Daniel O'Rourke was a new year present for someone in Leahy in 1904. But he could find Dan nowhere.

'Why would Dan's family not have registered his birth?'

'That's an easy one, Mal,' said Eilis proudly. 'He may have been someone else's son, given to the O'Rourkes. Or maybe the O'Rourkes weren't married themselves and were in, you know, disgrace. But I'm not sure it was altogether the done thing back then, you know, to register a wee child's birth as such. With the church, yes, certainly there would be a baptism somewhere and a record kept, but not necessarily with the authorities. They wouldn't have got on with them in them days, if you see what I mean.'

'Civil disobedience?'

'Would that be the name for it, Mal?'

'Or he wasn't a northerner at all,' Frank interrupted. 'We always thought the family was from Creenagh, but who knows?'

'It's amazing what you don't know about a person when you go looking.' Eilis got up to fetch something from the fridge.

'Dan was a famous Gaelic player. Did I ever tell you that? There's a rule in football, says you can't lift the ball straight off the pitch. Dan it was invented a way of picking the ball up with his toe. It's the way they all do it now, but Dan was famous for it. I remember reading an article in the paper about him: Gaelic All-Stars, or some such. It was a national paper, not just a Dungannon one or whatever. The reporter was all the way from Dublin. I kept it for a long while after. Your mother might even remember, but I can't think where we'd find it now. Patsy was a great player too, for the Fianna, in Coalisland. There's a book out about the team, I must get my hands on.'

'Phelim said Dan played in an all-Ireland. Can that be right?'

'Yes, he did. No, he never could. Did Phelim think that? Tyrone never made it to a final then. There mightn't've been so much county football then, what with the war with England. There was a lot of disruption in the game. Boys of the right age would have got mixed up a lot with that sort of trouble, and a lot of them were lifted by the Black and Tans and the local RIC, and the RUC after that. Dan wasn't the only one, although he was famous for it. Or rather, the Dan I knew was famous for it.'

'Why is that? Why Dan in particular?'

Frank paused. He was having to look at his uncle in ways he never had before. 'Maybe he wasn't, you know, maybe it's just as he was known to us. He was Dan, our uncle. I think he never compromised. Even when I knew him, and he wasn't involved in anything like the new IRA, he still hated anything British. He even hated seeing me play soccer. I remember I was kicking ball against a wall, and my mother calling me in because the Munich air disaster was on the news.'

'February 1958.'

'Yes, Mal. We were all big fans of the Busby Babes, seeing as there were so many Irish. But Dan . . . I remember the ticking off he gave me even yet. "What do you care about some English team? Sure that's not a game that should concern you.'" Mal could imagine his father using the same words with him. He felt reprimanded even for knowing the date of Munich. 'Dan wasn't an angry sort of a man, but you wouldn't have wanted to cross him either. I doubt we'll find he ever played soccer, or rugby for that matter.'

'That would be wrong? The 'Ban', right?'

'Yes,' said Eilis. 'At least that's what the GAA call it, Mal.'

Mal had never known his mother to take an interest in Gaelic sports. He, himself, had never played. 'Where did Dan live?'

'Were you never in Creenagh? It's near Edendork, where we…"

'Where we lived until the car . . . until I was six.'

'He had a, what I would call, a lean-to—a shed, more or less. Up at Creenagh, attached to the house where Patsy and his family are now. You know, for keeping hens or pigs. God, it wasn't fit for living in. Damp running down the walls. Do you remember, Eilis?'

'I remember Dan, of course I do.' Eilis had offered Mal a glass of Bailey's. When he declined, she poured herself one anyway. 'We used to walk up to the sawmill, or to the old house in Creenagh from your mother's place in Edendork where Ann is now. That's not a walk I would do nowadays. Dan had a nice wee room there, did he not, Frank?'

'Not fit for animals even.'

'He had his bed and pictures on the wall and a rug on the floor. It may have been a dirt floor, but then, lots were in those days. I think he was happy in there. I remember his sister too, Bassie. Did you know Bassie, Mal? No, you weren't born yet. Bassie was a great one for stories. Dan too. And songs. God, I remember his ghost stories, and we'd have to walk home that dark lane after, and not a light anywhere. And I was only a wee thing then, just courting your father.'

'He was most likely drunk most of the time. I remember that.' Frank's memory was flitting under his wife's influence. 'He always had sweets for the children, for Ann and Phelim and all the kids in Coalisland. I wonder where he got the money from, for he never did a day's work in his life. I wonder did he have an IRA pension. You could find that out.

'It's curious he never married. I think he may have been on the run for some time, you know. I might be wrong, but I heard he was meant to follow Molly out to America. She worked out there, earned the money for the ticket, sent it back home, but Jim took it. Jim was there nearly all his life and hardly saw Molly once. She wouldn't have it. Instead, Dan went to gaol. I wonder if Dan wouldn't trust folk after that.'

'How did he die, Dad?'

'I have that here.' Frank pulled, from a mound of papers, a piece of foolscap trimmed with red.

Daniel O'Rourke
Died 2/ 11/ 1967
At 6 Ardmore Road, Coalisland
Bachelor. Aged 66 years.
Retired Timber Merchant
(Coronary Thrombosis)
Reg'd by P. O'Rourke – sister-in-law
Coalisland Bk 28 E132

Mal read it aloud to himself to check if he had understood it correctly. 'So he was born in the twelve months after November 1900. The O'Rourke business was timber. I hadn't realised that Dan had worked for them. He died of a heart attack, which seems about right for a man who's lived a hard life, and who has been as drunk as much as he had, as you say, Dad.' He was a bachelor. They would have been shocked to find anything different. And they had an address. Little else. A name. An address. An age. A marital status. An occupation. A friend. A date and cause of death. 'So this is how they certificate a life.'

28 March 1922

On the Run

The open air is overrated. I hate the open air. Give me a warm fire and a roof over my head any day. I don't ask for much, I can't afford to be that fussy. Someone will tell me how long I have been out. Bradshaw will know. The B Men know everything, apart from where I happen to be at any given moment. I have been leaving out the back door of Mummy's and Daddy's, as they have been barging in the front door. If they only remembered their manners, they might have caught me before now. They don't waste their manners on the likes of us.

My boots are wet. They have been wet since September, and it's now March. They are the boots I wear at the sawmill when I am working there, so they are strong boots made with real leather. When I bought them in Dungannon, I rode all the way home to Creenagh in them, cutting my heels; and Daddy tore strips off me because he said they were too tight and too fancy. But he was wrong, they were good timber boots, they even smelled at first of new-cut wood, sweet. When was that—it could be years. They don't smell sweet any more. They stink like a sewer. From standing in bogwater, and never drying them or treating them. 'Are those your new boots, Dan?' Mummy asked one time I was home, when I needed tea and feeding. She worried about me, but said it about the boots instead.

MARK QUINN

I am not often home. The neighbours talk. Bradshaw even said as much at the Moy Fair when my father was there trying to get back some of the business he has lost on account of me being on the run. Mullins, McHughs, the other O'Rourkes. I wouldn't trust any of them not to tout on me to the B Men. That's their look-out, I don't judge, the bastards.

They don't have anything on me. They wanted me for internment, but now there's no internment, they just want me. I did Englis' breadvan on the Killyman Road, and the Dungannon to Strabane train, but they know nothing for sure about those. The breadvan was a waste of time and effort. Could have gotten myself killed for a pan loaf, which was all he had, so burning the van out was the least I could do. The Strabane job was another affair altogether. Boys came up from the South for that, saying they were from Collins, and that Michael Collins had sent them. I don't know about that, but they had guns the like of which I've never seen up here. From the landing at Howth, they said. I still have my Colt from that wee adventure. We got the train stopped, and the cigarettes—you've never seen so many in one place. The boys counted every box. You wouldn't have wanted to take any for yourself, on account of them now being needed for a greater cause, and my arse not being worth it. Shiels, the driver was named. He never put up much of a fight, and he's probably in trouble for it now. Good man.

After that, the RIC started paying their visits, though they never had the pleasure of finding me in. I'd be out lots with Daddy, cutting timber in Aughnacloy or as far as Tandragee or Cave Hill. We'd be away days, and get back to Creenagh and find Mummy all quiet. Jim nowhere to be seen and Molly squealing about the house, what she wouldn't do to those B Men given half a chance. Apparently, even Mullin from the nearby scutch mill at Twyford, had come calling for me. That's the younger one, not the Da. He's RIC now too, so it seems. Said something about me to Molly, and how he could be helpful if she was sweet with him, the bastard. I'll have him. He's picked the wrong girl there but, no fear, he'd be creeping back to his mummy with his hands between his legs. Internment. For the

FINDING DAN

maintenance and preservation of order. Arrest without charge. Imprisonment without trial. Lock 'em in the dungeon and throw away the key. Wouldn't be the only one from round here; they've already picked up Joe Cavanagh from Old Engine and Joe O'Neill, and put them in Ballykinlar. Quite the lads about town now, those two, everyone hanging off their every word. They deserve their moment in the sun, now it's over, I suppose. But that's not me. I have no intention of seeing the inside of one of their dirty gaols. I have heard about them, and I don't like what I have heard. I don't need much. My kit: boots, the coat with deep tool-pockets, the canvas satchel I use for lunch when cutting trees with Daddy. I don't want to carry much because I am faster than any of them when I'm travelling light, all that kicking ball did me more good than Mummy said it would. I miss the football, though I haven't missed it, there hasn't been any since the Government of Ireland Act. One time, we would have played all round Dungannon parish from Drumglass and Tullyniskin in the north to Killyman in the south. Too few of us around now to make up a team, there being too many of us raiding police stations and the like to make training. I played for the Clarkes against the Mitchells a year ago, but that wasn't official. Was that before or after I went on the run?

It's cold. The whole thing is cold, you never warm up, even when you do find someone willing to take you in. You shiver, and they think you are frightened, or at least nervous, or perhaps overwhelmed with gratitude to them. They can't imagine how cold you can be under big Tyrone skies. It's cold even now, late morning in late March. Every few minutes, I check in my deep pocket for my Colt, even though its weight is always on my lap, and it's cold too. It's never been warm in my hand: I've never used it, but I'd use it if I had to. Assuming it's not too cold. Waiting makes me ache. I am crouching in a ditch by the side of a road, knees locked up to my chin. My muscles are crying, they are so sore, I am sure they can be heard from the road. The two RIC men, walking home from their nightshift, are bound to hear. The two I'm waiting for, guns swinging, waiting to be plucked.

MARK QUINN

I slept one night under an upturned boat at Bracka, joined by other creatures that liked my idea for sheltering from the rain. It was dry and tight as a boat should be, but a boat rocks, even when upside down and there's no sea. For two nights, I made my home under the canal arch in Coalisland. The water there runs slower, brown and heavy from the coal. I could even have lit a fire there on the yard of shore with the pebbles of coal you can find that the scavenging children leave. But that would be asking for it. The RIC station is high above the opposite bank. Instead, I collected the few coals in my satchel. After all, there's never any lunch in there. Sometimes, I can persuade someone to take me in if I offer them some coal. Biddy and Annie Harkness will take me in, and they don't need so much persuading. They don't get a lot of, let's say, masculine company; apart, that is, from the old man who sits all day with the sow in the corner. 'Come on on in, Dan, and sit yourself down here beside me,' one of them will say. 'And we'll hear no talk of them B Specials you say are after you.' They will offer me a bowl of suet pudding, and I'll eat it anyway, though they won't have boiled it properly. And tea will be poured, though you will look in vain in that hovel for anything like a kettle or a teapot. They have two buckets, one for slag the other for embers. They have a grand enough fire crane, but hanging from it are only a hearth shovel, a poker, and maybe a pair of tongs. A box for matches and one for knives. The fire doesn't so much burn as smoulder, smoky from the illicit turf they cut with their own slane. To their stolen turf, they are grateful to add the coal I've gleaned from the canal-side. The pig farts. It sleeps in its foul straw, and I have the ledge above it. 'You'll be warm up there,' says a voice, and I realise it's the old man. 'Goodnight,' I say back.

There should be two RIC this morning, but there could be one, or three, I'll be ready in any case. I'll hear them coming from way up the road, as it's quiet here and they won't be fussy about disturbing the peace or who knows their business. They think they own the place. I won't know their names, they'll be association football men. That's fine by me. Nothing personal. It's their uniform, and their badge, and the way they walk that I hate. And talk. And the way

FINDING DAN

they get all nervous when their chief comes over from Omagh. I have watched it all. Knowing your enemy, that's called.

Charlie Magee taught me that. He spends his life watching folk from behind his bar in Aughnacloy. The Diamond Main Street. But for the time he did for firearms possession, I don't believe he ever comes out from behind that bar, like the captain of his ship, he'll even rather send one of his dozen offspring down the cellar to replace the one keg. Charlie keeps the place nice, mind, there's always fresh sawdust on the floor, which you can't often say about other places that smell of the piss of the last man who's been in. What he serves from his bottles, mind you, is anybody's guess, there hardly being a label among them. Thomas Hughes, the shoemaker, I happen to know is fond of gin, but I am positive he is served from the same bottle as Bernie Conway who will avowedly touch nothing other than vodka. If one or other turns their nose up at their glass, Charlie will be right on them with, 'No one's forcing you to drink it. If you can find another bar open on a Sunday about here, you're welcome to try there I'm sure.'

'No, no, Charlie, this is fine, it's lovely,' they'll quickly say, apologising for their offence. Charlie's not much of a strong drink man, to be fair—he's there mainly to watch.

Not that anyone worth watching would ever stray into his bar, only our own. He can count on that even on a Sunday when he shutters up and serves sly ones to his colleagues. Magee's lock-ins are famous for those in the know. I would cycle the whole trek to Aughnacloy for one, indeed I have, and that's a fair old jaunt on a bike with hard tyres. There's not much option for a man, such as myself, with so many RIC desirous of my acquaintance, and the Protestant churches fairly determined on it to keep us from drink on the Sabbath. I enter by their house door at the side. Medbh will let me in, and sit me down with a cup of tea and some fruit bread, or else potato soup ('to warm you'), and she'll chat away under one of her numerous Brigid Crosses even though she has a team of youngsters hanging off of her. She's a fine woman. The country will be safe so long as there are the likes of her in it. Mind you, she'd clip me round the ear if she heard me saying it, 'You wee skelp!' I like sitting there with her, filling my stomach with more food than I suppose they have to spare. And part-listening to her chat of the dances she holds to make some money for the families of the interned. 'Daniel, there's women there desperate 'cos their husbands have been put away, and they with no news nor nothing.'

Charlie himself would box my ears if he knew what I really thought of her. 'You sure you took enough tea back there, son? Anyone would think you'd gone off your drink. Your stout's been sitting here waiting for you. I don't want to hear your complaints about it having no head. Now, young Daniel, sit opposite us here, and let us hear some more of your adventures.'

That man travels miles in his imagination to make up for his general intransience. He can tell stories of cattle-rustling in Argentina, whore-mongering in Barcelona, and of the filthy priests of New York City. The Manhattan brethren were depraved in ways, he said he didn't want me ('one so young') to know about, yet he spares me none of the details of the ladies of Las Ramblas. He never leaves me wanting more. He knows everything important about anything, befitting of an IRA intelligence officer. People, it seems, just walk off the street into his pub and pass him information. He has only one licensed rival on Main Street, Matthew Lenny; and since Lenny is also in, let's say, a similar line of work, the rivalry is friendly enough.

I'm telling Charlie the one about the train to Strabane (he's already heard it), and there's the Conway boys there too, and sniper Mohan and Hughes the Shoe, and doesn't only Paddy Cassidy walk in with his one eye. I could've spat my beer clean out. Cassidy's a Brit—or ex-Brit, as he would have it, having fought for the Empire in Belgium. Magee says he's fine, and sure, didn't he have his left eye shot out by an Orangeman. Might have shot the both out, and I wouldn't have minded. Magee trusts him, but that doesn't mean I have to. There's not many you can trust these days if you know what's good for you. There was a time when everyone you knew was on the same side, and those you didn't were your enemy. Now we have the border. Nice and neatly drawn on the new maps with twenty-six counties down there and six up here, and you'd think everyone would know where they were, but no one does.

'Collins will not forget us, not him,' says Mohan.

'He's going about it a funny way then,' says one of the Conways, Thomas or John. 'No one made him sign the Treaty if he didn't want to.'

'I don't think we can be sure of that,' says the other. 'Dev put him up to it. Michael may be no negotiator, but he's a clever big bastard, he'll have a plan for us yet.'

'I happen to know that Michael Collins and James Craig have met and agreed a secret pact not to make incursions across the border at each other. As long ago as January.' Everyone looks at Cassidy, and he looks back, I swear to God, even with his missing eye.

'How could you know that, Pat?' asks Hughes the Shoe, but it's more an accusation. 'Where would information like that come out of?'

Cassidy dabs at a trail of yellow wetness from under his useless eye socket. 'That sort of top secret stuff they only write about in the newspapers. You should have a look, Thomas.'

'That's Craigite propaganda,' Mohan this time. 'Pat, sure, even you can see that.'

'Now, gentlemen, there's no need for rudeness in my bar.'

'I didn't mean . . . Patrick, you know I wasn't talking about your eye. I swear on the life of my wife and four kids, I wouldn't be offensive like that. I was just saying how even a moron would know not to believe a word written in the Unionist press. No offence intended.'

'None taken.'

I say not a word and just get drunk. The chat turns to carrying on the fight. Who do we fight when the Brits go home, will they ever, there are some who care more for the fighting than for the cause, we'll fight them or their proxies 'til there's none of them left, who then will there be only ourselves, so we'll fight amongst ourselves. To listen to de Valera, that's what's ahead of us. We'll wade through Irish blood, is what he says. I'll bow down before no Englishman, but I'd sooner be spared that.

I could stay there all night, and I think Medbh would let me, but Charlie will have none of it. He sets me on my bike and gives it a shove. I'm not far out of Aughnacloy before I fall off. I climb back up, but of course, it's pitch black and the moon is no help, and I'm riding on field as much as I am on the road, going no speed at all. Before I know it, there's a torch in my face.

'You're not from around here.'

'No.'

'Where are you going in this state?'

'Not far.'

'I don't recognise you. What's your name?' It's a policeman.

'As you say, I'm not from around here. I'll be on my way.'

'You better had. And on a Sunday, too!'

I scramble to get back on my bike, but in the dark, I keep missing the pedal. Then, when I do get started, he calls me back, 'Hey! You were going the other way!'

'So I was. Thank you very much. I'll just...' And I struggle to swing the bike round, and set it back on the road straight again. I swear, there and then, if I had my gun and I could see him right, I would take a pop at him right here on this road and leave him bleeding to death, I don't care if he does have children and a wife, I have my dignity too. But he has turned his lamp off, having lost interest in the drunk Fenian with the stolen cycle. Before long, I am lost in total darkness again, and pretty much the only noise is that of my own swearing.

It's like this for hours and the cold, I mentioned that, before I ride straight into a ditch, and collapse with the bike twisted round my left leg. The pain makes me vomit right there. The next thing is I'm waking up in the same ditch with the bicycle wrapped round me like a metal blanket, and I think, so much for being on the run, I couldn't run now if a dog with an RIC badge wanted a bite of my trousers.

FINDING DAN

Now I'm in a different ditch, still with my limp. I notice it's worse in the cold. Maybe one of these days I'll be warmed, and the left peg will not give me gyp. Chance would be a fine thing. Lying in a big warm bed with heavy big blankets weighing me down, and maybe one of those big roaring fires Mummy puts on when Daddy's not around, and only me in the bed not fighting for room with Jim, and certainly none of the girls with their peculiar smells. I can't mind now whether I've ever had a time like that.

Right. Footsteps there, right. Sit up. Now, hold on, the steps are too quick like they're skipping. A policeman skipping—now that I'd have to see! Jesus, it's Mary Finlay! What's she doing out here of a morning? That's Dan Dynan she's with, the Fianna man. Never played in his side, bit before me, but I saw him plenty and he was a good player. I never knew he knew Mary. By the looks of them now, I wouldn't say they had just met. She is wearing his coat against the cold. He is trying to lay a hand on her shoulder, but she is turning away, sniffing loudly. She looks too sore to touch, but big Dan hasn't the wit to see that, and he throws two giant arms around her whole body. She squeals like in pain, and I swear he still hasn't cottoned on, and I am about to get out and save her myself. I have seen Mary in Derry, Coalisland. Obviously, she is older than me, but I have seen her smile at people she's got that sort of nature. He's let her go now and is keeping his distance for a change. Wise move. Maybe the first one he's made. She said something to me once, now come to think on it. What was it. 'They'll be telling stories about you, Dan O'Rourke.' Something of that kind, although she couldn't have, for I never told her my name unless someone of her friends did. She wasn't telling me off, I think she liked it. As I say, she has that sort of a nature. Dynan must have done something bad if she won't even let him lay a hand on her shoulder, and she wearing his coat. I won't take sides; it's none of my business. They're gone now in any case.

This waiting isn't good. I don't like it that they are not here yet. Where are their manners, keeping a man waiting all this while. Ach, we've waited eight hundred years, we can wait a while yet. That's what Collins might say if he were here. He would approve of my patience. In fact, I know for a fact he's been in ditches, not unlike this one waiting on policemen for a reason not unlike mine. If it's good enough for Michael Collins, it's . . . only what he'd say about it all now, who's to say. That Pat Cassidy at Charlie Magee's saying as how Collins and Craig have an understanding on the border situation, we're not to know what we should be getting up to up here. Collins' people have been saying, if we hold tight, the six counties will come back and join the rest. De Valera's lot have called this treason and say we should fight on. Only I've never seen myself as a de Valera man. Anyway, I don't see as how I have any of a choice. It's not as if the B Men will see things my way if I just turn up at Creenagh and say sorry. The war can't be over so long as one side keeps fighting it.

Get him!
Pin him down there where he is.
There! Watch his right hand, he has a gun in his pocket.
The bastard will use it on himself if he can't use it on us.
Here, lift him up. I want to see his Fenian face.

'Do you have any Hail Marys before we take you away? What's wrong with you, O'Rourke? Don't you recognise your own neighbour?'

Is he a friend of yours, Sarge?
Shall we go easy on him, seeing as he's a neighbour and all?
Let me have his gun here.
What's he got? A Colt.
Loaded in four chambers. He was ready then.
Only, he wasn't ready for us.

'Give you a nasty surprise, did we, O'Rourke? Waiting for your own B men coming your way, and there's us coming at you from behind. I thought they trained you better in the IRA than that.'

Grab him. He's a slippery bugger!
Take him into the Orange Hall, and hold him there until there's someone ready at the station to take him off our hands. Tie him right. Make sure you do.

FINDING DAN

'You haven't got much to say for yourself this morning, Dan. That's not much like an O'Rourke. Usually can't shut you papists up, always got an opinion or a remark to pass. Can't I tempt you? Haven't you heard the news? You're at war with yourselves now. The IRA aren't going to support Collins' government. That'll learn him for thinking he could play at Lloyd George's game. It will make a nice change, watching you lot tear strips out of each other for a change.'

It's warmer here at least. That woman, I recognise her from somewhere, keeps plying me with breakfast—you'd think I hadn't eaten in a month or I'm not going to. Soda farls, fadge, eggs—two of them. I swear she's glad to see me. Maybe it was her who put me here, someone must have informed on me. Thinks to herself I'll forgive her if she keeps the tea coming my way. I won't, but I'll take the tea anyway. Ballynakelly Orange Hall. There's Orange Halls all over the show, but I've never been in one until now, and it takes me to be arrested. A floor like in a school gym, and schoolhouse chairs, and a long folding table they could use for committee meetings, or else for papering the walls. They have a painting of the King high up on the wall at one end with a British flag and an Orange flag on either side, bowing at him. I don't know what they must do with all this space. There's a bunch of them talking at the other end, and they're certain to be talking about me in just their normal voices, not trying to be quiet or anything. But I can't, for the life of me, work out what they're saying. I'd like to know, but the hall is so big, their voices don't carry this far. I should tell them to speak up. I bet this is what they do: they'll keep me here for a while, leave me alone, feed me up, not say nothing to me, get my hopes up that they might just let me be on my way, and before you know it, I'll be before the registered Magistrate in Dungannon dealing with questions from the District Inspector. They'll have their flags and their pictures of the King in the court, no doubt too. I'll tell them I don't recognise their British court, and if they ask me about my revolver, I'll tell them I'm only sorry I never got a chance to use it. Then they'll lock me up. Who of us is free in this country anyway? What Irishman in the six counties can be free now that they've condemned us with this treaty? That border, it's like a rope hanging loose around all our necks, and they're just waiting their chance to pull it tight.

Molly should leave if she gets the chance, and even Jim, though Daddy will need him now at the mill. Molly has been saving for the boat to America. They say there's work there for Irish girls who are well-brought-up and she is that. Mummy might need her at home now if I get put away, not that I've been any use to anyone at home this past while. If I'm in prison when she goes, that'll be it. I'll not see her. But this is no country for a girl like her. I wouldn't say no to going myself.

10 August 1998

Winnie

Frank did most of the talking in the car on the way to Coalisland. When Mal was six, they had left Edendork, and found a house in Ballymena on a brand new estate with a mound in the middle the shape of Slemish. Driving out of Ballymena now, they crested the hill at Moneyglass with its long and dramatic drop down to Toome on the northern edge of Lough Neagh. In the old days, with the little Mal rattling about unbelted in the back of the Viva as they made their dutiful visits to relatives in Tyrone, Frank used to switch his engine off to see how far the hill would take them. Past the telegraph pole, which was re-erected after Eilis skidded on black ice and knocked it down, past the bungalow with the orange garage door, past the crossroads. Never as far as the church at the bottom, at which Mal learned to bless himself, after the manner of his father. From the top on a clear day, you could get a view of counties Antrim, Derry, Tyrone, and Armagh. It was clear and hot today, but still, there were rain clouds over the far side of the lough. Through streaming sunlight, the rain fell in quiet diagonals over Washing Bay and Coalisland. Two rainbows arced the lough, touching down in each county. This was the view that Frank never failed to point out was like no other in the world. To Mal now, in a less romantic frame of mind, the scene was a stereotype. It was green, it was wet, it had fucking rainbows in it.

'Toome is the smallest town in the world with a one-way system.' If Mal had said this, it would have been to dismiss the place as preposterous. As it was, it was Frank who said it, and he meant it to impress.

'And the biggest RUC station per head of population,' Mal rejoined, as they passed the enormous police fortress with its crown of barbed wire. They crossed the bridge over the Bann, the river that cracks the country east from west. A bit wilder on the other side, Mal always thought. Just out of Toome, they saw two police vehicles positioned across each lane of the road, about twenty metres apart. For a moment, Mal entered a fantasy where his father was doing what he would never do: swerving his car between the armoured cars and tanks and guns as through a chicane then taking off at high speed down the long straight road to Magherafelt. Mal would duck in the passenger seat, as the volley of shots smashed the windscreen in front of them, fired from the roadside bushes where teen soldiers from Dagenham and Maidenhead crouched nervously.

If Eilis had been with them, she would have insisted on taking the road out of Toome through Magherafelt, Cookstown, and Dungannon. Alone, Frank always opted to drive along the west coast of Lough Neagh through Ballyronan, Ballinderry, Coagh, Stewartstown, and on to Coalisland. Skirting the lough, the heat had stirred the midges, as it often did this time of year. The midges folded through the thick air in their instinctive formations, detonating in tiny deaths: a red massacre on the windscreen.

As they approached Coalisland, the town he grew up in but never lived in as an adult, Frank felt a tight warmth gathering in the base of his throat like a blockage. The place had a way of confounding him, as if making him pay for his leaving of it. The unease was about this. It was about his son too, peering through the passenger window like a tourist. He wanted to say something to Mal, to tone him down.

'Maybe we should widen the scope of this now,' Frank suggested. 'The Main Street in Coalisland had a different story happen in it every day. You could write a whole book just about the people who

FINDING DAN

lived there, and what they got up to. There were other old IRA men knocking about too, not just Dan. They're dead now, I'm sure. Paddy Crawford, Joe O'Neill, Frank McQuaid, Sean Hughes. John Haughey: now I'm sure he was interned on the *SS Argenta* with Dan, or so I heard. And old Joe Cavanagh. As wee lads, we would have shown a respect to the likes of them, you know. And we would give the RUC man the run-around all the time. Constable Foster, it was. Father McGarvey, the parish priest, would say on a Sunday with a twinkle in his eye, "The young people should have a bit higher regard for the police. Sure, don't they have a bad enough time of it just being police?" And then he would name people from the pulpit, young people who needed to behave.'

'Did he ever name you?'

'Me? No, never. I should think Phelim got a mention though.'

'Was he bad?'

'Not bad as such, but he'd be in trouble as much with the boys as with the police.'

'The boys—the local IRA?'

'Aye, the boys.'

'You should write that book of tales, Dad.'

'That's more your thing, is it not?'

After a pause, Mal said, 'Perhaps that comes from you.' He had had the last word, which, with his dad, was always a mistake.

Main Street might not have changed much over the previous thirty years or more, apart from the cars parked double and the Heritage Centre. A travel agents, a pub, a vacancy where a building must once have stood, a hardware store, a supplier of electrical goods, and across from it—and bearing the same name—a tiny petrol station, *Shaun Quinn & Sons*. This last seemed to peer over the canal wall at the RUC station on the other side. Not that there was a canal. Where it should have been, there was now a car park, its white lines all paid out and displayed. A stream was allowed to struggle on through banks of twisting grass, and a smart arse from the council had put a pointless bridge across it.

They were met at the porch by Winnie; her daughter, Dorothy; and grandson, Andrew. Winnie was, by far, the largest physical presence. Dorothy stood out by standing slightly to the fore, practised in upstaging her mother. Andrew was there behind the darkened glass of the porch, so he could not really be seen.

Inside the house, Frank was guided into the living room, while Winnie took Mal with her to the kitchen. It was warm from the oven, and from the warm smell of baking bread. A stack of four or five baking tins, charred greaseproof paper licking out, was cooling near the sink; puddles of flour had still to be cleaned from the surfaces. As Winnie sat, her skirt billowed and raised a small cloud of flour around her. For a woman in her eighties, her hair was strangely dark and lustrous. Her face, though large, still bore most of the traces of a much younger beauty. She was tall. Her knees and hips struggled with their burden, as if one pair of legs was not quite enough. She pressed her left hand flat on the table, as she lowered herself into her chair. She offered Mal some fruit bread.

'I'll have a little piece, I wouldn't have too much of that.'

'There's Dan for you. Your daddy has been speaking to Molly. He's expecting her to send him over that memoir or whatever. He could be waiting a while yet!' Winnie laughed to herself. Mal said nothing. 'Well, she had better get a move on, she'll not get any younger!'

'Molly. Is she not well, Winnie?' Something had happened to Mal's voice, and he noticed it. Not just the accent, but the pattern he put the words into. He couldn't explain it, but it was mixed up with how much he liked his great-aunt. He wanted her to like him back.

'Molly's a horse! Dan, now, he was a good-looking fella.' Winnie paused, as if to allow Mal to take notes. 'He suffered in gaol, like,' she continued. 'That's how he got injured, lying in the water. They flooded his cell. You know, whenever he wouldn't wear the uniform, they flooded his cell. That was in Derry. And then, de Valera wrote to him telling him to come off the hunger strike. That letter was all wasted, wherever it is.'

FINDING DAN

'From Eamon de Valera, you mean? Was that letter sent to the prison?' Mal was excited that his father may have overlooked the letter in Dan's PRONI file, one from the Irish president at that.

'It would have been sent to the IRA business... I don't know who they were... and Dan was told to come off the hunger strike. But then, Looney's . . . Master Looney's father was governor of Derry gaol. Jack Looney was a headmaster in Coalisland, but whenever he went to Derry gaol, this old Martin Looney was the governor. And he says to Dan, he came in, "We've tamed lions here." And Dan says, "There's a lion here you haven't tamed yet."

'I heard tell, years later, when Master Looney had hung up his chalk and become a policeman, his da, the governor, got remarried. Now get this, Mal, the woman he married was Katherine O'Rourke. Not your grandmother, but the same name as. Isn't that funny!'

Sounds of laughter, drifting in from the living room, punctuated their talk. 'You've not brought your girlfriend to see me?' Mal shook his head. 'What's her name?'

'Rosa.'

'Ah, an English Rosa!' Winnie was amused by her joke. 'You want an English girl, Mal. You don't want an Irish girl bringing you back here.' She touched his hand on the table, squeezing gently. 'I say, Frank', she shouted to the next room, 'Mal'll not take an Irish girl!'

Winnie laughed again. Mal suggested they join the others.

The room, though actually quite large, seemed too small for everything that was in it. Furniture from more than one suite, a low ceiling, and only a single standard lamp offering any light, and a sideboard bristling with family photographs. One of these, in black and white, showed a smiling young man with shoulder-length hair parted in the centre. Long nose, big, white shirt collar—it reminded Mal of Bobby Sandds, the IRA hunger striker. A plate of biscuits, another of sliced cake, a tray for tea. There was too much of everything, and it felt like Christmas rather than the middle of summer.

Frank's cousin, Dorothy, was already in charge of proceedings. The standard lamp exhausted all its energy just on lighting her. 'Mummy, where are they all from? Dan and Molly and that, you know, originally?'

'Dan was born in Dunman. There was four of them born there, Molly and Dan and Bassie and Jim. And they lived there. My father run a mill there. My grandfather and my Aunt Roseanne lived at Creenagh at that stage. My Aunt Roseanne, who married an oul' RIC man, a boy named Campbell. And Dan…he'd never admit that. Then they left Dunman Mill and come up to Master Kelly's house, the schoolhouse. They lived in Master Kelly's house until Roseanna married, and then his father sent for us to go and live up at Creenagh.'

'So who was the eldest, then?' This was Mal.

'Jim,' said Frank.

'Dan, I think, was the eldest.' Winnie was unsteadied by Frank, but she was certain enough. 'There's ten months difference between him and Jim. And then Molly and Bassie. The rest of us were born in Creenagh.'

Frank wondered whether he had been looking for Dan's birth records in the wrong place. Mal decided to have a second slice of cake. Winnie leaned back in her chair, her eyes closing. Someone touched their teacup down in its saucer. Dorothy cleared her throat.

'It turns out Dan was not the only one of us to have a run-in with the Brits. Mal, you're not offended if I call them that, are you?' Breathing in crumbs from his cake, Mal didn't manage to say anything. 'Do you know who was the first person ever to be extradited within Britain? Well, you should all be ashamed of yourselves if you don't.'

'Brian O'Rourke?' her son guessed.

'Well done, Andrew, but you have heard this before from me. It was the same Brian O'Rourke, sheriff of Leitrim and last Lord of West Breifne, Mummy's ancestor from the sixteenth century. That makes him the ancestor of everyone in this room. They say he had a beautiful wife and was very handsome himself. So we did all

FINDING DAN

right there. He was described by his enemies as "the proudest man this day living on the earth" for refusing to submit his kingdom to Queen Elizabeth. Are you following me?' She had slowed down for Mal. He was wiping his eyes, having choked on the cake. 'The L*evant* . . . L*evant*? Is that how you say it, Mal, L*evant*? So, as I say, the L*evant* squadron of the Spanish Armada ran aground off the west coast of Ireland, and Brian O'Rourke helped more than eighty of them to escape back to Spain, including one called Captain Francisco de Cuellar. God, my Spanish is awful, isn't it not, Frank? De Cuellar: there's a story there too, if you've time. Cuellar had been sentenced to death for breaking formation in the North Sea, and was on board a galleon that ran aground off Sligo. Hundreds drowned and were washed ashore, while other survivors were beaten by locals who had come on to the strand for a bit of looting. With another survivor, he was set upon by four locals who stripped him of his clothes and valuables, and wounded him in the leg. A woman came, returning his clothes, and he gave her a locket with holy relics, which she hung around her neck. His wounds were tended by a boy, who also fed him with bread and butter and milk, and who warned him not to enter the village, as the English were there. So he went on, living off wild berries. When he was attacked again, and stripped again of his clothes and remaining valuables, he made a skirt for himself of grass and ferns. Eventually, he met a man who spoke to him in Latin, and he was taken to meet Brian O'Rourke in Breifne. In Breifne, he earned his keep by singing and telling stories and predicting the future. They say he foretold the terrible death of his host, O'Rourke, in London. Despite this, or maybe because of it, O'Rourke's wife is said to have fallen in love with the Spaniard who had hair as dark as a raven's. That could be where we get ours from because some say she bore him a child. But no one knows the truth, or otherwise, of this. What is not denied is that O'Rourke treated him well, and arranged for his safe passage back to Spain. Cuellar later wrote that Breifne was savage and lawless, but that the people were kind and believed in God.

'Anyway, none of this did Brian O'Rourke any good. Richard Bingham, the English president of Connaught, sent an army to occupy Breifne, and O'Rourke fled to Scotland to try to raise a force of gallowglasses—mercenaries if you will. He hoped to gain the sympathy of the Scots King James VI, but he was refused an audience. Instead, James was fooled by the English who said they would treat O'Rourke leniently, and the Scots delivered Brian to the English crown forces. The whole of Ireland was outraged: there were riots in Glasgow and attacks on Scottish trading boats.

'They held him in the Tower of London, and tried him on three counts of treason, aiding the Spanish enemy, trying to raise a mercenary army, and what they called 'treason of the image'. Apparently, he had tied a painting of the queen to the tail of a horse and had it dragged through the muddy streets. Too good for her.

'Of course, Brian didn't speak English, so the court employed a native Irish speaker to translate the charges for him. The court entered a plea of not guilty, but some said that Brian refused to recognise the court unless there was a jury and the queen was the judge. Well, they wouldn't have that, and they went ahead and found him guilty. He was sentenced to death. They dragged him by horse over the dirt to Tyburn. They hanged him then they cut him to pieces.

'Do you like that story now, Mal? I know you write a wee story yourself. Would you ever get one published for us, so we can read it? I'm sure they're marvellous.'

Mal had heard the word *Breifne*, but had always taken it for some mystical Irish place like a Tir-na-nog or Mag Mell. He was impressed by Dorothy's story, by the detail in it, and the way she told it. But he couldn't know it had any connection to them. Dorothy declared that they were descended from Brian O'Rourke, but that did not make it so. But she believed it, and so did Winnie, and so presumably had Dan and all the rest. Mal wondered that his father had not known any of this.

A cuckoo clock chimed. Andrew was now sitting on the floor by his mother's legs. Frank and Mal shared a sofa, each leaning back

FINDING DAN

into opposite corners, so as to avoid sagging into each other. Winnie was again seated in her upright armchair.

It was Dorothy who called her mother to speak next. 'Mummy, tell us about the time Dan was on the run.'

Winnie jammed her elbow into the headrest, and applied the back of her hand to her forehead like a southern belle cooling herself. 'Jack Bradshaw was one of the head B Men, and he met my father at the Moy Fair. And he says to my father, "Dan was home the other night." Dan was on the run, you see. And he says, "I have some of your neighbours here. Some of your neighbours saw him." You could stand and look round Creenagh and see who the neighbours would be. You couldn't get one to take you in. You wouldn't get a safe house. The only people who kept him in Creenagh were Biddy Harkness and Ann.'

'Oh, God! I wouldn't have stayed with them!' Dorothy laughed. 'If there was nobody else in the world...Oh God! Oh, they were awful dirty women, Biddy and Annie Harkness. They had a fire actually, I remember, was a hole in the ground. Seriously, they had no fireplace.'

'They used to scrape their legs with a knife and butter bread with it.' Winnie could not control her laughing. 'I remember going and I didn't like the tea. It was smoked in a can, and there was a hole in the welly, and they put the tea into the welly, and it came out through the welly. And they gave me Christmas pudding that hadn't been boiled.

'And Dan would have slept there. No one else would take him in. There was a fella who went there one time to ask Annie her hand in marriage. Arthur Campbell. And the father, oul' Barney, he was in the corner. But the sow, who had a litter of three, she was in the corner. Oh, God, they were all in the corner! And he never asked. He went in and sat down. And the sow got up and started to grunt, around him, Arthur. And oul' Barney says, "Oh, sit down, she knows the boy's strange. When she gets used to you, she'll go down again." She lay there anyway, and there was tea made and Annie got washed and all. But the way Annie was making this tea and setting it all up and all, Arthur didn't like it. Arthur put the tea aside, and he got up and he took the stick and away out. He didn't ask for her. He had seen she had dirty habits.'

Frank thought they would be interested to hear about the research he and Mal had already done. 'The boys that arrested Dan… there was a guy called Mullin around here. Mullin. From Dungannon.'

'Aye, they were down beside them,' said Winnie. 'If you continue on down the lane at Creenagh, you cross that road, and down there's Mullins. They were a scutch mill for flax. Owen Quinn lost his arm at it.'

'Is that Twyford Mill?' asked Frank. 'Did the Mullins own Twyford? The record in Belfast said Dan was arrested by Mullin, and they owned Twyford Mill.'

'Oh, my father never went near to Mullin after Dan was arrested.'

'Where was this that Dan busted his leg?' asked Frank. 'I mind he had a limp, and hearing as how it had been busted when he was on the prison ship, on the *Argenta*. Where did he hurt his leg?'

'While he was in gaol, they flooded his cell, his room was flooded, you see. And lying in water, paralysed his…'

'In Derry?' Frank interrupted his aunt.

'Dan was about twenty-something when he went there, to Derry gaol, and he was there over a year… and they were there on the ship, the *Argenta*, with Joe Cavanagh and anyway, they used to warm old iron they had and it killed the legs of them.'

'Weren't they protected?' Dorothy asked her mother.

'They had nothing to protect their clothes, to protect their legs. The ship was that dirty. The English treated the Irish worse than the coloured people. Oh, by Jesus, they hated the Irish. He wouldn't take a state pension when he was older, and he never got an IRA pension. John Haughey and them all got it. You know Tommy and them all? He applied for it, and he never got it.'

Dorothy mused. 'How much would he have got? By the time de Valera got a cut out of it, there would have been little left.'

FINDING DAN

'He wrote to...whether President de Valera wrote to Sinn Fein or whoever he wrote, for Dan to come off hunger strike. Where is that letter now?' Winnie was suddenly angry.

'Would that have been on the *Argenta*? 'Cos I know there was a hunger strike on the *Argenta*.'

'There was a hunger strike on the *Argenta*.' Mal noticed how Winnie had not answered his question. It seemed unlikely, if Dan had starved himself on the prison ship, the most notorious part of the internment network, that he did not receive an IRA pension. Mal suspected that Dan had his reasons for keeping his money quiet.

'Once he hurt his leg when he was on the *Argenta*, was he able to play football again when he came out?'

'Actually, Frank, he hurt it in gaol in Derry. His cell was flooded, you see. He lay in water. He was a broken man whenever he came out.'

Frank was perplexed. 'So was he able to play football when he came out again? Was he fit to play properly?'

'Oh, he played afterwards.'

'Because he was very bad when I knew him, he had a bad limp.'

'He wasn't as good. He was a broken man when they let him out.'

'He played for the Clarkes in Dungannon and the Fianna in Coalisland and he played for Tyrone too.' Frank had not expected his aunt to shed much light on Dan's playing days, but he could not see how he could be a broken man, and at the same time, a county footballer. And given he *was* a county player, he could not have been broken by his time in gaol.

Winnie left to use the loo in the hallway, announcing this, and getting her grandson to help her out of her chair. In her absence, they needed to work harder to keep the conversation going. Dorothy remembered that Dan had lived in a pensioner's flat before he died.

'Before that, he lived in Creenagh in a wee lean-to, and he was happy as Larry. We would wend up to Creenagh, and that's where we went. Into that wee lean-to, you would have stayed in there. And Patsy was with the family in the home. It was basic then, very basic. But he had his bed, and the house then would have been fairly basic itself. There was no running water or anything, but Patsy would have different views upon Dan, and how Phyllis and all was, you know, treated. Patsy had a family there. He had Phyllis and the kids, and there weren't that many rooms in the house. And he sort of . . . Dan just lived in an outhouse. You should talk to Patsy about that one.'

Dorothy paused. She glanced at the door to the hallway and lowered her voice.

'She did tell me about maybe a family, a child. Dan. Maybe he had a child out of wedlock.'

'Dorothy, did I tell you that Molly had written a memoir? Bram wouldn't have it, so he had it burned. Maybe that would be why. If there is a family, does your mummy know who they are?'

'I think so, Frank, I'd have to go over it with her. But why would Bram do that? Burn his own mother's story?'

'He'll have had his reasons. But she is writing it again, or so she indicated to me. The problem is she can't have long left.'

Winnie came back into the room, not looking at anyone in particular, but with something round in her hand.

'Mummy, girlfriends . . . what about Dan's girlfriends?' Dorothy hadn't the patience for subtlety.

'He had a few girlfriends.'

'Any offspring?'

'He had a girl in Rostrevor called Kathleen Jackson. They had boats there. We used to be there in our school holidays. A lovely, sweet singing voice. She was a great woman for Dan.'

'But he never married her? Or thought about marrying?' Frank this time.

'No, he never took her.'

'Why did he never marry?'

Winnie threw something to her grandson. It was a stress ball. He threw it back.

'She used to make great apple tarts,' said Winnie, catching the ball.

Dorothy pressed on. 'Why did he never marry?'

FINDING DAN

'He had a different view of marriage. He couldn't see marrying or supporting a woman or things like that. He didn't like that.'

'Did he never get close to marrying?'

'No.' She threw the ball to Mal.

'Or was she not close to marrying him?' Frank again.

'Oh, she would have married him,' Winnie declared. 'She would have took him.'

'What about playing around?'

Mal lobbed the stress ball back to Winnie. She missed it, and it struck her harmlessly on the forehead. Andrew rolled around the floor laughing, and Mal and Winnie joined in. The question was finally lost.

Within ten minutes, Mal and Frank were at the front door. Winnie was playing like a little girl with Andrew, Dorothy was making Frank promise he and Eilis would call in to visit her soon.

Although he would have preferred to drive straight home, Frank had promised to leave Mal off with his sister, Ann, in Edendork. Ann was younger than Frank, though not by much. Her bungalow had belonged to her mother. The young Mal would call in on his aunt when out wandering the wilderness of Edendork, and he remembered from those times the cracked tile in the hallway, which rocked when you stood on it. He could still hear it in his head, evoking clothes brushes on hatstands and mirrors with faded edges.

'I never knew about a lassie in Rostrevor,' said Frank, after he had told Ann everything else.

'I can do better than that, I'm afraid,' his sister countered. 'You know Patsy's son, Jim O'Rourke? He's been telling anyone who will listen that he overheard Johnny Early recently declare in a pub in Coalisland that "my wife is the daughter of Dan O'Rourke." Now, did you know that one, Frank?'

'No, I did not. Johnny Early . . . we are talking Damian Early's father here? I'd rather not believe that.'

Mal was undeterred. 'If Dan had a daughter, she must be in her seventies by now. How could you keep a thing like that secret? Unless it's no secret. What was Dorothy talking about back there?

She said something about Dan having a child out of wedlock. Winnie must have said something to her she didn't want to say to us. Out of wedlock, why not then get married?'

'Because the girl was a Protestant,' said Frank reluctantly. 'I'm sure Johnny's wife was Protestant before he married her. I went to school with Damian Early, their son. If she was Protestant, then so was her mother. Dan would have bother with that. No, he couldn't have. And we'd already know if he had.'

'You can find out for yourself, Frank. Patsy would know. You really ought to speak to Patsy.'

Frank knew the truth of this. 'Patsy is an old man, and I'm not sure he's the right one to remember Dan. I'll go back to Belfast. The records will have what we need.'

Frank hoped the post would bring a letter from Molly, and an end to it all.

An Irishman in an English Gaol, 25 November 1925

By Malachy Quinn

Why Seamus Hegarty killed his wife is not known. What is known is how and when and where he killed his wife, and what happened to the daughter they shared, but whom he hadn't seen for any of the previous ten years.

Seamus Hegarty carried out the brutal assault on his landlady, Flora Tucker, exactly one week after he had celebrated his twenty-fifth birthday (during which he had drunk away all the rent money he owed to her). Flora was a large lady, given to turning sideways as she passed through doors. She did this partly to avoid the door frame, partly to offer a favourable profile of her bosom to any man who might be in the room she was entering, but mostly because it had long ago become her habit; and Mrs Tucker was, above all else, a woman of regular habits. She demanded rent from her tenants on the same day every month, and sex from her husband on the same day every week. It was an aspect of her character that Mr Tucker, her late husband, had never reconciled himself to. His habits were more *irregular*, and his early grave was a blessing to them both. 'That's the sort of husband a woman is better off without,' her priest had said, and she had felt consoled and absolved. In the main, Flora had considered her bulk to be an asset. Whether she would have thought this, as Hegarty was repeatedly and viciously laying into her with a fire iron, is impossible now to know. She was not asked the question at Hegarty's trial in Limerick district court on 25 May 1913, and she died almost exactly three years later of injuries, which, fortunately for Hegarty, the coroner decided were unrelated to the original assault.

Before Hegarty was obliged to await his trial in Limerick City Gaol, his home had been 31b River Walk, Limerick, County Limerick, Ireland. His home was a single room, square, one window, one bed, one table, two chairs. The second chair was for Helen, his wife. The paper on the walls rippled with damp, and the rug moved with them as they moved across the floor. Helen was nineteen, and after one year, still hated the rhyme her name now made. And she especially loathed how her husband aspirated it, *Helen-Hegarty-Helen-Hegarty*, as he made love to her on the bed. Below in 31a, Flora Tucker listened to the rhythms above and rolled over on her hand.

Few details emerged concerning Hegarty's background and character during his trial. The judge could not have read from his smooth, yellow skin and bony, angular forehead that he had been a near-mute as a child, having to live with one parent or other, as they travelled their separate ways around the counties of Limerick and Clare. No journalist in the gallery (three had come from as far as Dublin) commented on the third place the defendant had achieved in a national spelling contest when he was a child. Instead, they mentioned his apparent lack of remorse, his failure to put a case in his own defence, and the absence from the court throughout proceedings of his young wife. The basic facts were quickly agreed. Hegarty had no money for his rent, and had attacked his landlady when she came to collect it on the agreed day. The judge pronounced him guilty, sentenced him to a lengthy stretch in gaol, then retired to his chambers to sleep for the remainder of the afternoon. Officers of the court already knew that there was no available cell in the local prison, and after seven days were advised that neither Tralee nor Galway could accommodate the prisoner. Under these circumstances, the procedure was to accompany the prisoner (handcuffed) by train to Dublin, from where port authorities would

FINDING DAN

escort him to Holyhead before setting him on the long rail journey to London. Helen Hegarty waived her right of appeal against this extreme separation from her husband.

Hegarty (Prisoner I:146001) spent three years in Pentonville prison. He was kept apart from other Irish prisoners. Some were being held for their gun-running exploits, other 'politicals' had been detained for anti-Home Rule conspiratorial activities. I:146001 shared a cell and a wing with other violent offenders, assorted arsonists, and anarchists. Being Irish, he was not offered the opportunity to rehabilitate himself through military service in France, as others of his colleagues did after March 1916. Following the Easter of that year, he might have noticed a sharpening in attitudes towards him of his warders, but the few records relating to this period of his incarceration mention only that he had requested to work in the prison library (denied), and that he wrote frequent letters to his wife and child in Ireland. And one other, protesting his transfer late in 1916 to Parkhurst prison on the Isle of White. The containment of German prisoners of war and Irish Easter rebels was putting enormous strain on the United Kingdom prison and internment camp network; and prisoner I:146001 was a casualty of the effort.

Several reports were filed on Hegarty's conduct over the first six months of his sojourn in Parkhurst. He was variously described as 'difficult', 'aggressive', 'unbiddable', 'intemperate', and 'typically Irish in demeanour'. He became involved in fights in the canteen and exercise yard, and spent several short periods in solitary confinement. During this stretch, he wrote his first letters to the prison authorities requesting transfer to an Irish gaol. He was missing his wife. A daughter, born after he was first imprisoned, was now approaching her third birthday, and had never seen her father. Sometime in 1917, Hegarty (E:45002) befriended Father Cathal Keenan, the Catholic chaplain assigned to Parkhurst. E:45002 started to assist Keenan in the weekly mass, but judging from the letters that the priest began to write in his support, the two met more frequently than that with the chaplain acting as both a spiritual and literary mentor. Keenan described his younger friend's thirst for betterment through reading as 'unquenchable'.

'Upon Seamus' request, I have brought him great classics of world literature such as Dostoevsky and Chesterton, as well as less celebrated works by Joseph Conrad and a little-known author from Ireland, James Joyce. I have also been able to interest him in some more obscure passages from the Old Testament. Though a quiet man in himself, I believe Seamus is learning to understand himself, and his past actions, through reading.'

Only one letter from Helen Hegarty survives from this period, apparently edited at that. 'Isabella [daughter] spends most days with my mother and is thriving. I am still working in the bakery, and they let me bring treats home if they're damaged. Do you remember old Willy McKenna with the bike and the eye? I saw him the other day. I reckon he would have asked after you, but he was ashamed to. Everyone remains very good to us considering the trouble. They say your mother's now in Cork, or Cobh.'

It must be assumed that the conduct of prisoner E:45002 improved over the ensuing years, as the only reports referred to his ongoing campaign to be removed to an Irish gaol. It appears the governor of Parkhurst was indifferent to the repeated requests, having no say over it in any case. Through 1919 to 1920, as war raged against British rule in Ireland, Hegarty succeeded in recruiting to his cause certain British parliamentarians who harboured well-known Irish republican sympathies. Captain Wedgewood Benn wrote to the Colonial Secretary's Office, 'As we seek to conceal our Irish shame by heaping upon ourselves yet more of the same, as we wage this doomed war against a people who ought to be our dearest cousins, it is obscene that we hold this man, as if a hostage, in an English gaol.' The Liberal MP for Oxford, Frank Gray, spoke in the House during passage of the Government of Ireland Bill. 'Seamus Hegarty is an Irish man. He committed his crime against an Irish woman in an Irish town. If there was any doubt before, there can be none now. He should serve out his time in an Irish prison.' (Hansard, 20 October 1920.) The liberal press,

FINDING DAN

based mainly in Manchester and Glasgow, intermittently took up the cause. And these newspapers attracted the supportive comments of Shaw and Yeats and Webb. Gray was perhaps speaking ahead of himself. The Anglo-Irish Treaty did not follow until December the following year, and the year that followed that was marred by civil war. But his point held. Hegarty had committed his crime at a time when Ireland was wholly a part of the United Kingdom when it existed as an outline on a map, or reclined as a lump of earth in the ocean, but not as a place that made its own laws. He could therefore be imprisoned as easily in London as in Limerick. However, by 1923, Ireland had sat up. E:45002 was now incarcerated in a foreign gaol.

Father Keenan remained faithful to his fellow exile. In October 1923, he sought the support of the acting president of Ireland, Padraig O'Ruitleis, employing new legalistic arguments.

'A t'Uachtarán. For ten and a half years now, Seamus Hegarty of Limerick has languished in English gaols. During his original trial for the assault of a woman witnesses were inadequately cross-examined. The judge preferring to interpret as criminal character Mr Hegarty's natural reticence, a condition he had borne since a childhood of parental neglect. No one sought to question the character of the alleged victim who, I am told, had repeatedly assailed Mr Hegarty with sexual advances. Testimonials were not taken at the time as to the defendant's previous good character with, for example, no reference made to his nationally recognised academic achievements.

'I have known this man for seven years, first as his priest, then as his friend. We have read together, and we have prayed together. He has allowed me to look into his soul. If he did wrong in the past, he is a good man now. He is also a husband and a father who has not seen his wife in ten years nor his child at all. He does not ask for his freedom, just the right to be imprisoned in his own land.'

Unsurprisingly, given the times, there is no evidence of a reply to this letter. Ireland, it appeared, had things on its mind other than the return to its shores of convicted felons. By the end of 1923, a note on the governor's logbook confirms that the English were keen to be rid of E:45002. 'Arrange for immediate transfer upon formal request.' The English no longer wanted him, but the Irish, by now, had more than their fill of hard men.

By 1925, Hegarty had done twelve years, and he was eligible for parole. He appeared before a judge in Southampton who asked him if he desired to be set free.

'No, Your Honour.'

'You do not?'

'No, I do not.'

The judge had before him a file containing many years of pleas from the prisoner himself, and from others of undoubted good character. He thought the man before him should be in prison in Ireland, and that the Irish had no right to insist that he stay where he was. If he could not put him in an Irish gaol himself, he could put him out of an English one, and let them deal with the consequences.

'But I do not wish to be released. I have not completed my sentence.'

The English judge ran his finger down the notes made by an Irish judge twelve years before. No minimum sentence had been decided, no tariff set. 'It's my view that you have.'

The train took Hegarty first to London then to Cardiff. He was escorted further to Holyhead, and on to the boat for Dublin. No official waited for him there. He somehow found his way to Limerick where, it is believed, he lived rough for four months. He was ineligible for any state benefits, having lived abroad for the previous twelve years, and having no address. He was found asleep below a bridge over a bend in the river on the northern outskirts of the city. He was arrested and taken for questioning in the central police station where he admitted to the murder of Helen Hegarty.

Seamus had surprised his wife in the same rooms they had shared at 31b River Walk. She had not been informed of his hearing in Southampton or of its outcome; she did not know that her husband was in the city. Hegarty told the police that she had said she was glad that he was back, but that she wanted him not to live with her and her daughter. He had left at that point, and over the next

FINDING DAN

few weeks had found shelter in some of the city's plentiful slums. He did not see the girl. Willy McKenna, an acquaintance who had also fallen on hard times, told him that the girl was not, in fact, his daughter. A boy from the bakery where Helen worked was believed to be the father. Seamus did not prosper outdoors. He had grown accustomed to the constrictions of a prison cell and of prison life. He found that he did not prefer to be in Ireland.

He returned to 31b River Walk with the intention of killing his wife. He had not expected to see flowers (he said they were white and yellow) in a huge vase on a table in the centre of the room; and the girl, tall and in a party dress, arranging them. He realised it must be her birthday, that she was twelve, and that it was only November. He admitted to the police his sorrow that the girl had to witness what happened next. He swept the vase of flowers off the table, the glass cracking in large fragments on the rug. He noticed how the water sat up in pools on the soft pile. He cut his own hand (his right) as he gripped one shard, and stabbed it into his wife's throat. Blood dashed against the yellow painted wall like raspberry in custard. It was two o'clock, he was hungry, so he left.

Once the girl had reported the murder, it took the police two weeks to find him. Although she could give them a clear physical description (dark curly hair, pronounced temples, about five feet six inches tall, a jaundiced complexion), she had not known the man's name nor his relationship with her mother. She had not known the man who had given her her name.

Selected bibliography

Glasgow Herald, 4 January 1921
Hansard, 20 October 1920.
Maloney, E. Shaw in Ireland, in Collected Essays on George Bernard Shaw, Dalriada press, 1967
Manchester Guardian, 21 October 1920

Thanks to the Public Records Office, Kew, London.

1922-1924

Argenta

Derry/ May 1922

Dear Molly,

They have had me here a few weeks already, but it feels like a lifetime. I'm not used to being cooped up all day, all them months spent on the run have given me a taste for it. I never thought I would say that. There is no fun in hiding out in a drainage ditch by the side of some farmer's field, and the cold (did I ever tell you about the cold?). Still, it's got to be better than this. What they call food is often little more than potato skins or porridge in plates they don't bother to wash. I'm in a cell of bare bricks. If I lie on my back with my arms stretched out, I can nearly touch its four walls with my head, my toes, and my fingers. A wee bit of carpet would be nice, or some photographs of you all for the walls. But that's not what they are about here. I do have some furniture: a chair I can sit on and a cot I can sleep on. Do you think that's too good for the likes of me? The warders seem to think so. Occasionally,

FINDING DAN

they remove the bed and the chair, and take a big water hose (like they have for putting out fires) and they flood my cell with it. This is not a kindness, a straightforward way of cleaning up after me, or ridding the cell of fleas. (They could boil my sheets for that, but as yet, they haven't bothered.) No, it's my punishment for behaving like an animal. I won't wear their prison uniform. As I see it, they have no right to hold me here, they are not my government, and I have committed no action unreasonable to a free man acting like a free man. Their laws don't apply to me. I'll not have them describe me as a criminal, so I'll wear no prisoner's uniform. I have fashioned my own range of clothing. You'd be proud of me Molly. A sheet when passed around the waist and knotted makes for a decent skirt. At nights, I could be mistaken for an old woman seated at the end of my bed with a blanket over my shoulders for a shawl. It's fine for now. My mistake has been to let on to them that it's fine. This is why they clear out the cell and flood it with water, taking the blankets and all with them. They kick my scrawny arse back in the cell to see how I like it like that for a night.

You oughtn't to be going away with the idea that I spend my days relaxing in the comfort of my hotel room. The magistrate in Dungannon said something about hard labour, but he never went into detail. I'll spare you too. (There is only so much that can be said about breaking rocks down into smaller rocks.) But this is no holiday. They take it as their job to break us, and they think they have a reputation to uphold. You'll never guess who's in charge here. Old Looney, you know, Master Looney's father. If I'd've known his da was going to end up running this place, I'd have given Looney a harder go of it in the school. That's despite him having a soft spot for me. Rather the Looney I had then than the Looney I have now. 'We've tamed lions here before, you know,' he said to me when I was brought in to him at the beginning. I could believe that, but I wasn't for letting on. 'There's a lion here you haven't tamed yet,' I said back. He's not for taming me, Molly. None of them is.

I'll be out one day, and you'll see, I'll be just the same as before. Hopefully, I'll be able to stick around Creenagh more than before. I should help out more at the timber mill. The work suits me, out in the open. I suppose Jim is having to lend a hand more? It wouldn't be before time. Tell Daddy not to put up with any nonsense from him. I'll sort Jim out when I get home. Are you still helping Mummy with the girls? Give kisses to Kathleen, Margaret, Betty, and little Winnie for me. Molly, I know you'll think you have to stay on, now that I'm in here, but I don't want you missing your chance just on account of me. If you save enough money, I want you on that boat to New York. And one day, I'll come and join you. I've always fancied a cruise.

God bless,
Dan

Letters: October 1923

13 October 1923
To Sir Richard Dawson Bates

<u>Recommendation for Internment</u>

Minister,

Daniel O'Rourke of Creenagh, Dungannon has been known to me for several years. While living

FINDING DAN

at that time in Brackaville, he was a pupil at my son's schoolhouse in Coalisland where he showed some academic promise. He took and passed the scholarship exam, but his father withdrew him to work in his timber mill.

Prior to the 'truce', O'Rourke was renowned locally for involvement in activity prejudicial to the peace. Though not proven, it is believed he intercepted a goods train to Strabane and passed the proceeds to the IRA. He ambushed and burned out a bread van. He was wanted for internment at that time, but evaded arrest by going 'on the run'. Fortunately, he gained little support locally and was denounced by a neighbour in Creenagh. He was arrested by a B patrol near his home, found in possession of a serviceable Colt revolver, which I am certain he would have used, given the opportunity. At his trial, he refused to recognise the court. His sentence was eighteen calendar months hard labour.

He therefore had a reputation as a 'hard man' when he arrived in Derry in April last year. I recall upon our first meeting telling him we could make a man of him here. I would rather not repeat his reply. Indeed, he has been a most difficult man to deal with. He has associated with James Cuskeran of Draperstown whom we also recommend now for internment in Larne. They have collaborated in damaging their stone-breaking tools. He has befriended the five 'Rule 11' boys sent here last October from the *SS Argenta*: Arthur McLarnon, George McCann, John Boyle, James Nolan, and George Hamill, though he did not join their six-day hunger strike. O'Rourke would become very agitated by their stories of conditions on board the prison ship. I would suggest O'Rourke would consider it a mark of honour to be interned there, so that he too could regale others with similar tall tales. For that reason, I would advise his internment in some other camp, perhaps in Larne. Under the influence of such men, he has refused to wear prison garb, and on occasion to leave his cell bed. We have flooded his cell and removed his cot, as per custom, but he has been hard to break. However, he now walks with a significant limp.

There is a strong likelihood that O'Rourke will, upon release, seek to destroy Twyford Mills in Dungannon owned by Mr J. L. Mullin, the father of his arresting officer, Sergeant Mullin. O'Rourke remains a dangerous Republican, and I recommend his expeditious internment under the special powers invested in you.

Martin Looney.
Chief Warden, Derry Gaol.

10 October 1923

I, John M Regan, County Inspector of the RUC for the County of Tyrone, being Chief Officer of Police for the said county, do hereby recommend that for securing the preservation of the peace and the Maintenance of Order in N.I. Daniel O'Rourke of Greenagh, Dungannon, in the County of Tyrone, who is suspected of being about to act in a manner prejudicial to the preservation of the peace and the Maintenance of Order in N.I. shall be interned.

Rank: G. Inspector

FINDING DAN

Crime Special 24/5480
Co. Inspector's Office
RUC Omagh
12.10.23
Subject: Daniel O'Rourke, Greenagh, Dungannon
DI Dungannon,

In your minute of 5th Inst., you state that above named was one of the most dangerous characters in the district. Please supply by return of post further information as to how he is considered dangerous, and any particular reason for thinking he would be dangerous now.

Co Insp.

District Insp. Office
Dungannon
13.10.1923

CI
Submitted.

On 28 March 1922, O'Rourke was held up by a B patrol near his home, and was found to be in possession of a serviceable Colt revolver, which was loaded in four chambers. Having regard for the happenings then in vogue, there is little doubt, but that an ambush of B men was in contemplation tonight. O'Rourke, when before the RMs, in reply to a question by me, said that he didn't get time to use his revolver or else they wouldn't have taken him so easily.

O'Rourke is a most dangerous type of man, and prior to the "Truce" was wanted for internment, but evaded arrest by going 'on the run'. The sergeant of the B patrol, who arrested O'Rourke, is a son of Mr J. L. Mullin of Twyford Mills Dungannon, and Mr Mullin is very much afraid that O'Rourke might have revenge by burning down his mill. I certainly think that O'Rourke should be interned for the present because if Mullin's mill was burned, whether by accident or otherwise, it would naturally be attributed to O'Rourke; and in that event, there would certainly be reprisals.

2DI

Belfast
17 October 1923

Internment Order

Whereas it appears to me on the recommendation of the I.G. RUC that for securing the preservation of the peace and the maintenance of order in Northern Ireland, it is expedient that Daniel O'Rourke of Greenagh, Dungannon, in the County of Tyrone, who is suspected of being about to act in a manner prejudicial to the preservation of the peace and Maintenance of Order in Northern Ireland, should be interned.

Sir Richard Dawson Bates, Min. of Home Affairs for N.I. orders internment under Civil Authority (Special Powers) Act (N.I.) 1922, interns O'Rourke at the Workhouse, Larne …to be kept until further order.

FINDING DAN

<u>Derry/ 25 October 1923</u>

My dearest Molly,

I should have been with you by now, my eighteen months up (or 'served' as they call it). I had plans. Mummy needs a new fence to keep the chickens in, and Daddy is missing me with the lumbering. Is anyone teaching Winnie her letters? I had meant to see you before next week. Don't you go changing your mind just because I'm not getting out as I had hoped. I want to see you in New York one day. Molly, they'll love you there. You'll knock them out with your looks and your sharp tongue. They'll try to make you famous, but don't you go and let them change you. You can't change an O'Rourke that easily!

The wardens gave me a terrible beating. They injured my leg, my left one, and left me with bruises everywhere. I'm not sure what this means for the football, or for one or two ladies I had my eye on! Molly, there's some injuries that mend themselves, and there's some that don't. It was one of those times when they took me out of my cell to flood it. This time, I must have made them really cross because they took my bedclothes, and left me naked in the flooded cell for days. When they came back for me with a prison uniform all folded neatly for me, and I refused again, they laid into me. Those wardens have heavy boots like the ones they issued soldiers with in the war. For now, I can't use the leg at all, and it's been a while. They had a doctor in to look at it, but I don't think he could have looked too closely. I don't suppose they pay him to look too closely.

I am being interned. They won't tell me where to exactly. I'm hoping for the *Argenta*, the prison boat. They do terrible things there. I have mates here who were sent from there, Charlie Burns and Geordie Hamill and others. They say there might be 500 or more on board with nothing to do, so fights break out on a frequent basis. The warders have them divided pro-Treaty and anti-Treaty. We are always being split up. I think we have a sort of talent for it.

We are hearing rumours here of a hunger strike going on on the *Argenta*. If I get there in time, I'll be joining in. The word is, the food there is even worse than it is here, it'll be no hardship to give it up.

I miss you, sweet Molly. Tell Ma not to worry for me. I dream of you all day.

Dan.

<u>Northern Ireland Home Office/ September 1922</u>
5 September 1922
Home Office, NI
HA/32/1/75

The Nationalist press, both north and south of the Border, has been passing increasingly critical comment upon our policy of internment and the conditions endured by the internees. This is despite the almost identical policies of the Free State government, which has imprisoned and even executed erstwhile comrades in arms. We have received no credit whatever for our even-handedness in interning not a few Protestant loyalists.

In Belfast, the *Irish News* and its scurrilous *Searchlight* column is waging an insurgent campaign-of-words against the government. By way

FINDING DAN

of example, in August, they posted a report entitled 'Craig's Deathtrap for Political Prisoners' about the prison ship, *SS Argenta*, moored in Larne Harbour. In summary, the *Irish News* made the following allegations:

I. Non-National movement prisoners recently admitted have been making a din at night so that the others cannot sleep.
II. Inmates have to eat off the floor; the bacon and cheese is inedible; rations allow 1¼ ounce margarine per day for breakfast and tea, with dry bread at night.
III. An artificial light remains on day and night; very little natural light is getting in.
IV. They sleep in crowded bunks.
V. There are only three isolation 'cages' for the sick.
VI. An outbreak of scabies was ignored for ten days.
VII. The library holds just eighty books for 330 men.

With your permission, I will investigate these claims, and report again early in the New Year.

Major EW Sherwell

<u>Aughnacloy/ September 1922</u>
Colonial Secretary
HM Government

Dear Mr Churchill,

I write to you humbly as a mother of eleven children and wife of a man currently interned in the prison ship, the *SS Argenta*.

My dear husband, Charlie Magee, was wrongfully arrested in May this year, interned in the general sweep which followed the assassination in Belfast of Mr Twaddell, the Unionist MP. Charlie had nothing whatsoever to do with that. Before his internment, he was a publican, a respected and law-abiding member of our community. Since his confinement, he has suffered terribly. He is much older than most of the others there, and decides not to bathe with them in the cold seawater provided for that purpose on the deck. He prefers to stay in his bed, and because of that he now is afflicted by the body and head lice. His cage-mates call his 'The Orchard', as they can pluck the lice clean off it. He has not informed the Medical Officer, for he fears being separated from his colleagues.

We have been given no clue as to when my husband might be let go. In the meantime, I have no income, and so, no means of feeding my children. My neighbours have been very kind, but there is a limit to the charity they can offer me. I can now afford to provide for my little ones only one meal in a day. If they have some stale bread with sour milk, they think they are in heaven that day. Today, I do not know how I shall feed my children tomorrow.

I remind you that my husband has been charged with no crime, and his wife and children are most certainly blameless. I beg you to find some means to relieve the suffering of my family, and to compensate the other innocent families caught up in this unfortunate business. We are desperate.

Yours sincerely,
Mrs Medbh Magee.

FINDING DAN

<u>Northern Ireland Home Office/ January 1923</u>
23 January 1923
Home Office, NI
HA/32/1/75

I have now completed my investigation into the allegations made variously in the *Irish News* and other Nationalist press concerning conditions faced by internees aboard the *SS Argenta*.

In general, I find the conditions to be good and (with the possible exception of the arrangements for taking meals) all that could reasonably be expected. The food itself is of excellent quality and well-cooked. For this reason, the decision by the governor to refuse the prisoners' requests to receive food parcels over the recent Christmas was wholly justified. The sleeping arrangements are fully adequate for the numbers held, which varies with transfers within the internment camp network. The Chief Medical Officer reported independently, following revelations of severe illness among the internees, and I can disclose his main findings here. Most ailments he found to be colds with a few cases of bronchitis. This is to be expected at this time of year and would be typical of the population at large, particularly amongst the social orders prevalent on the *Argenta*. Lack of exercise has caused ill health on board the ship. This problem is less acute in Larne Workhouse. A number of inmates have emerged as significant troublemakers, and have agitated for Christmas gifts and improved exercise facilities. These have been denied. Warders, who were found to be passing on letters for prisoners, were dismissed earlier this month.

This prison hulk continues to perform an important role in the maintenance of order in Northern Ireland.

Major EW Sherwell

<u>Belfast/ February 1923</u>
Dear Mrs Magee,

I refer to your letter to the Colonial Secretary, Mr Churchill, of September last. I am sure you can appreciate he receives a great many letters of this kind, and he has passed it to this office for handling.

Our colleagues at the Northern Ireland Land Registry inform us that a quarter acre of land is held in your husband's name in Aughnacloy. This is in addition to the public house, which as you pointed out, your husband owns and runs. We recommend that you could act to alleviate the suffering of your family by selling either, or both of these properties. You might also be able to sell fish by the box if any of your children are capable of catching it. Otherwise, for so long as your husband is held under the Civil Authority (Special Powers) Act, I suggest you take yourself and your family to the nearest workhouse.

With kind regards,

TA Simms
Assistant Secretary of the Cabinet of Northern Ireland

<u>Dublin/ October 1923</u>

FINDING DAN

The Irish Independent
Monday, 29 October 1923.

>Acting President
>Of the Free State
>Padraig O'Ruitleis.
>Open Letter
>Support for Hunger Strike
>In the North

Uachtarán Padraig O'Ruitleis, having already published his support for the hunger strikers in Mountjoy and the Curragh at the Sinn Fein *Ard Fheis*, has written an open letter to the internees of prisons in the north. While Eamon de Valera continues to languish in Arbour Hill Military Prison, the acting president of the Free State has spoken out for those still opposing the Treaty.

>Open Letter

'All good republicans of Ireland should, today, proclaim clearly their support for the brave men and women of the north who prolong the struggle for a truly free Ireland. In cages and from behind bars, they have found their voice in the hunger strike. Their dignity and humanity should surely move us all, perhaps even those stony-hearted tyrants in Stormont. We recall that they are guilty of no crime; that instead, they are the innocent victims of a cowardly regime determined to use their autocratic powers singularly upon the Nationalist community.

These internees act on personal conscience. They follow no orders from Dublin. *Sinn Fein* neither demanded them to strike nor can command them to bow to the will of their warders. They possess their own sovereignty. In doing so, they act as free men and free women throughout Ireland should.'

Hunger Strikes
Not Coordinated

There is understood to be no connection between the hunger strikes currently ongoing in Mountjoy Prison, the Curragh and Newbridge, and those spreading through the north. Reports reaching Dublin say there are men refusing food in Derry Gaol, Larne Workhouse, and the prison ship, *SS Argenta*. They are protesting the fact of their continued incarceration without charge, their conditions, and the terms of their release.

Larne/ November 1923
13.11.23
From: I D Drysdale, Governor of Larne Internment Camp
To: Secretary of Min. of Home Affairs, Belfast.

I list for you (overleaf) those men who were conspicuous during the recent hunger strike, and those who have been leaders in fomenting opposition to authority. I recommend that these men be transferred to the *SS Argenta* where they can be dealt with separately. At unlock this morning, there was quite sufficient vacant accommodation on board the ship.

Four internees were transferred to Larne Workhouse from the *Argenta* at the peak of the recent difficulty. They are Alphonsus McCartan from Kilkeel, and John Keenan, John Flanagan, and Patrick Reynolds, all from Belfast. At the same time, we received from Derry Prison James Cuskeran from Draperstown, and Daniel O'Rourke from Dungannon. I recommend that these men should, for now, remain interned here at the old workhouse.

I D Drysdale,
Governor of Larne Internment Camp.

<u>Argenta/ January 1924</u>
Letter to Frank Gray, Liberal MP for Oxford City
From Cahir Healy, MP for Counties Fermanagh and Tyrone

Dear Frank,

I need you to speak for me in Parliament when it sits again on the fifteenth. Tell them that my constituents will be disenfranchised if I cannot represent them in Westminster. Remind them I was first elected in November 1922. For all that time, I have been interned in the workhouse in Larne, or on board the brutal prison ship, the *SS Argenta*. I have been charged with and convicted of no crime.

500 men and women are currently being interned across a network of near-secret prisons. On the *Argenta*, we are caged below decks and above, incarcerated alongside infected men who should be in hospital. What they laughingly refer to as the library consists of a mere eighty books for all the men here. It's little wonder so many here joined the hunger strike. Those men deserve a voice. It is not acceptable that innocent men should have to beg to an Advisory Committee for the freedom they were born with, that they should have to leave their homes to live in the Free State for two years. You may have

noticed how unwelcome those men are made to feel there. Some will find work with the Garda Siochana, but for most, they have swapped prison here for destitution there.

They have let out the few dozen loyalist gunmen they interned at the start, and offered them new lives in the colonies. Why was this? Because these same Orangemen could have named the respectable local businessmen who bought them the guns. We Nationalists are being held just long enough to settle the border question—until the Boundary Commission have come up with a solution to the Unionists' liking. That's why they lock up the likes of me, a Nationalist and an MP to boot!

If this letter reaches you, it will be because I have found a way of smuggling it out. If the fact of it is ever revealed, I know you will have to proclaim it a hoax. That is the country, or the countries, you and I live in. You have been a friend to the Irish and to the internees, and I know you will not flinch from the matter where the parliament would prefer not to discuss it. You have assumed a heavy burden on our behalf. I am sure that if you shared this letter with Captain Wedgewood Benn, he would shoulder the burden with you as he has in the past.

May God bless you,
Cahir Healy

FINDING DAN

<u>Larne/ May-June 1924</u>
Letter to Daniel O'Rourke
From his mother

Crenagh, 16/5/24

"I believe the B men are a calling up. I suppose they are for the frontier but I do not see how [who?] is going to fight."[1]

Letter to Daniel O'Rourke
From Annie Timoney
Garvagh, Barnes More, Tir Conaill, 20/6/24

"I know what a letter means to a prisoner, being one myself for almost 9 months in Mountjoy, Kilmainham, and NDU internment camp, and everybody deprived of their liberty have my deepest sympathy. Anything I can do for you I will be proud to do."[2]

<u>Limavady/October 1968</u>

Laurence O'Kane of Irish Street, Limavady was arrested in the general sweep following the assassination of Unionist MP, William Twaddell, in May 1922 and was interned in June. When the hunger strikes gripped the internment camp network in October 1923, he joined them. In 1968, with the help of notebooks compiled by fellow ex-prisoner, John O'Donnell of Castlereagh, County Tyrone, O'Kane did his own research on the *SS Argenta*.

MARK QUINN

Notes on meeting with John Haughey:

John Haughey is from Main Street, Coalisland. He has lived there all his life, apart from the period of his arrest and imprisonment. He says it is the most Republican of towns, supplying many other internees from the period such as Pat O'Neill, Joe O'Neill, Frank McKenna, and Dan O'Rourke.

John is remembered for one of the more hopeless escape attempts from the prison ship. Nets were set at an angle all around the deck of the boat to prevent inmates from throwing things (such as themselves) overboard. Still, he managed it, along with two others, whose names he has long forgotten. These two, however, were anchors rather than lifebuoys—, neither being a swimmer. They clung to Haughey for dear life. Despite growing up beside the canal that carried coal from his home town to Lough Neagh, Haughey was no more than competent himself. The hapless trio were gratefully plucked from the water.

John Haughey was thereafter transferred to the Larne Workhouse, which long since had been employed for internment purposes. There, he conspired with a namesake, Thomas Haughey from Clady, near Strabane. For some forgotten transgression, they were both stripped of their boots. The exercise yard at Larne was a floor of sharp grit and pebbles: to walk on it barefoot was to render them bloody and useless. This, of course, was the point of their punishment. Resourceful as they were, they took to their beds and stayed there. 'Lions couldn't drag us from there,' he told me. Fearing a repeat of the hunger strikes the previous winter, the warders brought them their meals in bed, but authority would not suffer that type of indignity for

FINDING DAN

long. They were transferred to Derry in June 1924 with all privileges withdrawn.

The mystery is that John later had these privileges reinstated for good conduct.

Larne/ November 1924
Letter to Daniel O'Rourke, from Charlie Magee Aughnacloy, 17/11/24.

'It's amusing when you take a walk up town to see the people peeping from behind the blinds. Some of them glad to see you, and others wouldn't touch you with a forty foot pole. A lot of the leading Nationalists welcomed me home, and said they were opposed to the penalising of Catholics. I must say I was better received by them than my own side.'[3]

Larne/ December 1924
The Secretary
Ministry of Home Affairs NI
Belfast

22nd Dec. '24

Return of Internees in Custody, week ending 20/12/24

No. in custody at unlock (8 a.m.) 13/12/24 31
Admitted ----
Total 31

Discharged during week ending 20/12/24 20
Remaining in custody, 8 a.m., 20/12/24 11

Particulars of Admissions and Discharges
…

/1009 O'Rourke, Daniel, Greenagh, Dungannon, Co. Tyrone

...

Vacant Accommodation: 273
Drysdale,
Governor.

[i] The Ulster Special Constabulary was established as an auxiliary force for the Royal Irish Constabulary, functioning in the north of Ireland. Its principal remit was to carry out anti-IRA operations. The B Specials was one of four sections. Its officers were unpaid, part-time, but armed. It recruited almost exclusively from the pre-War Ulster Volunteer Force and the Orange Order. When this letter was written, Molly was about 19 years old, and Bassie just two years younger. Molly had already left for America.

[ii] The Gap of Barnes More is a beautiful spot in the low mountains of central Donegal. Being in the Free State, but near to the border of the new Northern Ireland, the area may have been thick with activity despite its remoteness. Timoney is writing to a stranger in this letter, one with whom she has a connection only because she too has been interned. Mountjoy, or The Joy, is in the Phibsboro area of Dublin. Many anti-Treaty rebels were held there by the Free State government during the Civil War. These included the four members of the IRA Army Executive – Rory O'Connor, Joe McKelvey, Liam Mellows and Richard Barrett – who were executed on 8 December 1922 in reprisal for the assassination of Sean Hales and injury to Padraig O'Maille. Kilmainham Gaol was equally notorious, being the scene of the executions of all the principals of the

FINDING DAN

Easter 1916 Rising in Dublin. Women were interned in the North Dublin Union from June to December 1923, sleeping not in cells but in dormitories that the Countess Markievicz said were "haunted by the ghosts of the broken-hearted paupers." The Union had previously been a poorhouse. Annie Timoney would have cut quite a figure in Donegal, or 'Tir Conaill' as she preferred to use the original Gaelic name.

[iii] Charlie Magee was a publican from the Diamond, Aughnacloy. He was the father of eleven children, and had had previous convictions for firearms offences. He was a suspected IRA intelligence officer. He was released unconditionally from the *Argenta* on 8 November 1924. One month later, he wrote to Winston Churchill, the Colonial Secretary, seeking compensation for prisoners such as himself who had been wrongfully interned. His letter found its way into the *Irish Independent*. Neither the London nor the Belfast governments ever paid reparations to the internees or their families.

Spot Dance, October–November 1923

By Malachy Quinn

The man dropped his copy in the tray and stood for a moment. 'Thank you as ever, ladies,' he declared, wanting to make further conversation, but again failing to. The typists, all four of them, continued with their work, barely lifting their eyes above the pages in their Olivettis. Slemish fumbled for the door to leave, pushed it when he ought to have pulled; and from the corridor, he could hear the tittering of the typists mingle with the clicking of their machines.

The man was tall. Through his teens, he had been only average in height, but into his twenties, he had begun to grow again, leading some to doubt he was as old as he claimed. On the day he had moved to Belfast to become a staffer on the *Irish News*, he had celebrated his birthday alone in the Grand Metropolitan hotel further down Donegall Street. That was a few years ago, but since no one had asked, and he had not celebrated his birthday since, he had more or less forgotten how old he was. He counted time by the dateline. The boss had named him Slemish.

'You say you're from the country, in Antrim? I'm no good with names. You're tall and broad-shouldered, like the mountain. You can be Slemish to me.' And the moniker had stuck. When he got his first by-line, 'Slemish' was at the foot of the column.

FINDING DAN

He had waited two years for that by-line, under a report on the first sitting of the Belfast parliament, in City Hall. The editor was impressed and gave him better assignments. Then in March last year, he had covered several of the murders in Belfast. He had been a regular at MacMahon's pub on Austin Road, so he had been the one to report on the murder in his home of Owen MacMahon and four members of his family. The *Newsletter* and *Sixth Late* had carried the story too, but only he had filed copy revealing that the murderers were uniformed, and thought locally to be RIC. The commander, Johnson, had called round personally to the office on Donegall Street, demanding to know who this 'Slemish' was.

'I hardly know him myself,' the editor had protested. 'And I would not be telling you if I did.'

At that moment, Slemish was probably in *Printers* pub, drinking alone, as had become his custom. He was certainly there a week later, drinking his Bass, standing at the bar. The man next to him had in his hand a whiskey, without water. It was only late afternoon, but already, Slemish was well on the way to drunkenness. Even so, he was watchful. That was the word his mother had once used about him, and he had decided then and there to become a reporter. He watched his neighbour now. He was about five feet seven inches. His clothes seemed suited neither for city nor country work, so that Slemish wondered whether the man had come off the boat from America and found himself here. Certainly, he wore no hat. And he had a beard, a full untrimmed brown beard, the like of which Slemish had never seen with his own eyes in Belfast. As the man got up to leave, he had stumbled slightly, and apologised as he placed his hand on Slemish's shoulder to steady himself.

Slemish rented a room in a two-storey house on Jaffa Street, off the Crumlin Road. He returned home drunk most evenings, and each time he had to let himself into the living room where old Mrs Gaston sat alone, without a fire on, wrapped in most of the clothes she owned. She did piecework for a textile firm, working in lace, sewing tiny bows on ladies' undergarments.

'Late home from work again, Mr Slemish,' she would say.

'Another hard day, yes, Mrs Gaston,' he would reply.

'Will you be for church this Sunday, do you think, Mr Slemish?' she would enquire.

'Not this Sunday, no, Mrs Gaston,' he would say, and he would take the steep stairs up to his room to preclude any further conversation. Sunday would come, Mrs Gaston would walk to church, and Slemish might treat himself to a day out to Cave Hill to the north of the city, or even the short train to Bangor. He liked too to watch Joe McKelvey and the boys down at the O'Donovan Rossa GAA club on the Falls, before, that is, Joe got mixed up in the fighting in Dublin and at the Four Courts.

That evening, Slemish emptied his pockets on to his bed then lay down fully clothed. He slept. He woke when it was still dark, the moon the only light. On his bed, with his wallet, pencil and pad and door-key, was a neatly folded piece of paper. He opened it, not remembering what it was, or how he had come by it. He took it to the window, so he could read it.

'*Bomb in Brown Street. Tonight. Get it right and there could be more.*'

He had not yet slept off the alcohol he had drunk earlier, and he nearly kicked over the washstand as he doused his face in cold water. A moth tapped silently on his window, trapped by the light of the moon. Brown Street was in the Millfield area, back towards the city centre. The trams would have stopped running by now; he could get there in twenty minutes on foot. He looked around his room: the single iron bed, the washstand, the two-drawer chest where he kept all his clothes and everything else he owned. Nothing in the room made him want to stay. But still, he reluctantly refilled his pockets, crept down the stairs, so as not to rouse his landlady, and let himself out into the frosty air of the Belfast night.

He did not rush. He lit a Gallaher's Blue against the night cold, and counted the gas-lamps along the Crumlin Road. He wore his hat low over his brow, but he had lost his coat in some bar somewhere, so he dug his hands deep into his jacket pocket to keep them warm. In his right pocket, he clutched his notepad. He had left the note

FINDING DAN

folded in the bottom drawer in his room. For some reason, his mind was on the girls who worked the typing pool at the paper. The one who sat nearest the door, Nuala, never turned her head to him when he entered; so rather than her face, he called to mind her loose brown hair, fashionably short, and her pale narrow neck. The other men talked of Nuala and recounted conversations they had had with her, and even drinks they had shared with her. Slemish thought he might ask her out.

Long before he reached Brown Street, he could see the smoke and hear the muted screams of another urban tragedy. Women, neighbours or family, stood around at a remove from the house, at a respectable distance. Children ran in and out between them, some of them still dressed as if they had never gone to bed, all of them excited at breaking the curfew. The house was gutted, the fire already dampened but still smouldering. A bomb thrown through the kitchen window, the women agreed. A man was standing in the doorway to the house, shifting his weight from foot to foot, alone but for a large bundle he was holding to his shoulder. Slemish could hear a wailing, like the sound of a wounded animal. To one side, Slemish recognised the members of a medical team from the many hospital calls he had written up for the inside pages. On the ground before them were three bodies, two of them—girls—sitting upright, having their wounds tended to. The third body lay flat, covered, already dealt with.

'Hey, mister, you a reporter?'

'Yes, I am.'

'Your friends have already been. You're too late.'

'Who's that man?'

'Francis Donnelly. Those are his kids. Played with our kids. Twelve, the older boy. The little one was three, or not three yet. It would make you cry, so it would. You writing any of this?'

'What's he holding?'

'Francie never hurt a soul. Never got mixed up in anything.'

'What is that wailing? Where's it coming from?'

'That's Francie holding his little one. You sure you're a reporter, mister?'

The morning editions of the *Newsletter* and the *Belfast Telegraph* both carried the tragic tale of the bombing on Brown Street, with the deaths of Donnelly's two sons and the injuries to his daughters and himself. The desk at the *Irish News* pieced together a story from those reports, and carried it in later editions. Slemish wrote nothing, and told no one of his presence there. His boss considered sending him to cover the funerals, but Breen went instead. There were scores of other killings in Belfast to write about that month, and Slemish got his fair share. Someone would be shot, Slemish would be sent if he was in the office, he would come back and write three hundred words, leave his copy with the ladies in the pool, then go to a bar and drink all night. There was a pattern to his day. In the city, you did not have to try too hard to get a story, and Slemish wrote easily in the style favoured by the editor. In the bars on Victoria Street, Waring Street, Skipper Street, and the Docks around the Ormeau Road, Fitzroy Avenue and the Markets, Slemish was a regular. Some might have said they knew him there.

In May, the editor had been satisfied with his report on the setting up of the Special Constabulary. And then, on the internment of three hundred IRA suspects after the assassination of Twaddell, the Unionist MP, he wrote:

'Exciting early morning drives'
Familiar Coercion

Alarm was created in many internees when night visits were made to the rural districts of the six county area, remembering the previous outcome of many of these unusual calls. This was the serious feature of the wholesale arrests during Tuesday night. When it was understood that nothing more than arrest was contemplated, the proceedings occasioned no great moment.

FINDING DAN

And he concluded the piece by listing nearly all of those interned: the forty-six from Armagh, the thirty from Fermanagh, sixty-three from Tyrone, forty-two Derrymen, and the rest from Belfast. The ironic tone of the article could not disguise its seriousness, and each one of the names would raise a cheer in the bars of the North where the *Irish News* would be taken and his piece read. Slemish had a good ear for the political sensitivities of the readers of the *Irish News*.

That was last year. Now the pogroms were over, there was peace on the streets, and even many Nationalists assumed the question of the boundary had been settled. Slemish found himself filing feeds from the news wires. He still had his contacts with the police and the local hospitals, but there was little to report.

'Sorry, Slemish. All we've got is a woman in the Markets area who's fallen from a bedroom window. Any good to you?'

'Catholic Defenestrated in her Underclothes. When it's quiet, the boss will take anything.'

Slemish, like just about every other reporter on the paper, wanted the *Searchlight* column. For as long as anyone could remember, the column had been the preserve of Tom Breen. Breen was universally loathed; even the editor barely attempted to disguise his detestation. In his absence, he was referred to in the lowest language. When he was in the office, which was rarely, he mistook everybody's name and resorted often to calling people 'boy' or 'young lad'. He would slot a *Fisherman's Friend* into his mouth, suck on his yellow teeth, then try his breath out on Nuala and the other typists. He was untouchable. No one had better sources, and his writing was beautiful, his style bereft of modern turns and catchy phrasings. The boss knew better than to question where Breen got his breaks from. Commander Johnson would call in and make his demands, and the boss had nothing to hide. Johnson, who was himself, almost certainly, one of Breen's trustiest snouts. Lying in his bed, stupefied by drink and kept awake by the troubled snoring and moaning of Mrs Gaston, Slemish would plot appropriate deaths for Breen. In one, the veteran was found spread across the hot metal of the press; in another, he was crushed in an avalanche of newsprint bales. In each of the scenes, Breen would begin by making some smart comment to a printer or cutter, and proceed to drive the man to mad distraction until, with one push, the murder was complete. As if Breen demanded to be killed. In his favourite scenario, it was Nuala who played the murderess, plunging the pin of her hat deep into his rival's heart. She would be carried off by the police, face fixed in defiance. A jury would find her guilty of a crime of passion, the papers dubbing her 'The Hat-Pin Assassin'. Shunned by society, only Slemish was there for her, and they would get married as soon as she was free from gaol. Slemish could awake from this, drunk more from the dream than from the beer he had taken, his head and his heart pounding.

When Breen was found, late on a Saturday evening, with an editor's spike sunk deep in his chest, Slemish experienced a thrill of recognition. The corpse was slumped forward at his desk. Pinned to his body, impaled on the spike with him, was the story Breen had written on the funeral of Francie Donnelly's boys some year and a half before. That evening's paper lay beside the body, folded open at what would be Breen's last *Searchlight*.

PRISONERS REMOVED

Hunger Strike Extends to The Curragh and Newbridge

SCENES AT MOUNTJOY

'Upwards of 200 prisoners were transferred from Mountjoy Prison last night to an unknown destination. The previous day, a similar number was transferred, including Larry Breen, brother of Mr Dan Breen, TD. The groups did not include Mr Austin Stack, Mr Ernie O'Malley, or any of the more prominent figures. Eight men were released

FINDING DAN

on Thursday, and it is stated some of them signed an undertaking. A man named McDonnell, from Clare, was taken to hospital to undergo an operation for appendicitis. So far, the hunger strike has not been attended by any severe illness.

Sinn Fein headquarters reported yesterday that sixty prisoners were unconditionally released the previous evening. The hunger strike has extended to Tintown Camp, the Curragh. Whether there is to be a general hunger strike in all the Free State jails, Sinn Fein says is a matter for the prisoners themselves.'

Johnson came to take personal charge of the investigation, deeming the death to have occurred in suspicious circumstances. He took initial statements from Slemish, Nuala, the boss, and everyone else employed at the paper. He wanted to know who else had been in the offices that evening. With no Sunday edition, it was rare for regular staffers to wander in. Slemish had named several of the public houses he had patronised, but past about seven o' clock, he could not be exactly sure. Johnson looked into some of the stories that Breen had recently worked on, chasing down obvious sources in Nationalist and Republican circles. He uncovered a family life of mutual devotion, unusual (in Johnson's view) in the worlds of politics and papers.

Monday was 22 October 1923. Whenever anyone again asked him his birthday, this was the date he told them: the day he was given the *Searchlight* column, the most prestigious feature in one of the most revered organs of the Northern press. To celebrate, he invited Nuala to join him after work for a drink at the Grand Met, and she accepted—Mondays were good for her. There was a spot dance at the Lecture Hall in the Ardoyne every Monday from eight, 1s 6d in, but there were special prizes. Would he fancy that next week? Yes, he would, and he hoped she would teach him what a spot dance was. She lived with her parents in the Ardoyne. He could meet her at the dance. And tonight, he could ride the tram with her up the Crumlin Road, past Jaffa Street to Ardoyne, and walk her to her door. He was in his room before the eleven o' clock curfew, happy and sober for the first time since he arrived in Belfast.

The next day, Slemish arrived early at the offices on Donegall Street. He found himself reading Saturday's edition, and in particular, Breen's piece on the hunger strikes in Free State prisons. He felt sure that some of the Northern detainees would want to emulate and support their Southern counterparts. He placed a call with the Home Office, and by late morning, he had concluded his first interview with the minister, Richard Dawson Bates. The bastard had said very little. Was there a strike in Belfast? Definitely not. In Larne? Likewise. Would the minister like to comment on reports that internees in Derry had joined the hunger strike? It would be wrong to speculate upon reports, which themselves may be spurious. That had been enough for Slemish, and it formed the centrepiece of his first *Searchlight* on the Wednesday: DERRY JOINS HUNGER STRIKE - Minister Maintains Silence.

He had wanted to celebrate with Nuala, but she was not keen, so he went alone to *Printers*. He sipped his Bass in a snug. Several men sat on stools along the bar, one of whom he was sure he recognised. When he turned to Slemish and raised his whiskey glass, he revealed an untidy beard, and Slemish remembered him as the strange man he had bumped into in this same bar over a year before. The man came and sat with him.

'Do you mind?' Slemish shifted along the bench in his snug. When the stranger sat down, Slemish was left in the corner, his legs uncomfortably crossed.

'You're the man they call Slemish.' Not a question.

'What do they call you?'

'You don't really want to know my name. Let's just say, I know enough for the both of us. You got lucky on that story about the hunger strike in Derry Gaol, am I right? You didn't know, you guessed. Well, you guessed right this time, but that's not going to keep your column going for long now, is it?'

FINDING DAN

'You seem to know a lot about me. Does that mean I should be scared?'

'A wise reporter should always be at least a little scared, don't you think? Your friend Breen is a case in point. Always looking over his shoulder, at the police, the Volunteers, even his colleagues.'

'What had he to fear from us?'

'I should have thought that was plain by now. Turned out all right for you, didn't it? Him, dying sudden like that. Like a dream come true, wouldn't you say? Very fitting, that spike.'

'What are you suggesting? I had nothing to do with Breen's death. Are you suggesting I had anything to do with that?'

'Where were you last Saturday night?'

'You're RUC! Johnson sent you to spook me.'

'You can believe that if you like, for now. Do you know where you were?'

'Here.' Slemish had meant to be emphatic; instead, he had uttered a question.

The stranger was shaking his head slowly. 'Is there anyone here who would confirm that? You work in an office not fifty yards from here—does anyone here even know who you are?'

'I'm a reporter. Anonymity can be an advantage.'

'Says the man who slogged for three years to get his name in print.'

'It's not my name.' Slemish imagined this proved his point. 'It's not about renown: quite the opposite. I get the story and I write it, and as much as possible, I stay out of the way. Unobtrusive.' He had never spoken at such length to anyone on this subject before. He felt exposed.

'You've seen Slemish, I suppose? I mean the mountain? In among the gentle curves of the Antrim Hills, it sticks out like a whore's nipple. Unobtrusive, it most certainly is not!'

At this, the two men laughed. It did not last long. 'Do you know where you were last Saturday evening? Not with that typist you like, not yet. Not tucked up in your single bed. You put that off as long as you can each night, and I don't blame you. Not with friends from the paper. You never tell them where you go drinking. See a picture? What did you see? Who was playing at the Alhambra? Were you there, or were you just sneaking about the sad streets of Belfast sniffing out another family tragedy, leering at their loss, composing some poetry about them in your head before dismissing them, and not writing a word? It wasn't his story, but Breen at least went to the Donnellys' funeral to cover it for the paper.'

It came like a smack in the face. The time he had met this stranger before, the tip-off about the bomb on Brown Street, the folded note.

'I gave you that story as a test. You failed. Now you've got the biggest break in your life, and you will fail that too. Breen was double the man you will ever be. You have no right to his column, to the respect it commands. If the best fucking informant in the North sat down beside you and stuffed a fucking story in your hand, you still wouldn't fucking know what to do with it.'

The stranger moved to leave, but the journalist stopped him. 'You know what happened to Breen, don't you? Then you must know it wasn't me. You know about Derry too, don't you? You could tell me about Larne, and the *Argenta*, and the whole network of internment camps. Tell me and I could write it.'

'I know everything worth knowing about those prisons, what size they are, how many men they have in them, the names and addresses of every man who works in them. I know stuff about you that even you have forgotten. Where you're from, where you drink, and where you piss at night. I do not know that you did not kill Breen, but I will. Until then, I suggest you keep an eye out for me.'

The man left. Slemish looked around at the others in the bar, none of whom were paying him the slightest attention. He appreciated this about the city's public houses. It was his job to know other people's business, and it helped if they did not know his. But the bearded stranger had unsettled him. If he had to prove to Johnson that he was where he said he was, or that he was *who* he said he was, he was no longer sure he could. He looked again at the

FINDING DAN

men standing and sitting around him, and longed for just one of them to look his way.

Breen had paid him no attention either when he was alive. When Slemish had started getting his name in print on a regular basis, there were no words of encouragement or guidance from the veteran hack. He would suck on his menthol lozenge, and raise his hat in that betters-to-lessers way he had, but would never trouble the younger man with conversation. Slemish thought it slightly odd now that Breen had volunteered to cover the Donnelly funerals, routine page-filler that it was. 'I'll have that one,' and he had practically snatched the chit from the boss' grasp. Slemish had not read the resulting story. It was a mystery to him that this was the story that found its way on to the spike that found its way through to Breen's heart.

Slemish decided he needed to see the stranger again. He did not call into the office on the Thursday, but instead, lifted the collar of his suit jacket to the nape of his neck and walked the slippery cobbled streets of the city, his hat pressed firmly down and forward. He stood around York Street and Ship Street, watching the mill girls arrive for their shifts at the flax spinning mills. 'No Pope Here', their walls declared. He strolled down Royal Avenue, impressed by the bustle of the traffic and the policeman's attempts to control it. Robb's department store was doing good trade. At Donegall Place, Anderson and McAuley's were promoting their 'Value Week' with discounts on ladies' gloves and hats. He didn't think the mill girls would be shopping there for their winter clothes. The great clock atop the corner of the fifth floor proclaimed it was nearing one o' clock. He had not yet filed his column for tomorrow's edition. He still had nothing to write. He reversed direction, and decided to order a sandwich at the Grand Met. They were used to journalists meeting there, otherwise they might have commented upon his disorderly appearance.

Slemish sat alone at a table, partly obscured by a tall decorative plant. His sandwich and jug of beer arrived.

'Where have you been?' It was the bearded stranger. 'Right. Take this down. The boys on the *Argenta* and in Larne want out by Christmas. They have heard there is a chance that the government is looking for a way to let them out. They have now gone on hunger strike to press their demands. That's all for now. See what you can make of it, and I'll see you to more details. Now, eat up and go.'

Slemish finished off his pint, wiped his mouth of foam and crumbs with his cuff, grabbed his notepad, and walked the short distance to the offices of the *Irish News*. Within the hour, he had dropped his copy in Nuala's tray. The next morning, Friday, 26 October, the men and women of Ulster could find this in his *Searchlight* column:

> "I learned last night that a hunger strike is going on in the Larne Workhouse and on the *Argenta*. The last official statement in the Northern Parliament gave the number of men in the workhouse and on the ship as about 500, but it is not known how many are concerned in the strike.
>
> I am given to understand that the men determined on the step they have undertaken in order to force their unconditional release before Christmas.
>
> So far, the Minister for Home Affairs has made no reply to the questions I put to him on Tuesday regarding the hunger strike in Derry prison. Perhaps, Sir Dawson Bates thought that in this case, silence was golden.
>
> If, however, he considers that he can continue to disregard the ordinary canons of humanity, and throw a veil over what is happening in the workhouse, on the ship and in the Derry Prison, he is mistaken.'

Slemish

FINDING DAN

Slemish enjoyed that final flourish. More elaborately phrased than perhaps Breen would have allowed, but with a hard edge too. It put the story out, and challenged the authorities to silence him. On the other hand, he knew almost nothing about conditions on board the prison ship or in the workhouse, and realised his article exposed his ignorance. He hoped the stranger would be able to help him there.

Nuala surprised him by agreeing to go with him to the Alhambra Theatre on North Street.

'I love the pictures,' she exclaimed. 'Especially the comedies. Sometimes I nip out with the girls at lunchtime to the Alhambra, as it's just around the corner.'

The picture house was showing *Souls for Sale* that evening, starring Eleanor Boardman as Mem Steddon. She elopes with a man, and then realises he marries women just to murder them and claim on the insurance. She escapes, is stranded in a desert, and finally finds herself starring in motion pictures in Hollywood. When she gets herself involved in a love triangle with Richard Dix (playing a film director) and Frank Mayo (a movie idol), her jealous ex-lover returns and attempts to blackmail her. There is a lightning storm, which causes a fire in a circus, and Mem throws herself in front of the director to save his life. In the end, her ex-lover dies having repented, and the director turns the camera to the fire, so he can use the footage in their film. Other real life actors and directors like Charlie Chaplin and Erich von Stroheim make appearances in the film playing themselves. Slemish found the film confusing and struggled to stay awake. Nuala, however, was captivated by the effects and by what she saw as the clever device of making a film about how films are made.

'You'd make a good actress, Nuala,' Slemish told her as a compliment when they were sitting in the theatre bar.

'You're a tease, Mr Slemish. How would a girl like me go about getting into movies?'

'You have a nice face. What else would you need?'

'You know how to give a girl confidence, I don't think! This is Belfast, no one makes pictures about dreary places like this.'

'Haven't you ever sat at the docks and seen those great big ocean liners they make right here in Belfast? Where do you think they go? America!'

'You mean, like how we built the *Titanic*? We saw what happened to that! You want to send me to America now, do you? It's all right, Slemish. I'm quite happy just being a wee typist.' She sipped at her drink. 'What about you, Slemish, what plans have you got?'

The question came as a surprise. He had not thought to have any plans. 'Like you, Nuala, I'm happy just being here. I don't expect to go anywhere, or do anything very remarkable.'

"Some would say you already are. Writing, and getting your name in the papers almost every day. That makes you famous.'

'For today, perhaps, and tomorrow if they put my stuff in again. You're only famous for one day in this business, Nuala. Nobody's interested in last year's news.'

'You sound sad.'

'Sad? I hadn't thought of that. Sometimes, reporters get lucky when they chance upon a story that people will look back on years after. The thing is you can't know that. You just go about your job day by day, writing what happens. You write in obscurity, and leave it to history to decide if any of it matters.'

'But you're doing *Searchlight*. I know reporters who'd kill to do that!'

'Do you?' Slemish turned in his seat to see his informant standing behind him. He was dripping wet, evidently from the night rain. 'You must be Nuala. Slemish has told me so much about you. Do you mind if I join you?'

Slemish did mind, but Nuala had already moved up on her seat to make room.

'Have we met somewhere before?' The stranger was still addressing Nuala. 'I never forget a face.'

'I'm sure you would remember me,' she replied, visibly stiffening. 'Slemish, have you forgot your manners? You haven't introduced us.'

FINDING DAN

Slemish stumbled, 'Nuala, you know. Nuala, this is …'

'McGuffin. People just call me McGuffin.'

'I'm beginning to question the company I'm keeping. Why is it I am the only person around here with a real name?'

'Because you are the only one with nothing to hide?'

'What do you have to hide, Slemish? Nuala and I would be most interested to hear.'

'I was talking figuratively.' Slemish felt defensive. 'As you know, Mr…McGuffin, my job is to reveal what others would seek to hide.'

'Quite so, and what a fine job you do too. Rather enjoying your new platform, I see, challenging the powers that be. Let's hope you continue to do so. Nuala, you must be proud of your young man?'

'My young man?' She blushed, and was cross with herself for doing so in front of McGuffin.

'Quite a week it has been for him, has it not? Walking out with you, getting the most sought-after column in the Nationalist press, all after the mysterious death of his illustrious colleague, Mr Breen. Of course, Breen was your colleague too. A sad loss for you all, I am sure. Brave of you too, to put it all behind you so soon, not allowing yourself to show grief in public.'

'I didn't know him well.'

'No, no doubt you were with Mr Slemish last Saturday, while Breen was being attacked in the office?'

'With Slemish? No, I'm not sure we had really met by then. I was at home, minding my little sisters. Slemish, if he wasn't working, was probably in one of the town's bars.'

'Slemish?' McGuffin parried the question on.

'I am not Nuala's "young man", McGuffin. She has been kind enough to share drinks with me on a couple of occasions, that's all, and to see the picture with me.' Slemish hated the way McGuffin was looking at Nuala, hated the fact he was looking at her at all. 'And as with most Saturday evenings, I was blind drunk in some bar somewhere. Not at work.'

'And half the city could testify to that, I'm sure. You must be reassured, Nuala, to be dating a man with so many alibis. Yes, the film. Any good?'

'I thought so,' replied Nuala coolly. 'The main player is a woman, a woman called Remember. She meets a man, and is attracted enough at first to be taken in by him. But, Mr McGuffin, she is a good judge of character. She sees him for the charlatan he is. It's in his eyes, in his manner, in the way he ingratiates himself into her company. The man gets his comeuppance, and she is there to make sure he does. I'll leave you two alone, I have…' and she clutched her bag. 'You have things to say that you don't need me to hear. But don't be long, I want my young man back.' She leant in to kiss Slemish on the cheek and was gone.

'You want to keep an eye on that one, Slemish.'

'You want to mind your own business, McGuffin, or whatever you're called.'

'Now, if I did that I would be of no use to you and your precious column, would I? Talking of which, the people I speak to think you aren't trying hard enough, not causing a big enough stir. If you want more of this, you need to deserve it more.' With that, he slid a brown envelope across the bar table. It slowed in the wet ring left by Slemish's glass. 'They're trying to break the strike by moving the leaders from Larne and the *Argenta* to Belfast. They're in a bad way. Also, Craig has gone quiet on an early release. The men are demoralised, and they need pressure put on the government. That means you.'

'Me?'

'Craig and the whole government in Belfast are still denying the strike is going on. They are still presenting the *Argenta* as a model prison ship. You know they have drafted journalists in from England to give them a tour of Crumlin Road gaol and briefings on their internment policy. They're stooges. Anything the IRA says will just be dismissed as propaganda. *Searchlight* is respectable enough to be noticed. There are MPs in London and congressmen in America who can quote you and speak to their people and help us that way.

FINDING DAN

'Right. I'm off. Give my love to Nuala. By the way, what's her surname?'

'I don't think she would want you to know that. McGuffin: was I there? Was I in the office last Saturday with Breen?'

'You weren't in the Met or *Printers* or here. You were in none of the places I have seen you. You don't remember doing it, but you do remember dreaming it, I'd bet. I won't see you for a few days. Do some digging around for yourself. Try Larne.' He was gone.

Slemish slipped the envelope under his jacket when he saw Nuala returning.

'What did he give you? No, wait, I don't want to know.'

'You'll be reading about it anyway. He knew you, didn't he?' Slemish found he was testing her.

'No, but I know him. Or rather, I've heard tell of him. The young lads round our way, you pick up talk from them. Slemish, I wish you didn't have to know men like that.'

'I wish you didn't. I'll walk you to your tram'

'And you?'

'I'm heading back to the office. I've got a story I'd like to see in the morning paper.'

INTERNEES RELEASE TERMS

'I received yesterday a copy of the conditions of release handed to the men interned in the workhouse at Larne, on the *Argenta* and in Derry Prison. It is an amazing document, and had it been deliberately arranged for the purpose of preventing any self-respecting man from signing it, it could not have been more harsh, not to say vindictive. Before an internee is released, he must agree to one of two conditions: first, to leave Northern Ireland altogether; or second, if he does remain in his native Province, to find bail for his good behaviour for a term of two years, confine himself to a radius of two miles from his home, and report at stated intervals to the local police barracks.

In plain language, these conditions mean that the internee must exile himself from his country for an indefinite period, or consent to be treated at home as a ticket-of-leave man. Yet, Sir James Craig promised us a 'model' government! As has repeatedly been said, no charge has been made against any of the internees, and therefore, they have not been brought to trial. The government possesses, in the Act of Parliament hastily passed during the first session, more drastic powers than those held by any government in the British Empire; and if it had been possible to bring any charge against a single internee, it would have been done.

REASON FOR STRIKE

The fact that no charge was laid is the best proof that none could be brought; so that as far as the internees are concerned, there is no law in Northern Ireland. A short time ago, it was hinted to me that the government proposed to release the majority of the men, and I was waiting every day to see this being done. But if the government ever had such intention, and I am doubtful, the idea has evidently been abandoned.

It is now believed that the rumour of their intended release also reached the ears of the internees, and it was only when they found no action being taken that they decided on the drastic step of a hunger strike. The Home Office, presumably, relied on its ability to prevent any news from reaching the outside world, but it failed. The information as to the strike did come out, and I was informed yesterday that it was still in progress.

Last night, I also heard that the leaders of the strike on the ship and in the workhouse had been removed to the prison on the Crumlin Road and that several of them are in a low condition. The position has now become a serious one, and still, the Ministry for Home Affairs simply looks on, sullen and aloof, and says nothing.

I suggest to the well-known journalists now visiting Belfast that they should ask the Northern Government for facilities to visit the workhouse and the ship, and for permission to question the internees without a third party being present. The newspaper men would, I am sure, learn something they do not know of the conditions in the workhouse and on the ship, and what is more important, of how law-abiding men were taken from their homes without the slightest justification, and kept in custody for the past eighteen months to two years without any attempt being made to prove a single illegal or suspicious act against them.

[Our Derry correspondent wired last night: twenty internees from Larne were conveyed under strong police escort by the Midland mail express today and lodged in Derry jail.]'

Slemish

The *Irish News* hit the streets with their story on Saturday, 27 October. The Home Office immediately published their denial in the *Belfast Telegraph*, stating there was 'no truth' to the hunger strike story. Mysteriously, the evening paper also quoted the Belfast Government as saying the *Irish News* claim that there were five hundred on hunger strike in Ulster was 'grossly exaggerated'.

Slemish's appeal to the 'well-known journalists' visiting Belfast provoked a response from the Rothermere press, in particular the *Daily Mail*. Its Ulster correspondent pronounced himself unconvinced by Craig's internment policy.

The editor of the *Irish News* sat with his feet on his desk, his hands clasped behind his head in a pose he imagined all self-satisfied editors struck. Sales were up. On his desk was a small stack of chits, calls to be returned: to the Home Office, to Johnson, to the RUC chief of police. All due to the *Searchlight* column, and the story it had broken over the hunger strikes among the internees of Northern Ireland's prisons. In truth, down to him, the editor: he had been the one to spot Slemish, nurture his talent on the small stuff, give him his chance when a vacancy arose. He was pleased with Slemish, and he had just had him in the office to tell him so. Shy, he was, about his sources, but he respected him for that. Actually, he was more interested in what he, the boss, felt about Breen.

'You don't have to worry your head about that business, Slemish. Johnson will pore all over it, and then decide on "death by misadventure". Breen had big boots, but you're filling them rightly for now.'

'Thank you, sir. Has Johnson questioned the staff again yet?'

'He has been making the usual nuisance of himself, naturally. Actually, he has asked after you. He'll catch you again when you're about. I explained that I don't necessarily desire for my best reporters to be knocking about here too much. I want you out there getting the stories.'

'Has he mentioned anything out of the ordinary?'

'Johnson? About Breen? Apart from being found dead with my spike through his heart, you mean?'

'Your spike?'

'You had noticed, I hope, Slemish, that I am the editor about here. Of course, it was my spike. There are no others to my knowledge.'

'I haven't seen you with one.'

FINDING DAN

'That's your good luck, Slemish, if you have never had one of your stories spiked since you joined us. Not many can claim that.'

'Could Breen?'

'No, a fine writer, don't get me wrong. But not even Tom Breen escaped the spike. I beg your pardon, God rest his soul. I mean even Breen had stories cut. In fact, it was one of his that was on the spike that killed him.'

'The Donnelly funeral.'

'How did you know that?'

'I'm a good journalist. You didn't print that story, why not?'

'Because the funeral wasn't the bloody story. Every paper but ours got a first-hand account of the bombing. I think Breen blamed himself for missing that one, that's why he volunteered for the funeral. Where were you that night?'

'When Breen died, or the Donnelly murders?'

'You're edgy, Slemish. That's good. That's what separates the good reporters from the hacks and has-beens.'

'I don't remember.'

'Which night don't you remember?'

'I don't remember.'

'Slemish?' The reporter stopped at the glass door. 'When should I tell Johnson you'll be here?'

Nuala sat at her desk—the one nearest the door to the typing pool. She was working, so didn't notice Slemish creep up behind her.

'Jesus, Mary, and Joseph! Don't do that!'

'Don't you like surprises?'

'Can't you see I'm working?'

'Can't you take a break? I want to talk.'

'I'm a typist. We type. Reporters take breaks. During which, no doubt, you read yourselves in the paper.'

Slemish chose not to interpret this last comment. 'Are we still on for tonight then? The spot dance in the Ardoyne?'

At this, the other ladies all simultaneously stopped typing, leaving a white space for the question to hang in.

'We? Now, who would "we" be exactly? I mean I know who I am. But I am not sure who you are. Where you came from, where you go after work, how old you are, even what your real name is. That McGuffin seems to know more about you than anyone here does.'

'Has he been getting at you? I'll kill him!'

'Would you? Would you really?' Nuala started typing. 'Not tonight, Slemish, all right? I think I had better . . . I'll be staying in.'

Slemish was already at the door, retreating at the mention of his source's name, and recoiling from the woman's questions.

'Just one last thing,' he said. 'What is a spot dance?'

Without looking up, Nuala replied, 'You dance with one partner, and you move about each other, but you keep to the one area or spot on the dance floor. One very restricted area all the time. It's very popular these days.'

Slemish was gone.

He took the mid-week Antrim Coaster, the train from Belfast as far as Larne. He stood outside the gates to the Workhouse. But for a thin wisp of smoke from one chimney, there were no obvious signs of life. The workhouse—the last resort of the destitute and starving—seemed an appropriate place for a hunger strike. Slemish walked out to the pier. Moored in the Lough was the wooden hulk he knew to be the *SS Argenta*. The sea was unsettled, and the sky above threatened a storm.

'It's bad weather we're having,' he said to a group of fishermen mending their nets.

'The fish aren't liking it', offered one, 'so the catch is good. It's bad though if you're stuck out there.' And he pointed out to the prison ship. 'I don't know who to feel the sorrier for. Those they took off in the gale, or those they left behind.'

'What? They released some of the prisoners?'

The fishermen turned in on each other at this, and Slemish was worried he had lost this unexpected source. Then one, the same as before, said, 'Don't get me wrong. I'd rather they were locked up in there than let free on the streets. But that's not the king's justice, the way them men were treated last Friday.'

FINDING DAN

'Did you say they were let off the boat?'

'There were over a hundred of them, I'd say. Let off? No, they were under guard still, being moved to Belfast by the look on it. You remember the storm on Friday night, teeming it down it was, and blowing a gale. Those men were barely dressed, and some were barely fit to stand up. They may have been dangerous men when they went in, but they're broken men now, I tell you.'

'You saw this yourself?'

'We all did, around midnight. We'd been hoping to go out, but thought better on it.'

'It's the same at the Workhouse,' volunteered another. The others muttered their consent for this new story to be told. 'On Saturday, a police van—a tender—was leaving the grounds, and stopped to beat and cuff one of the prisoners in the yard. I know it sounds funny, but it was no such thing. It's a disgrace to Crown forces. The prisoner had only bent down to fix his trousers or pick something up, and the guard set upon him. No one deserves that, not even the muck they keep in there or on that ship.'

Slemish sat alone at the end of the pier. The prison ship was anchored far enough out, so that voices from land would not carry to it, and voices from on board would be lost on the waves. Despite the reports he had already, he knew next to nothing about the men on the ship, why they were there, and what conditions were like. For that, he needed McGuffin. But he had come to fear his source, this stranger. If he, Slemish, were guilty of Breen's murder, it would be through McGuffin that he learned of it. Slemish was aware that he was drawn to the very man who could take away his life. He would get the truth from McGuffin, and he would dare Johnson to find him guilty. He threw his empty stout bottle far out into the Lough, and he shouted after it, 'Come and get me, you know where I am!'

On Thursday, McGuffin found Slemish in O'Hara's in the Millfield area of the city.

'You've been drunk in fancier bars than this, Slemish.'

'I find the drink gets me drunk wherever I am. What have you got?'

McGuffin spoke for over an hour about how the hunger strikes began, how many were still interned, and about the state of the men who were removed from the boat in the rain the previous Friday. And for the first time, he talked to Slemish about life on board the *SS Argenta*.

'I'm telling you this, but if you write it all, they'll never believe you. The detainees are divided on board, pro and anti-Treaty. The antis are pretty disillusioned with their boys in the Free State. They say de Valera has abandoned them. Of course, he's in Arbour Hill. For them all, the boredom's the worst. They have only a tiny area above board to exercise, and that is caged. The *D* is porridge and bread for breakfast, soup and bacon for dinner. They eat off the floor: they are not allowed chairs or tables because these could be used as weapons. The medic on board is an alcoholic whose stock of meths has made its way into a drink the men have made using potato skins. The guards are civilians, but many are B men, and they beat the internees up for making trouble. The authorities won't improve the conditions, but are panicked lest someone dies. Jeremiah Tipping from Lurgan is in the Mater Hospital along with the boy O'Donnell from County Down. Michael Keating and Billy O'Hara from Belfast have simply been released, as have the Toome man, Henry Carey, and Terry Mackle from the Moy. They've let out Philip Murphy too from Castle Coole, too ill to keep him in. Two men have already died since their release, the young boy, Gillespie from Sion Mills, and Billy Hyndman from Belfast. No man will ever come off that ship the same way they went on.'

Slemish stopped his pen and looked at his pint.

'I've noticed you don't drink. You come into all these bars, you get a glass, and you leave without touching it.'

'Not when I'm working, which is all of the time. It's a lesson you might learn.'

'I've never missed a story for being drunk.'

FINDING DAN

'We both know that's not true. You may have missed the biggest story of your life.'

'I want to know.' Slemish was imploring his informant to become his accuser. 'And I want to know how you know.'

'If I told you that, you would never need me again. I am the source. If something becomes known, it is because I allow it to be so. Though you barely knew it, you wanted Breen dead, and you planned it, though only in your dreams. You knew he would be in the empty office that Saturday night because only you understood why such a man would rather work alone. He was the master. You were in none of the bars of Belfast because you wanted to see how Searchlight wove magic into his words. No one would think it was you because no one thinks of you. You can bear the guilt of the crime, but feel no regret because now you are Searchlight. You are now writing the words that Breen was not ever going to write.'

'Why are you sure Breen would not write this for you?'

'Because he also got the note telling him to go to Brown Street. Like you, he missed the story of the Donnelly killings. But unlike you, he never even showed up. He had to go. He had to go to make way for you, so that this story could be written.'

'You killed him.'

'No. But he had to die.'

The Irish News. Friday, 2 November 1923.

LARNE HULK TO BELFAST JAIL
Origin and Course of
Hunger Strike.
240 INTERNEES
Losing Hope, Take a
Desperate Course.
DRENCHED IN GALE.
Midnight Journey of Weak
And Poorly Clad Men.
FACTS AND FIGURES.

'In view of the attempts of the Unionist press to minimise the seriousness of the *Argenta* hunger strike, and to misrepresent the attitude of the internees taking part in it, the following recital of the facts, as authoritatively ascertained, has become necessary:

THERE ARE 131 HUNGER STRIKERS IN BELFAST; 70, APPROXIMATELY, IN DERRY; AND 40 IN LARNE.

The strike began on Thursday, 25 October, when 150 of the internees on the *Argenta* refused to take food as a protest against their continued imprisonment without trial.

Swoop on Committee

On the previous day, 24 October, the Northern Authorities having learned of the impending event, made a swoop on the Committee, three prominent members of it first being removed from the boat, and subsequently the other members, five in number, and taken to Belfast Prison. How the authorities procured the names of the Committee is not known. The removal of the internees mentioned aroused much resentment among those remaining.

Deputy Governor Notified

On the Thursday, an internee notified Captain Long, deputy governor, that 150 of the 258 men then on board were going on hunger strike immediately, and the strike was accordingly begun. It is to be remembered that the strike is in no sense 'sympathetic' with any similar movement in the rest of Ireland, as it comprises internees of both

Nationalist and Sinn Fein sections of opinion, although there is a statement that papers were found by the authorities to show that the move had been suggested from Republican quarters in Dublin. In any case, the men lost patience after

SEVENTEEN MONTHS' INTERNMENT WITH NO SIGN OF RELEASE IN SIGHT.

In fifteen months of that period, there has been almost absolute peace in the North-East. The majority of the internees are Constitutional Nationalists, and as for those alleged to have been IRA men, it is felt that having been in custody for such a long time, they should be regarded as having earned the right to resume liberty as citizens. This continued detention without hope of release has convinced the internees that they are being held either for some sort of 'deal' on the Boundary question, or merely to satisfy revengeful feeling.

Taken off in a Gale

On Friday night, 26 October, at midnight, in a downpour of rain and with a gale blowing, 127 hunger strikers were ordered out of their beds and taken off to Larne Pier and thence to Belfast. Many of them were poorly clad, and all were weak. Their clothes must have been sodden. This 'delivery' left 115 on the *Argenta*, as twenty had already been sent to Derry Jail for another reason. On Monday, 29 October, four further hunger strikers were taken from the ship and sent to Belfast Prison.

MARK QUINN

In Larne Union, on the same morning upwards of seventy went on hunger strike, and they have probably since been removed to Belfast. Many of the latter were before the Advisory Committee and agreed to give all undertakings asked, but have not been able to secure release.

Intolerable Conditions

The conditions in the camps are intolerable. On the *Argenta*, the only exercise ground the 270 men had were two strips of a deck 40 by 38 yards wide, so that when all were up, there was just standing room. No blankets, sheets, or pillowcases have been supplied, and only once in sixteen months have the coarse black rugs been replaced. The health of the men has been much undermined in consequence of being penned down for eleven hours daily in what is a dark hold of an old cargo boat purchased for £3000. The food is the regulation prison diet known as *D* and is very poor and coarse. Many of the men have dependants outside who are in want, and this is, needless to say, accentuating their feelings of despair.

Total of Internees

A year ago, there were 500 internees; today, the number is the same, for although about 100 have been released, another 100 have been arrested. The conditions of release include reporting weekly to political opponents and neighbours, the B men, after the manner of convicts-on-leave, procuring bail, and being subject to a limit of two miles radius.'

Slemish

FINDING DAN

For the first time since he became *Searchlight*, Slemish had written less than he knew. He hoped that, by holding back on some details, other sources would come forward. That weekend, he went to all of his usual haunts, and some new ones, but he tried to stay off the drink. He was working, gathering information, cultivating his sources, doing his job. He had other reasons too to keep his mind clear.

'Great job, Slemish. This is really exciting our people.' The editor had called his protégé into his office. 'I want you to keep on this story as long as it lasts. You can consider the column your own.'

'Thank you, boss. But it is not up to me how long the hunger strike will go on for.'

'Oh, I don't know about that. Dawson Bates is in trouble over the publicity you have brought to this. He could declare release dates, and the strike would end like that.' The editor snapped his fingers.

'And my story would be over just as quick.'

'You'll have others, son.' The editor leaned back in his chair, and blew a smoke ring from his cigar. He looked upon the young reporter with something approaching pride. To Slemish, it appeared more the look of ownership. That word, *son*. He had never heard it spoken to him by another man.

'Will that be all, sir?'

'How are you handling Johnson, Slemish?'

'He hasn't questioned me, not since that first weekend when he called in all the staff. Has he been looking for me?'

'He's just keen to make a name for himself, that's all. To be honest, I think they are more concerned by the pieces you have been writing than by Breen's untimely . . . you know.'

'Death, sir. Can't the porter tell him who was in that night when Breen was at his desk?'

'It was Terry. You know him?' Slemish shook his head. 'Terrence has been with us for twenty years in the same chair, no disciplinaries, not even a day off. Knows the name of every beggar that's ever stepped foot in this place, yet, he can't recall the man whom he saw follow Breen in that night. Gave Johnson a description, but no name. Johnson says Terry must have been drunk.'

'Maybe he was.' Slemish spoke to the back of his boss, who was now standing at the window. Below, a tram was rattling up the street. Early Friday evening, traffic was taking workers home for their weekend.

The editor took a deep drag of his cigar, and blew his smoke against the glass. 'Terry is a pioneer, took the pledge at eleven. He's never drunk a day in his life. He says the man had a hat, but no coat. And that he was tall.'

The November gloom was fast descending upon the city. Slemish had walked as far as Great Victoria Street. He was cold, so he slipped into a coffee bar for a Van Houten's. Across the street was Matcham's Grand Opera House, and near it, the Hippodrome. He didn't fancy another film. The billboard outside the Hippodrome announced that the famous Harry Lauder was performing in music hall that evening.

'*Stop your tickling, Jock*! Oh, that's a funny one.'

'McGuffin.'

'Don't sound so pleased to see me. Anyone would think you were ungrateful. We, by the way, are not at all ungrateful. Your piece today was just right. I have some more. Here, a letter. No, don't open it in here. We haven't time. Let's go.'

'Let's go where? It's raining. I've lost my coat. I haven't finished my coffee.' But despite these protestations, the reporter followed his informant back on to the street. The smaller man was moving quickly against the wind and the rain, heading north across the Grosvenor Road into Millfield in the direction, it seemed to Slemish, of his newspaper office. On Clifton Street, the man stopped suddenly, holding out his arm to halt the reporter.

'There. There they are.'

Slemish counted twenty-seven men huddled around a broken-down charabanc. The men themselves appeared broken down: soaked by the rain, heads uncovered, in scant rags. And totally silent.

FINDING DAN

'They are from Larne, on the train into Midland Station. They have been here forty minutes, waiting for another motor to take them to Crumlin Road Gaol. They are too weak to run.'

Slemish saw them in a sepia light, gathered under a gas street lamp as if for warmth. The rain drove hard on the road that separated him from them; the occasional motorcar, scoring through the puddles, underlined the distance. Four or five guards stood loosely together, the orange dots of their lit cigarettes making unconcerned circles like fireflies. After some time, a high-sided van pulled up, and the men were herded on the back. Its engine reared, loud and rude, and it was gone.

The reporter followed the route of the prison van as far as Jaffa Street, and let himself into the house. Mrs Gaston was not in her usual seat, and as he ascended the stairs to his room, Slemish was aware that the house had recently been occupied. The door to his room was hanging off one hinge. The washstand had been pulled to the floor, the jug and basin lying in a shattered mosaic. The contents of his drawers were scattered on the bed. The note informing him of the bomb on Brown Street had been taken. He experienced a pang of elation. This was the note that connected him to the dead body—to Breen. It might all be over soon. He wouldn't be sorry. He propped the door back against its frame, pushed his clothes to one side, and lay down on the bed. Through the pillow, he sensed a hard lump against his head. He felt for it, and pulled out a small paper bag of sweets. They were *Fisherman's Friends*.

Slemish stayed away from the office on the Saturday. McGuffin had told him that his column had alarmed the families of the men on hunger strike, and that many were converging on the city to demand of the Home Office news of their sons. Slemish took the tram to Cromac Street and entered the bar of McGlade's Wine Merchants. For an early afternoon, it was already fairly filled, and Slemish reckoned that these people were not from Belfast. They were smartly dressed, as if for Mass. They were speaking, not in the bored tones of familiars, but in the animated fashion of strangers who have discovered matters in common.

Slemish ordered a short from the bartender.

'You're strange here too, I see,' said the man, sliding the glass to Slemish.

'No,' Slemish replied. 'Where are these people from?'

'Derry, Tyrone, Fermanagh. Their boys are interned. They've read that they have stopped eating. They have come looking for answers, but they are getting nowhere. Still, they are good for business.'

The reporter leaned his elbow on the bar, the better to survey the others. They were men and women, all looking old in their forties or fifties. While some raised their voices, as if the government itself might hear them, several stood sullenly, nodding into their glasses. Slemish wondered if he should take out his pad and pencil, or even tell someone who he was. For a moment, he wanted to. The whole assembly would turn to him, perhaps in applause. They would plead with him for information, for he had access, he had channels to those who know. And he could startle or reassure them depending on his whim. He might call them all to silence now, rally them. Or he could take over a snug, making it a temporary office, and take down all their stories. He really might do this, but he became aware that someone was addressing him.

'Is your brother in there?' this man asked. Slemish felt the way a boy does when someone throws a rubber ring over his head and draws him to shallower water. Swimming in the bay at Cushendall, bobbing over the gentle breakers, in too deep, clutching the shoulder of a taller boy, his brother maybe.

'No, I haven't got a brother. Is it your son?'

'He got this postcard out to me. "Pray for me", it says. What's a father to make of that? I've told them I'm not leaving. I've been to the Home Office, and I've told them I'm staying put till they let me see my son, or tell me how he is. He was meant to be out last week. He was in Derry. Then they interned him, and sent him to Larne. "Pray for me", it said. They won't let on if he is on hunger strike, and they are not letting anyone in. I'm going nowhere, till I hear something.

FINDING DAN

It's the same for all these people. We'll sleep in the church if we have to. Can you do that here?'

'I have no idea. I don't know what to suggest.' Slemish put his glass on the counter and turned back to the man, but he was already gone. The reporter tried breaking into other conversations, but once he revealed he had no connections in Derry or Larne or the prison ship, the talk moved away from him. Everywhere he looked, he saw mothers and fathers without sons, sisters without brothers, daughters and sons without fathers, wives without husbands. They had lost what he had never had. He tried again, but it was as if his accent, or even his language, couldn't reach them. Damn you! He thought. I know more about this than any of you can know. You know only what I have already told you. Slemish felt the cool sourness of the gin on his tongue. Your sons have only the voice I have given them, a voice shouting at the doors of power in Belfast and London. The gin slipped like oily shellfish past his throat, tight in rage. They are safe in their cells and in their numbers, locked together, their families to pray for them. He was alone, watched by the police, and watched over by the IRA. The gaslights were lit in the bar. The crowd had changed. The ungrateful families were gone, and now, the men were the local men of the Markets, drinking down their week's wages. His throat was tighter still, allowing the slick of gin to just trickle through. Slemish breathed in the bar air, suffused with alcohol and burnt gas. The fumes lay heavy in his lungs, and in his head, flooding the convolutions of his brain, pushing at his scalp. He stood as well as he could and headed for the brightest light. He was on the street. By instinct, he kept the docks to his right, so as to head north. A clattering charge and urgent bells, and just in time, he fell to the ground away from a tram—the last tram, not stopping, heading home. Beneath his jacket, a tickling warmth told him he was bleeding at the elbow. But the jolt had cleared his head somewhat, and soon, he was at the grand double doors of the *Irish News* offices on Donegall Street.

'Can I help you there, sir?' This was the doorman.

'You don't have to call me that. You can use my name.'

'Yes, of course, sir. Now, what would that be?'

'You know who I am. I work here every day, passing through these doors. You are Terry, aren't you?'

'That's right, sir. I'm sorry that your name slips my mind. Every day you say, sir?'

'And this night, two weeks ago. You saw me then too, didn't you? Tall, no coat, just as now. I came through these doors, and up those stairs to the news desks. You saw me. Say you did.'

'I can't honestly say I did, sir. Mr Breen was here that night, God rest him. And the boss, of course. I'm sure I would remember seeing you, sir, if you were here. Never forget a face, me.'

Slemish felt alone with the voices of the night, as he neared his room on Jaffa Street. The linen mills of Belfast groaned in the background, while straining above them were the higher notes of the cranes in the docks, heaving and winching and cranking out their hard lives. The filthy air laid a heavy film on every thing. His eyes were sore from it. His feet ached from cobbles. His shirt clung to his elbow.

'I've tidied your room, Mr Slemish.'

'Thank you, Mrs Gaston, I'm sorry about that.'

'I'm used to young men, Mr Slemish.'

'Yes.'

'Will you be for church in the morning, do you think, Mr Slemish?'

'I shouldn't think so, no, Mrs Gaston. But it's kind of you to ask.'

'Another time, perhaps.'

'Yes, perhaps.' As fast as his aching body would carry him up the narrow stairs to his room, Slemish collapsed face down on his bed. He cried. He cried like no other time in his life he could recall. He cried until he ached no more, and he was asleep.

Nuala had agreed to take dinner with him at the Linenhall Dining Rooms on Donegall Square. The food was affordable, within the reach of a hack reporter and a typist. But sitting in the wood-panelled rooms, with City Hall filling the view from the window, they could pretend they were living it up.

FINDING DAN

'Thanks for coming,' said Slemish.

'This means nothing. You know that. I'm just taking pity on you, as you're lonely.' And Nuala gave him a smile, which said she meant it, but not unkindly. 'Will McGuffin be joining us?'

'Possibly. I never know. I hope not.'

They both ordered the same: pork chop, boiled potatoes, peas, gravy. Slemish wondered when was the last time he had eaten such a good meal with company he was at such ease in. When he had been with Nuala before, in the typing pool, in the bar at the Alhambra, he had wanted to kiss her. He could still see that she was beautiful, but he no longer desired her. It was as if he had lost all ambition in that area. She saw this new mood as limpness.

'You want to give yourself a good shake,' she declared, as their plates were being cleared away. 'No one would know that you had single-handedly forced the government to tell the truth over internment. Where I come from, you're a hero.'

'I don't need to know that. I never asked to be a hero. I was happy when I was allowed to watch what was going on and write about that.' As he said this, he saw through the window that McGuffin was heading their way up the street. 'I want you to go now, Nuala. It has meant a lot to me having you as a friend. McGuffin is here now, and I don't want him seeing you. I never wanted him to see you. I thought I wanted a life, as well as a job. Now, I realise that I don't have anything except when I'm working. And right now, he is keeping me in work.'

Without saying anything more, she got up, placed her napkin by the side of her plate, and clutched her bag. She hesitated for only a moment before leaning to his cheek and kissing him, for the second time.

The moist trace of her kiss was still cool on his face when McGuffin entered the dining room and sat in her place.

'Dining alone?'

Slemish didn't respond.

'You will be filing a report today.' Query and command.

The merest nod from the reporter.

'Did you hear about Johnny McQueen? He was found for that payroll robbery at the mill. One of us, it turns out, though I never knew it.'

'I thought you knew everything. You losing it, McGuffin?'

'We have our cells, Slemish, as I think you know. It can be dangerous to know too much.'

'It's the knowing too little that bothers me.'

'Well, you should have plenty for your report today. We are eleven days in, Slemish. Eleven days into the hunger strike. The men are getting desperate. There's one hundred and ten not taking food in Belfast. The authorities have decided against force-feeding: they got too much bad press from the women in England a few years back. We've heard they want to close Larne down altogether. Did you pick that up? I don't think it will be long now. You've done well. Have you read the letter I gave you?'

Again, Slemish nodded. He wanted McGuffin to be gone. He wanted Nuala to be back. He knew that just as soon as his source left, he would head back to the office and write up another report. Then he would leave it to be typed, walk out, and catch a train. Maybe go to Cave Hill like he used to. It was Sunday, after all.

The Irish News, Monday, 5 November 1923.

'News, Comments, General,
Local and Impartial'

'The grim struggle for unconditional liberty continued in Belfast Prison during the weekend. There are now, in round figures, 110 men in Crumlin Road on hunger strike. Yesterday was the eleventh day of the fast, and as was inevitable, many of them were in a low condition, but the spirit enabled them to carry on against the odds of fast weakening physical strength. On Friday, twenty-seven more men were brought from Larne Workhouse Camp to Belfast. They were taken from the coast town by train, and from the Midland Station in Belfast, to the prison by charabanc, which broke down in Clifton Street with the result that the men had to wait in the rain and cold until a fresh motor was procured. It was evident that a number of the men were in a poor condition, but they helped and consoled one another and not a murmur escaped them.

From all parts of Northern Ireland, relatives of the internees came into the city during the weekend, anxious to get news of any kind of the men. A County Tyrone man, to whom I spoke, said he would not leave Belfast until he knew how his son was doing. He had, he told me, received from his boy on Thursday past a postcard dated Wednesday with the deeply significant words, 'Pray for me.' When he arrived in the city, he called at the Home Office where he was told by a clerk that the highest authority absolutely refused to allow any visitors into the prison. The experience of the Tyrone man was that of scores of others, whose anxieties were thus increased tenfold by the unnatural refusal of the authorities to give any information. There was only, so far as I was able to gather last night, a single exception—one woman being allowed to see her husband.

It seems from what I heard last night to be the intention of the authorities to clear the Larne Workhouse altogether. As I have already stated, twenty-seven were brought to Belfast on Friday night, and forty others were transferred to Derry Prison on Saturday forenoon when the weather conditions were again most unfavourable for the removal of the men who were obviously very ill. As a police tender was passing from the Workhouse grounds to the street on one morning last week, one of the internees bent down, apparently with the intention of lifting a parcel or fixing one of his lower garments. Immediately, the guard seized hold of him and handcuffed him. Several spectators of the incident, obviously from their conversation Unionists, expressed themselves in strong language regarding the incident, which was obviously no credit to the powers that be.'

BELFAST HUNGER STRIKE
Letter from Argenta Prisoners Now in Crumlin Road, Belfast

An internee removed from the *Argenta* in Larne Lough to Crumlin Road Prison in a letter says, 'We pledged ourselves to one another to be released, living or dead. If they don't release us living, well, they can't keep our dead bodies. As there is no charge against us, we are justified in making any protest against our imprisonment. We are now seventeen months held without any charge. We would like the Rosary to be said each night for us. We are all isolated and not allowed to correspond with anybody.' The internee complains of the treatment they received when leaving the *Argenta*, and alleged they were kicked and beaten by their custodians.

The Derry Prisoners

It was learned in Derry yesterday that the political prisoners in Derry jail on hunger strike are in a serious condition. A party of prisoners from Larne were brought to Derry on Saturday afternoon under a strong escort and conveyed to the prison. At a representative meeting of Nationalists in Derry last night, a resolution was passed 'that having regard to the fact that peace has been restored throughout Ireland, all political prisoners should be immediately released.'

Slemish

Slemish had the need to leave Belfast. He wanted to be away from McGuffin and his story and his guilt. He did not feel brave, though it took some of his courage to board the train north for the short journey to Cave Hill. It was already late afternoon, and almost all the Sunday walkers had left. He did not care that he was not dressed for hill walking in November nor that he would have trouble finding a late train home. He had not noticed that it was raining. He wanted out of the city. He followed a dirt track that ran alongside a farmer's field, binoculars knocking gently against his chest. He had found them hanging from a coat hook in the office, looking uselessly to the floor, and had decided they wouldn't be missed. All the land here belonged to the Earl of Shaftesbury, and he still lived in the castle that stood proudly ahead. It was more a grand, turreted house dubbed a castle by the Victorians who built it.

Slemish stopped when his view of the castle was not obscured by hedgerow. It cropped out from the foot of the hills, its pale sandstone a contrast to the black basalt behind. Then, as the early evening sun made a last effort before resigning below the horizon, the castle blazed a glorious orange—a stubborn molten eruption.

Slemish flinched when a light came on in a downstairs window, and he sought cover as a trespasser would. He became agitated at last by the rain and the wind that were soaking his clothes. To the left of the main building, there was a carriage house, and attached to it, a further room with a sloping roof. He went in, finding the door unlocked. The walls and floor were whitewashed, and hanging from the ceiling beams were dozens of game birds, unplucked, drying. Closing the door, the room was sealed. The wind dashed pellets of rain against the high window, but inside, the air did not move. Mountain midges were choked in the gauze of the window, shuttering the first glimpses of moonlight. He shifted his weight to remove his jacket, scraping his boot an inch across the floor. The sound was crisp, but died instantly against the deaf walls. A low bench ran across the middle of the room, and he sat and then lay down upon it. He eyed the rows of condemned birds, hanging not by their feet, but by their broken necks, heads angled as if whispering unlikely last words to their friends.

He slept.

Human noises infiltrated the game larder: the gardener and the gardener's boy, the laundry maid and dairymaid, the steward, the groom. Soon, the scullery maid would be coming to the larder for grouse. He sat up on his bench, and felt the stiffness of his shirt dried overnight. First checking that the courtyard was clear, he let himself out of the larder, taking care to close the door behind him. Within seconds, he had found cover among the hedges, which ringed the house. In its basement rooms and outhouses, the castle was awake and working. The day, however, had barely announced itself, the sun still slumbering in the lough. He hunkered down in the hedge where he felt safe, where he could watch without being watched. He slept again.

The slip of wheels on wet pebble woke him. A car had driven up to the front entrance to the castle, and two men had climbed out. He thought he recognised the first, a stiff-backed, if somewhat tiredly dressed, gentleman, a man who had fought wars and lamented their passing. The second was taller, though he carried himself as a smaller man. He was in police uniform. Slemish glanced back at the first man and recognised him as Johnson. A slight breeze picked up across the dewy field behind him, and Slemish felt the short coldness of the hairs on his neck. He watched them being admitted into the big house before scuttling across the field and into the embrace of a dark forest. His heart pounded high in his chest. The pine needle carpet stifled most other sounds. The wood was dark, but he could

FINDING DAN

see with brilliant clarity the low grasses and fallen trunks and hollowing stumps of his new habitat. They would not find him here.

He walked a little way and found his stride shortening in front of him, the ground rising now quite steeply. The tops of the trees juggled the pale grey light that indicated the sun had risen. There was no path here, slowing his progress. He knew the Caves would be ahead. And then they were. Four, then the fifth cave, hewn from the rock by miners' hands and prospectors' tools. Many fugitives had found their way here in the past. In one, he found the remains of a small campfire, and he was warmed just by his imagined communion with these previous occupants. He wondered then if he would come across any walkers today. It was Monday; people did not have the leisure to walk here on a Monday. The train only ran for those working on the Hill. He should be safe. So he sat on a log, the dead fire between him and the huge sky. He had no way of calculating how long he stared into this blankness, but at some point, he was taken by a desire to climb further. Keeping the caves to his right, he made for the promontory known as McArt's Fort. It was a treacherous climb, and an apron of loose scree was spread as if to bar him. As he scrambled, he lost his footing, and he slid alarmingly fast down the escarpment. He came to a stop some way down, and stayed there on his back. He did not bother to move. His ankle hurt, probably sprained, but he did not care to see to it. Above him, the low cumulus was plump like a cushion; below, a blanket of mist was rolling steadily up the hillside towards his feet. He thought of his narrow cot in Mrs Gaston's house, and was content to be here in his bed of cloud and fog. Time passed. The mist crept under his shirt and cooled him like a sweat. It ran its damp fingers through his hair. It gripped his ankles with its cold hands, and he again felt the pain. This time, he chose not to ignore it, so he dislodged himself from the side of the hill, and limped until he reached the lowest of the caves. He sat, just inside, his back comfortable against the cave wall, and he let the rest of the day slide away.

Other days passed. On one, he discovered an abandoned hovel— that of a shepherd. Outside, a bucket had collected rainwater, and realising he was parched, he drank for the first time since he had arrived on the Hill. He was hungry too, but the pain in his gut gave him an odd pleasure. The hovel had a fireplace, so he limped into the forest in search of firewood. He heard the sawing, the rhythmic see-sawing before he got sight of the two men. They were heaving at either end of a long crosscut saw like competing oarsmen. When the tree was felled, they set on it with axes and hacksaws, stripping it of minor branches. They were joined by two or three other men, who cut the tree into logs and piled the logs onto a wagon. It took hours and the men worked without a break. When they were done, they hitched the wagon to their horse, and gently guided the load down the forest track. On the gate at the back of the wagon, he made out the words 'Timber Merchants, Creenagh', below a name he could not decipher. When they were all gone, and their noises gone with them, he stepped into their clearing to gather some of their discarded branches for his fire.

The hovel was little more than big stone set upon big stone, but the thatch of the roof was more or less intact, and the door closed tight in its frame. With the fire burning, he sat in the doorway looking down the hill towards the city. The cranes of the shipyard performed their dumb show, raising their arms and dangling their loads from their fingertips. Stacks of chimneys spewed a pall of smoke, deadening everything beneath. Buttons of light ran along chaotic seams, street lamps on a map he didn't recognise from here. The whole town was like a toy he could hold in his hand. He extended his arm to eye level to rest the city in his palm, and he thought only of children playing. He could die here.

On perhaps his fifth day, his gut was hurting more, but his ankle felt strong again. He decided he would try again to reach McArt's Fort. This time, he turned right at the Caves, and took the longer but gentler route. It was a narrow sheep's pad, muddy from the rain, and he fancied his shepherd had walked this path from his hovel. With ease, he reached the ancient rath at the summit of the hill. A huge ditch protected it on three sides, and on the fourth, a sheer drop. He scrambled up to the enclosed area, flat and expansive.

FINDING DAN

He breathed in the big air, stood as high on his toes as he could, and stretched out his arms to embrace the sky. He was greater and smaller than he had ever been in his whole life. He was full up with the words of *Searchlight*, of McGuffin, of words he had written and not written yet. He shouted with all his might, but the wind lifted his words and dispersed them in tiny, soundless fragments. He stood with his feet on the precipice and lifted his binoculars to his face. The sky was brilliant and alive, carrying light enormous lengths on its hum. Beyond the city, he saw the long wicked finger of the Ards Peninsula, pointing down, down to the Mournes. Spinning westwards, the hole of Lough Neagh shimmered darkly and past that the Sperrins. Then further north, the slopes and valleys of the Antrim Hills and Glens. And a mountain he was sure he knew, feminine, with a name that came to him slowly: Slemish: a sound shaped like the thing itself, gentle at the start, rising in the middle, falling away at the end. Symmetry.

He collapsed where he had stood. The sun warmed his face before clouds crossed his brow. Then a gentle drizzle dotted his chin, and over hours, ran in the creases of his neck. His mother had run a rough towel over his neck and shoulders and back, rubbing life back into him in front of a stacked kitchen fire. And your brother helped you? You sure he wasn't holding you down? No, Mother, he saved me. Why did he have you that far out in the sea at all? But I was swimming, Mother. For a while, I was really swimming! Did you know they have sharks and octopuses and even crocodiles? You're having me on—in Cushendall? And she rubbed away at his legs and feet, celebrating the life still in him. Shh now, enough of your chatting. You'll have yourself and me worn out. Shh. The drizzle glistened on the granite of his chin and gathered in the crevices of his neck. He wanted to be rock, willed himself to become inanimate. His pulse slowed, and his mind simplified. Shh. Only his gut would not relinquish its pain, forbidding sleep. Strong arms gathered him in and lifted him from the precipice. Slemish. They carried him past the Caves, then off the Hill. Slemish. They transported him back to a single bed in a darkened room with a washstand and chest. 'Slemish, you're safe.'

Slemish was nursed by Mrs Gaston over the weekend. She would allow no visitors, not even the man who had rescued him. At first, he could not keep down solid food; his body rejecting everything but water. But slowly, Mrs Gaston won that battle, and by Sunday morning, she felt able to leave his side and go to church. His rescuer returned with a message. Slemish was dressed by the time Mrs Gaston got back, and all she could do could not stop him going out. He walked into the city, bathed as it was in glorious winter sun. Terry greeted him by name in the entrance to the *Irish News* building. Nuala was not in the typing pool; another woman was in her place. Half an hour later, he was gone, having filed his latest report as 'Slemish'.

The Irish News, Monday, 12 November 1923

HUNGER STRIKE ENDS

'The hunger strike of the internees in Belfast Prison came to an end on Saturday when a number of the men had been fasting for seventeen days. I am told that the men were led to believe by the officials that their protest would not be in vain. Several of them were in a serious condition, but it is expected that they will soon recover.

Only an overmastering sense of injustice could have induced the internees to make their protest in the form of a hunger strike, which had certainly the effect of drawing the attention of the British and American people to their plight. I understand that steps are being taken to raise the question of the internment of the men in another form.'

Slemish

FINDING DAN

Two days later, Slemish was feeling much stronger. At lunchtime, he bought a stack of newspapers from Easons & Sons, and walked through the Corn Market to one of his favourite haunts on Victoria Square. Outside Richmond's Spirit Vaults, horses were pulling carts laden with piping, coal, and vegetables. Some were bound for grocers in the city, others headed down to the Lagan. By the Jaffe fountain, two boys were selling apples from a barrel. In the bar, Slemish read the papers and took angry notes on his pad. Since he had broken the news of the end of the hunger strike, he had received two calls from government offices. He would speak again tonight to ascertain the terms of the men's release. He had not seen McGuffin and was impatient for him to show up.

'I see you are back to your usual habits,' McGuffin said, when he finally arrived. On the bar table in front of Slemish stood four empty glasses.

'My work is done, McGuffin. I think I have done enough for you. The men are eating, and soon they will be out.'

'We are very grateful. Their families are very grateful, Slemish. But the story isn't over.'

'It is for me.'

'You're a reporter, Slemish. You only exist for the story.'

'Is that what you think?' But even as he said these words, Slemish knew the truth of them.

'You are a conduit. Events unfold in their own way and in their own time. You place them in neatly turned sentences. That's all. You have your name at the end because like all newspapermen, you fear you will otherwise disappear. Without your name, you are transparent.'

'There's more to it than that,' Slemish found himself shouting. 'Events happen, but they happen silently, secretly, away from where people can know them. That's where we come in. We give your events meaning, a place in people's homes. As for being transparent, how I wish that were true! You are here now because there is something more you want me to write. Some additional secret tragedy, or tiny human story that, without me, would remain secret and tiny. And utterly meaningless. And forgotten. So, just tell me it, and you can go and read it in your paper tomorrow.'

McGuffin told his story. When Slemish got up to leave, he stopped him. 'And what about your story? Breen? You have done well for yourself out of this, Slemish, but never forget it's a dead man's words you have been writing. Since you say my story is finished, perhaps it's time to bring your own to a conclusion. You can. You can know everything if the reporter in you still wants to know and if the man in you is not too scared to know. Be in the Waverley Hotel tomorrow, by the Docks. You may pack a bag, for you won't be going home. And do be a good man, and say goodbye to Mrs Gaston."

McGuffin left, leaving Slemish alone at a table full of empty glasses. Slemish got up to go, but was called back by the barman.

'You going to pay for those?'

'I suppose I'd better.'

Outside, one of the barrow boys was feeding a rotten apple to a horse. The horse's flanks steamed in the cold air. Slemish dumped his newspapers in a horse trough. He walked to the office, compiling the column in his head.

The Irish News, Wednesday, 14 November 1923.

TERMS FOR INTERNEES

'I learned last night in official circles in Belfast that the Northern Government has definitely decided to offer terms to the internees in Belfast Prison. The exact nature of the terms has not been disclosed except to those immediately concerned, but I understand their principal feature is that the men will be immediately released, provided they agree to find two sureties that they will keep the peace for two years.

FINDING DAN

Why cannot the government take its courage in both hands, and disregarding that section of its supporters, which sees red every night in every street lamp, give the men at least the same terms as those imposed by the Free State; viz. immediate release on signing an undertaking not to take up arms against the government and not to support any such movement?

If every one of the internees was released tomorrow, there would not be the slightest trouble, apart from the fact that they would only be a handful compared with the armed legions of police at the disposal of the Northern Government to say nothing of the British Army, which is also at the back of Sir James Craig. I have good reason for believing that the terms will also apply to the men interned in the *Argenta*, the Larne Workhouse, and the Derry Prison.

PRESS GAG WITHDRAWN

The Home Office gag having been removed, the Belfast Unionist Press yesterday gave their version of the strike and its end. The *'News-Letter'* sneered at the men having 'yielded to the good things of life', and asserted that 'their courage had not proved equal to the self-imposed strain': a characteristic observation to come from the mouthpiece of a government whose minions used every device during the second week of the strike to break it. The statement that men who deliberately fasted for seventeen days lacked courage was a nice example of the mentality of the defenders of the government who evidently do not have the faintest idea of the meaning of the word courage. Quite in keeping with the whole article in the paper named was the insinuation at the end that if the hunger strikers had not been closely watched by the prison officials, concentrated food would have been conveyed them by their friends, and of course, used.

I heard yesterday an interesting story of how the mother of one of the men forced from the Home Office a permit to visit her son. Letters and personal calls at the Home Office, having failed to secure any information as to the whereabouts of the young man, she called on Friday at the department mentioned and declared her intention of waiting there until she was given the necessary passport to see her boy. The officials expostulated with her and told her that she would not be given the desired permission. But she stuck her ground, and eventually was given the permit and visited her son in the Belfast Prison on Saturday.'

Slemish

If he were to go to prison, he would be ready for it. He paid his rent arrears to Mrs Gaston, and two further months in lieu of notice. He thought she stifled a tear. In his room, he stripped his bed and rolled back the mattress. He opened the window to let in some air; a moth skittered up the glass and out. He saw the folded blanket he had placed on the bedspring, and decided he might need it. He would leave some extra change for Mrs Gaston on the chest of drawers. He packed his other clothes, his comb, his toothbrush. He didn't much mind if they were to take these items from him—he had no sentiments for things. He wished he had a coat; it could fill the space he still had in his bag. And he was sure he would feel the cold. When he went downstairs, his landlady surprised him with a brown paper package containing cheese, bread, cold meat, and a small bottle of whiskey.

FINDING DAN

'I want you to look after yourself, Mr Slemish.'

'Don't I always, Mrs Gaston?'

'No, you do not. I hope you will be happy in your new place, Mr Slemish.'

'I have been happy here.' And again, he noticed what he thought must be a tear. 'Are you all right, Mrs Gaston?'

'Of course, I am. Why wouldn't I be? Now, you run on. Oh, before you go, I want you to take this. It was Mr Gaston's, so I doubt I'll be needing it any time.' She handed him a long black woollen coat.

He wanted to protest, but also wanted the coat. So he thanked her by trying the coat on, and showing her it was a perfect fit. He shouldered his bag, said goodbye, and left her at the door. Some way down Jaffa Street, he looked back, and Mrs Gaston was still standing at the door waving vigorously. Involuntarily, he lifted his own hand and waved.

He walked the long Crumlin Road towards the city, putting distance between himself and the notorious prison, which lay in the opposite direction. He called in to the office.

'Slemish, great work again,' said the boss. 'Any other stories like that in the pipeline?'

'We'll see what comes up. Has Johnson been looking for me?'

'He's a persistent bugger, and you're an elusive one.'

'I'll be at the Waverley Hotel by the Custom House.'

'Your bag's packed. You moving in there? We must be paying you too much.'

'Not moving in, just seeing a source. Anyway, I'll see him there if he calls in.'

'Right.' The editor was keen to get back to work.

'Goodbye then,' said Slemish awkwardly. The boss ignored him. In the lobby, Terry was more talkative.

'I like the coat, Mr Slemish. Well-earned it is too, if I might say so.'

'Thanks, Terry,' said Slemish not caring to set the man straight. 'You look after yourself there.'

'I am off early today, Mr Slemish, on account of it being my birthday. I'll have a nice dinner at home.'

'Just you and your wife?'

'No, there is no wife, Mr Slemish. I'm happy on my own.'

'I see. The right girl never came along.' Slemish thought of Nuala, and the girl sitting in her chair.

'No, sir, I'm fairly sure she did. I just let her go. That's what happens when you're not careful.'

'I'll bear it in mind. Goodbye, Terry.' And he dropped a coin in the dish beside the doorman.

Slemish was glad of his coat against the chill wind, although his walk to Custom House Square Gardens was a short one. In the Waverley Hotel, he passed the reception desk where several men and women were waiting to check out. He reckoned they had travelled up from the country yesterday, stayed the night at the hotel, and would shortly be taking one of the ships of the White Star Line to New York or Canada. At the bar, the steward could have worked on the White Star Line himself, crisp white collar and waistcoat, standing in front of an impressive bank of bottles. Slemish ignored these and ordered a Bass and sat in a low armchair by a window. The view was dominated by a liner in the dock. Like bees around a hive, men were busy loading it with cases of wine, crates of fruit, bales of white linen and towels, casks of aerated water. The ship idled, being served. Back in the hotel, at the reception, a young woman was checking out. She had two large cases, and no porter was there to help. Slemish watched to see how she would manage. She could do little more than push the luggage across the polished floor.

'Can I help?' he called over from his armchair.

She glanced up at him, but did not answer. He tried again. She ignored him again.

'Can I help you with those bags?' Now he was standing beside her. 'If you'd rather I didn't, you might say so.' She looked up at him, but still didn't speak. She stood at an angle to him, her best foot forward. Her clothes were cheap, and under her hat, her hair was wiry and black. He thought she couldn't be more than about

FINDING DAN

eighteen. She had been told by her father to rebuff the advances of men. 'You are really not going to get those bags to the quayside by yourself, you know.'

'Look, mister, I have no intention of carrying these cases any further than this lobby. When I have to go, I have a porter ready to carry them for me. It's been arranged.' She straightened up, perhaps realising she didn't need quite so sharp a tone. 'Thanks all the same.'

'Can I get you a drink then?' He saw her blush: her father would disapprove, she wasn't sure she wanted to, she wouldn't know what to ask for. 'They are still servicing the boat. You have at least an hour.' Slemish looked behind the bar and saw an advertisement. 'Have a Ross's ginger ale. That'll help settle you for the voyage.'

She felt she had been given an acceptable choice, so she sat with him by the window. 'My name's Molly. If I'm going to have a drink with you, I should know your name.'

'People call me Slemish.'

'It's a good enough name. Do you often hang around hotel bars helping girls with their bags?'

'There aren't so many girls in the bars I usually hang around in. At least not so I've noticed.'

'You look like you have seen the inside of plenty of bars.'

'Thanks.'

'It wasn't a compliment. You look terrible.'

'I know it wasn't. I suppose I do. I haven't ever thought much about the way I look.'

'You should.' Molly looked at him hard. 'You'd look all right if you tried.'

'What country are you from, Molly? For I've never met a person like you.'

'Just the same as you, Mr Slemish. I'm sorry if I act a bit presumptuous. That comes from having big brothers that let me tease them.' She talked for a while about her family in Tyrone, about her brothers and sisters back home, and about her eldest brother who was interned.

'Are you sure, Molly, you want to be telling a stranger that kind of thing? Where is he interned?'

'He was doing time in Derry before they interned him last month and sent him to Larne.'

'Was he on the hunger strike?'

'We don't know. He was moved to Larne in the week it started. We heard de Valera wrote to the boys, telling them to come off the strike. Do you think that's right?'

'Why would I know a thing like that, Molly?' Slemish stared at the girl over the rim of his glass. 'Have you heard any other news like that?'

'No, just the stuff you'd know yourself if you read the papers. Mr Slemish,' she was looking at his bag. 'That's not a lot to be taking with you to America.'

'I'm not going to America.'

'Oh, but you should! Haven't you seen the advertisements? There is work there for young people like you and me who can talk, who can get along with people not like ourselves. I'm sailing right into New York, and that's where I intend to stay. I'll get a job, they pay good wages for hardworking girls, and I'll send money home for my brother to come out and join me. The one in Larne. It'll be a new life for him there, away from the Brits, the yellow dogs. You should go, Mr Slemish. Life could treat you much better there.'

'I'd have no one to go with, Molly.'

Molly looked at the man, his grey pallor, and limp hair. 'Have you anyone here to stay with?'

Slemish looked for her blush again, but this time, she was resolute. 'I can't go,' he said at last. 'I'm not free to go.' Now she did blush. 'No, Molly, I haven't a girl,' he said, sparing her. He wasn't free; he hadn't a girl. After these few minutes with Molly, he yearned to know what he was and what he had. 'There are simply things I have to face first here.' He looked at the girl in front of him and wished she were not so young. He might be able to talk to her, she might be able to understand, and he might not have to be so attracted to her.

FINDING DAN

A porter had arrived in the lobby and called a name. 'Was that for you, Molly?'

She nodded, stood, straightened her hat. 'Mr Slemish, I don't want you to think I was making an inappropriate suggestion. I have no experience of men in bars, still less of travelling, and no doubt you have saved me from a terrible embarrassment.'

'I hope I don't come to regret my good deed, Molly.' She offered her hand, and he shook it. He remained standing by the window, as she walked out of the hotel followed by the porter with the bags. After some minutes, he saw her cross the gangway on to the ship and disappear. He ordered another drink at the bar and sat back where he had been, waiting for what he was not sure. New York would be cold at this time of year, he supposed.

'A very pretty girl, Slemish.'

He turned, expecting to see McGuffin. 'Johnson? Of course, I forgot.'

'Are you quite recovered from your stay on Cave Hill? Everyone was very worried for you. Will you have another drink?'

Slemish nodded, surprised he had finished the one he had just bought himself, and sat again in the armchair. When Johnson returned from the bar, he asked 'Do you always offer drinks to men before you arrest them?'

'Arrest, Slemish? I have no desire to arrest you. God, man, I would have tracked you down long ago had I wanted to arrest you. No, I have questions for you, and I reckon a man is entitled to a free drink in exchange for free information.'

We use the same currency, Slemish thought to himself, somewhat ashamed. He allowed himself not to listen to his interrogator. He thought instead about Mrs Gaston and her husband's coat. He couldn't remember where he had lost his own. He was grateful that the woman had shown him that kindness. He wished he were lying down now somewhere with the coat pulled over him. He felt he hadn't slept since he was on the mountain. And the drinks he had just taken, and all the drinks he had taken in all those bars, were welling inside him. Johnson was talking. He was asking him about his home, about Antrim, his family.

'You're a mystery, Slemish. I don't mind telling you.'

The journalist was assailed by a need for it all to be over. 'The man is dead. My success at the paper was all down to him. I have no alibi. The doorman has a description. There's your mystery.' Slemish was resting a hand on each knee, and brought each wrist together as if to be cuffed.

'That would be a great pity, Slemish, as I was hoping to be introduced to your informant. However, I am quite sure you are mistaken, as he was spotted with you only yesterday.'

'Not him, you idiot. Breen! How is it that you can strike fear into the hearts of half of the North, and yet you be so clueless about straightforward murder?"

'Breen wasn't murdered, Slemish.' And Johnson laughed out loud. The reporter sat confounded, disoriented by the simplicity of the policeman's words. 'For a while, he had us fooled. But then, one of these clever blokes the police employ these days decided to take a look in his gullet. It was one of those lozenges he sucked, *Fisherman's Friends*. He choked, and apparently lunged forward, and impaled himself on the spike. Quite beautiful really. If only all deaths could be so appropriately arranged.'

Outside the window, the gangway was being slowly withdrawn. Some people were on the quayside, waving to their relatives on board.

'So, I'm not guilty?'

'In my book, you're as guilty as bloody sin for writing all that seditious crap about the hunger strike. Unfortunately, it was also the truth, and not even our repressive regime in Belfast has gotten around to criminalising that.'

The ship's horn blasted, making the window tremble. The tethers were slipped over the moorings, and the boat slid imperceptibly away from the quay. People stood in clusters, waving at other people on the deck. Dockworkers and uniformed employees of the White Star Line busied themselves with clearing away.

FINDING DAN

Slemish opened his eyes, and suddenly, the absence in the dock was a chasm, as the boat crept irretrievably down the river into the lough, and out of Belfast.

Selected bibliography

Bardon, Jonathan (2001) <u>Belfast: A Century</u>
McGuffin, John (1973) <u>Internment</u>
O'Donnell, Feargal, (1998) <u>A Holding Pen for Innocent Men: the Prison Ship Argenta</u>
The Irish News and Belfast Morning News, October–November 1923 (Searchlight column)

13 August 1998

McConaghy

Mal woke up in his aunt's house. Ann had invited him to stay in Edendork, close as it was to both Coalisland and Creenagh. While waiting for Molly's new memoir to arrive, and for his father to arrange a visit to Dan's brother, Patsy, he could speak to people who knew Dan; and he could begin to write. He had begun already. Conversation was reaching him from the kitchen.

'The last time I saw him he didn't give any indication that he was anything other than his normal. He always looked a fairly strong and robust sort of man, although in later years, I suppose he moved fairly slowly. He didn't exert himself much.' The voice, an old man's, laughed at that. 'He might have had some physical condition I wasn't aware of, you know. You never would have seen him move very fast. I mean in those days he was. Well, he was in his late sixties, which in today's terms isn't a big age.'

'Art, this is my nephew, the one I've been telling you about,' said Ann loudly, directly into the man's ear. 'Mal, Arthur McConaghy knew Dan before he died. Art ran all the football around here for years, so knows that side of things too.'

'I remember him quite well, Ann, to talk to quite often, I'd be talking to him quite often.' Mal was not sure the man had noticed

FINDING DAN

him. He was little more than five feet tall, had no hair, and was very old indeed.

'I would say there was a very stubborn streak in him in a way. Would you agree with that? That's right, and in a sense, I would have got the sense that although I would have spoken to him often, you would need sometimes to watch what you said to him. He would have been not so much touchy. He certainly wouldn't have been diplomatic. He would disagree, he wouldn't *have* to agree with you.' Then, as if to correct an impression, he added, 'He had a good sense of humour, to my mind a quiet sense of humour, but you wouldn't see him throwing his head back and laughing too much.'

Ann had offered Arthur a seat, but he preferred to stand, as if sitting down meant he had to stay. Mal noticed how he kept glancing over his left shoulder.

'Arthur, Mal here is interested in how Dan would have been remembered.'

'Just like that Lenehan man before you. You're not in newspapers, are you?' Mal assured him he was not. 'Anybody who would be a fan of the Coalisland football team today, and a serious one, especially anyone who is around about middle age or older, would be very aware that Dan O'Rourke had been a big football man. And people like that would be aware of the book that has been written about the club, and so on, and they would remember him. And as well as that, I think a lot of people who would be interested in the republican tradition would also be aware. I remember Dan wore his IRA medals at the commemoration of the Easter Rising in 1966. Not all would have done that. They unfurled the Irish tricolour outside Quinn's filling station that day. Any old information you came up with, they would be very interested to read about it, you know.' Art looked at Mal for the first time. 'I was looking at his picture there again in the *Fianna* book. Dan's picture, in that team, and he was a very fine looking fella. There's one in particular where he's in the 1928 county championship winning team. He's in the very front row, just himself, and it must have been

Captain Devlin, Frank Devlin. Dan's on this side and Frank's on the other side and Dan looks a fine man.'

'Was he popular?'

'I would never remember Dan with a friend. You never saw him walking in the street with anybody else. He would have been walking on his own. Or he may have been sitting on the windowsill, and somebody would come along and join him. It's a strange thing. Dan was lonely. He was a loner.'

'Winnie says he was a broken man, Mr McConaghy, after he came out of prison. He was on the *SS Argenta*. They say he was broken by it.'

'Would Winnie be your Aunt Winnie, Ann? She's a fine one!' He laughed again. 'Now that you mention it, he did have a sort of a limp. Did you hear he wouldn't come off the hunger strike on the Argenta until de Valera sent word to him? He was sixty-three days, seemingly, on hunger strike. Like Bobby Sands in 1981. They thought he was dead. He was prayed for in Edendork chapel as a dead man. "The recently deceased, Daniel O'Rourke." I mean I can't say, you know, I have documentary proof.

'Or again, you see, it could have been the football. So many footballers have bad knees and ankles and all that afterwards. But gaol leaves its mark, you know. And when your aunt says when Dan came out he was a different man, he could still have been, you know, physically intact. Maybe he had football about him yet. His brother, Patsy, would be the man to ask about that.'

'For his own reasons, my dad seems reluctant to go to see Patsy, or at least to talk to him about Dan. Because Patsy, or Phyllis, put Dan out of the house.'

'Art, will you have a seat now?'

'That's fine, Ann, I won't be staying. I don't want to be keeping your young man from London.' Mal was drinking coffee. More significantly, he was still wearing the shorts and T-shirt he had slept in.

'Mr McConaghy, I used to live around here.'

'I'm sure that's a fact.'

FINDING DAN

'It would be a pretty republican area. Would Dan have held those views to the end, do you think?'

'Well, he had his pension, Ann,' said Art. 'His IRA pension.'

'My Dad said he'd heard that Dan had refused his IRA pension for whatever reason,' Mal said. 'And Winnie said they refused him an IRA pension, and he wasn't on a state one either. I asked her directly about it.'

'A Northern Ireland state pension? Of course not.' The old man sounded ashamed to utter the words. 'I don't think he would take it. He wouldn't vote in elections to Stormont. I know that now. I heard the only thing he lived on was his IRA pension. Dan, even when I knew him in later life, would still have been known for having been on the run. I don't think that ever left him. Now here's an interesting fact. Cahir Healy, who spent time on the *Argenta* with these men, he was elected to parliament from his prison cell. That helped them to end the whole internment thing then. He became MP here after the War, in about 1950, I suppose.'

'Like Sands?'

'Well, yes, but there was Rory O'Brady before him. Do you remember O'Brady, Ann?'

'The name would be familiar, Arthur.'

'Ruairí O'Brádaigh stood and lost here as an Independent Republican in 1966, having recently been IRA Chief of Staff. Ten years before that, he had led the Teeling Column attack on the RUC barracks in Fermanagh, which killed an RUC man. He did time for that in Dublin's Mountjoy, and from there, was elected as TD to the Irish Dáil.'

'It seems the best way to get elected. Bobby Sands did the same here, did he not, when he was on hunger strike in the eighties.'

'He did, but that would have been after O'Rourke's time, I suppose, Ann?'

'He had been dead fifteen years by then,' Mal confirmed. 'Arthur, I am sure there is much more you could tell us about Dan. But I will need to get dressed first, and you will need to accept Ann's offer of a chair and a cup of tea.'

'Well, if there's tea going, I'll stay a wee while longer.' Arthur McConaghy sat down. 'What did you say your name was?'

'Malachy Quinn. Mal.'

'And why, Mal, are you here asking questions about Dan?'

'I'm a writer, or that's what I'm trying to be. I want to write about Dan.'

'Writers! It's always writers with Dan. Well, I hope you are more use than the last one.'

'Maybe, Mr McConaghy, you can start by telling me about that journalist?'

11 September 1932

Bob Stack

'You must feel right at home in this kind of company, Dan. Players more of your own calibre.'

'Aye, right you are, Joe.' Joe McAnespie can talk some shite like all men from Cookstown, like all referees.

'Surprised you're not, you know.'

'What's that, Joe? What's that you're surprised at?'

'You know, what's the word I'm looking for . . . mingling. That's it. I've noticed you're not mingling, Dan.'

'Not much gets past you, Joe, does it?' He taps his nose like I'm not to let others in on his big secret. 'Excepting, of course, that goal you allowed Donaghmore in the O'Neill Cup.'

'Jeez, Dan, you're a harsh man. That was three year ago, and it didn't stop you winning.'

'Fuck off, will you, Joe.' He does. I'll mingle if and when I want to, and not before. It's not as if they need me for their big party. All the bigwigs are here from the county and from the Ulster game, rubbing shoulders with the Wexford boys and the Kerrymen. They have really rolled out the red carpet, I can't remember the last time we had both the Donaghmore Pipe Band and the Ancient Order of Hibernian flute band play the night *before* a big game. What must they be making of us? Especially the Kerrymen, it's not as if they aren't used to being played in by a flute and a pipe, they've been hearing plenty at Croke Park over these last years. Those boys must be laughing at us and our wee Tyrone ways. At least the speeches are over at last. All that how honoured we are to be hosting the three-in-a-row All-Ireland champions from Kerry, graced by the presence of the latest heroes from Wexford, that noble footballing county. They have managed to lure two of the biggest football teams in Ireland all the way to Coalisland, and they can't quite believe it themselves. Christ. Bring on the céilí, let's have a dance and a mingle. Better still, a drink. At least the beer is free if you know the barman.

'Would anyone be allowed one of those?' It's a Kerryman.

'Don't you have the big game tomorrow?'

'Don't you?' So he has spotted me as a player. Give him some credit.

'The Fianna against the Clarkes is only a big game if you've lived here all your life and never seen anything else.'

'The guy giving the speech said it was the final game in your senior championship.'

'It will be. What the gobshite didn't tell you was that it's the only game we'll play this year, there being only one other team entered. You needn't listen to him.'

'So it's not true what he told me that you're the best man they have here, and a regular for the county and for Ulster? I'm Bob Stack, by the way.'

'Are you, now? Well, I'm pleased to make your acquaintance. Here, have my beer while I grab another.'

Bob Stack, five times winner of the Sam Maguire, unbeatable partnership with Con Brosnan in the Kingdom side's midfield. He's drinking my beer. And he's heard I'm pretty useful too. Good man.

'What are the girls like around here, Dan?' He's still here.

'You've met them already. They're all in camogie teams, and they were there on Main Street to greet you all tonight, somewhere between us and the pipe band.'

'They looked big.'

'What can I say? That's how they are bred here.'

'Do you have a sweetheart, Dan?'

FINDING DAN

'I wouldn't put it like that. There's a girl in Rostrevor who sometimes thinks of me. I don't like to be tied down. I might travel.' Now that I have said it, that sounds less of a prospect. I could have gone to New York, but Jim went instead to see if he can be as useless there as he was here. 'I fancy New York. I have a sister there.'

'You should go, Dan, they'd like you there. It's a great place if you are young and have a head for heights. They are building towers there so high they are calling them skyscrapers. You stand on the street and look up, and you can fall over for trying to see the top. They finished one just last year, a hundred storeys up it goes. They are getting used to the Irish now too, I think. There was a time when we were just thought of as monkeys who laid Tarmacadam and pissed our wages away on a Thursday. It was true enough, I remember it well.'

'Come again?'

'I'm a New Yorker, Dan. Born and brought up there, and even played football there before coming to Kerry.'

'You're a long way from New York now. St Patrick's Hall, Coalisland is a long way from anywhere civilised.'

'Not from where I look at it. I arrive here on a Saturday night, and all the girls in town turn out in their nicely pressed camogie jerseys to see us, and they lay on some speeches, a céilí and all the free beer I can drink. I promise you, Dan, I wouldn't have got that if I'd stayed put in America. And we don't get it now when we travel there as a team. Sure they applaud us and are glad when we come, but it never lasts. They don't remain interested in you for long.'

I take his hint about the beer, and prise two more out of the barman's private stash. Bob Stack from New York? Now I would never have thought that.

'Molly O'Rourke, Bob, did you ever hear tell of a Molly O'Rourke? She's worked in hotels there. Some of the finest, she tells us, done very well for herself, saving money and everything. Molly. O'Rourke. Dark-haired girl.'

'In hotels? You do find that Irish girls tend to get work like that. They are all dark if they're not redhead.' He gulps from his second bottle. He can put his beer away, for sure.

'Molly. She's younger than me. You'll hardly have met her.'

'It's a big city, Dan.'

'Of course, I know that. Skyscrapers and all.' Let the subject drop.

'Your little sister? I'll certainly listen out for the name.'

'It's a big place, as you say.'

'Molly O'Rourke. I'll look her up the next time I stop by a swanky hotel.'

He's being nice. I'm not sure I'd trust him with my sister. I'm not sure he stops in swanky hotels. 'If you're used to such places, you'll feel right at home at the Lough Neagh Hotel in Maghery. That's where you are tonight. I hear it's so swish even the midges from the lough have moved in.'

'You are a cruel man, Dan.'

I thought he might suggest joining in on a dance, as most of his teammates appear to have, but he doesn't. He seems happy to hug the wall with me, sharing my beer.

'You have any trouble finding your way here, Bob?'

'When you're on a train, you leave that sort of thing to the drivers, Dan. They seemed to have no bother, though. We came into Dublin last night, and left there this morning. It got quite interesting in . . . what's that place called? Begins with a *P*, Portadown would it be?'

'It couldn't have been Portadown if it was interesting, Bob. Are you sure you got that right?'

'I mean we got the type of reception, which said we were less welcome there than we are here.'

'That'll be Portadown then. Was there trouble?'

'Maybe after we left. Not while we were there. It was them boys you have here like the Orangemen. The guard called them Black Preceptory, would that be right? They had some banners asking us politely to go back to our own country, and others with little citations from the bible and the like. They tried to stop the train out of the station. You know, Dan, the funny thing is I think they were scared of us.'

FINDING DAN

'Good if they are. They have had charge of the North for ten years now, and they're still frightened of losing it. They can't see where the threats are coming from, but they act like the war's not over. If we tried telling them we had no fight left in us, they would not believe it. They'd ask us, So when are you going to stop talking your peasant language? And, Why are you still playing your Gaelic games, if you've stopped the war? Talking and playing football are all the fighting we do these days. You lot in the South seem to prefer it that way.'

'I reckon you are right, Dan.' Bob Stack is not from the same country as me, and not simply because he is American.

'How good are you, Dan? You look like you could handle yourself on a pitch.'

'I have maybe another year, perhaps two, in me. I'm carrying a bit of a limp now. It doesn't show when I'm playing, but I take longer now to get over games.' I don't want to brag, but how can I in front of a man like Bob Stack? 'I have played centre half back for Tyrone these past six years. We played the McKenna Cup against Monaghan in July there. And I got a game for Ulster in the Railway Cup in '28.'

'Leinster beat us all that year.'

'They did. But you won it the year before.'

'That was a tough game. I've had a few too many tough games, Dan, if I'm truthful. I can't think I'll have too many more.'

'Will you beat Wexford tomorrow?'

'No, we've left too many of our big boys behind.'

'And against Mayo in two weeks' time?'

'We'll beat them. All-Irelands are what we're good at. Croke Park in Dublin feels as much like home turf as the Austin Stack in Tralee. Christ, Dan, you should play in front of a crowd like that. The noise is like a howling gale, it can knock you back on your heels, or it can lift you clean out of the stadium. If you had feathers, you'd fly. Did you ever get a crowd like that?'

'Only in my head. Bob, what will you do when you stop playing?' He looks offended, like he hasn't already told me what he has. Or perhaps it is something other than offence: fear, or shame.

'Men like me have been taken on as bookkeepers. Firms feel their clients can trust us. Or there's always teaching. A change from this anyways.' Bob looks like it's a change he'd rather put off.

'What about you, Dan? What are your prospects? Something similar?'

Buses came and took the players to their hotel in Maghery. The céilí band packed their gear away, and the barman heaved the remainder of his beer onto the back of a wagon. I have the walk back to Creenagh ahead of me. On Main Street, the bars are empty and shut up. Bunting is still fluttering from between the telegraph poles, as no one has been given the job of taking it in. Way off from Annagher direction where the games will be played tomorrow, some young boys are already in full voice.

ooO0Ooo

There can't have been many Sunday games I have played without a sore head brought on by drinking on the Saturday. I have a sore head today. Bob Stack will have a sore head too. Not a great way to get ready for two important games, but then again, neither game really matters at all. You can't say that to the punters who have travelled from Fermanagh, Armagh, Down, and Antrim; who have taken the special trains from Donegal and Monaghan, Drogheda and Dundalk; who left Derry on the one-off fare of 5/- and got here passing through Strabane, Sion Mills and Victoria Mills, Newtonstewart, Omagh, Beragh, Sixmilecross, Carrickmore, Pomeroy, Donaghmore, and Dungannon, gathering fans all the way. They will want to see the Wexford boys, Crean and the Walshes. But it's the Kerrymen, the soon-to-be four in a row men they have really paid their money to watch: Jack Walsh, Con Brosnan, Bob Stack. They'll have their eye out too for Jack Flavin, Eugene Powell, and one or two of the others like Paul Russell. The man from the *Tyrone Courier* reckons there must be ten thousand here already, or on their way. He has consulted with his rival on the *Ulster Herald*, and that's the figure they have agreed. A pity the *Dungannon Democrat* is no

FINDING DAN

longer in business. They could cover a GAA event and do it properly. I notice the RUC are out in force, not surely out of interest in the game itself. I'd like to think that a crowd this big would give the old bastards some work to do.

They could start by solving the Case of the Vandalised Football Posts. They have been patching them up since this morning when young Patsy McDonagh reported the news to his dad. Patsy had fancied kicking ball on the Annagher ground, so as to say he'd played on the same turf as the All-Ireland champions.

Dungannon Clarkes took to the field first. I know all the boys, or I know their older brothers, having played for them for so long. They weren't happy when I left them for the Fianna, as it's not the usual thing, and Creenagh is officially in Dungannon. I don't much mind who I turn out for, I'd play for Edendork if they could muster enough men for a team. So there's a bit of needle, but I can handle it. I have always been taller on the pitch than on the street. The game is going our way. I leap high in the air to catch the ball, and handpass it twenty yards, turning defence into attack. The trombones of the Dungannon Brass Band tune up their applause. I can pick out my name in the crowd when they cheer a punt upfield leading to our first point. The crowd is thickening, and lends its voice to the breeze. When they cheer our next score, it is loud and prolonged and feels like the crowd I have played before all my life, the crowd I could have played before. I bend to catch my breath and look towards the pavilion, but Bob isn't there, he'll be with the rest of the green and gold jerseys, maybe warming up or just drinking tea before his game, whatever ritual he follows. The ball skids in towards me, followed by a Dungannon man. I don't catch his face, but I catch his boot on my left knee. The game carries on, and I do too, uselessly. The Clarkes, however, have given up on winning. The whistle blows, and there is a loud cheer for us. I raise my arms, but the pain makes me wince. I look to the crowd to celebrate, but they have turned away. They have moved their attentions to the next game, the game they really came for.

Sunday, 10 April 1966

Thirty-Seven Seconds

The last person left Saint Patrick's Hall two hours ago. In one corner, a stack of wooden chairs, the sort found in schoolhouses, leans at a precarious angle. Several other chairs are scattered randomly, some facing the walls, others upended with their legs aimed like missile launchers. Empty beer bottles have been brushed with the dust into a pile in the centre. Three foldable tables are arranged in a U.

Five men and one woman enter and take their places at the tables in a manner, which suggests they have done this before. The mood, as determined by most of those present, is jubilant. O'Connor and McQuaid are respectively the Chairman and the Secretary of the Tyrone 1916 Commemoration Committee. Early and Corr (the woman) are veterans of the Easter Rising in Dublin. McGarvey is a priest. The youngest man is called Maguire.

O'Connor: Well, well, well, well, well. Well. I think Mrs Corr, gentlemen, I think we did it.

McQuaid: I think, Mr O'Connor, we can all agree that you did it.

O'Connor: Jim, that's kind of you as always, but I can only take so much of the credit. You all played your parts too. And before we forget, I think we should ask Father here to say a few words in thanks to God for the part He played today.

FINDING DAN

McGarvey (*clearing his throat*): Yes, quite. Dear Lord, we would like to thank You for Your blessings upon us today. For bringing all the people safely to our wee town today, and ensuring there was no trouble with our friends in uniform. For inspiring some fine words from our guest, Mr O'Brádaigh. For putting on a nice sunny day for us, for we haven't had many of those lately. (*General mumbles of agreement.*) We thank You also for the lovely catering, which Mrs Corr and her team pulled off. Last, but not least, we are thankful for the glorious example of the men and women of 1916, in whose honour we gathered here today. We thank You, Lord. Amen.

Corr: Those were nice words, Father. And I know, in your heart, you also remembered our President, Mr de Valera. We would not be here without *him*, most of us would agree.

McGarvey: As a priest, Mrs Corr, I prefer to steer clear of politics. But for you, I could add a few words to the Lord now, you know, out loud?

Early: Oh, God!

O'Connor (*diplomatically*): Given the time, we might be better off adding our own words, you know, to ourselves. If that's all right with you, Father.

McGarvey: Oh, yes, I'm not one to stand in the way of progress and modern ways.

Early (*just audibly*): Not like de Valera then.

O'Connor: Right! Moving on! Item one on our agenda. We do have an agenda, I presume, Jim?

McQuaid: As always, Mr O'Connor. You wouldn't be without one. We've done item one.

O'Connor: We have? Remind me.

McQuaid: 'Father McGarvey will thank the Committee'.

McGarvey: Christ! I don't think I did that. I was so busy thanking God and everyone else...

Early: And Corr.

McGarvey: ... and Mrs Corr, I think I left the rest of you out.

O'Connor: Well, I think, Father, we can assume you had us in mind too. Jim, can you ensure the minutes reflect that please. Item two?

McQuaid: Item two is 'Chairman's Business'.

O'Connor: I think we can all guess what *that* is tonight! Well, well, well. I think we outdid even ourselves today. Rarely can Coalisland have had such a day, a 'day in the sun', you might say. I thought the Edendork Pipe Band were a worthy accompaniment to our own Ancient Order of Hibernian flutes despite their lack of practice. And the crowds! I have never seen anything like the crowds, fifteen thousand I'd say.

McQuaid: I told the RTÉ people seven thousand.

O'Connor: Did you, Jim? I told *The Courier* fifteen, and they seemed to take my word for it.

McQuaid: I'm sure you are right, Mr O'Connor.

O'Connor: When, Jim, were you speaking to the television people?

McQuaid: At MacRory Park during the speeches. They said they needed to speak to someone from the Committee, and as I was available...

O'Connor: Was I not? Was I so hard to find, Jim? You see, this is why we need a structure, an organisation to avoid conflicts such as this one. Now, if you had called me, I could have told them, as I did the men from the press, that there were in fact fifteen thousand people here today, a *historic amount* and not a mere seven thousand, which could, in future, be overlooked. I take it you did not say it on film?

Early: He did.

McQuaid: I did look for you, but you were busy with *The Courier*.

O'Connor: The Tyrone *Courier*! Get that? Not Radio Telefis Éireann! Not the *Irish* Courier or the *Dublin* Courier, but our own wee *local* paper that doesn't even come out every day!

McQuaid: It should have been you, Terence, I'm sorry. It won't happen again.

O'Connor: No, it never will.

FINDING DAN

Early: I thought you were magnificent, Jim. Much more entertaining than O'Brady giving his speech, which the camera seemed to miss. What was that line you gave? *"We believe in starting our own traditions here in Tyrone.'* You certainly made sure they heard that one. Twice you said it. Genius!

O'Connor: Well, if Quinn shows up, we'll all have the chance to hear it. Ah, speak of the Devil (forgive me, Father), and there he shows up.

A man, Quinn, enters. He is pushing a television cabinet into the hall on a makeshift trolley. He struggles with the doors, which keep closing on him. He looks to the members of the committee, appealing wordlessly for help, but none of them moves.

O'Connor: Quinn here has kindly agreed to fix up a television set for us, so we can watch our moment of glory as it goes out on air. *(Quinn continues to struggle getting the set through the doors, but still, none of the members rises to help him. He is grunting. O'Connor tries to ignore this).* Mrs Corr here volunteered to have us round to her place to watch the programme, but I wouldn't hear of it.

Early: No, indeed.

O'Connor: So, Mr Quinn, it had to be. Nothing electrical is too much trouble for you, is it Mr Quinn?

(Quinn is the other side of the doors, still pushing the television cabinet into the hall. He answers only with another grunt.)

McGarvey: Is Quinn's television equipped to pick up an RTÉ broadcast?

O'Connor: He has thought of that, Father. Quinn has a small supply of aerials, which can pick up the signal from Dublin loud and clear.

McGarvey: Is that not strictly speaking illegal, Terence?

O'Connor: Only strictly speaking, Father. And sure, a crime committed in a good cause is scarcely a crime at all, wouldn't you say?

McGarvey: Perhaps, but morally . . .

McQuaid: And it's hardly a sin if no one else gets to know.

McGarvey: Maybe not a sin exactly. I have to say I don't know where to stand on this. It is, after all, a form of theft, of piracy.

Corr: Father, could I be allowed an opinion on this, would you say, theological point? RTÉ is the state broadcaster. That is the *Free* State broadcaster. I think that entitles us to freely enjoy the benefits of it, as Irishmen and women, wherever we happen to be. Sure it's only the people in Stormont (*she looks for, and gets, nods of recognition from O'Connor and McQuaid*) who put up barriers along the Border to block the airwaves. 'Sound barriers', isn't it, Jim?

McQuaid: I've heard that told, now, but I couldn't say I know it for myself.

Early: Christ, help us!

Corr: What's that, Mr Early? Have you some wisdom you'd like to share with us? Perhaps some technical, even political insight you have kept hidden from us?

O'Connor: Now, now, Mrs Corr, Mr Early. We don't need any unpleasantness on this day of all days when we remember those of all parties who fell fighting for Ireland. Now, while I'm sure Quinn will work as quickly and quietly as he can, (*Quinn promptly, briefly, falls silent.*) I will proceed with chairman's business. We have, I see, forty-five minutes before the programme goes out, and we wouldn't want the meeting to overrun and miss out, would we? I think, for the minutes, we should record what happened during the day as it unfolded. We began this morning up at Brackaville with players from Tyrone and Derry and Mr Maguire here, and some of his friends at the front of the parade.

Early: In uniform. We agreed no uniforms.

FINDING DAN

O'Connor: No, it wouldn't be fair to call it that—Jim, the minutes, not 'uniform'—I think we can say the boys were smartly attired in matching trousers and jumpers.

McQuaid: And dark glasses? Do we want the minutes to say what people were wearing, and if so, should we record the wearing of dark glasses?

O'Connor: What does the Committee think? We could get away with not mentioning glasses?

Corr: Then there are the Easter lilies and the IRA medals. Some were, some weren't. Of course, it may not be fair to refer to individuals *not* wearing their medals, if in fact they never received them in the first place.

Early: I'll ignore that remark.

O'Connor: Mr Maguire, would you like to add anything at this stage?

(*Maguire, who has yet to speak, lifts his stare to O'Connor, but remains silent. Early offers a cigarette to the priest and lights one for himself. Quinn can be heard muttering occasional profanities, as he struggles to install the television. McQuaid puzzles over how to account for this hiatus in the minutes.*)

Corr: May I offer my own observation? I thought it was refreshing to see so many young faces out in force today. Speaking as a 1916 veteran, it is very gratifying to find the youngsters still interested in their history. And if they bring their own flavour to the proceedings, I can't see any harm in that, so long as it is within reason. Don't you agree, Mr Early?

Early (*reluctantly*): We were all young once. There was a time when we all thought we could change the world. It didn't last, but there was a time.

O'Connor: Thank you for that, Mr Early, and before that, Mrs Corr. Those of us who, let's say, 'missed the opportunity' being that much younger, have so much to be thankful for. Don't you agree, Jim?

MARK QUINN

McQuaid: Oh, yes, we thank God we missed it, terrible time!

McGarvey: I don't think that's what Terence had in mind, Jim. As I said at MacRory Park earlier, we all owe a debt today to those who went before us who showed us the path. They had no maps, they hadn't much idea of where they were going or even what they were doing, and as we know their paths diverged, but where would we be today if it wasn't for those brave men and women who led us here?

O'Connor: That's surely something to think about, Father.

McQuaid: It made me think.

Early: Me too!

(*A terrific clattering, as Quinn empties an entire bag of tools on the floor.*)

O'Connor (*checking his watch*): How far did I get? Yes, Brackaville. Mr Maguire and his associates made their contribution, and then we were off. By the time we reached the Gaelic ground, as I informed *The Courier*, there were 'in excess of' fifteen thousand people there. A lively crowd, I think we could characterise it. But the bands served to mute some of the more raucous behaviour, I would say.

Corr: If I may interrupt again? There's no one here a more enthusiastic supporter of the bands...

McGarvey: No, indeed, your tea is legendary.

Corr: ...but... Sorry, Father, I don't follow.

McGarvey: Don't mind me, please.

Corr: To get to my point, wasn't eighteen bands a bit excessive?

O'Connor: I have no objection to you interrupting chairman's business. You know that I like to steer my committee according to democratic principles, and your interventions carry all the more weight for coming from such a patriot as yourself, Mrs Corr, but we did discuss this matter at length during the planning phase when we balanced the merits of ten or fifteen or even twenty-five bands of varying seniority and musical

FINDING DAN

heritage, and arrived by a process of near mathematical deduction at the number eighteen. Now, it's all well and good after the fact with the benefit of hindsight, and so on, to say that you could personally have done with fewer bands. But I ask you, Mrs Corr, hand on heart, would you like to be the one to say to any of those bands, 'I'm sorry, Mary,' or 'I'm sorry little Declan, but your services are surplus to requirement'? No, that's what I thought. Jim!

(*McQuaid drops his pen on the minute book. Corr sits in red-faced silence.*)

Maguire: I thought they were grand.
O'Connor: That's settled then. My personal highlight was when Father led us in a decade of the Rosary...
McGarvey: In Irish.
O'Connor: ... yes, in Irish. Thank you, Charles. Are those the beads you used?
McGarvey: They are, yes. (*He spins them round an extended finger, building speed.*) I was given them by the bishop at my ordination. They're something of a lucky charm for me if I can put it that way. It's not true that superstition has no place to play in modern religion. I know the pope has his views, but I have my own.
Early: You may want to keep those to yourself, you know, Charles. Another? (*McGarvey accepts another cigarette.*)
McGarvey: Anyway, it helps settle any nerves I might have, you know praying in public, if I have my lucky crucifix with me.
O'Connor: No one noticed any nerves, Father, nor remarked on any mistakes of pronunciation you might have made.
McGarvey: Did I make any mistakes?
O'Connor: Just the one that I spotted.
McQuaid: I spotted the same one, I imagine.
McGarvey: Which was that?
O'Connor: 'Mary', or 'Mhuire'. You forgot to aspirate.

McGarvey: How many times? (*He spins the beads even faster.*)
McQuaid: Just each time.
McGarvey: Ten times! Per decade! For Christ's sake, I could be defrocked for this! (*The beads fly off the end of his finger, and slide across the floor to where Quinn is still trying to fix the aerial.*)
Early: You and I both know, Father, you would have to try an awful lot harder than that to get defrocked in this country.
McGarvey: So much for my lucky Rosary. (*He stays in his seat, leaving the beads on the floor.*)
O'Connor: Well, as I say, it was a personal highlight of the day if that's any consolation. Then Mr Crawford read the Proclamation.
McQuaid: Now, I know we debated this earlier in planning, but has anyone had any second thoughts about this? Is it still necessary, do you think, every anniversary to read out the proclamation of the Provisional Government of the Irish Republic? Given that the Republic has moved on since then?

(*Maguire releases a single roar of laughter. Everyone else stares at McQuaid in silence.*)

Corr (*gently*): I think, Jim, it is good to recall the words, the intentions, of the men and women of '16 during what is, after all, a commemoration of 1916. Traditions may come and some may go, but that's one at least I think we should hold to.
McQuaid: It's just . . . (*he pauses to see if he is allowed to talk*) with the deepest respect, I think there might be ways of marking the anniversary without dwelling too much on the event itself. (*Again, he pauses, expecting to be interrupted.*) Or we could concentrate on the more positive aspects. We could have some people walking into the Post Office, you know, going about their business, then . . . (*he tails off.*)
Early: Do you have any suggestions for how we could represent the brutal murder of the rebel leaders, or the years of war and civil

war, the bloody mayhem of it all. Which positive aspects might we pick out of that? Should we have some Irish dancers do a reel for us and call it 'Internecine Strife'? Or get our Unionist brethren to come along and bang their Lambeg drums to symbolise the British warship on the Liffey? Patrick Crawford reading the Proclamation does it for me, thank you.

Corr: Whereas I agree with you, Mr Early, that the Proclamation is one tradition we would do well to hold on to, there might be some scope for bringing some of the more noble events back to life. May I elaborate?

(O'Connor checks his watch again, and again looks anxiously in the direction of Quinn who is now sitting on the floor reading an instruction manual.)

Corr: You won't need reminding, any of you, that I was with Commandant Eamon de Valera at Boland's Mills that week. That it was us in the Mount Street Bridge area who inflicted the most casualties on the Tommies and alone remained undefeated. There is glory in that, and I, for one, would not object to some tasteful re-enactment of the event.

Early: And would you faithfully recreate the Commandant President having his nervous breakdown in the middle of it all?

Corr: He never did! I won't have you say that, I won't! De Valera is a hero to us all, and first of all, to the women and men who served under him.

Early: These would be the same women and men who have been telling Max Caulfield that Dev was mentally exhausted and had to take rest?

Corr (*shouting now*): I don't need to read what some reporter puts down in a book to tell me what happened. And I don't need you either. If it wasn't for your lot, hiding in the GPO, and then surrendering...

Early: Hiding?

Corr: Hiding, yes, and then surrendering when there were plenty around Dublin and elsewhere who were willing to fight on. Surrendering was all Collins and his men were good for.

O'Connor: Now, if we could just get back to our agenda...

Early: Your agenda can go frig itself, O'Connor.

O'Connor: Today is not about digging up the past, poring over the details, or working out the whys and wherefores. Not the did-hes or shouldn't-he-haves. A commemoration such as this ought not to be looking backwards, or lingering on divisions, which belong in the past. If I might put it this way, our anniversary should have nothing to do with history, as such, and I think in this I am beginning to see where Jim was coming from (though I disagree absolutely with how he put it.)

McQuaid: Thank you, Mr O'Connor.

O'Connor: No, that's okay, Mr McQuaid.

Corr: Oh, shut up, you old fool. How can you be chairman of a commemoration committee if you are too scared to even look at past events. Mr Early and I disagree on many things...

Early: On everything.

Corr: ...but we can agree on this, that we will get nowhere as a country if we are ashamed of our history.

McGarvey: In our own ways, Mrs Corr, I think all of us here would agree on that one. The past is a wonderful and fascinating country, as scholars have told us, and we visit its more interesting places from time to time, sipping its wine, eating its exotic food, taking quiet moments in its palaces and churches, perhaps sending a postcard to a special friend. And then we come back, hopefully refreshed, with a bit of colour in our cheeks, to here, Coalisland. And everything is exactly as it was before.

(Quinn has discarded the manual, and resorts to slapping the side of the television set to get it to work.)

FINDING DAN

O'Connor (*tentatively*): Then Ruairí Ó'Brádaigh gave the address. (*He looks up, anticipating interruption.*) Any comments?

McQuaid: Should I write that in Irish or in English? Can I just keep to Rory Brady? It's easier.

O'Connor: I did notice a stronger than necessary police force. Did anyone think to count how many?

McQuaid: About one hundred and fifty.

O'Connor: And not one thing for them to do.

Corr: It might just be worth noting for the record, Mr McQuaid, that, technically speaking, we did just veer from our original plan with that one.

O'Connor: How so, Mrs Corr? I recall distinctly almost from the get-go, we always intended to have Mr Ó'Brádaigh come up from Longford to address us. A most appropriate choice, we were agreed. Elected a TD from the Mountjoy Prison, an internee at the Curragh, escaping with Dáithí Ó'Conaill, and going on the run...

Early: To become Chief of Staff of the IRA.

O'Connor: ... It's a familiar story to many here.

Corr: He's not the MP. You promised in the planning stages that we would have the local MP give the address.

O'Connor: I surely cannot shoulder the blame for that, Mrs Corr. That is the business of the electors of Fermanagh and South Tyrone who made their decision, what, ten days ago. If they voted against Brady, that's hardly my fault.

Corr: No, I'm just saying, technically speaking, we agreed to invite the local MP to do the speech and we never did.

O'Connor: The Marquess of Hamilton is our local member of parliament, Mrs Corr. Are you now putting to this committee that we should have an aristocrat from the Ulster Unionist party address the veterans of the Easter Rising?

Early: We shouldn't put it past her.

O'Connor: Do we have anything to say about the speech itself? McQuaid, I know you were too busy with the RTÉ people to be listening. Mr Maguire, was this your sort of thing?

Maguire: I'd like the priest to put out his cigarette. (*To Early*) And you too.

McGarvey: Of course, child, if it bothers you.

Maguire: It bothers me. Strong drink bothers me. They bother all of us who believe the body must be strong to take the fight to the British. And the soul.

O'Connor: Do you have a view, Father, about the speech?

McGarvey: The speech? Ah, yes. Well, he spoke very well. Mr Brady has a nice way with words and of putting them together. As to what he said, he went a little further than I would have done, with the idealism and the rousing rhetoric. I don't quite see myself as a priest in the political mode. I'm more of your practical sort of curate. In so far as Mr Brady is a man who gets things done, I think you can admire that.

Early: That'll be like raiding arms for the IRA and murdering a constable in Derrylin. That's to be admired, is it, Father?

McGarvey: No, I never said that, Mr Early, and that's mischievous of you to suggest it. I'm merely proposing that a man who has principles and acts on them is a man who can be looked up to.

Early: Is that your moral position?

McGarvey: I'm not saying morals have anything to do with it. I think, in matters such as these, in *national* matters or *existential* matters, let us say, that there are different kinds of rights and different kinds of wrongs, and adopting too rigidly a moral stance is helpful to no one.

Early (*to Maguire*): I don't expect you would disagree with that. But what about the rest of you?

Corr (*after some hesitation*): I'm sure if Father McGarvey said it, it's what he believes.

O'Connor: Are you okay there with the minutes, Jim?

McQuaid: Just dandy, Mr O'Connor, don't you worry about me.

O'Connor: So moving on, we moved on from MacRory Park and back into town until we arrived here, just outside, in fact. And Joe O'Neill unveiled a wee plaque on the wall for the veterans from hereabouts who met here, in this room, to organise

FINDING DAN

their response to the events in Dublin in 1916. And it was a generous touch, unbidden by any of us here, for Joe to call to mind at that stage the contribution of veterans from Antrim and South Derry. Should we have the wording of the plaque for the minutes? I don't see why not. 'This plaque is erected to commemorate the assembly of Irish Volunteers in this hall, Easter 1916, prepared to give their lives for Irish freedom. Got that, Jim?

McQuaid: Word for word, Mr O'Connor. And may I add, too, how proud I am to be sitting here alongside two such people as Mrs Corr and Mr Early who, despite their differences, were also prepared to give their lives for Irish freedom.

Applause from all present—apart from Quinn who is entangled by the aerial. As the clapping fades, only Maguire continues, slowly and ironically.

Maguire: And so the celebrations drew to a close, and all the old volunteers were wheeled home, much drink was taken, and the Committee retired to Saint Patrick's Hall to give itself a pat on the back.

McQuaid: Don't be hard on yourself, Maguire: the minutes also show we patted you on the back.

Maguire: If you think I seek or accept approval from any of you lot, you are mistaken. What we have been engaged in today gentlemen (*he ignores Corr*) is a charade. If it were a decoy for some more meaningful activity, it would not be so bad. But it was not. It was a mere game. While the bands played and the girls danced, while Father here did his prayers, and you unveiled your wee plaque, the English must have been laughing at us. 'There's the Fenians,' they'll be telling themselves, 'making do with their songs and their speeches. We'll just stay here lording it over them.' Well, the time for talking and for singing is over.

O'Connor: May I just remind you of the time, Mr Maguire...

Maguire: Did I ask you to speak? You can have your moment of fame with the *Tyrone Courier*, O'Connor. After that, I suggest you stay at home. The cause will not be won by the likes of you.

McQuaid: And I suppose we should look to the likes of you for that, Maguire?

Maguire: When it comes to it, McQuaid, you will not be asked for your opinion. The course is already set. We will speak to the English in the language they understand. We will meet their terror state with our own brand of terror, and they will wish they never set foot in this country. We will hit them from behind when they are sleeping, when they are going about their own business in their own streets, we will chase them out, and even then we'll not let up. And after that, you can have your fiddle and your wee colleens and whatever else you need to make you feel Irish.

Early: There's no Irish sentiment in you at all, is there?

Maguire: Sentiment doesn't come into it. I know how to defeat the Brits, that's all. If I was a Brit myself, I'd know exactly what I'd do with you, and I'd do it. You understand me, don't you, Mr Early? You're a Collins man.

Early: Michael Collins would have had nothing to do with the likes of you.

Maguire: He was a thug.

Early: He had ideals!

Maguire: He was a thug like me. And I guess, so were you. He was ruthless when killing the English, and when he'd finished with them, he was as ruthless when killing his own lot.

Early: That's just not true! Michael hated civil war. He was pulled apart by his doubts.

Maguire: And that was his deadly flaw. There must be no room for doubts. They only make us weak and sympathise with our enemies. We must be brutal and impassive when we look at the face of our enemy. That's the only way we can win.

Early: Is that all it means to you?

Maguire: There is nothing else.

FINDING DAN

There is a sudden blast of music from the corner of the hall where Quinn has been working. And then, faintly at first but then quite clearly, a picture appears on the television screen.

O'Connor: Hush, everyone, it's on! Mr Quinn has come good!

O'Connor, McQuaid, McGarvey, Corr, and Early all pick up their chairs and sit on them in front of the television. After a short while, Maguire joins them, standing.

McQuaid: May I just say, sir, whatever happens, it has been a pleasure serving with you.
O'Connor: Oh shut up, McQuaid.
McGarvey: Should I offer a quick prayer?

(They all stare at the priest, to say 'no'.)
The music continues. A title appears on the screen: 'Spoken of among Their People'.

Corr: 'They shall be spoken of among their people. The generations shall remember them and call them blessed.' That's Padraig Pearse. Isn't that beautiful?

'There now follows a special programme from the Newsbeat team bringing reports from commemoration events around the country. Today, we had our cameras in Coalisland, Cloughjordan, Dundalk, Enniscorthy, Galway, Kiltyclogher, Limerick, and Cork. First to Coalisland in County Tyrone where seven thousand people turned out for a parade.'

McGarvey: Never mind, Jim.

A road sign: 'Coalisland' fills the screen.

O'Connor: That's us!

MARK QUINN

The sign is replaced by a tricolour flag.

Several: Aha! They never got that one!

A small group of young men, including Maguire, are seen marching on the spot. They are wearing berets and ties and are carrying flags. The film is mute.

Maguire: What's this, Quinn? There's no sound.
O'Connor: That is a kind of uniform, Maguire. Were the berets really necessary?
McQuaid: The RTÉ people did tell me there might be problems with their sound engineer. It's very complicated, you know.
Corr: Shh. There's Main Street and more flags. Oh, it looks lovely!

The film shows the parade down Main Street. Close-up of a policeman. Hearty clapping from onlookers. The parade passes S Quinn & Sons filling station.

Early: There you go, Quinn. You're on nationwide television.

The front of the procession has surviving 1916 and War of Independence veterans, including O'Rourke, Haughey, Early, and Corr.

Early: You're looking well there, Mrs Corr.
Corr: As are you, Mr Early.
McGarvey: This is all after the gathering in MacRory Park, is it not? They've missed your interview, Jim, and they've left out Ó'Brádaigh's speech, and my prayer. God, my Irish was so bad they were too ashamed to use it!
McQuaid: You were fine, Father, and I never wanted on anyway.

Close up of the plaque mounted on the wall of Saint Patrick's Hall.

FINDING DAN

O'Connor: And that's where we are right now, in that hall. And to think that the country is watching these pictures, and don't know we are inside watching them too. Isn't that marvellous!

Fade to black-out. The programme continues with footage from Cloughjordan with sound.

O'Connor: That'll be enough, I think, Mr Quinn. You may turn it off now. (*Long pause.*) It wasn't very long, was it?
Maguire: Just thirty-seven seconds.
O'Connor: Thirty-seven seconds. Write that in the minutes, please, Mr McQuaid. Well, well. Well, well, well, well, well. Do we have any further items on the agenda, Jim?
McQuaid: Only the one further item, Mr O'Connor. Next year's anniversary.
O'Connor: Then I move we postpone that item until our next meeting.
Early: Seconded.
O'Connor: Shall we go home?

The five men and one woman return their chairs to around the tables then slowly leave, politely showing each other out of the door. The room is left to Quinn, now standing beside the television set with his hand on the aerial.

Quinn: Bugger.

Finding Dan O'Rourke, October 1961

By Malachy Quinn

The boss wants me out of the way. He said it in the kindest possible way. 'You're a wreck and sad to have around. Get out and stay out of this office, and don't come back until you've sorted your crash of a life out.' Or words to that effect. When I didn't run and he didn't bark, I asked if there was a story he wanted me on. 'You know, one that will take me out of circulation for a bit?' I tried hard to disguise my desperation. I have some pride left.

The boss was holding his cigar the way some hucksters handle a billiard cue. He jammed it in his mouth to free up his right hand with which he reached for a card folder labelled 'Players of the Past—Munster'.

'You're sending me to Munster?'

He aimed his cigar at me to shut up. He was rifling through loose papers and cuttings shaped like *T*s and *L*s. I was getting a follow-up, a story usually reserved for a rookie or a grateful tea boy. When I was on the *Independent* scribing the leaders, this was the sort of thing we would give to the old soaks who patronised the pubs of Temple Bar for a living, sucking their stories out of brain-damaged old sluggers and rheumatic past players. Fossil hunting, we called it. So I'm a fossil hunter now.

FINDING DAN

I'm stopping these days in a boarding house in Donnybrook. Lenehan, a commercial traveller, is in the next-door room. He invited me in once. 'This new toilet water has to be experienced,' he declared mysteriously. I didn't go in, but I noticed he was growing a plant on his windowsill. Mrs Rooney, the landlady, has her rooms on the ground floor, but she allows her daughter Polly the run of the room under mine when she has no guests in it. 'To keep it warm and aired' is how the practical Mrs Rooney puts it. Polly is seventeen. She cooks and cleans the rooms for her mother during the day, and at night, she plays rock and roll records while bouncing joylessly on her bed. Between them, the Rooneys manage to keep the debt man at bay. 'We are a team, Polly and me, you understand,' says Mrs Rooney when she calls me in to share her gin. I am well looked after. I have no complaints on that score. My wife is also happy with the arrangement. All she demands is that I call in on the house in Stillorgan every so often to see the baby, and to tell the neighbours about how my work has kept me away so much lately. 'It's the least you can do to keep me honest,' she says, as if any of this was my doing. The baby has fair hair like her father. When she cries, the wail vibrates from the pit of her empty stomach, and I want to hold her. Rosa, her mother, snatches her up, the crying momentarily appeased by the shock. It was like this yesterday when I saw them last. Was it yesterday or last week? The baby's tear-brimmed eyes scrutinising me as through heavy lenses.

I packed the usual: a toothbrush, a spare shirt, some pencils. I also had the papers the boss had given me with the notes written in the margin. When Bob Stack, a hero of Kerry's four in a row from 1929 to 1932, had been featured in 'Munster Players of the Past', he had named Daniel O'Rourke of Tyrone as the player he would have liked most to have played against. He recalled playing in an invitation match against Wexford in O'Rourke's town, Coalisland, and seeing the local man play halfback for his home team. 'You could tell he had been a great player, and he was certainly a great man. He became my friend.' He was quoted saying this in the article. 'Croker', the reporter, had evidently pencilled notes in the margin relating to the man O'Rourke. 'Girl in Rostrevor' and 'try Dungannon' floated above the end paragraph. The boss wanted me to track down this Daniel O'Rourke. 'If he's alive, we don't know where. Find him and talk to him, and we'll have a look at what you come up with. If you draw a blank, at least I won't have had to look at you lurking around here like bad luck.'

I draw looks while driving my ancient Standard Eight saloon even through the centre of Dublin. The leather of the passenger seat is burst, and I reckon the front springing won't last me this journey. I thought about calling in on Maggie, but there'd be questions. 'Is it me you're running from, Con? For I'm not the one you want to be running from.' I could do without that, but still, I should have seen her. I'll explain when I return, and I'll sort things and ask her to marry me. 'Aren't you forgetting something?' she asked the last time I proposed to her. I was drunk, of course, but meant it no less. If I find a telephone, I will call her.

I can take the T1 trunk to the border. After that, I'll need my map and my wits. The North has always sounded like some sort of fairy tale kingdom to me, distant, perilous, and sealed off from the real world by a jagged border. Stories occasionally reach the outside of every house wired for electricity, some even plumbed for gas, and the roads are like ribbons of tarmac. There are places, I am informed, that will take my punts, but I won't get far before needing to exchange for sterling. When I requested an advance in English from the boss, he told me to 'ask in accounts', but I didn't bother because I knew he would get to them before me. He did tell me to pack my passport, the easier to get past the border with all this trouble going on.

I left early, so I could eat breakfast in Drogheda. I had sausage, bacon, and fried bread in a café house opposite the church—the one that keeps the shrivelled head of St Oliver Plunkett in a casket. They have it displayed like in a trophy cabinet. I wonder do they polish it up. The tea was good, and I took a second cup, as they said I needn't pay for it. I left a few coins in the saucer, the way I used to when I was on a proper paper, and Christ! I even tipped my hat to the waitress on the way out. The saloon was running smoothly, hitting fifty, and I slid the roof back to let in more of the day. The air carried a mingle of warm dust and hay fever grass, cut and juicy. At that speed, not much can be heard above the engine; but when it sings, it is sweet. Coming into Dundalk, it was warm, and the chatter from the people on the pavements was like birds chirruping. Even the grey granite of the town walls joined in, reflecting flecks of sunlight. I hadn't any business to do in Dundalk but fill up with petrol; but I hung around in any case, putting off crossing the border. I can't say why, except to say I had never crossed it before, and I'm not much one for foreign travel.

I stopped in a bar called Brannigan's. The men at the tables sat in threes; those at the bar stood alone. It had the look of a place that people go in only if they have been in it before: every seat seemed taken or reserved for someone not yet arrived. I stood at the far end of the bar to the door and hoped the barman would make his way down to me.

'What are you having?' he asked after making me wait five minutes. 'We've only Guinness on tap.'

'That'll do me,' I said, trying to sound grateful.

'There's other places if you'd rather,' the barman said, walking away. I wasn't sure if I was ever going to get my stout, but he came back with it sure enough. 'You from Dublin?'

I nodded. He nodded on to his other patrons, as if confirming a bet I hadn't seen them make. 'I'm going North after I've had this,' I said, offering conversation. Instead, the barman moved away again into a back room. The other conversations in the bar had resumed, and I imagined I had been left alone.

Then one spoke up. 'Is that business you have up North, or would that be pleasure?' He seemed a short man and far from the oldest one present. He was at a round table.

I may only be a sports hack, but I have learned in the past that strange men in bars don't talk if they think they're talking to a reporter. 'I'm a commercial traveller. In toilet water,' I said it like an old joke. I hoped Lenehan from the boarding house wouldn't mind.

The man laughed, signalling to his colleagues that they should join in. 'I'm carrying a box over the border in my boot,' I added.

At this the man stopped laughing, but a thin sort of smile was left there on his face. 'What did you say your name was?'

I hadn't. 'Lenehan.'

'I usually call my friends by their Christian name, Mr Lenehan.'

'I prefer to use my professional name.' I didn't know what Lenehan's mother had called him. 'When I'm working.'

'Is that what this is, Mr Lenehan, business? Have you a proposition to make or a service to offer? There's people here who could be interested in that boot of yours, if not your toilet water.'

I'm paid to write about football or boxing, and I read my papers the way I write them, from the back. There might be a story to be had from this bar, but it wasn't up to me to write it. 'No, no proposition. No service. Unless you want some scent?'

At that, my companion withdrew.

Perhaps it was the stout, but my car ran less smoothly after that. I stayed on the T1, heading for Newry over the border. Maybe I strayed from the main road, for I found myself in Jonesborough, a village in the North, without apparently crossing the line. Then I was back in the Republic, the road, the air, the light not obviously different. It seemed, though, as if the border was tangled round the road, tightening around it, pulling tight. I finally came upon the border post, some few miles short of Newry. There was no barrier, but a Nissen hut to pull up at. A man, thirty years my junior and wearing a uniform of indeterminate origin, appeared from behind the hut and motioned for me to lower my window.

'Where are we off to today, sir?' he asked. His tone was bored. He wasn't asking to climb in with me.

'I have no definite plans. I thought I'd go to Rostrevor first.' Thinking that this had somehow failed to convince, I added, 'It's a nice day. I might see the boats.'

My man was no analyst of human nature even though he must have seen plenty of it pass his hut. He restricted himself to simple, pointless enquiries. 'Travelling alone, are we?' He glanced at the

FINDING DAN

foam stuffing erupting from the passenger seat and let that be his answer. 'Carrying anything today?'

I nodded to the back seat. 'Just a bag.'

'No meat, dairy, fruit or vegetables, no flowers, no plants, no animals, stuffed or living, no materials to be put to a terrorist purpose. No antiques or national treasures without a licence.' There was no priority or special emphasis in his recital. And he didn't ask for my passport. He stepped back, tapped the saloon twice on the roof, and waved me through with a flourish like he suddenly had an American song in his head.

To get to Rostrevor, I had to drive on to Newry before heading south again towards Warrenpoint, keeping the narrow needle of Carlingford Lough on my right. The holiday trade finished five weeks ago, but I found a guesthouse still open to custom. I was exhausted from my day's driving, so I wasted no time in stripping down to my vest and climbed into my bed. Behind my closed eyes, I could see a child, the child ignored by Rosa and abandoned by me. Her body convulsing with the effort of crying, silent at first, and then (I suppose I had fallen asleep) loud and hoarse and empty. When I woke, my pillow was moist with my own tears, and I was more tired than before. It was dark, and I couldn't find my matches to read the time. The moon shone sick and yellow in my window, and on the unbroken waters of the lough, its reflection appeared like a spotlight on a greasy dance floor. I returned to my bed and slept deeply through the remainder of the night.

Enquiries at the post office the next morning offered up no Daniel O'Rourkes in Rostrevor. At the GAA ground outside the village, I found two youngsters hurling a sliotar at each other. The goalposts at one end were an inadequate frame for the Mourne Mountains behind. The boys directed me to a bench of old guys sitting outside the club changing rooms. I asked them did they know a Daniel O'Rourke, or had they ever known someone of that name, a player from the old days.

There were three of them, and although all of them made noises, only one actually spoke. 'I would know if there was a Daniel O'Rourke living in this town, and I can tell to you now there is not.'

I turned to go, tipping my hat for thanks.

'That's not to say that there never has *been* a man by that name living here. That I couldn't be sure of, and I don't know if anybody could be that sure.' Noises came from out of the other two. 'But if there was any man I'd advise you to enquire of on the matter, that would be me.'

'But you have never met a Dan O'Rourke here?'

'What gave you that impression? I would estimate that I have met at least three men of that name. Which, if any of them would be your man, I could not tell you, and I wouldn't wish to lead you astray. There was an O'Rourke, Daniel, I'm sure, who ran a small hotel on the quay for a short while. There were problems with money there, I'd imagine, and that was that for him. Many years ago, there was a Daniel O'Rourke who would drink in all the bars along here, complaining of his work being thirsty work, and threatening to saw the fingers off of a local bobby who tried to apprehend him drunk and disorderly.'

'And the third? You said you knew three?'

'I did, but I was mistaken. The other that I knew was a timid little thing that used to work in the sweet shop, and she got taken up by the wrong sort of man who didn't treat her right, and now she has to take what the doctor gives her to keep her from embarrassing herself.'

'She'd be called Danielle O'Rourke, would I be right?'

'An awful sad case. Was that any use to you now?'

A strange notion took hold of me then. 'Would there be any women living in Rostrevor, say in their early sixties, who aren't married? I mean, who never married?'

The bench of men shook with the laughter of one. 'You don't find the sort of woman you're after in a wee place like this. In Dublin maybe, and no doubt in Belfast, but that sort of thing hasn't reached us yet, and I suspect it never will.'

FINDING DAN

'No old maids then?'

'An old maid can be an old maid without having to have another old maid keeping her company, so to speak.' I had scandalised the man. 'Jesus! Are things that bad in Dublin already?'

I could not explain myself to him. To him, I was an envoy of Satan, come to plant a modern hell right here in Rostrevor. I was made to feel filthy, by the look on his face. I went to speak again, but he raised his hand in a halt, shaking his head in slow disgust. And so, I merely walked away, retracing my steps to town. Ten or a dozen strides on, the three men were laughing again, calling out, and—I felt—taunting me.

I walked to the quayside. I didn't hold much hope that I would find the hotel that the old man had said was once run by a Daniel O'Rourke, but I had nowhere better to go.

The quay ran for forty yards or so. It boasted five metal benches, all facing the water, and recently painted blue. The buildings along the quay were mainly boarded up, some permanently, others for the season. One of them could have been a small hotel, abandoned many years ago with its faded sign swinging arthritically in the lough breeze: *The Silver Ship*. A paper was pasted to a board where the window should have been, indicating that the site was now the property of the council. I sat on one of the benches with the retired hotel behind me to stare at the boats. I don't know what I'm looking at when I'm looking at boats. Some are sleek and look sharp enough to slice the water in halves, some are bashful and need to be painted. I prefer the bashful sort. I spotted one, shorter than my saloon, with a little cabin on top to sit in. It was moored less severely than some of the others on a single tether that paid it out and sprung it back in again. Again and again, tirelessly, without learning its lesson. I wondered if the boat knew better than me, that one day its tether would snap, and it would drift down to Carlingford; and from there, sail across the Irish Sea, or better still, slip around and voyage the Atlantic. Then it might get lost, tossed on the ocean, and crushed by its rippling muscles. The boat would be unremembered, its sticks washing up on shores here or there, thrown back into the waves by people amusing their dogs. Better to stay moored to play with its length of rope, more fortunate than most.

I was the only resident staying at Jacksons' Guesthouse, so the landlady made a fuss of me. She looked younger than older women usually look to me. The wide belt of her dress divided her body in nice halves, still good to look at. Her hair was white, but recalled the blonde she surely once was. But she wore no make-up, at least none that I could detect. I sat invited in her sitting room, the walls of which displayed three framed photographs: one of herself, younger and serious; another of her with a tiny girl, both laughing wildly; the last, apparently more recent, showing a family group including two children.

'You don't have a picture of your husband,' I ventured.

She laughed. 'Oh, there was never any husband. 'Mrs Jackson' is more my professional name. You're thinking of Katherine's father of course. I'd have married him if he'd had the guts to ask me, but he never did. He didn't hang around after that.'

'He would have been lucky to have you.' I was looking at the photographs.

'He would.' She smiled, and I blushed, but she was not being flirtatious. 'Some men just lack the courage to take on a woman, Mr Lenehan.' I had given her that name. She used it like she didn't really care if it was my name or not. 'They can take on the world, the Germans, the British, whatever, and they can even go into space. But put them in front of a woman with a mind of her own, and they go weak, or they just go. Anyway, he was from the other side, a Roman Catholic.'

She spoke without fear of offending me and without bitterness.

'But you would have married him anyway?'

'There was a lot of good in him, Mr Lenehan, and he was a handsome man. I say 'was': he may still be alive for all I know. He was strong, you know, physically, and I'm pretty sure he was in love with me. But he was young—a good few younger than me—and there was the religion nonsense that bothered him a bit, a lot, and he had sisters who, I imagine, were jealous of me. That was all too

FINDING DAN

much for him to stand up to. I never told him I was expecting a baby. I knew already by then that he wasn't for hanging around, and I didn't see the point in making it harder for him. Word got out, unfortunately, after I left. Things were said, I'm sure of it. I was glad to miss all that, but for him, it was different. Or so I heard. They beat him. I should have gone back and cleared it all up. I thought about it often enough, but in a way, we had both made our decisions, and I was stubborn then. More so than now, I think. Stubbornness is a kind of cowardice, the worse for pretending to be brave.'

'Do you regret it now?' I ask questions all the time of people when my only interest is in how their answers will fill my column. It's a professional habit, and I'm good at it. But I wasn't writing a piece on Mrs Jackson, and here I was asking the most personal questions.

I thought I saw pain in her face. 'Forty years is too long alone to spend in regret. I've had a contented enough life. Katherine was always lovely. She'd get taunted, you know the way children do, and sometimes she'd tell me when she was upset. And we'd sit down, just here, as a matter of fact, and eat some cake bought in a shop as a treat. We never argued, not once, and she never complained about having no father about.'

'Did she ask?'

She was about to speak, but found herself surprised by her answer. 'Do you know, I don't think she ever did. Is that strange?'

She waited for me to answer. 'I don't know, Mrs Jackson. I'm not used to answering hard questions like that.' I had told her I was a sports reporter, but we hadn't talked further on the matter. Until now.

'You're wearing a ring, Mr Lenehan, but you haven't mentioned a wife. I know men who are married who won't wear a ring, so you must be very devoted.'

'I live alone, Mrs Jackson. My wife prefers it that way.'

'And children?'

'I'm sorry, Mrs Jackson. Like I said, I'm not used to answering questions. It's not in my nature or my line of work.'

'That's not very fair, is it now?' Her ears reddened a little. 'So you watch other people doing things, and you listen to other people saying things, and you say that's your nature, your line of work.'

'That's about it, yes. Not much, I grant you.'

'Not much at all, Mr Lenehan, and you so clearly an educated man. I'd say that's not work at all if you'll forgive me.'

'Nor life at all, Mrs Jackson. I quite agree. And you've said nothing for me to forgive.' I gestured around the sitting room, and to the view through the window. 'Is this what you live for, Mrs Jackson?'

'You do ask the queerest questions, Mr Lenehan. I make beds, and I cook breakfasts, so that once in a while, folk don't have to. And some stay or come back, so I suppose they are grateful. That's a little thing, I know, but it's something. Katherine and her family, do I live for them? Not at all now if I'm honest. They know I'm still here, and I dare say they are happy enough to know that, but it's a distance for them to travel down here, and I don't expect it. I'd be glad to see them, sure, but I don't sit waiting for it. What do I live for? I can't say I can answer that, but I know I *am* alive. And I know I am glad about that. Would you say that's the same for you?'

Once again, she had posed me a question when I had been lost in her answer. 'I know I'm alive when I'm working when something appears in the paper with my name on the top of it. I already know what that says about me.'

'Mr Lenehan, please don't go feeling sorry for yourself. It's not attractive.' And she smiled a smile that conveyed nothing, but the happiness she intended. 'I don't think it's so bad to want to put our name on what is ours. You've seen my sign?'

'Jacksons' Guesthouse, the writer in me was expecting more than one Jackson.'

'That was the sign writer's mistake, or he felt it lent more respectability to the establishment. It was only ever meant to be about me.'

'So this is your thing, Mrs Jackson, your article.'

FINDING DAN

'I like that way of putting it. Yes, Mr Lenehan. I don't know about you, but I'm ready for another cup of tea. I'll make fresh.'

My eyes followed her out of the room, the hem of her dress, her right ankle, her flat shoe. I listened for the tinkle of china cup on china saucer, as she conveyed the crockery on a tray to the kitchen. I heard cupboard doors open and close, water running into a kettle.

I stood up for something to do, and walked the two steps to the window. The view was of the lough, violent and metal in the squall. For a moment, I was in a boat thrashed by the sea-spray, holding on. I rested my fingertips on a side table. I pressed harder to correct my balance. This was an absurd thing I was doing. Getting out of Dublin, avoiding my boss, escaping Rosa and Maggie and a screaming child, turning my back on all that. There was a man who existed only in the scribbled margins of another man's story, and somehow, that's why I was here now—a two-night guest in a room with a single bed and a toilet on the landing. I turned from the window and looked back at the room, at the photographs on the wall, at the furniture bought and paid for. I could be happy here, I suddenly thought. I smiled (and I thought of the smile on the woman's face). The child, who'd never known me, would never miss me. Rosa might be permitted her divorce. The friends I had, had other friends. Maggie, Maggie, Maggie. It was a younger man than me that she needed. I smiled again, and my heart pounded in my ears and a knot of something held my throat. Wasn't she back yet, the woman, from the kitchen? No, I could still hear her slicing something—cake perhaps with efficient strokes. The air felt still and hard to breath, so I turned back to the window. Its latches were glossed shut, but a draught seeping through the frame kissed my face. There was another door leading straight into the hallway and up the stairs to the guestrooms. I wondered whether it would be best to leave now, to pack my bag, and leave a note with the money. And I knew that was ridiculous, an unnecessarily dramatic move, which no note could hope to explain. Just to stay, not to have to make a move, that's what I wanted.

Mrs Jackson was at the sideboard now serving apple tart onto plates, now bending her head into the cupboard for the cups and saucers, reaching above for the sugar with an unseeing hand, knowing exactly where everything was. She was humming.

'I'll be driving on tomorrow, Mrs Jackson. I thought you should know.'

'Yes, as planned, Mr Lenehan. Of course, you're welcome to stay.' I felt for a pause, but there was none. 'I shan't be letting the room to anyone else before Christmas.'

'No, I should be going. You know, work and all.'

'It's what you live for, Mr Lenehan! As you said previously.'

'Must keep moving! I'll head for Dungannon next, that's where my man might be.'

'Your man?' We hadn't discussed it.

'An old footballer from those parts I'm hoping to meet. He had some connection to Rostrevor in the past, we believe. Not much to go on, just a name. But I'll see if my old reporter's instincts are still in working order.'

Mrs Jackson continued pouring tea into two cups and dividing the cake between two plates. 'You'll need to head back into Newry then take the A28 for Armagh then the A29 straight to Dungannon. A couple of hours is all it should take you.' She spotted the surprise on my face. 'I haven't lived in Rostrevor *all* my life, Mr Lenehan.'

That night, as I lay trying to steal some few hours' sleep from the night, I heard soft music eddy up from the rooms below. A sweet, steady voice joined the melody, and then I was asleep.

I was on the road early the following morning. I wasn't yet out of Rostrevor when I saw from the car a widow (or at least an old woman in black mourning weeds), bending down by the side of the road. I thought she must have flowers and was laying them by a shrine. The morning breeze caught her shawl, lifting it over her head, and this made me want to slow down to help her. As I did, the wind rose again. Her shawl, her skirt, everything flapped up; and to my astonishment, I realised she was not a widow at all nor even a person, but a ripple of crows, maybe twenty or more, gathered around a fresh loaf of bread presumably dropped there by the baker or his boy earlier that morning. The crows were picking furiously at the glazed crust of the bread, none giving up until the crust was broken, and the birds could tear at the white flesh within. Each with its morsel, they flew off in disparate directions, leaving no trace of their crime.

I followed Mrs Jackson's advice, and drove my Standard 8 through Newry and Markethill into the ecclesiastical city of Armagh, at which point I got lost. I had already reached Caledon before I realised I was still on the A28 and heading for Aughnacloy. In a yard advertising 'monumental concrete' and 'resurfaced gravestones', I turned the car around and drove back into Armagh. I still could not find the sign I needed. A little outside the city, I approached hopefully what I thought was an ancient milestone, now five or so yards off the side of the road it once would have marked. I pulled up the saloon and found a gap in the drystone wall I could clamber through. The pillar stood taller than a milestone normally would, and it was more rough-hewn. There was no writing, but I found a series of nicks and notches running nearly its full height along one edge. They were like scars, or the shadows of wounds inflicted upon a body lashed to the stone centuries ago. The wind fell away at that moment and clouds masked the sun. I was left utterly alone. I could have been there in that exact place, in a time before history, before the building of walls and roads and cities, before the need of anything like a milestone, but when people had an impulse to mark a place and erect a tall stone on it, and on the stone to write something in a script that itself would be lost when they died. The clouds darkened and turned to rain, and I was forced to leave the stone and get back to the car. I turned the saloon around again, knowing that wherever I was going, it was not in the direction of Dungannon.

So it was for the third time that day that I entered Armagh, each time on a different road. It was proving a hard place to avoid. On my fourth attempt, I spotted a road sign for Dungannon, but decided against driving on straight away. I was hungry. I would find somewhere to eat first. I found a teahouse called 'Millie's' or something like that, and I ordered a bacon roll from a girl in a black skirt and white blouse.

'If that's what you want, Mister, you'll have to ask for it from someone who works here.' With that, she sat with two other girls dressed in the same uniform, and obviously not waitresses. I liked that 'Mister'. That showed respect.

I was relieved to be leaving Armagh behind me, and to be sure I was on the right road to Dungannon at last. I had begun to feel that only there would I get close to my story. I knew that O'Rourke had played in Dungannon for the big local team, and if he deserved any of the praise Bob Stack had heaped on him, people there would remember him.

But first, I had to get into the town. Approaching from the south, the road swept along the bottom of the town, allowing no way in. Streets, which promised to lead to the centre, were one-way going out; road signs pointed consistently right for the Town Centre without leading me any closer to it. I decided to park my car and walk.

I heard the cries and laughter of children, and correctly guessed I was nearing a primary school. The black Victorian building stood three storeys tall, and in front of it was a man, also dressed in black, hands buried deep into the crotch of his cassock. One hand emerged to lift a cigarette from his mouth. A fine drizzle was falling here, the kind that forms in silver beads on your shoulders. Some children were running around or kicking a ball; some others, younger, I estimated, were eating their sandwiches huddled under the school walls for some shelter. One boy, perhaps 6 years old, was having his head knocked repeatedly against a wall near the gate. An older boy had his chin in his hand, the perfect grip for the task. I willed the priest to see what was happening (I almost called out to him), but he wouldn't be disturbed. The beating went on. I wondered at the power of the youngster to remain on his feet. His face was red, and there was a trail of red showing on his shirt collar. Maybe it was the grip of the older boy that was keeping him upright. Indeed, it

FINDING DAN

was this second boy who seemed to be making the greater effort, grunting ever more loudly with each thrust of his right hand into his victim's face. The intervals became longer, his breathing became heavier, and the bashing became easier to endure until, finally, it stopped. The younger boy remained there, as if awaiting permission to leave, while his assailant was slumped double recovering from his ordeal. The Brother left his post, the other schoolchildren went on eating and playing, and the drizzle laid its gauze over the whole scene.

Across the road was a Catholic church. I went in out of the rain, blessed myself at the holy water font at the entrance, and brushed the grains of damp from my jacket. I sat in the last pew, remembering at the last minute to genuflect. Then I knelt, the better to appear occupied.

'Not from here?' I jumped, not expecting to be spoken to. 'You not from here?' the voice repeated.

'No, I am not,' only at the end, finding the place to direct my reply. My interrogator was seated in the gloom behind me, in pews beneath the organ balcony that I hadn't seen on my way in.

'You looked lost.'

'No, I'm not lost.'

'No, but you look it. There's no Mass on.'

'I didn't come for the mass. It was raining. I came in for some peace.'

'Well, you came to the wrong place for that!' As if to make its point, the voice stood up and became a body and stepped out of the murk to show itself as a woman. 'Now, you're not from here, so where are you from?'

'From the South. Dublin, in fact.'

'Dublin. Are you even a Catholic at all? You didn't seem so sure on the way in.'

'I haven't had a lot of practice lately. Were you watching me?'

'It's part of the job. There's people who come in just to steal the candles. You can never be too careful.'

'The job?'

'I clean. And I change the flowers when we have them. And I collect the takings.'

'There's takings?'

'From the prayer candles. Were you intending to offer a prayer?'

'Well, maybe a private one.' I wasn't intending to offer a prayer I would have to pay for.

The woman nodded. 'That'll be connected to your wife then.' She was happy to have sorted me out. 'Anything else I can help you with?'

I wanted her gone, but I looked at her again. She was so stooped I wondered how she could stand up without a stick. Her fingers, rested on the back of my pew, were so twisted and swollen it was impossible to count them. Yet, her mind was sharp and playful, and I realised that she might only be 60 years old.

'I am looking for a man,' I announced.

She glanced about to share the joke. Finding no one, she said nothing.

'Daniel O'Rourke. Do you know him? He played football.'

'I know a great many people.' The woman puffed with pride, and for a moment, almost reached her full height.

I tried flattery. 'There must hardly be a person round here that you don't know, seeing as you have such an important job. And did I say how spotless the church is today.'

'This church is spotless every day. Not that you would know that, only arriving here today as you have. I might know a Dan O'Rourke, but I wouldn't go telling a body's private business just to any blow in.'

I stood up slowly and walked to the side of the church to where the votive candles were arranged in their little grandstand. From my pocket, I pulled a handful of coins, which, one by one, and with a meaningful glance over my shoulder to the old hag, I dropped into the locked box. We both knew that as soon as I left this temple to the Almighty, she would be in there.

FINDING DAN

'I can't say as I know the man you are looking for, but if there is a man who does, especially if it is a footballer you are after, then that man is Arthur McConaghy.'

'Where could I find him?'

'Here. He's the sexton.'

'Is he here now?' There was no answer. I was about to ask again, but realised she was gone, disappearing back into the gloom.

Outside, it was still raining. The small churchyard catered only for deceased priests, and their magnificent stones stood all the prouder, glistening wet. I saw an open door, and guessing it led back to the vestry, I went in.

I was not expecting to find what I did. Standing in a pair of polished, black brogues, socks gartered at the knees, was a priest. A pair of crumpled yellowing shorts covered most of his backside, a vest, and what looked like a nightshirt falling approximately over his belly. His arms were caught in a tangle with his cassock over his head. He bobbed and weaved like a drunken boxer, trying to relieve himself of his garment, and cursed too—loudly and clearly. I tried to back out, but succeeded only in walking into the door, making it slam shut.

'Jesus, Mary, and Joseph! An intruder!' The priest had still not freed himself, but the harder he pulled at his clothes, the tighter the knot became. 'What is it? Is it the wine you're after? I'll call the monsignor!'

'No, Father. If you hold still...' and I reached to release the button fastened at his neck.

A minute later, all vestments restored to order, the priest spoke as if the preceding events had not occurred. 'Arthur McConaghy, you say? Now I know I can help you there. On a Monday or a Tuesday or a Wednesday, Arthur can be a hard man to locate. If it's a Thursday or a Friday, there are options. On a Saturday or a Sunday, I would have no hesitation in directing you right here, as it's his busy time. Strictly speaking, he should be here on the other days, but there are things we can afford to turn a blind eye to, and things we cannot. And that, I would venture, falls into the former category. Now, what is it today?'

I realised I did not know. I had no deadline.

'Mrs Coulter is here, so it's a Wednesday. That's the rather frightening lady you met in the chapel. She sweeps on a Wednesday, and fills her pockets with the votive offerings. As, I'm sure, you noticed.'

'One of those things you can afford to turn a blind eye to?'

'In Mrs Coulter's case, I believe so. Now, as we have agreed that today is Wednesday, I suggest you look in the youth club. Arthur is often in there watching the youth of Dungannon punching the lights out of each other. He tells me he was a fine featherweight once himself, but we have only Arthur's word for that, if you know what I mean.

'Now, may I offer you a drink?'

After my tussle with a near-naked man of the cloth, a drink was in order. But Communion wine was not what I had in mind, so I declined. Instead, I accepted pointers to the youth club, which was apparently only a little further along in the direction of the school.

I found the club straight away, although there were few signs of any connections with the local youth. It was a brightly lit, overheated hall. Two middle-aged men, and one rather younger lady, all dressed in tracksuits too small for them, had taken up positions. One of the men was at the door checking names, the other man was hovering by a table tennis table, practising his swing with an imaginary bat and ball. The woman was standing on an exercise mat, stretching, but not stretching too far.

'How can I help *you*?' asked the man at the door with extraordinary emphasis on the 'you'.

'I'm looking for Arthur McConaghy. I've heard he works here.'

'Arthur, Arthur . . . ' He was looking down his list of names.

'He works here... he won't be on that list.'

My man with the list looked up, a little insulted. 'I *was* trying to be helpful,' he declared, again laying the stress in an odd place. 'Gabriel, can you help this *man*?'

FINDING DAN

Gabriel interrupted his game of ping-pong, but remained crouched, ready to receive serve. 'What does the man desire, Julian?'

'I'm looking for Arthur McConaghy. I'm reliably informed that he works here.'

'*Is* that so? Information, eh? Did you get that, Julian? Our visitor has reliable informants. Before we proceed, did you leave your name at the door?'

'My name? No.' I turned, embarrassed, back to Julian. I gave him the moniker I seem to be using now.

'I have it *now*, Gabriel. You can go ahead.' Julian motioned for me to enter the main hall.

I found myself at the other end of the table tennis table to Gabriel. 'The priest told me Arthur worked here. Sorry, I didn't get the priest's name.' I offered the apology to them all, but especially, I think, to Julian at the door.

'Was he wearing clothes?' Gabriel asked.

'He, umm . . . he was...'" I couldn't finish.

Gabriel and Julian together sang the name. 'Father Thomas!'

'Young Father Thomas!' This was the woman speaking for the first time, still limbering up.

'No, not so young these days, Maureen,' said Gabriel. 'We've been monitoring. Leaving that to *one* side,' he went on. 'Are you here for a game, or are you not?'

I quite clearly was not here for a game, but before I knew it, I had a bat in my hand and the man was advising me on my grip.

Young boys growing up in Dublin have few choices when seeking amusement. They can turn up drunk at the pioneers' dances. They can lose themselves in the mysteries of the Latin mass, while serving at the altar. Or they can do sport. That would be football and boxing and billiards and table tennis and soccer—all of them. That was how I chose to amuse myself, and while it broke my mother's heart that none of her sons was destined for the priesthood, it was a relief to her that I had not followed my father to the bottle. Of course, as I grew older, I learned to combine a passion for sport with an interest in alcohol, a convergence of pastimes, which suited perfectly my arrival on the back pages of *The Independent*. I had once felt at home at the table tennis table, every square inch within my comfortable reach. I played best when uninhibited, achieving optimum direction and spin only when really letting loose. Hesitating now, thinking too much about it, the feather-light ball became a capricious thing; and I could only pat it back, lest it embarrass me. I lost the first five points on his serve. He tossed the ball over the net to me, and stood noticeably straighter to suggest he would go easy on me. I removed my jacket and hung it on a peg on the wall (over the name 'Peter'). Gathering myself and shaking the tension out of my arms, I earned four of my own service points. He took three from his next set of serves, leaving the score at nine-six to my opponent. But I was back in the game.

'We play here to eleven. House rules, Peter. Is that *all* right?'

'That's hardly fair!' I blurted. 'It's twenty-one, or I quit now!' Dominic Slevin had tried that one on me in 'Twenty-Eight, almost cheating me out of the Donnybrook perpetual trophy.

'Now, now, Peter.' What was it with this 'Peter'? 'You know that's not the kind of behaviour we want here. If playing to twenty-one would be *helpful to you* then that's fine. Now, my serve, is it?'

'It's mine!' And I snatched the ball from the air, as it floated over to my side. I played now with considerably more aggression and took five points in a row. Eleven-nine to me—a winning score under house rules. I played the ball back for my opponent to serve, putting some wicked side spin on it just to emphasise to him that I could claim victory now if I was *that* sort of player.

The game was characterised by a mix of audacious offensive flashes and costly defensive lapses. At nineteen-twenty, I won the last point on my serve to save match point. I won the next off his serve. 'Match point to me,' I said, trying to remain focused and tossing the ball back over to him. He showed to serve as before, but at the last minute, he had a change of heart and switched to a Chinese style pen-hold grip. He smiled (somehow, this was also in Chinese style), and with his left hand, threw the ball high into the air, his eyes squinting against the artificial light in the hall,

FINDING DAN

following the ball in his vertical trajectory. At the other end, I was caught between preparing to return forehand or backhand. Jeez, he was devious! He was good! The ball dropped and met the pimple of his bat beautifully, as it pushed through with an outlandish topspin. The ping-pong kissed his side of the table and bounded off. I was still lost at my side, dazzled by his disguise, and almost dropped my bat. Then the most unexpected thing happened: the ball struck the top of the net and kicked up. As it descended, it hit the tape again and came down, not on my side, but his. I had won the point and the game.

'Yes!'

Maureen and Julian stood in stunned silence. This sort of thing clearly didn't happen very often here. More should have been here to witness it.

'How old did you say you were again?' This was Julian checking down at his list again.

'I'm forty-seven. But you didn't ask.'

'The maximum age here is twenty-one unless you're staff. This is a *youth* club!' Julian jabbed some piece of paper with his finger, as if this proved his point. 'I think, Gabriel, our friend played under false pretences.'

'I did think he played a more *mature* game than the average,' said Gabriel, trying to sound fair-minded.

'Allowing us to think he was Peter!' added Maureen.

'I only came because the priest suggested I might,' I protested. 'And it was raining earlier. I'm not from here, so I don't know the local rules. Nobody tried to explain the rules before we started. I was only trying my best. I am sorry to have bothered you, really.' I went on like this for several more minutes, desperately trying to remember my original reason for coming here. After the drenching I had received in the rain, I had overheated during the game, only to be attacked for defeating the local favourite. Maggie thinks I am running away from her. Maggie, who is smarter and less in need of me than any woman I have fallen for before. She once said she would never have married even if she had met me when I was young, handsome, and mainly sober. 'You worry too much over commas and semicolons,' she had said. 'You are too long on the pauses, and not long enough on the things either side of them.' Maggie preferred to live life with little or no punctuation. 'Until I hit the big, black full stop,' she said. 'And then they can bury me in it.' When Rosa learned of Maggie, she just laughed. 'When you can't keep up with that one, you'll be happy enough to come back to me,' Rosa had said. Rosa was always doing that, pretending that I was the one who had walked out on her. Even clutching the baby to her shoulder, she could stand there and call me all the names. And she never stopped that baby from crying. She barely even tried.

Good man that he was, Gabriel had recovered from his defeat. He found me a chair and sent Maureen off to get me a cup of tea. 'That'll settle you now. I wish Arthur were here, he'd know what to do about you.'

'Who's Arthur?' I asked.

'Arthur McConaghy, of course,' said Maureen with a cup in her hand. 'He's very practical in situations such as these.'

I had gathered myself sufficiently to know they were talking about me. 'Am I in a difficult situation then?'

All three nodded without quite looking me in the eye. 'Turning up in Dungannon with no place to go or stay, that's a situation all right.'

'And McConaghy could help me, you think?'

'*Most* certainly!' exclaimed Julian. 'But if he's not here by now, I doubt if he will be. You could try calling him if he has a phone, which I don't know if he has. You shouldn't just drop in on him, as he might think you were pressing yourself on him, which would not help you in your predicament.'

I looked to Julian, who looked to Gabriel, who looked to Maureen. Maureen broke the logjam. 'As it is Wednesday, and he is not here, my guess is that he is already at *The Taps*. Isn't that where he goes? Why don't you try there, Peter?'

There was general relief at this suggestion. Julian fetched me my jacket, and Gabriel guided me to the door with his hand on my

FINDING DAN

shoulder. He whispered directions in my ear, muttering something about them being duty-bound to remain at their posts in case the youth arrived, and with a gentle push in the small of my back, I was again out in the rain.

The Taps was allegedly in the centre of town, and the rain got heavier the nearer I approached. I had no trouble finding it, as it was the only pub open. On the outside, *The Taps* occupied a double-fronted building. Inside, however, the frosted glass door opened on to what could have been someone's living room, but for all the people crammed in there. A modest fire burned in the fireplace with a hearth set of shovel, brush, and poker standing sentry. Miniature farmers and ox-driven ploughs repeated across the wallpaper. A cat weaved between the legs of drinkers and stools. I ordered a pint at the bar.

'What is this, some kind of a joke?' Rainwater was puddling at my feet.

'I'm sorry about that. It rains a lot in Dungannon.' I asked the barman if he could point out Arthur McConaghy for me.

'Who would I be pointing him out to?'

'Me, I'm Lenehan... Peter Lenehan. I know he works at the chapel and at the youth club, though not, apparently, on this day of the week. I've been told he is a very practical man for my type of situation.'

The barman took in my wet clothes and my foreign accent. 'You seem to know a lot about a man you've not ever met before. What exactly do you expect him to do for you?'

I really did not know. I dimly figured I should know. I'd received a tip-off, that was it, from a lady (it seemed days ago) who said Arthur McConaghy was the only man who would do. She was the genuine deal, a reliable source. In all my years of reporting, I have learned that much at least: whom to trust, who my go-to people are, the leads worth following, and those that lead nowhere at all. Oh, yes, that much I have picked up along the way, let me tell you! These Northerners are tricky, I'll give them that, but they can try tricking

Peter Lenehan and see where that gets them. Not that that's who I really am—that's how hard I am to fool!

'Enda says you were looking for me?'

The man now standing in front of me was no taller than five feet and four inches. He was almost entirely bald. He was dressed in the same nondescript clothing as everyone else, as ready for the farm as for the factory as for the pub. He kept looking over his left shoulder and spitting. After he did this five or six times, I realised it was a sort of nervous twitch.

'Are you crying?' He stood back a pace, as if I might drop something on him. He motioned to Enda, the barman, to do something about me.

I wiped my face clean with my handkerchief. 'I've been in the rain,' I said.

'Right. What can I do you for?'

'Everyone says that you are the man who can help me.'

'That's a lot of pressure if everyone says it. Help you with what?'

'With what I am looking for, with the thing I need the help with.' It took me an eternity to get these words out.

'Enda, what have you given our friend to drink? Nothing from the reserve bottle, I hope?'

'That's for regular patrons only, Art, as you have reason well enough to know. He's had just one pint from the tap, though I can't vouch for anything before he got here. He looks no worse now than when he arrived.'

'Perhaps Dungannon isn't suited to your constitution, friend? Where does that accent come from?'

'It's Dublin. I'm from Dublin. I've driven north for my paper. That's it!'

'You're a newspaperman. What, a foreign correspondent?' McConaghy and the barman seemed to find this funny.

'No, sports, that's what I know about.'

'The man was right, Art,' said Enda. 'You're the man around here who knows about football and all.'

FINDING DAN

McConaghy withdrew somewhat at this. 'It's a long time since I bothered myself with any of that oul' lark, Enda, outside of helping out at the youth club now and then.'

'That's who sent me here, Gabriel from the club. And before that, Father Thomas in the chapel. And there was someone before that too.'

'Art here was secretary of the local GAA for donkeys' years, isn't that so?' Enda was shining a glass with a cloth, but he could have been polishing McConaghy, so proud was he of the man. 'Ran the Dungannon Clarkes more or less on his own.'

'So you knew Daniel O'Rourke?' The name slipped out without me trying to remember it. All this trying to track down one man, Arthur McConaghy, had led me to forget who it was I was really looking for. A near lost instinct made me reach into my pocket for a notepad and pencil. I sat down. Enda brought me a fresh pint. McConaghy sat down too, thus confirming he did know O'Rourke. He was quiet, I guess unused to being interviewed by a journalist.

Arthur agreed to help me find him. As far as he knew, O'Rourke lived with his brother's family in a townland between Dungannon and Coalisland, a place called Creenagh. He hadn't heard anything about him in several years, but he guessed he was still alive. 'If a man like Dan O'Rourke died, we should all be reading about it.'

'I don't understand. Why is that?'

'Dan was a hero. Don't you have that already?' he asked, nodding at my notebook. When I still looked blank, Arthur added, 'It's the man who was on the run you're after, isn't it?'

'On the run?'

'And when they arrested him, they gaoled him, and then interned him.'

'I don't think we can be talking about the same man,' I said, somehow apologising to McConaghy for his trouble. 'The man I am looking for was a great friend of the Kerry player, Bob Stack. This fellow you mention seems an entirely different character.'

'Well, please yourself, but there's only one Dan O'Rourke round these parts worth a newspaperman talking to him.'

I followed McConaghy's directions to Coalisland. I wasn't long out of Dungannon before the rain cleared completely, and I was in a rural wilderness bathed in late autumn sunshine. The local landmarks were few; a large-domed dance hall to the right, a small flint church set on a hill to the left. Entering the town was like coming in by a side door unannounced. Only the backs and sides of buildings presented themselves, keeping their names to themselves. Rather than look in any particular place, Arthur suggested I walk Main Street. Dan could often be found perched on a windowsill, or walking his bike between bars.

I didn't find him. I found a bunch of kids who said they knew him—at least they said they knew a man they called Dan O'Rourke. He was great to them, he always had sweets, and he never passed them by without a word. Sometimes, this was to scold them for playing soccer; and sometimes, it was to share with them a dirty joke. They knew this man, not for his football, but like McConaghy, because he had been 'on the run'. Outside O'Sullivans' Travel, I met a woman who told me that, of course, she knew Dan O'Rourke. Everybody did. Sure, wasn't he the father of so-and-so, everyone knew it, though no one was letting on. But you're letting on to me, a total stranger, I said. Aye, but you don't count, she said, you're from the South. I began to think that there might be several men of the same name. It was not likely that one man could bear all these things said about him.

At this hour, all the shops in the town were shut except for the bars. I passed a barber's, and beside it, a ladies' hairdresser's. A young stud pulled his car up at the kerb and left it there. It called to mind a cowboy and his horse from one of those westerns they show on the television. He stood alone, looking one way up Main Street, adjusted his hair, then turned and walked in the opposite direction. His sole purpose, to be seen walking there. Before he reached the bar at that end of the street, its double doors were flung outwards, and two men fell out in tandem, each on their backs. Noises of laughter, clashing glasses, and Irish traditional music followed the men out the door. I half expected a sheriff to come strutting down the middle

FINDING DAN

of the road, and for Wanted posters to be billed everywhere. In fact, there were posters from some distant election, framing the smiling face of the Sinn Fein man, Philip Clarke, and with some few words of Gaelic below which I could not read.

I decided to get the hell out of that town and head instead for Creenagh. McConaghy didn't know a telephone number ('In fact, I wouldn't be surprised if the place isn't wired up yet for electric.') so I would be arriving unannounced. The lane I ended up on was almost too narrow for my Standard Eight, the wheels of which several times nearly came off in the puddle holes. The word *Breifne* was nailed to a gatepost. I was in an awful sweat by the time I stopped the car outside a single-storey house. At once, out of nowhere about a dozen black, curly-haired children appeared and proceeded to climb on top of, and into, the saloon. A man arrived to swat them away.

'Are you here for the fencing?' he answered his own question with a doubtful look at my car. 'I imagine not then.'

'I'm looking for a Mister Daniel O'Rourke. Have I come to the right place?'

The man laughed, and with his hand, brushed his brilliantined hair across his head and behind his ear. 'Dan must have moved up in the world if he's been ordering a fancy taxi. Has he lost his bicycle again?'

'So he lives here in this house?'

'In a manner of speaking, he does, yes. And why might you be here asking all these questions?'

'Because it's what I do.' In under two minutes, I told this man who I was, why I was here, and how I had managed to get this far. I had sudden energy in my legs I didn't know what to do with, so I sprinted twice around the car, much to the amusement of the children.

'I'm Patsy, by the way, Dan's brother. You may come in for a cup of tea, for you may be waiting a while yet if you're expecting to see Dan this side of the dark. He'll be in one of the bars in Coalisland until closing. You may take a ride in if you like, or you may wait here. You're welcome either way.'

I was surprised by the man's instant hospitality. Everyone I had met had offered me some sort of help, but only after considerable persuasion. This man was different. He was happy to have a perfect stranger in his home.

He wasn't alone. We stepped through the back door straight into the kitchen where I was introduced to Phyllis, the woman of the house. She had two red, swollen arms dipped to the elbow in a washing tub of steaming water. And, if I say her smile was swollen too, all I mean is that she had a large face and stretched across it was a large smile. I soon learned that she was not house-proud, a sure sign being she let her husband show me around. The house was essentially two rooms (a living room and a bedroom), to which several more rooms had been added over the years. The children I had seen earlier were putting themselves to bed. I found myself looking for Dan's room.

'Dan will show you himself where he stays,' said Patsy, reading my mind. By now, we had taken armchairs in the living room. There was no central light. Candle lamps were placed in corners where their effect was minimal. A Brigid Cross was over the doorway, several photographs were hung on the walls or displayed on the mantelpiece. I picked up a football trophy from a side table, blowing away some dust to read the inscription.

'You won this? You played too?' I had expected Dan's name to be engraved on the plate.

'I was a fair player in my young days,' said Patsy, a little proudly.

'As good as Dan?' He stiffened, I thought. This was a comparison he was used to.

'It's hard to say. Football is a team game. It's fair to say that Dan played in better teams than I did. Then again, he was prepared to move about to find a team.' I indicated I wanted him to continue. 'I doubt there was a local team my brother didn't play for at one time or another. He even played rugby for the Swifts in Dungannon. He was very adaptable that way, if you get my meaning? There are some men who choose their side, or rather, they are sort of born into a side, and that is the side they play for till their playing days are over.

FINDING DAN

That wasn't Dan's style at all, but he was good. I'll grant him that. The earliest I remember him was for Tyrone against Antrim. They played at O'Neill Park in Dungannon, it may have been 1929, I was about only nine myself. Ned Magee was captain. Malachy Mallon scored a penalty, I remember. Dan was good that day.'

'Where are the trophies he won?'

'Phyllis wasn't keen on having the place cluttered.' I couldn't help but look around at the clutter that there was. Patsy met my eye with a smile. 'Let's just say she was less than keen on *his* clutter,' he continued. 'When my father died after the War I think, the house became ours. By then, my sisters were all moved away or married. I had a brother, Jim, who was in the States. Then there was Dan who, in those days, was a bit of a vagrant and not much given to settling down. That left me with a wife and family on the way. So the house became ours. You'll not put this in your notebook, I doubt, but this house has been in O'Rourke hands for centuries. How we came by it is something of a mystery, and I'm not inclined to believe stories that I'm told, but there was a priest in this parish in the penal days, a Father Phelan, and the only way he could keep the faith going of people around here was to give secret masses right here in this house. That's a thing to be proud of in my book, and so we moved in, so the house wouldn't be sold. There are some as are critical of Phyllis for that time, but she never forced Dan out. She gave him a home in her home, and he's been happy enough in there, he'll tell you himself.'

'His trophies?'

'He had all sorts. Trophies, papers, medals, medals too of a non-sporting nature. I don't know where they are now, for sure. There was a sort of cubbyhole in the wall behind where his bed is, which we found when we were making his room up. He could have put his effects in there, out of the way. A smart move if you want my opinion.'

'Why is it smart to hide away all the proof that you were once a great football man?'

'Because without the proof, he is free to tell anybody anything.'

'Is that what he does?'

'That's not for me to say. Let's just say there are plenty others willing to tell you what a great man our Dan was.'

'I think I met some of them already. The kids in Coalisland told me Dan was on the run. Is that right?'

'Some of those medals he hid away were of the political variety, that's true. You're better speaking to my brother about all that. I was a bit young at the time to appreciate it all. He was gaoled and interned, as were dozens of others from around here, you'll find. How hard done by at the time, I don't know, but he's had plenty of acclaim for it since, so he's done all right.'

'You don't see your brother as the hero that others do.'

Patsy was uncomfortable, unused to speaking unkindly. 'My Phyllis has been nothing but a saint regarding Dan. She cooks for him when he bothers to show up, and she washes for him. And for years, she's tolerated a man under her roof who can barely utter two civil words to her on account of her being a Protestant. You're a cultured man, Mr Lenehan, and you live in a modern country: surely to goodness we can put nonsense like that behind us by now?

'But not Dan.' He was finished. I had not taken out my notebook, but even without it, I felt the man's embarrassment. I doubt he had ever spoken at such length, and in such terms, to any man before on this subject; and for the life of him, he couldn't understand why he had spoken to me. I might have consoled him, saying this sort of thing happened often to me, that it was a fact of life for good reporters. But in truth, it hadn't happened to me in a very long time, perhaps ever only once or twice, and that at *The Independent*, when people spoke to me in the sure knowledge that it would find its way on to the pages of an estimable paper, certainly never during the long slide in my career, which had landed me in my current dead end at *The Gaelic Weekly*.

'Sorry about that.'

'That's all right.'

I stifled a yawn. I'd had a long day since I had left Mrs Jackson in Rostrevor.

FINDING DAN

'Unless you're booked in somewhere, I suggest you take the sofa in the living room for the night.' As if surprised by his own feat of hospitality, Patsy added, 'There'll be cats.'

'Is there somewhere I could book?'

'I have no idea.'

'Well then, I'll stay gladly. Cats?'

'Vermin. We are a sawmill, but we keep animals.'

'Right.'

'You might want to stay up a while for Dan to come back. I, if you don't mind, will take myself off to bed now. I have an early start.'

I only then became aware that the rest of the house had already gone to bed. The clock in the living room seemed to slow to a deep sleep rhythm. The cats were presumably still busy outside. I stood in the yard, as if that would speed Dan's return. It was a starless, moonless night, and the house was in the grip of complete darkness. But for the white wash on the walls, I wouldn't have been able to see it at all. I lit a cigarette, and tried to breathe the nothingness in to clear out the rubbish from my day. I wondered if I should leave now. I wondered what the point was of my being here, and recalled that my editor's main aim was just to see the back of me. I could return to Dublin, and not even be asked to produce a story. I had found the home of Daniel O'Rourke, though I doubted it could really be the same man as mentioned by Bob Stack. I had gone out looking for a great and found a journeyman. No one in the world cared that I was here, and, but for the dot of red receding down my cigarette, no one could have seen me. I took one final draw and watched the red glow orange then die to grey.

The first I heard was the groan of his wheels under his weight, then the clatter and curse of a drunk falling from a bike. I think he must have then abandoned the bike where it lay, for the next sounds were those of workman's boots on loose shingle, heavy and unlaced.

'Is that you, Patsy, you oul' bastard?' I closed my foot over the cigarette, thinking that way I couldn't be seen. Dan continued muttering to himself about how he had to do everything himself, even pick himself out of the ditch when he fell over. I said nothing, and was still not sure what I was going to say when the moment could no longer be put off.

'Patsy! I can see you're there. There's nothing wrong with my eyes!'

I, for one, could still not see him, and I could not locate him by other means for the sound of him filled the whole yard and the lane and the ditches either side, so that he might have been coming at me from the front, but just as easily from the right or the left. So I still wasn't ready when he planted a heavy hand on my shoulder.

'Holy Jesus!' I exclaimed.

'Hold still, will you? Till I get these friggin' boots off.'

So I held still, trying to make out his form, still blind. Though I couldn't see him, he bulked before me, filling the entire space. Like when a hand passes over your eyes when the lids are shut, his presence was a shade of black, flitting and formless. He smelled of grass and spirits and potatoes.

He was still talking. 'And before you ask, I have already eaten at Kathleen's, so I'll be needing nothing from the house. I shan't be bothering you.'

'Dan?'

'And who else were you expecting at this hour?'

'I'm not Patsy.' As far as introductions go, it wasn't the most revealing, but it was a start. Still, it had an unexpected impact on Dan.

'You've got nothing on me. Whatever it is I'm supposed to have done, I wasn't there and I didn't do it. What's more, I'll not be helping with your enquiries.' There was a pause in which Dan appeared to be contemplating further denials. Then, 'Are you RUC? You're not, are you?'

'No, I'm a journalist from Dublin,' I said, then quickly added, 'You're not in any trouble that I know of. I'd show you a pass, but you couldn't see it out here. Can we go in?'

I motioned to go in the door to the kitchen, but Dan shuffled off to the left, saying, 'Follow me then! From Dublin, that's a journey!

FINDING DAN

You'll be hungry, or I can make you tea. Let's see what we find.' I followed the voice.

With a big old black key hanging from somewhere by a length of string, Dan opened a door to what looked to me like a pig house adjoining the main building. With the deftness of a blind man, he found and lit a kerosene lamp and hung it from a nail on the wall.

'Come in! Come in!' he urged, and shut the door behind me. 'Have a seat anywhere.'

There was one armchair stuffed with cushions to make up for the certain loss of its springs. Assuming this to be Dan's place, I sat on a footstool. The floor was smooth, beaten earth. The night chill lay a mist on it, so that my boot left an impression. The walls were damp too, although they were covered in wallpaper, which reminded me of Spring. Behind the armchair was a cot, all ready to be slept in, occupying the entire width of the room. Dan was busying himself in a low cabinet from which he took everything he had to feed and water me with. There was none of the promised tea. He poured a brownish liquid from an unlabelled bottle, and he unwrapped some slices of cake from its paper, and he handed me my glass and plate and sat on the armchair with his own.

'There,' he said, contented. He ate his cake and drank his whiskey with the same mouth, unconcerned when they leaked from the corners of his smile. He no longer felt so large now that I could see him, but I still reckoned he could fill this space standing up. His hair was lighter than his brother's, even blond, although in fact most of it was probably white. His face glowed red and brown from spending most of his time outdoors, or spending most of his indoor time drinking.

I took out my pencil and notepad. He feigned shyness. 'Now, now, you'll be stealing my life away next.'

'I'm sorry, Mr O'Rourke, but I think I might be here on a false pretence,' I began. 'I don't think you can be the man I was looking for. I have been sent by my paper in Dublin to do a profile on one of the greats of Ulster football to recall some of his famous matches, the opponents and teammates, that type of thing. I have come a long way with not much more than a name to go on, and I have found you, but now that I am here...'

'I am your man all right,' Dan interrupted. He watched me as I looked around his room. 'You are wondering how the young man you set out to find could possibly have come to live in this hovel. Well, that's your story, mister, whatever your name is. And either you ask me the right questions, or you let me witter on in my own way, or I won't bother and you can leave. As for my home, it may not have all the modern conveniences people find so necessary these days, but I am happy in it, and I wonder if everyone else can truly say that about themselves. I wonder if you can?'

For a moment I was perched on the edge of my bed, in my room in Mrs Rooney's boarding house in Donnybrook, with Polly and her businessmen friends in the room below. I thought of the house in Stillorgan, of Rosa, and the baby, and tried to imagine a place for me there where the neighbours would admire my car and a little girl would hold my hand.

'Did you never want a family of your own, Dan?'

'I thought you were interested only in the football?'

'It's a paper for Gaelic games, sure. But for a profile, I need more background.'

'Oh, I can give you background!'

It was light by the time Dan had finished talking, though the kerosene lamp still burned. I had filled a notepad with the stories he told me about his football, and this had encouraged him to talk further. He told me about the harassment his family had faced at the hands of the Black and Tans during the bad times, and about how he had been arrested by his neighbour's son and carted off to gaol. He had been brutally beaten there, kicked and punched in every imaginable place where young men of his age need not to be kicked and punched, until it was almost a relief to him to be sent for internment to the notorious *SS Argenta*. When you woke up in the morning, you were taller then than you were in the evening, as you could tell by your head brushing the beams under decks. And

FINDING DAN

he told me too about the girl in Rostrevor, the girl he should have married, but for the things people were saying.

Dan didn't notice that I had stopped writing, or perhaps he presumed for me a reporter's gift for recalling tall tales. In any case, by the end, he had recounted for me an entire legend of a man savaged by the British, and made noble again through football. I had before me a man desperate to tell a story he knew few people still wanted to hear, and to tell it now before he lost his own grip on it. Somehow, I was the reporter he had told it to. Was there ever a time, even at *The Independent*, when I could have written this story? Was I ever that good? Maybe I should go into the boss when I get back to Dublin and say, 'Boss, that hunt you sent me on, to find the friend of Bob Stack. I found him. He has a story, but it's more than football. It's a life, a whole bad life, but out of it came a good man. Can you handle a story like that? Is your paper good enough to print a story like that?' He'll say no. He'll say, 'I sent you away to sort out your own life, not to go native on someone else's.' So I won't write it, or I won't write it really. I'll write something much less than that. It'll be just what the paper can handle, just what I can handle.

'Will that be enough for you, do you think?'

'Mr O'Rourke, it will be a marvel to our readers,' I assured him.

'Where will I be able to get a copy?'

'I'll send you one personally,' I promised.

Dan was uneasy. 'That would be grand,' he said slowly. 'I suppose I can share it with others who might be interested.' There was a quality about the man, which meant he would still enjoy the interest of others.

'*The Gaelic Weekly* does not have a wide circulation, Dan,' I said. 'But, for those interested in this sort of thing, it can be got north of the border as well as the south, so I'm told.' I saw the hope in the old man's eyes. 'I'll write it well, Dan, I promise.' And I meant the promise, though I knew I would not keep it.

We stood up and shook hands then walked out into the yard.

'That's a nice motor you have there. What is it?'

'It's a Standard Eight. It may not get me home in one piece.'

'That's the same with my bicycle. It never gets me home safe!' Dan laughed so loud it woke a cat and disturbed some chickens. I could make out the handlebars of his bike, attempting to haul itself out of the ditch by the lane.

'Can I give you something, Mr O'Rourke?'

'You mean, as a tip in return for my whiskey and my life story? I suppose I mightn't refuse.'

In my jacket pocket, I found an old penny. One my uncle had given me years ago, dated 1826. 'A hero gave me this,' he had said, or something like it, for my uncle was prone to wild stories. The coin seemed worthless in my hand, but when Dan slipped it into the pocket of his good tweed jacket, it gained value.

'By the way,' he asked. 'Why did you come here? Why me?'

'Bob Stack, the four in a row Kerryman, he gave us your name. He said he met you in 1932 in a famous game played here in Coalisland. He said you were his friend.'

'He told you that?' I watched thirty years disappear from Dan's face, from the slump of his shoulders, from the white of his hair; and when the years returned, they left him lighter. 'That's paying me a big compliment, that is.'

I climbed into my car and waved to Dan as I drove carefully down the lane. Out of habit, I felt for my pocket to check my notebook was there.

17 May 1938

Creenagh

Ann gave me a photograph. 'It could go in your book.' She knows the people in it, but not the occasion, so I speculate. It is about eight inches by six. It is slightly creased in the bottom left and top right corners from too much clumsy right handling. The black is brown and the white is nuclear, aflash. It doesn't have a frame, but the truer colours running the edge suggest it did have, once upon a time.

The photograph was taken at Creenagh sometime in the 'Thirties. There are seven people, three of them seated, around a folding deal table. They are drinking: it's a celebration. The people and the table are set amongst a rubble of off-cuts and deadwood. A fence of rough wooden Xes forms a sort of corral behind them or horizon. From the left, Kathleen is standing at Dan's shoulder, pouring drink into his raised glass. Seated opposite him is his father, Joe, and between the two is Winnie. Joe is holding his hat on his lap, as if back from mass. Winnie is having the most fun, and it seems that this occasion and the photograph are in her honour. Standing in trio behind her are Bassie, Joe Quinn (a neighbour known as Jack's Joe), and Patsy. They are all dressed in best, although Kathleen also has an apron and some form of head covering befitting her seeming status in the picture of servant to the others.

The occasion may have to do with Molly. Molly, the eldest sister, had returned home from the States to nurse her dying mother, and this would have been about 1936 or '37. But wouldn't they all want Molly *in* the photo? This might be (this *was*) the last time Molly would visit Creenagh. They would all insist that she take a drink and take a seat, perhaps the one that Winnie did. No, Winnie is the star of this event. While Joe and Bassie are posing with their glasses raised to the blunts of their chins, and while Dan has raised his to meet the bottle in Kathleen's hand, only Winnie is truly happily abandoned. She has not yet noticed how, from behind her, Patsy is reaching for her glass; when she does, when the shutter has snapped, she will swot him away. For it is her birthday, her twenty-first; and sure, isn't she entitled to a drop of alcohol.

<u>Winnie</u>

Winnie had her hair cut the day before by one of the Cullen girls. She would leave nothing to chance. She could rely on Kathleen to set it for her, but not to cut it. Kathleen was always busying about with things and would, as like, take a knife to her hair as a pair of scissors for all her rushing. To be fair to her, Kathleen had not let her down today. Winnie was very happy with her hair done in waves rather than curls, the way Molly had shown they do in America. Oh, she missed Molly! Molly was the sister she never knew, as she had taken the boat to New York when Winnie was still a tiny girl. But the way she said that word—'girl'—now! When Winnie said it, or when anybody else she had ever known said it, it could be a dog coughing, it was so abrupt and unwanted. But Molly spoke the word so it uncurled from her mouth in a great long roll. It might rhyme with desire. Imagine that! Winnie was sure that, given the opportunity, the first thing she would lose if she moved to the States would be her accent.

She practised it now, an American voice to go with her American hair and American clothes. Molly had been so good to her and her sisters. Kathleen too had loved the jackets and collars,

FINDING DAN

the skirts with the generous cloth. (Bassie never seemed interested, but that suited Winnie as it meant more for her). She had known for days what dress she was going to wear for her party today: the one with the lilac tartan pattern and white frill collar. In it, she felt sophisticated like a lady who might work in a grand store, like the ones on Fifth Avenue that Molly had talked about. And it would undoubtedly have the right sort of effect on Martin Quinn.

'You be sure he comes with you, Joe,' she had said to Jack's Joe the day before.

'And what am I to say to him, Winnie, to get him to come?' Jack's Joe had replied.

'Tell him that Winnie O'Rourke has invited him, as it is her birthday, and that she expects him to be here.'

'Winnie, you will be the undoing of my wee brother.'

'That, Joe, would be somewhere near my intention.'

And Winnie had laughed. Now, she was nervous, lest her being too brazen would put poor Martin Quinn off. Well, if it did, it would only go to prove he was no match for her. She didn't need a man who couldn't banter. Surely, Jack's Joe would find a nicer way of putting it to him.

She wouldn't put the dress on till later when everything was ready. She had work to do now, helping Kathleen with the house. There were carpets to sweep and floors to wash and laundry to fold and put away and food to prepare, and the hens would need feeding, and she was sure no one had checked on the pig. Daddy and the boys would be down at the sawmill unless Dan was already off fetching the booze. Bassie would be off gallivanting as per usual; it was anybody's guess if she would even show later. So that left her and Kathleen. Good old Kathleen. Since Mummy died last year, Kathleen had done everything and kept everybody together. She was only three years older, but there surely never was a time when Kathleen had not been at least twenty-one. Kathleen did everything for everybody else without a thought for herself. Winnie caught herself looking at her reflection in her dressing table mirror, surrounded by combs and brushes and Molly's cosmetics, practising her Brooklyn talk. Just how grown up can you feel at twenty-one? In some ways, she was the baby of the house. Patsy might be three years younger, but he was cut from the same tree as his father, strong and capable and going nowhere but right here. Where had he found the money to buy that wristwatch for her, she just could not imagine. And she could not imagine ever wearing it. Winnie felt she would probably always be just a girl. That meant she needed to move out. With all the determination she could muster amongst her combs and brushes and cosmetics, she resolved to go to America by twenty-five at the latest, or thirty.

With her hair already done (why had she allowed that to happen!), there was a limit to the jobs she could safely tackle. She decided to restrict herself to the kitchen, leaving the door open to keep cool. She was good with pies and pastries. Daddy and Dan always said they were as good as Mummy's, and Mummy's had been shown at the Moy Fair. On a Saturday, Patsy would have two before a game, saying he needed one to get him through each half. She had mentioned as a joke that he might like to take some extra to give to his colleagues, and he had taken her for serious and said he would work up a business proposal for her. That Pasty one, just like his father. The left oven was getting over hot, she would have to keep an eye out for it and make sure she remembered to put the trays on the bottom shelf.

She needed another egg for glazing, and she had run out, so there was nothing for it but she would have to go out to the hen shed behind the cow-house where they kept the pig. Kathleen was coming out of the cow-house.

'Oh, I didn't expect to find you in there,' said Winnie without meaning anything at all.

'I had to feed the hens, as no one else had,' replied Kathleen.

'Are the hens taking over the barn now, as well as everywhere else?' Winnie continued on her way to the chicken shed, not bothering to chat more, happy that her sister was getting on with things. No one was looking, so Winnie skipped the rest of the way there and back again to the kitchen. She was just in time to pull

FINDING DAN

a tray of smoking tart bases from the left oven. She would discard one or two, but she could get away with the rest once she had filled them with custard or sugared cream. 'Have you tried one of these, Martin?' her fingers stretching to the circumference of the big plate. 'You really must!' Preparing a meal for a man other than her father, or her brothers or cousins, that was a sure step up to being a woman even if it was just a pie. Martin would cover his lip in custard, and spit crumbs out with the compliment he would give, embarrassing himself. And Winnie sank to her chair in giggles just at the thought.

A car skidded into the yard. That'll be Dan. He'll have got the drink. He'll have taken some of it before he left Coalisland to come back. That's Dan, as everyone knows. Does no one any harm, and his self not much good. Leave Dan be, Mummy would scold whenever any of the girls had a go at him for drinking. He's had more life through his body than all the rest of you put together, it's only natural he should want to enjoy himself a bit now. Daddy would say nothing on the matter with Mummy around, but he wasn't happy, you could tell. Now Mummy's not around.

There were voices in the yard and in the house. Winnie counted off Dan and Daddy and Patsy, and that sounds like Jack's Joe already, and even Bassie has arrived. Kathleen'll be around some place too. That means everyone is here, and she's not even her dress on yet! She slipped the dress off its hanger, pulled the long zip all the way down the back as far as the hips, stepped her stockings in, and shimmied the Fifth Avenue dress up her woman's body. She had never smoked in her life, but she wanted a cigarette now. The powder brush was too fat and was more like a cigar, like a gangster's, so she slotted it back in its pot. 'Winnie O'Rourke, you're a girl!' she said, and she could be Molly in the room, it sounded just like her. 'You're a girl.' It meant she was ready.

There was no one in the kitchen. The noise was coming from the yard. There was the folding table covered in a freshly laundered cloth near by the fence. Kathleen will have done that. She hasn't even had the time to take off her apron, and she's not resting yet, what with making sure everyone has their glass filled.

'That dress looks so much better on you than it does on me,' said Bassie whose dress was not the same as Winnie's, being a different colour and having a wider collar.

Old Joe said, 'Kathleen, make sure my birthday girl has a proper drink in that glass. Now, Winnie, you sit there in the middle beside me.'

'Let me have a go of that,' said Patsy, reaching for Winnie's whiskey.

'Away on you, Patsy O'Rourke. Not before I've even had a sniff myself!'

'Smile!' Martin Quinn pressed the shutter button on the expensive camera, detonating a minor bomb of light. 'I think I got you fine, Winnie,' he announced.

'No, Martin, you haven't got me yet!' laughed Winnie.

Kathleen

Kathleen O'Rourke had been planning the day for over a week. She had moved the laundry day forward to leave her time to cook the meat and prepare the vegetables. She had pressed her own dress and Winnie's, although she was nervous that the cream colour was not going to work for her on the day. The men all had clean shirts. She had set them out of the way until that very morning, making sure they weren't soiled before they were needed.

As ever, she had to turn her hand to the business too. Not the cutting or hauling: she never, ever went down to the sawmill and would be hard-pressed to even describe what was there. But customers sometimes came up to the house to place an order, or collect one, and her father was not always in a state to meet them. Sometimes, Patsy would appear, and he would spirit them away and do whatever had to be done. Patsy had a good head that way. But last week, James Quinn, the carpenter from Main Street in Coalisland, had called up to collect his cut timber, and it hadn't been ready.

'I have more important customers to worry about than a small tradesman like James Quinn,' Joe had said when Kathleen told him.

FINDING DAN

'But he was cross, Daddy. He says he's sending his son up next week to get it, and it had better be ready, or he'll take his custom elsewhere.'

'I'll have Dan do it,' Joe had said irritably. He had his paper now, and he meant to read it. 'Which one is his son?'

'I think it's Shaun.' Kathleen knew full well it was Shaun.

'There are so many bloody Quinns, I can't keep track o' them. Anyway, if he's like his father, he won't be up to much.'

'They say James Quinn is a quality carpenter, and he gives you good business, Daddy. He sent up for orders every three month last year.' Kathleen tried to hide her knowledge of that family behind her knowledge of the business. 'Small tradesmen keep us going when the big contracts dry up.'

Joe eyed his daughter suspiciously. He had five daughters, and they all needed watching, especially since his wife, Margaret, died last year. 'Have you been in his house?'

'No, Daddy!' The heat of her denial made her face redden. 'What would I be doing in there?' She meant her question to be rhetorical, but her father was schooled in such distractions.

'There could be many things a young girl could be doing in a house like that, Miss O'Rourke. For one, you could be helping your sister deliver groceries there.'

Four months ago, James Quinn had walked into Winnie's shop in Coalisland and bought a box of potatoes and cabbage and onions. He already had a parcel of screws and hinges from Willie McCrum's hardware shop, and he was suddenly embarrassed that he could not manage to carry the box as well. Kathleen knew the man from his regular visits to the sawmill in Creenagh, so volunteered to deliver the box to his home at the bottom of Main Street.

She had arrived with the box at the carpentry shop. Someone there, sitting on a stool doing nothing, pointed her through the back of the store where she found stairs to living quarters. She knocked on one door and found a family of little children, clearly not the Quinns.

'No, dear, you don't want us or the next door. That's the Taylors. Take the next stairs and that's you.'

Kathleen felt bewildered by the interior. Three homes seemed to have been approximately hewn out of an old warehouse. She came across a low gate across an archway. Looking over, she realised the gate protected against a five feet drop. She took more stairs and found herself in a sort of loft. She was drawn to the only light—two tall windows garlanded with cobwebs. Above and between them was a mechanical contraption with a swinging arm and chain and hook.

'It's a crane,' she whispered. She reckoned that one time the windows would have opened out over the street, and the crane would have raised and lowered goods from the barges that scuttled up and down the canal. 'Linen,' she said, again out loud.

'You're very clever,' came a deep and amused voice from behind her. Startled, she dropped the vegetables, which skittered, embarrassed, across the floor. 'But easily confused,' the voice concluded.

Kathleen gathered the potatoes and cabbage and onions in a rush while the man let her. She had seen him before. She knew who he was. Winnie knew about him in the way Winnie always knew such things. She had said he was a charmer.

'Hi, I'm Shaun. You're Kathleen. Those are my da's vegetables.'

'He rents,' Joe said, as if that were all.

'I think he has plans to expand.' Kathleen made this sound as reasonable, as non-partisan as possible. 'He says people need bicycles, that that's the best way to get about around here.'

'Is this the old man talking here, or the young boy, Shaun?' Joe shook the creases out of his newspaper. His daughter imagined a shower of full stops scattering from its pages and knew this conversation was over. And every other possible conversation on the matter.

Kathleen O'Rourke was 24 years old; Shaun Quinn was twenty. They met again, first accidentally on the street, then secretly by the banks of the canal curving out of Coalisland. She acknowledged her family's opposition to the courtship by mentioning it to no one.

FINDING DAN

She found she enjoyed the necessary subterfuge, enjoying more the seeming contradiction to her character. 'Kate, you're an open book,' Dan often said, and she took it as a compliment. During their mother's long illness, the siblings naturally looked to her to arrange the mealtimes, and to keep Agnes McCarthy, their laundry maid, busy. Obviously, when Molly sailed in from New York, the older sister took over command. Kathleen would have questioned her no more than any of the others would. Molly had overseen her mother's death and left again. Joe and the boys and the sisters were bereft until Kathleen brought them back into line. Indeed, Winnie's party was really her idea. Winnie had needed no excuse to start enjoying herself again. Dan's drinking was becoming more sociable. Her father was recovering some of his old sharpness, although he was driving the business to ruination. Patsy spent his days down at the sawmill, helping where he could, Kathleen supposed. With Betty married and Bassie always out, that left a great big space, the house, for Kathleen herself. No one was curious about what she got up to. No one had to worry that she was too young, or too incapable to fend for herself. She put her father to bed in the way her mother had put her husband to bed, and no one, least of all Joe, thought this odd. She was an open book. So she had met Shaun Quinn by the side of the canal and no one suspected a thing. And no one would know tonight, as she met him again in their own cow-house in Creenagh.

She had everything prepared, even the pastries that she knew Winnie would be too distracted to bake properly. She retrieved the white linen cloth that she had reserved for the purpose at the back of the closet, and spread it over the card table she had placed in the yard with six waiting glasses. She, herself, would not be drinking. She spent several moments worrying that Dan would not make it back from Coalisland with the alcohol, or with the money she had given him for it. Dan, who could be so sweet when he was sober. She had sent Jack's Joe with him in Jack's Joe's car. That doubled the chances they would make it back in one piece, and doubled the chances they would not. Bassie appeared from nowhere wearing Winnie's dress, the one with the heather tartan.

'She'll not mind, she'll just be pleased I'm here,' said Bassie.

'She'll be pleased *and* she will mind. You are ten years older than her. Here, at least turn the collar out a bit further, make it bigger.' Kathleen helped her do it. 'Have you seen Dan?'

Bassie nodded gravely.

'Oh, God.'

'He was in Girvin's the last I saw.'

'Was Jack's Joe with him?'

'Aye, and Martin too,' Bassie confirmed.

'That should help. Can Martin drive the car?' Kathleen tried to imagine Martin Quinn tall enough to reach the pedals of Jack Quinn's vehicle. Was he older, or younger than Patsy?

'He's driven it before when he's had to, if you catch my meaning.'

Kathleen was afraid she did. As she had done everything she could do and just had to wait for everyone to do what they needed to do, she returned to the cow-house for the third time that afternoon. They called it the cow-house, although it was where their mother had always kept a pig. When she died the previous year, no one had felt up to looking after the pig, so they had had it slaughtered. So the cow-house, which was really a part of the actual house, had remained unused for several months. Kathleen had thought about it and decided not to think any more about it. She would make use of it, and when she had done that, she would invite the others to decide what should happen with it next. She fished for the old black key, which hung from a string, and let herself in. She made sure she shut the top half-door, which normally was never shut. She found an old carpet good enough to lie on the dirt floor. She found two crates and set them side by side. A white cloth from the linen closet, two empty glasses, and a candle in a makeshift beer bottle candleholder, a box of matches tucked thoughtfully beside. She was sure the candle would give exactly the right impression. And otherwise, without it, the room would just be a dark byre smelling of the pig that lived in it. On her way out, she met Winnie skipping across the yard to the henhouse. She might look like a Manhattan moll, thought Kathleen, but she was only a girl from Creenagh.

FINDING DAN

In the yard, she was alarmed to see Martin Quinn walking alone up the lane towards the house.

'Hello Martin, 's good to see you.' Kathleen battled to keep the rising dismay out of her voice. The party had to go well. Mummy would want us all to be enjoying ourselves by now, she was convinced. She had to keep everyone distracted if her plan was to work. 'I heard you were with your brother and our Dan?'

'They are on their way up now. We met someone on the way, and he took over the wheel. Says he knows Winnie,' Martin added after a pause.

The Quinns' motorcar came screeching into the yard like a fire-breathing monster, but with the wrong Quinn driving. Jack's Joe was perched on the bench at the back, evidently propping up Dan. At the driver's wheel was Shaun Quinn, looking proud and handsome. He leapt out of the car before its breathing had properly eased, and ran around the front of it to present himself to Kathleen.

'Hello, Miss O'Rourke! I am here on my father's business!' When they had rehearsed this line, it had not sounded so ludicrously formal. It did not help that Shaun completed the introduction with a deep bow.

'You must be Shaun,' Kathleen recalled the line with minimal conviction. 'I will fetch my father. And as you have arrived in the middle of this family celebration, you must stay for a drink.' (Kathleen could not help that the celebration was still yet to begin, and could not help notice that Shaun himself was complicit in the delay. She was glad of the chance to leave him there and look for her father.)

At least Dan had remembered his part. There was plenty of alcohol to get the party going. Dan recited a poem he had made up, and Bassie sang a song or two. Old Joe remained quiet mostly, but Kathleen thought he showed a contentment she hadn't seen in him since her mother died. Kathleen kept to her plan by refraining from drinking, and by keeping the others readily supplied. She could not, however, draw Shaun away. He wanted Dan to talk about the old days.

'My da tells me you were on the run,' said Shaun.

'He was for months. Or was it years, Dan?' Bassie's eyes sparkled liquid and brown like her drink.

'They used to call up for him here many's the time. His poor mother's head was turnt, may God rest her,' said Joe who then sank back into his thoughts.

'And they interned you on the *Argenta*? That's what people say. Did they beat you bad?' asked Shaun.

'They beat him till he was a broken man.' They all laughed at Winnie for saying this.

'No one ever broke Dan,' said Patsy. 'Isn't that right, Dan?'

'They kept trying,' Dan set them up. 'But I'm still standing!' And Bassie and Jack's Joe and Martin Quinn and Winnie and the rest of them cheered.

Her father had somehow gone back into the house during this. Now, he was coming out again bearing an object like it was a monstrance, lifting it slightly for their adoration.

'Molly's camera,' he said simply. 'She left it for us to use on special occasions. I reckon this is a special enough occasion.' He handed it to Shaun, as the others would have seen it before. 'It's genuine American.'

'Kodak,' Shaun said approvingly. This utterance alone implied sufficient expertise to confer upon him the privilege of using it.

The family instinctively herded around the folding table with the white tablecloth, trapping Jack's Joe in their midst. (Later, they would wonder where Martin Quinn had gone to as he missed the snap.) Winnie sat down like she was never going to stand again and laughed at herself for trying. Kathleen couldn't bring herself to stare at the lens or at the man wielding it. She was worried the photograph might betray her most secret thoughts at that moment; that someone, later, would read it and see that she was in love; that Kathleen O'Rourke was in love with the man you could not see, but that everyone else was staring at and admiring.

FINDING DAN
Patsy

Patsy hated working for his father, but he had no objection to making money for himself. In the forests of Lough Fea, Aughnacloy, Killyman he would trudge after the old man, dragging the crosscut saw behind him. 'Watch those teeth, Patsy!' his father would call over his shoulder.

Oul' Joe was an old man all right. He would forget where he had put his drink then he would forget that he had a drink. He was like that with the business too: he would have no recollection that a customer had placed an order, then he would deny he had ever met the man at all. 'It's Jim Canning, Da,' Patsy would whisper in his ear (or Brian Cavanagh or Peter McHugh), and Joe would shake his whole head and neck the way the old horse would. Patsy had recently taken to calling his father, Joe, or Old Joe, but only when talking to customers or to himself. It helped to define the business relationship between the father and the son.

'Now, take the other end of that!' Joe swung the end of the saw towards his youngest, and the two set immediately to work on a poplar. Patsy had to admit that however much his father had lost it in the head, he was still a physical force to be reckoned with. They would saw for ninety minutes without rest ('Why d'you think you got those shoulders?') as if anything less would be a sin. Joe would pull the saw towards himself, Patsy would pull it back; Joe drew the blade again, Patsy pulled it back. It's mine. It's mine. To survive the ninety minutes of labour, Patsy played this game in his head and imagined Joe must be too. With a two-man saw, one man cannot give up: both have to agree on the moment to relinquish. Many times, Patsy wanted to call a break, but the saw handle kept rebounding to his stomach, as if Old Joe were pushing the blade at him and not just pulling it from him. It's yours. It's yours. When time was called, Joe would sit confused amongst the fallen trees, wondering who had left them lying, resentful of Patsy for not clearing them away.

MARK QUINN

The poplar would get carted back to Creenagh, and his father would forget that he had it. Patsy, however, knew a Portadown man who would take it off him for making dartboards with. Maybe weeks later, Joe would ask whatever happened to that poplar wood we cut, and Patsy would pretend he hadn't heard. Patsy thought his father a fool for never writing anything down. In a cavity in the wall behind his bed, Patsy hid a ledger; and in the ledger, he kept accounts of the business he made. Under *income*, he recorded the £, s. and d. that he received from his man in Portadown, and the one in Pomeroy and the fruit and vegetables lady in Bracka. For *costs*, he made himself write down the hours he worked alone or alongside his dad, hours that cost his father nothing, but him, plenty. To Patsy, keeping the book was just sound business (keeping it hidden, he told himself, was also the wiser thing). So he also entered there the deal he did with his sister, to supply her shop on Main Street with the crates she needed for her mushrooms and apples and potatoes. Some old-fashioned reservation made him write a false name instead of Winnie. Winnie never knew about the book, and never found out she wasn't buying the boxes from her father.

Everyone, Winnie included, was therefore surprised when the little brother presented her with a bought gift for her birthday that morning. And what a gift—a lady's wristwatch from the jewellers on Scotch Street in Dungannon. It had a gold-coloured chain strap and a pearl white face. Everyone was not only surprised; they were envious, not of Winnie for receiving such a wonderful gift, but of Patsy for having the wherewithal to buy it. The girls had bought her slippers and a nightdress and other things appropriate for girls to buy their sister on her twenty-first birthday. Molly had left her the Kodak camera and Patsy was happy to concede that that was the superior present. But Patsy looked for, and duly recorded, his father's discomfort when he handed over to his youngest daughter the present he had bought when he had no idea what to buy. Nylon stockings. He had noticed Molly wearing them last year and had been subtly ashamed at his thoughts of how beautiful and womanly they made her look. He had gone to Dungannon and

FINDING DAN

then to Portadown and then to Armagh (all with other business in mind) before he had found the stockings and then the nerve to buy them. He never missed his wife so much as he did then. A lady sales assistant asked him who they were for and what shade he required and what size. He had wanted to shout an obscenity at her, for he thought the whole affair was sordid and obscene; and he found himself wanting his daughter not to like them, to think they were silly or too old for her. Of course, she had loved them, and had instantly unfurled them making a comedy of them, which Joe was glad for. She played with them like a little girl fascinated by their static and their elastic. Then when Patsy handed Winnie the red velvet box like a miniature treasure chest, and she opened it to find the watch inside, all the comedy of before was swept away. The girl of the house was no longer a girl, and the boy who gave it to her must be a man.

Patsy had logged the watch in his ledger under *costs*. He dimly calculated that Winnie would now buy more crates directly off him. Think of a cost as an investment, was what Jack's Joe had taught him. Jack's Joe now had a motorcar, and last year, he had taken a holiday in Rostrevor. He was planning a trip to Scotland, and Patsy, determined that he would do that too. There were plenty of forests there and the Scotch were renowned for their business sense. He would go there to learn, and then he would come back and expand the mill at Creenagh into a proper enterprise. With only a glance, Patsy could convert their three-room, mud-stepped cottage into a family home with curtains and electricity and plumbed water and a wife. Old Joe would be dead, of course, and the girls married off somewhere. There was no room in Patsy's vision for Dan. Dan could sharpen the saws. In fact, he had greater skill with a flat mill file than any O'Rourke, and he knew more people about than either Patsy or Joe from his old political days, from his football-playing days, now from his drinking days. But in Patsy's ledger (the one he kept in his head rather than the hole in his wall), the time Dan spent with these acquaintances was not investment, but pure cost. None of Dan's friends brought any business. Even Kathleen was more useful than Dan in that regard, having somehow secured regular custom from James Quinn, the carpenter.

Patsy had a GAA match that evening for Edendork against his old team, the Fianna from Coalisland. He felt strong. He had noticed the muscles in his shoulders growing from the long mornings sawing with his father. He was faster and more physically assertive than the other lads on the team. He felt sure he would soon be selected for Tyrone, as Dan had been. He saw no reason why he should not profit from association with his brother even if Dan was starting to be a public embarrassment. Patsy did not mind it when the old blokes, who stood on the touchline, said, 'You'll be as good as your brother soon.' It only meant they thought he was an O'Rourke, and being so, he was near ready for selection. Boys from the Tyrone Board would likely be at the game tonight, so Patsy was keen to be at his best. He would therefore stay away from the liquor that Dan was due back with at any minute.

Dan had persuaded Joe Quinn to take the motorcar to Coalisland for the drink, and it was Jack's Joe at the wheel when it came skidding into the yard, scattering chickens and Bassie and Kathleen alike. Patsy supposed Winnie had set up the card table with the white cloth by the fence. 'We can gather round that, and we can at last have a picture taken with Molly's camera,' she said. She established herself at the centre, and got her dad and her big brother to sit either side of her. 'The rest of you, bunch in.' She lifted her empty glass. 'Kathleen, have you a bottle there?'

'There's no one to take the picture,' said Jack's Joe, looking tall and handsome at the back. 'I'll take it if you like.'

'We can't have that,' said Winnie. 'Not with you in your best suit, dressed for it and all.'

'I'll fix it!' offered Patsy who already had the camera in his hand. Although it was Winnie's, a camera was a thing for a man. But a careful man, not a blundering one. Old Joe wouldn't do, gripping his glass with his whole hand, drinking the liquid with his whole mouth. Dan's hands were made of leather, or they were made of wood. Patsy noticed how fine his own fingers looked holding the apparatus, and how nimbly they nudged the dial and lever. Molly had shown him last year how to set the light and how to work the shutter delay. ('Winnie's a doll,' his big sister had confided. In that one word, Patsy had heard *moll* and *brawl* and *y'all*, and thought it contained the whole of New York City.) 'If I set it here, we can all get in.'

Patsy pulled open the top half of the cow-house door, briefly looking inside before balancing the camera on the lower door. Looks clean in there, he thought. Could be a decent room for someone someday.

'Right, everyone get ready! It'll go off any moment now.'

Dan raised his elbow and his glass, Kathleen poised over it with a spirit bottle. Joe and Bassie both lifted their glasses, wanting to be seen celebrating rather than drinking. Jack's Joe held his cigarette in his right hand then switched it to his left, inserting his right in his trouser pocket. Patsy pretended to reach for Winnie's glass, and held the pose until the shutter snapped.

'Is that it? Is it taken yet? Will it have caught us all?' Only Winnie had managed to forget about the camera.

Dan

Kathleen had wanted him to get the booze. Well, he could manage that! If there was one thing Dan O'Rourke was still capable of, it was procuring liquor. Even so, he had taken the precaution of commandeering the services of his neighbour, Joe Quinn who, in turn, had recruited his brother, Martin; and together, all three had set off to Coalisland in Jack Quinn's motorcar.

That had been some time this morning. They had kicked off in Girvin's with its off licence sales, imagining for all the world that that would be them for the day. But Bassie had spotted them in there, and she had brought over to their snug some of her lads. She always called them that. Dan assumed it was to avoid calling them by a real name, for these lads were notorious republicans, or liked to think they were.

'So you are the great Daniel O'Rourke, the one Bassie is always telling us about?' The lad who said this was no older than seventeen. Bassie sucked on her cigarette, filling up on nicotine and dignity. Dan had had this sort of thing before. He sometimes thought he must bear a chiselled inscription across his chest: the great Dan O'Rourke. To you, I am, he thought.

'Don't ask him too many questions, he won't like that,' said Bassie, inviting the opposite.

'Dan. Can I call you Dan?' began one of the lads without pausing for affirmation. 'Do you still hate the Brits as much as you ever did?'

'Dan, do you hope for the coming Emergency that it might be Ireland's opportunity again?' added another lad, plainly reciting the lecture he must have attended recently on the imminent war with Germany.

'I don't hope for war,' Dan began. 'Bassie, where do you pick these up from?' Dan said no more, confident that he had said enough.

'Of course, Dan, of course,' said Bassie, shooing the lads off. 'Don't forget to come home, Dan, will you?' she added. This time, like to a brother she was concerned about, and she waited until she saw a look on his face that assured her.

'God, save me from these people,' said Dan when he was alone again with Martin and Jack's Joe. There were few afternoons and rare nights when he was not approached in a bar by someone wishing to talk to him about his days on the run or his internment. These people were not the Cavanaghs or the Magees or the Corrs of this world, people with their own stories to tell, but who seldom had cause to tell them. Dan never found himself reminiscing with old comrades. In truth, even back then he had operated alone. Even in prison, he had been his own man. Relying on no one else was a way of getting through. Some of those young Turks that Bassie brought along from time to time were barely born when all that was going on, so it was no wonder they tended to romanticise it like it was already history.

FINDING DAN

Bassie's lads were still at the bar. One of them raised a glass to Dan, pointed at the glass, and then at Dan, as if he were offering to buy him a drink. Maybe the lad was not so bad after all, mused Dan. At least he took an interest in the old days. Dan shifted in his seat and felt the familiar pain in his leg. Surely, his best days were behind him. There would be fewer good days ahead. The lad had a smile that was friendly enough, and any friend of Bassie's couldn't be all bad. Maybe he had been hard on him. Dan considered joining the boy at the bar, but before he could move, the boy had turned back to his comrades to share a joke with them. The three of them laughed, and Dan saw how his sister tried to shush them.

'Shall we try O'Neill's, Dan?' Joe Quinn suggested. 'More our crowd there.'

O'Neill's was packed with men getting ready to watch the big game that evening between the Fianna and Edendork. 'Here's Dan!' someone called out when they entered. 'He's just the man to settle this.' And Dan quickly fell into chat about the merits of the two sides now, and how their players of today compared to those in his day. Patsy, of course, would be playing; and Dan, of course, would be there to see it, as always. Martin reminded him that he would be expected at Creenagh before that, as it was Winnie's birthday, and they all three remembered they had the alcohol to get for that. And then there was a round of drinks to celebrate Winnie being of age. Dan felt at ease in O'Neill's because the men there knew what they were talking about when they talked about football, they appreciated their football heritage, and they could hold their drink.

'You getting the rounds in today, Dan?' asked yer man Duffy. 'You win the sweepstake?'

'That's enough out of you there,' said Dan, avoiding the man's name, for he wasn't sure of it. 'I never let a man stand me when I have my own.' He rattled some coins in his trousers and allowed the laughter that followed to pass as good-natured. Duffy (it *was* Duffy) was not to know the money in his pocket was Kathleen's.

'That's a point, though, Dan,' said Jack's Joe, taking Dan aside to be private. 'Have you not had your welfare cut by the Means Test?

You don't need to put your hand in your pocket when I'm here, Dan. You know that.'

'What welfare? I have no Means Test. You're the last man that should be saying that to me, Joe, as you know well I've never put my hand out for any benefit from a British government. I get the money I need from the mill.'

'You mean from your da?'

Dan knew what Joe meant. He knew he meant well, and he knew he was as good as his word about Dan not having to buy drinks with him around. But he was enraged by the implication that his old man kept him (and ashamed again that he was drinking the money intended for Winnie's party). 'I work hard enough, and I get a wage. It's not a lot, but I put my hand out to no one.'

'So you won't be wanting one from me then?' said Duffy. 'That's noble of you, Dan.'

Dan would have gladly accepted a drink from Duffy for his thirst, but his principles so stood in the way Duffy already knew he was safe, and was now at the bar getting a drink for himself.

'Aren't you deserving of an IRA pension then, Dan?' This was Martin who only usually spoke when it was safe to do so.

'I would say I was, and there are plenty around here—witness the lads we met in Girvin's—who would say I was. Aye, and there's no shame in that.'

'Of course, Dan, of course.' Martin Quinn contemplated asking the natural next question, but considered Dan would have told them already if he had wanted them to know. The truth was, but for his drinking, there was not much Martin ever saw Dan spend his money on.

When Molly had asked much the same questions last year when she was over to nurse their mother, Dan had not lost his temper with her. Everyone commented on how she had changed, how she looked and sounded like something out of the movies, and Dan could see and hear what they meant. But to him, she had barely altered at all. The way she stood, not quite square on, but with one hip pointed forward: they all said she looked like a gunslinger, and had she met

FINDING DAN

Annie Oakley, but Dan remembered her like that twenty years ago when she would stand up from milking the cow they had then. She could knock a tin off the fence from ten paces, and all she would need would be one of her smiles. He hadn't known how it would be with her when she returned. Her boat had docked in Liverpool before proceeding to Belfast, and she had taken the train as far as Dungannon and a bus the rest of the way. 'Someone should go and meet her,' Kathleen had protested. 'If she can make it to New York on her own, she can make it back again,' had been Daddy's final word, and they all knew what he meant. Molly could manage absolutely fine.

As it was, Molly had had to ask a young man to kindly help carry her cases up the lane to Creenagh, and she had tipped him even though he was a neighbour and not portering bags for a job.

'A fine how-de-do this is!' she had called from the kitchen when she found it empty. Then everyone came rushing in to greet her, apart from Mummy who was too ill. Dan had felt nervous, but he drew comfort when he saw Patsy and realised the boy could have had no memory of his sister at all. Patsy always liked to play the big grown-up, but he was a tiny boy beside Molly, even after all these years.

'Come here to me, Daniel,' Molly said when it was his turn, and there was no American in her then.

For weeks after, Molly spent nearly every hour tending her dying mother; and when she wasn't, she was fetching water or boiling it to cook with it or clean with it. When she did have a free moment, it would be in the evenings when their mother was asleep and everyone had been fed. Dan made certain he was there. The others would be there too, but with the darkness fractured only by the turf fire spitting in the grate, Dan could imagine he was alone with her. 'Tell us one of your ghost stories, Dan, please,' she said, and he sensed a reshuffling of the gloom in the house, a closing-in on the fire.

'If you continue on down the lane from here and cross the road to Mullins', you'll pass on your right an old flax hole. There is no flax hole there as such any more, but the stench of it still lingers during the retting season, and I'll tell you why.

'That old flax hole belonged to Mullin who used it for his scutching mill. When I was very small, I used to watch him with his corn fiddle broadcasting the tiny flax seeds in his field. Every spring, this would come up in a beautiful blue flower then Mullin and his people would pull it up in handfuls. Five handfuls to a beet, he used to say. Mullin had made his flax hole by damning the stream that runs the length of the bottom of his field there. That hole was about two foot deep and the water was a shukh, so it stank even before they lay the bundles of flax in it. Nine days they'd keep it there under these boulders they would use for the walls, unless sometimes it took longer for the wood to leave the fibres. After that, they would lay it on the field to dry then take it up to the scutching mill. Why I watched all this, I can't remember now, but I learned to be sorry of it one night that I did.

'None of you is old enough to remember Father Freeland, and in any case, he was a rare visitor to Tullyniskan Parish here. Father Freeland was what you might term a priest of no fixed abode. He tended to bring bad luck down upon the people he administered to, and there's one thing you want to avoid, and that's an unlucky priest. There was one story I heard, told of a man name of Campbell who wanted his last rites. Campbell was in a bad way, having drunk himself into a stupor, so that his companions thought he was dying. Maybe they were the worse for wear themselves, but they took it into their heads to call a priest to give the man his last rites. The only priest they could lay their hands on was this same Father Freeland. Now, priests are many things, but they're not doctors; and Freeland took these men at their word that Campbell was at death's door and needed to confess and receive extreme unction. Otherwise, they had reason to fear the man would be making a short trip to hell. Now, Freeland was leaning over this man, saying his Latin, and laying on his oils and smells. And lo, didn't the man, Campbell, sit bolt upright, as he was, and start chatting away like nothing had happened.

FINDING DAN

'A man's reputation can alter overnight, and that was the case for Father Freeland who, the whole of the next day, went round every pub he could find telling all and sundry that he was a miracle worker. Sure, hadn't he brought a man back to life just with a few words of Latin, some ointment, and the grace of God? And if anyone should doubt it, here was the man in question, Campbell, standing right there. Not one to miss an opportunity for self-promotion either, Campbell allowed several drinks to be stood for him, until—would you credit it?—he collapsed again as he did the night before. Campbell's companions, wise heads that they were, having seen their friend's performance of the previous night, advised all to stand back and let the drunk recover in his own time. Father Freeland, unsure he could summon two miracles in succession, was persuaded to leave him alone. No Latin. No anointing. Well, Campbell died there and then. As I said you're better off without an unlucky priest.

'Feeland may not have been a miracle worker, but he had a talent for which he was called upon more often in those days than he maybe would these. He was an exorcist. Sure, exorcists are ten a penny, I hear you say. True, but not of this variety, for Freeland was an animal exorcist, livestock mainly, pigs in particular. You shouldn't laugh. Pork from a bedevilled pig is poisonous. They give off a certain squeal that you or I would just take for normal, but a pig man would know was satanic. Lopping their tales is often cure enough, but often enough, it is not, and that's when they need the exorcist. It's doubtful what view would be taken of this by the pope in Rome, but then again, Father Freeland was, in many ways, something of a freelance cleric. He favoured swine, but he would turn his hand to cows and horses and, at a push, have a go at hens too. If you want to know what a demonic hen looks like, just watch Winnie with them at feeding time!

'On this particular night, Father Freeland was passing down our lane, having successfully completed the exorcism of a litter of pigs up at McHughs'. He would have been feeling jolly, I would say, and the moon was full, which is advantageous for an exorcism. The moon shone brightly, casting ghostly shadows through the bushes. A strong breeze bent the trees to the ground, their branches scratching the soil like black fingers. Freeland's black cassock brushed across the ruts in the lane. He felt a tugging at the bottom. He kicked his foot out to clear the obstruction, but it pulled again. Thinking it must be a bramble caught on his cassock, he reached down to brush it off, and as he did so, a HAND caught hold of his. He pulled back, but it wouldn't let go. He pulled and he pulled and he PULLED and still it wouldn't let him free. He was screaming himself, but under his screams, he could hear another voice. And he knew to whom this voice belonged.

'"Campbell!' he cried. "Let go of my frigging hand!" For it was indeed the same Campbell, the man whose life he had saved in an apparent miracle, but who he had allowed to die without issuing him with the last rites. For some few seconds, the priest tussled with the dead man. He freed his hand at last, and with both hands, he ripped the cassock over his head and flung it into the field beside, cursing the dead man's soul. It landed in Mullin's flax hole.

'Freeland knew what had taken place. Having once received the last rites, Campbell's soul ought to have rested in peace. But in the twenty-four hours it took him to die, he must have committed some cardinal sins, for his soul was still in torment and clinging to the priest—the one man who might yet absolve him. He was now wrapped in the priest's holy garment, though how sacred the cassock of a self-employed priest is, even Freeland was not sure. Freeland, you can be sure, did not hang around to find out. And he was never seen again.

'Some years later—I do not know how many—I received this story from a most reliable source. As you know, there were times in the past when men, such as I, could not always come home, when a bed for the night might be found in a hovel, or even a hole. The B men were more frequent visitors here than me. Molly, you remember that, and Mummy would tell you the same. I was nearly caught many times before I was. On one occasion, and it was night of course, I was minded to sneak home for a bit of warmth when I nearly walked right into a B patrol. They would know me from sight,

FINDING DAN

for the neighbour, Mullin's son, was an RIC man himself. I had time just to hurl myself over the wall. I landed in a ditch, which I didn't know then was the very same flax hole I've been telling you about. I lay there as quiet as the grass. The other side of the wall I could hear the patrol talking. They had not seen me, and they had no idea I was there, but as long as they didn't move, I couldn't. The reeds in the hole were damp rather than wet, and I suppose I was lucky that the hole was no longer used for retting flax. I suppose I might have started to drift off. Believe me, in those days, I slept in worse places. Whether I was asleep by then, I cannot say for certain, but there was no mistaking the stench that reached my nose. It was the stink of rotting corpse.

'I wanted to be sick. I gagged, my stomach turned over. But I could not move, and I dared not make a sound. I lay there still, worried the moon might reveal me or the trees point me out. Then I heard the whispers, whispers from within the flax hole. I was not alone, and my next thought was that this other fugitive would betray me. It whispered again, and I felt behind. There was nobody there, no body there.

'How long was I there, maybe an hour. The B patrol moved away, but still, I couldn't climb out of the hole. I crouched there not looking behind, listening to the whispers, and listening to the story that the whispers told. The story of a priest and a drunk man, and the night the priest cast the man into a shallow hell.

'If you look in daylight, and I recommend you do it no other time, you will see the traces only of the old flax hole. It was abandoned soon after the night the priest walked past. It turned the flax too quick, or not at all. But for nine days every year, you will smell it. The smell of retting flax; the stink of rotting flesh.'

Dan stayed in O'Neill's Bar with Martin and Joe Quinn for most of the afternoon until all Kathleen's money had been drunk.

'Have you any money left, Joe?' asked Dan.

Joe shuffled some coins in his palm, but could not make them any bigger. 'I have some, Dan, but not so as to buy drink enough for a whole party. Sorry, Dan.'

'No, Joe, don't be sorry. It's not your lookout. It can't be helped. Something will turn up.' Dan paused for inspiration. 'Martin, have you any money?'

'No, Dan, sorry, Dan, I haven't a ha'penny on me.'

'No Martin, you never have. Never worry, it's not your fault. Now what shall we do?'

The three drunk men pooled all their mental resources. An *Irish News* hung from a stick near the bar, and Jack's Joe suggested taking it and beating money out of everybody until they had enough. They contemplated the pros and cons of this, finally dismissing it when Dan lit on an alternative.

'Give me that paper there.' Martin reached him the *Irish News*. Dan turned the pages expertly to the death notices. He scanned the messages announcing the deaths of the Catholic men and women of the North. 'Got one!'

'You seem pleased, Dan. Someone you know?' asked Jack's Joe.

'Someone I don't know, Joe, and that's why it is perfect.'

Five minutes later, the three friends had managed to find Jack Quinn's motorcar and were in it on their way to a wake in Pomeroy. Martin drove, while Dan and Joe rehearsed. They came upon a farmer who was steering his cattle down the road to be milked, their udders rubbing uncomfortably.

'What would happen if we drove into one of those cows, Joe?' asked Martin.

'It would end up on the seat here with us,' replied his brother. 'So don't go getting any ideas.'

Finally, they were there. They had no trouble finding the street, and from there, locating the right house was straightforward. 'There'll be one with all the curtains drawn, and maybe flowers in the window if they have no room left on their mantelpiece,' declared Dan, an old hand at this.

'Mrs Brady?' The woman at the door nodded doubtfully at the three strangers. She wore a black skirt and blouse, and had her impressively black hair pulled back into a clip. 'Mrs Brady, I'm very sorry for your loss.'

FINDING DAN

'As am I,' added Joe.

'Me too,' said Martin.

'Your husband...', (Dan allowed a pause for the widow to show her own sadness) '...he was a very dear friend of mine.'

'And mine,' chimed the brothers simultaneously.

'Robert.' Dan shook his head slowly, allowing the full weight of the deceased man's name to bear down on the occasion. 'Robert, Robert.'

The woman glanced at Martin and Joe, expecting them to add their own words of wisdom. None there came. 'Do you mean Bob?' she asked finally.

Daniel O'Rourke had been in tricky situations before. 'Mrs Brady, we regarded your husband with the utmost respect. To us, he was always Robert.'

This seemed to satisfy the woman who then, not failing to notice the three men were peering past her into her house, felt obliged to invite them in.

The three had hoped for a large wake, and judging by the elegiac notice in the paper ('Robert was renowned locally as a gentle giant'), they frankly expected it. However, counting them, the widow, two neighbours, and the corpse (upstairs), there were only seven there in total.

'We early?' asked Martin before Dan could stop him.

'I 'spect there'll be others later. Where'd you know Bobby from?'

'From work,' all three chorused at once. They had practised.

'Oh, you don't look old enough. Bobby left the brickworks fifteen years ago.' The woman looked especially at Martin. Martin—who had come close to catastrophe with his earlier comments—said nothing, just smiled.

Mrs Brady put the oddness of the three men behind her, deciding instead to be grateful for the numbers they added. She had wanted to send her husband off respectably without embarrassing him or herself, and to that end, had paid for a more creative death notice. She had bought in lots of food because that's what Bobby had liked most in the world, and she had, that day, received a crate of beer from her husband's former colleagues, but had so far failed to persuade either of her neighbours to drink it. She could tell (for she was not entirely naive) that she would not have the same problem with these recent arrivals. She led Dan by the hand to her pantry at the back of her house, and invited him to help himself to a bottle. 'And one each for your friends,' she added.

Back in the living room, Dan had modified their alibi. They didn't work in the brickworks themselves (having heard where the beer had originated from, Dan half expected a hod-full of brickdusted labourers to appear at the door). They supplied wooden prop supports from their sawmill in Dungannon. The fact that this was very nearly the truth made the crime they were planning seem less heinous.

'Oh, Jeez, where's my manners!' Mrs Brady shot out of her seat. 'You'll be wanting to pay your respects...*directly*, won't you?'

Dan was the first to understand the woman, then Joe, and then Martin the last.

'I'm not sure it would be what he wanted,' said Dan.

'I can be a bit funny around the dead,' said Joe, tapping his heart.

'I don't think he would recognise me,' said Martin. The widow took this last to be a joke, in bad taste as it was a wake, but a joke nonetheless and therefore something to ignore.

'Why would he not want it, a last visit from friends as powerful as you?' Dan looked at the widow, and knew it was her wish, and not necessarily her husband's, that they had to respect.

'Right, lads,' said Dan, mustering his men. 'Upstairs, am I right?' The widow nodded.

The three men ascended the unlit stairs and entered the room with the open door. The coffin, gleaming wood and creamy silk, occupied the space at the foot of the bed where a linen box might normally be. Its lid was propped behind the door, obscuring a mirror.

'I *am* funny around dead people, Dan,' said Jack's Joe. 'I wasn't lying, especially with drink on me.' He swooned backwards against

FINDING DAN

the door, upsetting the balance of the coffin lid. It slowly inexorably slid to the floor with a crash that could awaken the dead.

'For fuck's sake, Joe!' whispered Dan as ferociously as he could.

'Are you all right up there, boys?' called Mrs Brady, the saintliest woman in Christendom.

'We are. Yes, we are!' Dan called back, adding, unnecessarily, 'We won't be long!'

Martin was looking at the corpse. From toe to chest, it was swaddled in ivory satin. Above that, it wore a black suit and tie and a winged collar, just like the undertaker who would have dressed and put him there. Its face was hard and yellow. Martin Quinn queered his view to look again. 'Funny,' he concluded. 'I'd never have recognised him if I didn't already know.'

'If there wasn't already one dead body in this room, I swear I'd be making sure there was by the time we left here.' Dan pulled both his companions upright, so they were all three standing in a row along the length of the coffin. 'Now, pay your respects!'

Back in the motorcar (Martin at the wheel, Dan beside him on the passenger seat, Joe hugging a crate of Bass in the back), the three mourners considered the ethics of their current situation. Once they had satisfied themselves that they would make a better use of the beer in Creenagh; that, in fact, Winnie's twenty-first birthday party could be a more fitting send-off for the gentle giant than his own wake; that if they were going to steal beer, it was best to steal it from a widow with separate side access to her back yard; once they had talked it through, and Dan was already dozing in his seat, they made their way again to Creenagh.

Light had mostly slid from the sky by the time Martin skidded his dad's vehicle to a halt in the O'Rourkes' yard. Dan woke, responding to the screech, as well as to an instinct of being home. Winnie and Kathleen and Bassie, his dad and Patsy and some other guy, all came out to see him, as if *he* were the party they were waiting for and they could start now. Kathleen gave him a kiss then carried the beer crate away from Jack's Joe (who was still apparently stuck on the back seat of the motorcar). She tore the dedication, 'from Bobby's friends at Tyrone Brick', off the side of the crate and disposed of it. Winnie and Bassie (or was it Bassie and Winnie? They looked so alike today) took a hand each and led Dan to a table near the fence with a white cloth draped over it, and they made him sit there. A sister poured him a drink, others gathered around the table, and someone took a photograph.

'No,' cried Dan. 'We should wait for Molly.'

'It'll be too dark if we wait any longer. We'll send her the picture, Dan. How's that?' someone said.

Dan recognised his mistake, but thought it the sort of mistake anyone could make. He raised his glass and more whiskey—it was whiskey—went into it. He missed Molly for sure, but he was still lucky to have his family and his friends—yes, he had friends. Jack's Joe was always around when he needed him, and it was good of Martin to do all that driving, and he always had someone he knew when he was in the pubs in Coalisland who wanted his opinion on something or other. He had been abrupt with Bassie's lads that time earlier. Sure they meant well and had been respectful in their way, though they had laughed and kept the joke to themselves, which wasn't on. Winnie was the life and soul, Kathleen was an open book (they all agreed), and Patsy was a dark horse, he was always up to something. The evening was wearing on, and where was Kathleen with the beer? The old man was making a speech to his hat, something about Patsy being the best of the O'Rourkes, and the hat responded by jumping off his da's knee and lodging itself on a boulder, head-shaped. Dan laughed at the sight of it, a great big belly laugh, which amused him long after he noticed he was alone.

Joe

After the picture was taken, Joe carried Molly's camera back into the house and buried it safely in the hole in the cavity behind his bedhead. Joe regarded the camera as a sacred thing, and film he knew to be as precious as blood. He had allowed only the one photograph. Everyone who mattered to him—and Jack's Joe, who

FINDING DAN

did not—he had ensured was in the frame. He had lost Margaret last year, and already he had lived too long without her. He no longer touched anything alive. Before Margaret had gone, even in the long months when she was dying in bed, he lay in the bed with her, touching the last of her life, holding on to it for her. In the old days, in the mornings, he could run his fingers over the grain of her belly and hips; and down at the sawmill, he could handle a length of timber and feel it was alive. Now, the wood was lifeless. It was wood—it was wooden—the moment it was cut from the tree. He felt this way himself. He'd been felled. 'If you cut your finger, Joe', Jack Quinn used to say, 'there'd be sawdust instead of blood.' Jack meant his neighbour was a skilled tradesman, but now, Joe knew it literally to be true. He was dry on the inside.

Joe's great fear was that he could not die; that, though all joy had left him, he would endure like an old table. Patsy had told him, as a matter of fact, that his mind was going. He knew one end of a saw from the other, he always would, but he had lost the faces and names of his customers. Patsy was stronger than him, Dan was more skilled than him, Kathleen had more acumen for business than him. Of the three, Patsy had more of what Joe used to have.

Joe had originally thought it would be a good idea to have a photograph taken. With his wife gone now, it mattered that something like a picture should hold on to what he had left. Joe stared out through the kitchen window, and though he looked upon the people around the table, still arranged as they had been for the camera, he could only see the people who were not there. First, Margaret she would have taken the seat that Winnie had now, her glass would have been filled first, and she would have been the one to announce the toast, her lips pressed hard against a shortness of breath. Molly. Where was Molly? It seemed only yesterday she was here, bunching flowers in a long lost vase, brightening the day. Betty was missing too, but Betty was beautiful and married and therefore excused. Jim was the one who had no right not to be there. Jim, his second son, but no son, really, since he stole Dan's passage to America. Margaret could forgive that, but not Joe. Joe peered hard through the crooked glass, the figures shrinking to nothing, and stretching to the sky; and on the table was a white pall and a tiny box, and the old man wiped a tear away for the infant son who had died.

Joe removed his hat and dabbed at a brim of sweat. He was shaking. He poured a cup of water from the pitcher to steady himself, and it shook too. He had never felt as absent from the people here present as he did now. If he were not there, they would just count him amongst the others and raise a glass anyway. Three daughters, two sons, and a neighbour sat and stood around a folding table in one rubble-strewn corner of the yard: you could almost miss that they were there, they took up so little of the land that he had claimed at Creenagh. Joe tried mentally to allot each of them their share. Winnie was happiest when she was away in her shop in Coalisland. Patsy would convert an outhouse to an office, and run the sawmill like a business until there was none of it left. Kathleen would wait till his back was turned, then marry the carpenter's son, and settle into the house. As for Bassie and Dan, she was a gypsy and so was he. Dan had never stopped running away and was hardly fit to live in a house. Joe stood at the kitchen window, and saw how little he had left. Joe now knew it was a mistake to have the photograph taken, for it captured him alive, and he no longer wanted to live. He drank again from the cup, but the water passed his lips and tongue without wetting them. He would make a will, declare it now, tell them all what he intended to bequeath them: the shop, the house, the land, and the mill. The girls would find husbands, and they'd be taken care of, though God help the husbands. But if Joe were not there to give them away at their weddings, he would like to give something away to them as he died. Winnie would stay with the shop; she had a way with the customers in there, and she could make a fair go of it. Kathleen deserved a share of the money he had made from the mill, given as how she had helped keep it together over recent months. The house would be home to Dan and Bassie and Patsy for as long as they needed it, and Joe could not imagine Bassie or Dan ever needing a home provided.

FINDING DAN

Patsy would take over the sawmill. He had his own ideas. He was already diversifying (Joe had noticed.) Yes, he'd tell them now. He would walk back out into the yard and make them all listen to him. He would have to get Dan to shut up first, of course. That could be tricky because when Dan had drink in him, he got the devil in him too. There was the possibility of contention also. Dan and Bassie, and even Kathleen, might well object to it. Winnie and Patsy were, after all, the youngest, so why should the will favour them? Having posed their question in his own head, Joe struggled to remember why, only moments earlier, he had come up with this plan. 'There he goes again, speaking of death.' He had heard one of them say this before. It was only natural he should speak of death. He was acquainted with death. Death had paid his home a visit only last year. Death, he hoped, would come back sooner rather than later, and he intended to be ready for it. Why tonight though, Dad? Why on Winnie's birthday? He admitted some shame at this. Winnie, so full of life and on her twenty-first birthday, wouldn't thank him for this late (or would it be early?) extra gift. But he could not see how he would get them all, or as many of them as this, together again unless it was a similar, equally unsuitable occasion. Yes, he would stride out into the yard, clear his throat, and tell them. Stride, or strut. The business of putting one foot out confidently after the other, coordinating his pistons and levers, securing his ground, this took a courage he knew he had lost. He walked small now. Each pace was a concentrated, deliberate operation with success not guaranteed. If people looked at him when he walked now, it was for fear he might fall. It was the same when he spoke. He caught himself listening out for his own blunders, counting them, adding them to his running tally of decrepitude. When Kathleen listened to him, she nodded off each properly placed word, congratulated him for each well executed sentence.

He would not shuffle out into the yard to tell them that he wanted to die. They would think he had misspoken.

15 August 1998

Laming

<u>Molly</u>

Down through the centuries, the O'Rourkes suffered at the hands of the English. Their beautiful daughters were torn from their breasts and sold as slaves to the [?]. Their handsome sons shot like dogs. O, God, how they suffered, yet weren't defeated. Joseph O'Rourke, in the twentieth century, suffered. His eldest son, Dan, at the age of nineteen, had a gun placed in his pocket and arrested for carrying arms against the king of England, and given three years hard labour in Derry Prison. He was beaten by yellow brutes, the skin and flesh torn from his back. A man in for murder washed and cleaned his sores, and held him in his arms, while he cried for his beautiful mother. The man's name was Dominick Murphy[?]. He was a Catholic and killed a Catholic: he got three weeks.

Dominic washed Dan's cell, but they refused to let him dry it. They threw Dan on the wet cement floor, naked in midst of winter.

When Dan's time was up, they opened the door and threw him on the street. A truck driver, passing, picked him up and brought him home. No one knew him. Just twenty-one, [the] left side of his head turned grey, he dragged his left leg. He never mentioned what happened to him.

FINDING DAN

Time wore on. His beautiful mother's health failed, and she lived with too much trouble. She died in [the] year 1929, at the age of fifty-two, a casualty of war. She was laid to rest in the graveyard of Edendork by Joseph O'Rourke, who loved her more than life itself.

His trouble was far from over. A few months after his wife's death, his mills were burned to the ground, not by a 'B man', but a Catholic paid by the same man who arrested his son. At two o' clock in the morning, he said to his daughter, Molly, 'One heartache your poor mother was spared.' He never once felt sorry for himself.

That morning, he was off to Belfast to get orders for his timbermen. He kept things going, although his business suffered. [?] Protestants couldn't continue to deal with him.

Mrs O'Rourke's eldest daughter, Molly, cared for her in her illness and death. She listened to her sobbing for her handsome son, Dan, although she didn't know his agony. She left behind three young children, Patsy, Winnie, and Kathleen. Molly took care of them to help her poor father. She got them confirmed, and sent them out neat and tidy to school. But she saw them growing up, and herself growing older. She married a man, John Fox, who was home from America, and returned to America. She sailed Dec. 31 1932, 4 ½ months pregnant. A bit of a wild trip, but she made it. [Scored out: That 4 ½ month pregnancy is now visiting Ireland and a highly respected businessman.] She is very proud of him, with a distinguished naval career.

There were many O'Rourkes. One comes to mind. Owen O'Rourke lived in a fine house with his wife and four children. A fine horseman, the English put them on the street, and put a Scotch family in their house, name of 'Whiteside'. Owen O'Rourke tried to get his favourite horse out in the middle of the night, but was caught, tried for horse stealing, a rope placed around his neck, and hanged on a tree at his front door. That tree's never turned green, [it] always stayed red. His wife and children perished in the cold. They were found, their mouths green where they tried to eat grass. May the English rot in hell.

MARK QUINN

Times were bad. The Black and Tans raided our house every night, stole everything they got their dirty hands on. The Catholics had no say.

In the sixteenth century, an O'Rourke, name of William, built a house from mud and straw with his own hands. Called the Breifne in the townland of Creenagh.

Since that day, till today, an O'Rourke has lived in that house. The Name Breifne is from a king called Turlough O'Rourke from Leitrim, his ancestor. Today, the house is occupied by Patrick O'Rourke and wife and family of nine.

Patrick's father was called Joseph O'Rourke, the best man God ever made. He married Margaret McGrady in 1898, and they had eight children. A grandson called John Fox is presently visiting Ireland, and is the toast of the town. His mother was called Molly O'Rourke (an Irish beauty and very modest), still living at the age of ninety-two, and will beat her son up if he doesn't visit Creenagh.

The Breifne house windows were slits, so the yellow dogs English couldn't slither in and murder them in their sleep. That was the time of the long nights and Bloody Blankets. Seventeenth century times were very bad. A Catholic going to Mass or receiving Communion, was slaughtered on the spot.

Father Freeland [?], a friend of O'Rourke, said mass in the old house Breifne once a week. The Communion was made in the fireplace. He walked the roads dressed like a tramp. People came as far as ten miles with bags tied on their feet for shoes. Their fierce belief in their God and religion enabled them to stand up to the yellow English. The English tried, in every way, to get rid of them, but failed. They were burned out, and then starved to death in the eighteenth century. The O'Rourkes had flocks of goats and sheep, and made the English believe that they were diseased. That left them with plenty of food to feed the starving flocks. Everyone was given a bucket of soup and meat that kept them alive, along with plenty of oatmeal bread.

Getting back to Dan. England wasn't finished with him. They couldn't destroy his young body, but they could his character. He was accused of fathering a child of a young Protestant girl. He did not

FINDING DAN

deny it. He did not want anyone to know that the brutes in Derry Prison performed a vasectomy on him. He hadn't reached the age of twenty. He vowed me to secrecy, he was so ashamed, he thought he was like an animal in the fields. It almost killed my father, but I could not ease his pain. Dan would never forgive me. I can tell it now. Dan died at the age of 60 years, a broken man. May he rest in peace.

ooOOoo

Armagh

When they packed the car that morning, it was for a journey to Omagh. Several of the letters demanding that Dan be interned were written by the police there. However, calls to the RUC that morning revealed that they held no records open to the public. Ann suggested they continue their efforts at the Irish Studies centre in Armagh, a city she knew well.

The centre held a peculiar mix of unpublished manuscripts, doctoral theses, and miles of microfiche scans of old newspapers. Ann trawled the papers, looking for reports on Dan's playing days. She expected to find him in references to the Fianna, the Coalisland team. Instead, she found him listed in line-ups for their Dungannon rivals, the Clarkes. Winnie and McConaghy had suggested as much: Dan would play for any side at any sport.

Ann, then, moved to reels of old *Irish News* issues hoping to find a report on Dan's arrest. There was none. His internment and his eventual release also went unreported. The Centre did have a small collection of sources relating to the period of internment in the 1920s, and here she found dated manifests of inmates on the *Argenta* and lists of internees transferred there.

'I can't find Dan,' Ann announced after rechecking more than once. 'If we knew exactly when he was there, it would be easier perhaps to find him. Or if they had a list of every single internee. I suppose on the days I have here, he must still have been in the workhouse in Larne. On the transfer lists, they have prisoners moving between Larne and the ship pretty frequently. Dan could have been moved to the *Argenta*, and back to the workhouse without a record of it surviving, or even a record of it being made at all.'

'That can't be right,' Mal insisted. 'They would have accounted for every man they despatched and every one that arrived. Our problem now is that the records did not all survive, or if they did, we just haven't found them yet.'

'Here's something!' Ann called from one of the hooded cubicles scrolling through microfiche slides. She read aloud, 'The *Tyrone Courier*, 8 November 1967. Internee Dies. The death took place on Thursday, of Mr Daniel O'Rourke of Greenagh, Coalisland, a member of the Old IRA. He was sixty-six. Mr O'Rourke was interned on the Belfast Prison ship, *Argenta*, and in Derry Prison until his release in 1923. In his early days, he was a noted Tyrone County footballer. He is survived by two brothers and four sisters.'

This tribute, if only in the local paper, proved to them that Dan was highly regarded, that his passing was deemed noteworthy. And this was so, not just because he was a local man, or even that he was a renowned footballer, but because he had been an internee on the *Argenta*, had been imprisoned in Derry, had been in the IRA. Four decades had elapsed, and nothing the man had done since compared to that experience. A tribute in a paper, only a few lines long, still tried to convey the meaning of the man; and for the *Courier*, Dan was entirely the man he had been in his twenties.

'Sixty-six?' said Ann finally. 'That's not right, is it? And they have his release date wrong too. I have been spending this time looking for him on the *Argenta* in 1924 because Frank found at the Public Records Office that he was released just before Christmas that year. But it says here he was let out in 1923.'

'That's not so hard to believe,' Mal reasoned. 'It had happened forty plus years ago by the time he died. The person who wrote that report probably wrote most of the rest of the paper that week. Proceedings in the courts, beauty contests, road accidents, the lot. The ads too, I wouldn't be surprised. What interests me is who gave him the information? Who told him Dan was sixty-six and that he

FINDING DAN

was in Derry and on the ship until 1923? "He is survived by two brothers and four sisters".' Mal read again. 'Jim, Patsy, Molly, Bassie, Winnie, and Granny. It must have been one of them. There's no reason why they should remember exactly when he was released, but we might expect them to know how old he was.'

Ann had a possible answer. 'Jim and Molly were the two nearest him in age. In 1967, they were both living in the States, so they won't be the ones who spoke to the reporter. The younger ones, Patsy or whoever, may just not have known precisely how old Dan was. That's not unusual.'

'No,' said Mal. 'But it is a reminder of just how unreliable all of our sources are, whether they are the people we have spoken to or the records that got written down. Molly's memoir, if it ever arrives, will be no better. Actually, Ann, I wouldn't mind if she never sent it. I remember something Phelim said to me about how Molly's politics had become more radical the longer she lived away from home. She's an old woman by now, and I doubt the story is still straight in her own head.'

While Ann found and copied old Ordnance Survey maps of Dungannon and Coalisland, Mal looked further into conditions on the *Argenta*. They held a manuscript, a thesis submitted just that year, by Feargal O'Donnell, *A Holding Pen for Innocent Men: the Prison Ship Argenta*. McConaghy, in particular, had made a point of saying Dan had been on hunger strike, that it had gone on for sixty plus days, and that the congregation at Edendork had even been asked to pray for the happy repose of his soul. Winnie had claimed that Dan had to be instructed to come off the strike by Eamon de Valera himself. Mal made careful notes on what O'Donnell had to say. The hunger strike had begun on 25 October 1923 with 135 internees on the *Argenta* and twelve in Derry Prison. Within days, the strike had spread to Belfast Prison and Larne Workhouse. By 12 November, the strike had been abandoned. It had lasted a total of nineteen days, and O'Donnell at least made no mention of a letter from de Valera. Mal flicked back a few pages in the notes his father had taken. Dan was admitted to the workhouse in Larne during the week ending 27 October 1923, having been interned before his planned release from Derry Prison. According to O'Donnell, eighty-nine internees in Larne went on hunger strike in that same week. The majority were transferred to prisons in Derry or Belfast. Dan's file at PRONI did not say anything about further transfers, and Mal wondered how likely it was that he would have refused food the instant he arrived in Larne. On the other hand, Winnie had told Frank and Mal that when in Derry Gaol, he had objected to the prison uniform and refused to wear it; the same man could have made a similar protest in Larne, particularly as this time, it was an orchestrated campaign.

The Centre held another publication, *Internment*, by John McGuffin, written in 1973. And a search of the *Irish News* for the month of the strike offered up a series of articles in their *Searchlight* column all penned under the pseudonym of 'Slemish'. Although Dan was not mentioned in any of these, together, these sources confirmed much of what they had been told about his time interned on the prison ship. The inmates were caged below decks and above, medical supervision was cursory, the diet meagre, escape attempts few and unsuccessful. However brutal the conditions, the inmates there preferred it to the other camps, somehow enjoying their status. Cahir Healy was elected to parliament from there. It was the place to be. That was where the story was.

On the way back to Coalisland in Ann's car, Mal put the radio on to listen to the news.

ooOOOoo

Frank

Molly's letter, with the pages of her memoir, lay strewn across the bed.

'Not much of a memoir, really,' Eilis concluded.

Frank agreed: not really. There was the Breifne stuff, and there was the story about the flooded cell in Derry. Frank was sure she

FINDING DAN

had mistaken some of the dates. So not really much of a memoir. Bram had been justified in destroying it. Only he hadn't. Not quite. Dan was accused of fathering a young Protestant girl. That much Frank had already guessed. That would be Johnny Early's wife, as told to the world in a pub in Coalisland. Only here, Molly was saying it did not happen, it could not have happened. Because Dan's big secret was that he had had a vasectomy done to him in Derry prison. That would be why he had never married then. Frank felt a rush of something for Dan more than sympathy. He felt a deep, deep pity.

And yet, Frank could not be sure that Molly was right. She had also written that this had happened before Dan reached twenty, whereas Frank already knew that Dan was sent to prison in April 1922 when he was at least 21 years old. Frank realised he had a way of proving Molly wrong on this: he knew Damian Early, the man supposed to be Dan's grandson. He would, reluctantly, make another visit to Belfast.

At the General Records Office, in the birth index, Frank found a 'Damian Patrick Early', born 14 September 1942 in Derry, Coalisland. His father was listed as John Francis Early (a fitter); his mother was Catherine Early. So this Catherine was meant to be Dan's daughter, thought Frank. He remembered her and remembered thinking she was a Protestant. 'Catherine' did not especially suggest she was from the other side; it was his own mother's name after all.

'Are you done then?' said the GRONI man. He was tall, a bit stooped, his skin the colour of the pages in the ledgers. His name badge had him filed under 'John'.

'How could I find this woman's father if I wanted to?' asked Frank. He pointed to her name in the index.

'Look for her in Marriages,' suggested John, already reaching for another index. 'It gives, you know, father of the bride, that sort of thing. Was this one . . . Damian . . . was he the eldest, do you think? It might indicate a year for the wedding.'

'1942,' said Frank, dejected somewhat by the GRONI man's enthusiasm.

'1942. Let's try 1941. Here we are!' John slammed a ledger on the desk. 'Do you want to look, or would you like my help?'

The question was redundant. Before long, John had found a wedding on 14 May 1941 at St Patrick's Roman Catholic Church in Dungannon. It was of John Francis Early, aged 23 years and four months (a labourer in Brackaville); and Kathleen Dynan, aged 25 years and ten months (a factory worker). The groom's father was Martin Early. The bride's father was a Mr Daniel Dynan. Emphatically, not Daniel O'Rourke.

'Was that the man you were after?' asked John.

'You might say that,' said Frank. 'Is it possible that where it says 'father' there, a different man could actually be the father?'

'Oh, yes! We have a lot of people come in here and discover that type of thing.' John rubbed his hands and licked his lips at the same time.

'So if one man had actually fathered Catherine—or Kathleen—and another had reared her, the other, the second, might have himself down as the father of the bride?'

'That's right,' said John. 'Especially if he were the one that showed up at the wedding. Only right, even if it wasn't right, so to speak. So what you want is this girl's, Catherine's, birth register.'

'Can we do that?'

'Easy as.'

'No, but is it *allowed*?' To Frank, going back this far felt like prying. John just cast his arms over the shelves and shelves of registers, as if they spoke for themselves.

'So,' said Frank, steeling himself. 'We know how old she was in 1941. We need 1915.' Leaving John sat where he was, Frank fetched the relevant index and brought it back to the table. 'Right, I'm looking for July. . .Catherine, Catherine, Kathleen . . . here she is! Why does she keep changing her name like that? Common, I suppose. Right, born Kathleen Margaret Dynan in Derry, Coalisland on 19 July 1915. Well, that rules Dan out for a start. He

FINDING DAN

would have had to have been no more than fourteen himself when the deed was done, and I don't reckon on that.'

'Sorry. Who's that?' John was beginning to feel professionally excluded.

'Dan, another Daniel, never mind. So her father. . .yes, it's still Daniel Dynan, still a labourer. The mother, right, this is interesting. This is the one Dan is meant to have done the dirty with. Mary Dynan née Jackson.' Frank sat back in his chair in sudden need of a rest.

'I take it we're done then?' asked John.

'Yes, John, I think we are,' replied Frank. He was contented. He had disproved the Early connection. Case closed.

But not so fast, said the attorney in Frank's head. If Dan O'Rourke had nothing at all to do with Catherine Dynan, why had her husband, in a Coalisland pub, insisted he had? And if Catherine was born eight years before Dan went to gaol, why was Molly claiming a prison vasectomy as his main defence? It dawned on Frank that the castration story might still be true. His research had no bearing on that. Indeed, Molly might have been denying an entirely different paternity case. He had followed the Early lead because that was the only name they had, given them by the woman's own husband. Well, Johnny Early was wrong, conclusively wrong. He should learn to shut up.

It occurred to Frank that that might be good advice for himself to follow. He had been wondering how to tell Mal about the memoir. He had thought that his visit to the registry would prove that Dan had not been brutalised in prison. Now, he worried that Mal would want to hunt down this trail, attracted by the scandal. Mal had always been a teller of tales from the youngest age.

So Frank's mind was made up. He would simply tell Mal that the memoir had not arrived. He could (truthfully) report also that Dan was not the father of Catherine Dynan. No other word on the matter was necessary.

Perhaps, old newspapers would confirm at least one story from Dan's life, that he had taken part in the *Argenta* hunger strike.

MARK QUINN

On tall John's advice, Frank decided to make for the newspaper archive at the Central Library. He walked. He pushed his way through the shoppers on Donegall Place, piling in and out of Marks & Sparks. Even for Belfast, there were a lot of police about and army helicopters buzzing overhead. He looked for Anderson and McAuley's, as his landmark for Royal Avenue. But though he found a grand Victorian building, he seemed to have lost the department store. Nothing stayed the same even in Belfast, and that could confuse a man who preferred not to keep up with modern trends. Up ahead was a similar red sandstone edifice. Frank crossed to it and found he was on Royal Avenue already, outside the Central Library. An enquiry at the door sent him round the corner to what looked like a post office collection point, but was in fact the Newspaper Library he had been searching for.

To Frank, a library ought to be dim and serene with angled lights poised over readers' desks, concentrated and studied. Instead, he walked into a cube, lit yellow with a uniformed commissionaire surrounded by a counter in the centre. One other person was there, a woman reading an ancient *Belfast Telegraph* at a sloping desk.

'What can I do for you, sir?' asked the library attendant. He was in charge despite the 'sir'. He was standing now with his hands pressed down at angles on the counter in front: like a semaphore *N*, Frank thought.

'I really don't know,' admitted Frank. The *N* meant 'no way', 'not here'.

'Well, I'll need a bit more than that to go on. Are we talking 'old' here, or more recent?'

There was nothing all that hostile about the commissionaire, but Frank was suddenly self-conscious about the nature of his enquiry, and convinced himself that the man was a Protestant. No Catholic would wear a uniform like that—the uniform itself and the way he was wearing it. Frank stood firm and took his hands out of his pockets.

'1920s,' he said.

FINDING DAN

'Civil War or post?' The librarian was playing a game of twenty questions.

Frank was caught out by this. He ought to know his history better than he did. 'We're talking 1923, October–November. There was a hunger strike about then.'

'Indeed there was!' The man clapped his hands, pleased he was getting somewhere. 'So I imagine we are looking at the Republican press here, yes? Have a wee seat there, and I'll have a wee look.' He nodded at a lone plastic chair in the corner, and went to work at the computer keyboard on his counter.

Frank sat on the orange chair. The woman reading the *Belfast Telegraph* raised her head to him, and he raised his to her like truck drivers do when passing each other on the road. She showed only professional disinterest when the commissionaire spoke again.

'Right, okay, fine. This could be your boy. There was a publication named *Eire: the Irish Nation*, which covered your period. It's under 'Republican and Radical press, post-Civil War'. Catalogue number 13. We have it on microfilm.' With Frank's approval, he repeated this into an intercom, looking at the blackened reinforced glass panels of the double doors behind him. Then he smiled at Frank, as he would at an expectant father.

Minutes passed without the film arriving.

'You not found it yet, Sammy?' said the attendant down the intercom. 'Hold on there, I'm coming in.' He signalled more semaphore to Frank and the *Belfast Tele* lady—*stay where you are, don't move*—and disappeared through the double doors. Now there were just two of them, they had to decide who was in charge in case anything should happen like, say, someone else walking in. Frank would have happily ceded to the lady, the senior on account of her prior arrival, but she chose that moment to step outside with her packet of cigarettes. She had left her papers open on the desk. Frank could not resist a look at his fellow historian's notes. They concerned a terrible case, like Frank's also from the early 1920s. A Mr Seamus Hegarty from Limerick had brutally assaulted his landlady, for which he was sent to prison in England. He was befriended by a prison chaplain and drew the support of prominent British parliamentarians who campaigned for his removal to an Irish gaol. The parole judge in Southampton, instead released him altogether, and he returned to his wife and child in Limerick. Some time thereafter, Hegarty murdered his wife in full view of his daughter. Frank wondered what would entice a woman to uncover a tale like this. He thought perhaps he should be careful with this one. She came back in, scented in smoke, but not before Frank had retaken his neutral seat.

Frank wanted to talk to someone. Actually, he regretted Mal wasn't there right now because he reckoned they could have had a decent chat even though they were in a library of sorts. This place was something of a find, the type of place that the writer in Mal would have revelled in. Frank almost spoke to the woman. My son is a writer. Perhaps you have read his work? Mainly Irish themes, though he chooses these days to live in London where it's easier to publish. You don't know him? No.

The commissionaire's worried head appeared at the door. 'We can't find Number Thirteen,' he declared. 'The computer says we have it, but it's not in the drawer. You can come in and have a wee look if you like.' Frank sprang to his feet. A glance to his left revealed surprise and envy on the face of the lady reader. He followed his man back through the doors.

He entered a warehouse. The air was conditioned cool, and dustless, the floor was sucked clean. Shelves were caged high with bound copies of old newspapers saved here from extinction. Frank was escorted through to a simple metal drawer cabinet where Sammy stood.

'This *is* the right drawer,' said Sammy without introductions. 'No question. But you see, the reels only go up to twelve.' He wasn't wearing white gloves, but he handled the little white boxes like museum specimens. 'Number thirteen is missing, so that can only mean it's been *misfiled!*'

Sammy exchanged meaningful looks with the commissionaire, and in unison, they announced, '*Nigel!*'

FINDING DAN

Frank understood Nigel was a third colleague, fortunately for him, off today. Without thinking, Frank slid the drawer of the cabinet shut and pulled at the handle of the drawer above. He walked his fingers over the microfilm boxes, counting the numbers in his head until he reached one at the back of the drawer.

'Might this be it?' It was.

Back in the yellow reading room, Willy (the commissionaire was called Willy) fed the film into the reader, and let Frank get on with it like a trusted co-worker. The prison research lady was still there, now with a notebook. Frank wondered if she ever left this place except for the occasional cigarette.

Frank took a while to master the controls. The lightest nudge and *Eire, the Irish Nation* would spool too far forward; tip the dial the other way, and time would flash back again, the words and pictures in too much of a hurry. At length, he reached 10 November 1923 and a headline, 'The Men Who Hunger Strike for the Living Republic'. There were mugshot photographs with captions and lists of names in divisions. Frank took out his notebook to record the men from Coalisland and Dungannon, listed within the ranks of 'Second Northern Division'. He would not let his eye skip forward or scan for his uncle. He wrote the names one at a time like he might honour each in that way. He knew a few, fewer than he thought he might know, fewer than he would have known if he hadn't moved away from Coalisland and settled in Ballymena.

Coalisland: Pat O'Neill, F. McKenna, J. Haughey, P. Hanlon, F. Cory, J. Cullen, Joe O'Neill, Mick O'Neill, Edward Haughey, M Dillon, D O'Neill.

Dungannon: W. J. Kelly, John Mullan, Joe Devlin, P. Hughes, J. Skelton, P. Mallon, Neil McKenna.

Right. That was that, then. No Dan. Somehow, it was as he had expected. The British, in their official papers, didn't have Dan down as a hunger striker; and neither, it now transpired, did the republicans in their newspaper. All these others were and Dan wasn't. There might have been a small space in Frank's mind where he could have tried to contain this information, but he eschewed the effort. It was out there already, all over the show. Too small to bother with, you might think, and before you know it, too big to get your head around. Frank didn't care that Dan had not been on hunger strike. Plenty others hadn't, and it was easy to excuse. But no hunger strike meant there was no letter from de Valera, probably no *Argenta*, no prayers for Dan from the pulpit in Edendork, no basis for the decades of stories told by his mother and every aunt and uncle and Dan himself.

Frank wanted to slam the microfilm reader. He was about to, but stopped himself just short, in the end giving the dial just a mild tap. It barely expunged his frustration. The reel whirred like a roulette wheel slowly coming to rest on an article dated 25 October 1924.

Republican Prisoners in the Six Counties

The headline intrigued him enough, but unlike with the article on the hunger strikers, Frank felt no duty to read it word for word. His eye scanned down the piece for stand out detail. Then with sudden fury, he gripped his pencil and nearly drove it through the pages of his notebook.

> ". . .Larne Workhouse, a place built for the detention of tramps, bleak, unheated, with broken windows and leaking roof, where in wet weather nearly every prisoner falls ill.
> It was in Derry that Dan O'Rourke of Dungannon was lamed for refusing to wear convict clothes. His own clothes were taken from him, and his bed was removed; he was left without covering of any kind for days in the cell. Once a warder poured cold water into the cell, then they kicked him until he was so injured that his left leg became half-paralysed. In December 1923, when his sentence expired, he was interned in Larne and is still a prisoner there.

FINDING DAN

It was in Derry Jail that three of the criminal prisoners, their endurance broken, tried to escape by gassing themselves, and a fourth attempted to cut his throat.'

Frank rested his notebook on his knee and read back the words he had written, checking each against the text on the screen before him. He expected to see the name slip, or some other crucial detail falter, stumble erroneously on to his page. He lined up all the principals to make sure they were present and correct: Dan, O'Rourke, Dungannon, Derry, Larne. There could be no mistake. As sure as Dan was not included on the role of hunger strikers, here he was now being beaten half to death in Derry Jail. It was just as Winnie had said it. Dan had refused to wear the prison garb; he had been stripped, and his cell had been flooded; and then they beat him until he couldn't walk. Frank wanted to celebrate, and only faintly did he feel sorrow for the Dan in the article. This, Frank was sure, *this* was Dan's defining moment. This denuding, this deluging, this *laming*—this was the signature, which stood for everything else Dan had done or was said to have done. This was the story, retold faithfully by Winnie to him and Mal only last week, and again in the memoir sent by Molly, which had drifted into other tales, less true, but no less suggestive of the man he truly was.

And perhaps, to be 'lamed' was the castration, or the 'vasectomy' that Molly had written of. It was a direct punishment for refusing the governor's orders. It was a year and more before any of his family would see him again, by which time his half-paralysis had become a bad limp in his left leg. And some time after that, he would take up the football again, and he would play for a while, as if he never had been assaulted. But all the while, he was not the man he had been when he went in. To Winnie and the others, he was 'a broken man'. But Molly knew it for real, or thought she did.

On the way home to Ballymena, Frank put the radio on to hear the news.

17 August 1998

Patsy

It rained all the way to Creenagh. Frank drove with Eilis beside him, gripping her seat and keeping an eye on him. The rain smacked the windscreen and flew with wings along the length of the car. Frank experimented with alternating blasts of cold and warm air to try to clear the condensation. Eilis helped by wiping the corners of the windows in front of her and to her left with an old chamois leather.

From Ballymena, it is downhill most of the way. Dungannon, Coalisland, Edendork, Creenagh—all lie in the shallow shores of Lough Neagh, none far from the others. When it is hot, the midges scout the area in sorties, spreading the swamp like a disease, hanging the air out to dry. It is not often hot. Even in August, the rain can nip. The cold gets into your socks, grips your calves, and itches your knuckles. They talked about Dan.

'Phelim asked me right at the beginning whether I thought there was less to Dan than meets the eye,' the son began. 'I think, in some ways, he is right.'

'What would Phelim know? He must barely remember him.' Frank snatched the chamois from his wife. 'You don't think he was on the *Argenta*?'

'Did you hear him say he was?'

FINDING DAN

'I never listened to him much at all. I remember he would watch me play Gaelic every week, but shout at me if he saw me kick a soccer ball. He did tell stories of being on the run, but no, I don't recall him talk about prison or anything like that. Others said that. My mother said that. Is that not proof?'

'Yes, it is. It's proof that people *said* he was on the *Argenta*—that they *thought* he was on the *Argenta*. But the fact that lots of people have told us that is only proof that lots of people said and thought it, not that it was so.'

'You haven't found the records?' Frank's tone suggested failure. 'For all your looking, you didn't find it?'

Mal felt defensive. 'We found the records. It's just that Dan wasn't there. He was in Derry, and then in Larne Workhouse, and then he was released. Meanwhile, internees were coming and going from the *Argenta*, but he wasn't among them. Plenty of others from Coalisland and round about were...'

'But not Dan? So maybe there was less to him.' It seemed a conclusion Frank could accept. 'What about the hunger strike? You don't think he was? Didn't Winnie say she saw the letter from de Valera?'

'President O'Ruitleis published an open letter. That's maybe what Winnie had in mind.'

'There are lists of people on hunger strike, but Dan's not there,' said Frank. He revealed to his son what he had found in the newspaper library. 'There were plenty of names I did recognise from Dungannon, Coalisland, every bloody place. But our Dan was not among them. I can't understand how an idea like that can take hold if it's not true.'

Frank glanced at Eilis. Mal thought he reached for her hand, but he was only changing gear. 'Do you know, I remember one incident that I have felt bad about ever since. I was courting your mother, and she was round the house. I had planned a night in with her, but Dan showed up drunk as always. He was for going nowhere. I gave him the change from my pocket and told him to run off and have another on me. Like you would dismiss a child with some sweets.

I was being flash in front of your mother. Of course, he left happy enough, but I always mind that time. We were taught to respect Dan, you know, for what he stood for and what he had done. But what had he done after all, and what sort of principle is it that leads a man to sleeping in a cow-house and drinking his life away?'

'Dad, I think a man who can inspire those stories to be told about him has something about him even if the stories aren't all true.'

'Are you going to tell his story?'

'What would you think, Dad?'

'You don't care what I think!' He must have seen in the mirror the wound this inflicted because he went on. 'I mean, Mal, you'll write what you want to write regardless of what I think.'

'You don't sound as if you would want to read it.'

'It's probably better for you to imagine I won't. Anyway, why would I? I know how it ends!' Dad laughed at his own joke.

'Unless Patsy can tell us different,' Eilis interrupted.

Frank brought the car to a gentle stop in front of a single-storey house. Its walls were faced with white and grey pebbledash. A back door appeared where the front door ought to have been. Patsy and Phyllis were already standing there, as if they had been waiting for them for days. They came rushing up to the doors of the car, young again, and eager to greet them. Patsy was virile, looking like he had just been chopping wood (which he very likely had been). Phyllis loomed large in a print skirt and turquoise T-shirt. There are times when a child gets to spectate as their parents perform. Mal's mother was polite, recoiling only slightly as first the one then the other, encroached on her space.

'You've done the yard nicely, Phyllis. It's cleaner...'

'When would you have been up here last, Eilis?' Phyllis was not making an accusation. 'It's years since we did this!'

'Well, it must be years since I was here last!' Both women seemed happy to have agreed on something already. They hurried in out of the rain.

FINDING DAN

Frank was already in a deeper conversation with his uncle, checking on the whereabouts and wherewithal of his various cousins. Although it seemed that Frank was the one struggling to recall all the names, Mal understood that he was in fact testing Patsy, assessing his soundness.

'So, Patsy, what do you remember about Dan then?' This was Eilis, no mucking about, the moment they were in the house. 'Mal here has been researching into him and has some questions for you.'

Mal had been nervous already. Now, his mother's boldness drained him of his own.

'What do you want to know about Dan for?' Phyllis asked. 'He's dead these years, there can't be many that still remember him anyways.'

'We have met plenty that still do,' Mal tried. He hadn't rehearsed the next, but he reckoned it might make all the difference to the success, or otherwise, of their whole visit. 'I'm not sure "why Dan?" He was the one Dad always talked about. I don't remember Granny at all. There is a photograph of me beside her outside the house where Ann is now. I have this awful bump on my head, and I'm wearing a sky-blue jumpsuit that Mum must have made me. I used to think I recalled the day itself, but now I guess it's just the photo: I've seen it that many times, I've come to recreate the day in my head. I've met you, Patsy. Over the years, I've seen Winnie quite a bit, and Molly has always had some glamour about her, living across the Atlantic and never coming over. I never had the chance to know Dan, but he always seemed an interesting character, and we decided to find out more. We hoped you might help. But, of course, you were twenty years younger, you might hardly have known him yourself?'

'Aye, well. I knew him rightly, though we were not friends as such. Brothers first, and maybe friends some way after.' Mal recalled what Phelim had told him at the beginning of all this. It had been Patsy and his wife who had put Dan in the cowshed—there were things they might want to hide. Mal sensed they would talk to him, but, as Phelim warned, they might tell him more than they wanted to. But Patsy had started. Mal tried to note down as much of what Patsy said as he could. He knew already that if he ever wrote a book on Dan, this would form the last part. Patsy didn't speak alone, Phyllis had plenty to say too, and Frank and Eilis also recalled times they thought they had forgotten. But Mal had decided that this chapter was Patsy's.

Dan was twenty years older than me, but he might as well have been older still, for all I knew or saw of him when I was growing up. Dan was something of a legendary figure even then, you know. His fighting days behind him already, so to speak. I don't recall him talking much about it then, not directly at any rate. Bassie and Kathleen, and Winnie (though she was hardly any older than me), they were the ones always going on, 'Dan this', and 'Dan that'. I couldn't complain about anything, or one or other of them would be reminding me what a hero Dan was. Trouble was he never seemed much of a hero in my eyes. I did see him play once, I guess right at the end of his GAA days, and he was good all right. He came to see me play too, and he was never short of advice. I don't think I ever minded that. Other old guys told me I should listen to my brother, and I reckoned on that score, I could probably learn something from him. Trouble was I was good too, and he never would give me credit for that.

My sisters couldn't have seen much of him either when they were young, if their stories of him on the run are to be trusted. According to them, he might spend weeks at a time in a waterlogged ditch; he couldn't come home, the B Men were after him. Was he not on hunger strike? Are you interested in that now? Dan did forty-seven days on hunger strike, and only come off of it when he got a letter from de Valera. Do you believe that one now? It's Winnie I heard tell that one. He never could feed himself, my sister Kathleen would tell you that, and Phyllis could too. If someone didn't bring him his food and practically feed it into him, I doubt he would have ate at all.

Not that he would ordinarily have taken his orders from de Valera, but I suppose by then, Collins had been assassinated. Dan was a Collins man, as were we all. My oul' da used to talk about the time Collins was here in Creenagh, in this very room, apparently.

FINDING DAN

Hard to credit that one now, is it not? It would have been during one of his recruiting campaigns in the North, for he did do that—that's a fact. Well, Daddy used to say that Collins spent the night here in Creenagh on that there sofa, only not that sofa, but the one that would have been there then. You can believe that one if you want to. What is true, I'm sure of it, is that Dan never took his de Valera pension. Whether he was ever offered it for real, I can't say, but Dan himself was fond of telling all and sundry that he wouldn't take any money from Dev. I'm not sure he would have gotten it anyway, did you not have to have held a position, or whatever, before the Truce? He wasn't a commander or a quartermaster or anything; he was more a free agent, I would say, when he was on the run. He wouldn't have a state pension either, so I can't say how he funded himself. He worked as little as possible, let me tell you. He was happy enough to live off of my da while he was here, and off of us too for as long as he could before . . . well, before we had our own family.

Frank, Eilis, you know Phyllis here was a Protestant. That sort of thing would never have bothered you, you being open-minded in that way, living in Ballymena. Dan, though, could not abide it. 'Patsy, you're a fine fish, and that Phyllis has caught you,' is what he used to say. I was felling in Scotland, and Phyllis followed me out there. We had to come back to get married, and of course, we moved straight back into Creenagh. Bassie and Dan were still living here then, but there was no room for us all, what with the baby being born and another not far away. But there was the cow-house, which hadn't been used for keeping animals for years, probably since Mummy died. We hung a proper locking door on the external doorway, and put in a new door connecting it to the main house with a wee step up and down. We took up carpet from our own bedroom and put it down for him, and Phyllis, herself, found some lovely patterned paper to put on his walls. Daddy's old armchair, he had that, and he made himself up a wee bed frame from some spare timber, and we went out and bought a mattress special to fit it. I reckon Dan was as happy there as he had been anywhere. He called it 'my outside room', and when you think of it, that's exactly what he would have wanted. That's also when we found the Mass goods.

Did you ever hear of those, a gold chalice and goblet and wafer plate? There was an old Irish coin, and I don't recall what else, all hidden in a cavity in the wall like a cubbyhole. They must have been there since Father Phelan used to give his secret masses here in the penal days. Daddy always said the O'Rourkes had been here for centuries, and we had hid the priest here. And there we had it—proof! I don't mind telling you that it had a strange effect on us, finding that treasure. I'm sure Dan felt some connection to that fugitive priest, as he saw himself in the same mould. But he would say, 'You, Patsy, live in the holy house, whereas I live outside it.' He meant it as a complaint, but I don't mind hazarding that he said things like that because he wanted us to think that way about him. It also gave him another stick to beat my Phyllis with: what was she, a Protestant, doing occupying the place? 'Christ, it's practically a chapel!' he said more than once. And he called the cubbyhole a tabernacle, which I suppose it was really. I can't show you any of it now, as we gave it all to Maynooth Seminary. That was on the advice of Father McGarvey. He said we could expect a spiritual return on our donation to the Church, whatever that meant. They have it to this day, or so I hope they do. You should check that one out. There was a lot of old stuff, which we decided to get rid of. Those pewter dishes Mummy used to have on the dresser, they were no loss. Books. Dan used to have a load of old letters and medals. Did you rid those out too, Phyllis? Those might be worth a look at now if we still had them, but there you go. When the other children came, we couldn't keep everything. Dan said, 'Since you have me on the run again, I can't be weighed down by all this stuff. A man my age has no need of baggage.' He said it the way a young man would say it, not an old man, which he was by then. After that, when he moved into his own place on the Ardmore Road, he was never as happy. It was always too big for him.

Did you know he was a drinker? For nine years, Dan didn't drink; then for eleven, he didn't stop. Frank, you'll remember he

FINDING DAN

drank. He could be fair company, but you wouldn't cross him. He'd be telling one of his stories, or singing one of his made-up songs, then you'd realise all of a sudden that he was going on and on and he wouldn't stop. I mind once a reporter from Dublin tracked him down to here, wanted to hear about Dan's old football days. Dan kept him up all the night, talking about God only knows what. I have that piece still somewhere. In the end (it was your idea, Phyllis), we had to take him to St Luke's Asylum in Omagh. I had the notion of leaving him there, but for Dan, he wasn't having it. 'You're not leaving me in another prison,' is what he said. It was a hospital, not a prison! We met a very fine man there, Dr Moriarty I remember his name was. He took a shine to Dan straight away. Said his own father, also Dr Moriarty, had been on the Argenta, and would surely therefore have known Dan. Dan had said, 'Yes, I recall your father. He gave medical to us all when the authorities wouldn't.' Dan had no problems going back to Omagh after that, and enjoyed his little chats with Moriarty. But he kept on with the drinking, though Moriarty did his best. Moriarty would talk about other old-timers, how they had come to a sticky end, and Dan drew comfort from that fact that he was still alive. Moriarty's point was that better men than Dan had been driven to drink, and worse, down the years. At one meeting (I suppose it was the last), he told Dan, 'Either you manage this yourself and probably kill yourself, or you sign yourself into St Luke's. We've tamed lions here,' he said. Dan was having none of it.

That's what did for him in the end. They said it was his heart, as if he worked himself to death, but it was the drink.

'Haven't you seen Dan yet, then? Frank, if you don't mind us tagging along, we could all go down to the graveyard in Edendork. Would you like that, Mal?'

And so they did. Frank parked the car in the roadside with the church perched above among the trees. Patsy led the party into the graveyard, the five of them, their feet grinding the gravel. He could not find the right stone at first, but they kept the group intact rather than split up to look for Dan.

'I've found him, Patsy,' called Phyllis quietly. 'Here he is.'

The five gathered around the plot, two along each side with Patsy at the foot, standing opposite the stone. Eilis pulled up some few weeds and held them in her hand until she could find somewhere to place them. Frank peered through the trees, scanning the horizon, picking out Edendork and the dance hall, Ann's house, Coalisland over to the left, Dungannon unseen in the distant right, a small world left behind. Mal clasped his hands, conscious of his boots sinking in the soft earth. Patsy breathed deep, as if to becalm a breeze. He read the inscriptions aloud like a eulogy:

>'Erected by
>John Oroark of Creenagh
>to the memory of his beloved
>mother Mary Oroark who
>depd this life March the 28th
>1841 aged 77 years. May
>she rest in peace, Amen.'

Below that he read:

>'Margaret O'Rourke. Died 9th Oct. 1937
>Her husband James Joseph O'Rourke
>Died 26th Jan. 1944'

And as a footnote to the main stone, another had been added:

>'Their sons:
>Dan O'Rourke Died 1st Nov. 1968
>Owen Roe O'Rourke Died 1906.'

'Owen Roe was my brother,' continued Patsy. 'He died an infant. Maybe in childbirth, I don't know.' His eyes traced the stone upwards. 'My father lived too long after my mother. He had no interest in living after she was gone.' From the top, 'This John Oroark, I don't know of him. He seems keen for everyone to know

FINDING DAN

he was the one who looked after his old mother when she was gone. Nearly a hundred years—strange, isn't it before Margaret is laid beside Mary. And the others, Bassie, Kathleen, Betty, Jim: not one of them wanted to be buried here. Not a popular site, this one.' Patsy nodded to Phyllis for her to take note. 'Do you know, I must have been here for at least three funerals, but I can't remember one of them. By this, I was seventeen when Mummy died. I never would have said that I was that old. You'd think I'd remember an occasion like that and in a place like this.'

Patsy did not acknowledge that this was because the plot was in a ditch at the foot of the sodden hill. The laces from Mal's shoes sucked water from the ground. The sod here undulated in a still ripple. It was no place to rest in peace. Nor did Patsy or Phyllis point out the plain fact that the gravestone was wrong. Frank had found the register that said that he had died on 2 November 1967, a whole year before the date there. Of all the witnesses to the life of Dan O'Rourke, this, his gravestone, had finally got him wrong. The epitaph was as unreliable as the earth it was stuck in.

'There you are then, Mal,' said Frank. 'There's Dan.'

Finding Dan, Thursday, 2 November 1967

By Malachy Quinn

The woman had already wrapped the cut from last night's joint in brown paper, and put it carefully in her string bag alongside the dozen eggs she was taking to her sister-in-law. She then wrapped herself in her long serge coat and knitted scarf and hat. She said goodbye to the empty house, pulled the kitchen door shut, and walked down the long muddy lane towards the main road where she hoped to catch the bus into Coalisland.

The seats were hard, and inside, the air smelled of fuel. The others on the bus had got on at Dungannon, and had already fallen into a pious gossip that she found hard to break into. Some women were talking of All Souls' Day. They were off to tend the graves of their dead and claim their indulgence. On their laps, they held baskets and garden trowels and tiny bunches of winter flowers. The woman gripped her bag of eggs and meat on her knee, nursing it like a pagan offering.

On Main Street she called in as always to Winnie's fruit and veg shop. She had the meat already, so all she wanted was a handful of potatoes, maybe two carrots, and an onion. There was no point in cooking Dan more than one meal at a time. He was like a goldfish, he would just eat everything put in front of him. On her way out, she spied a leafy big cabbage and decided to have it too. She would cook

FINDING DAN

it tonight for her own family, and have it with the meat gravy she still had and the sausages her husband would bring back later from his rounds. Her mouth watered. Could she hope for some bacon too, would that be expecting too much?

As she stepped outside, a curtain pulled across the sun: there was a total solar eclipse going on on Main Street. She remembered one of her sons talking about it that morning at breakfast. The moon passes between the sun and Earth, and as the diameter of the moon appears slightly larger, it can completely block out the light from the sun. He described the pinhole camera that was safe to use to study the effect of the eclipse. On no account must you look directly at the sun, even in November when its rays were less powerful. The woman walked cautiously up Main Street, head down, anxious to avoid the others who were straining to see what they should not see. The temperature dipped sharply, so she pulled her scarf tighter around her neck. The birds on the canal fell silent. In the entry by Girvin's pub, a horse sighed, ready for sleep. In the pub, lamps were lit against the dark, as dim as night. The woman went in and bought two bottles of stout for Dan. He didn't need them, for sure, but he had been good of late, and there was little point in denying him what others would give him at any rate. By the time she was out again, the moon had moved on, and the living had returned to Main Street.

Thursday was her day for cooking for Dan. As ever, she bought the ingredients in Coalisland, or brought them with her, and cooked his dinner at Kathleen's. On other days, Kathleen cooked or one of the nieces. Together, they made sure Dan was right, and always he took it for granted. But it meant he could stay in his new home, and that was a small price to pay.

She walked through the Quinns' electrical store, and let herself through the door at the back, which led up to the set of rooms that the widow shared with those children of hers who hadn't already grown up. She passed two other doors belonging to two other families before she reached Kathleen's. The door was open, and through it she could see a vase standing empty on the table by the window.

'Kathleen! Hello, it's me!' the woman cried. She entered the kitchen. Kathleen was dumping flowers in the bin.

'Cheap rubbish, no doubt!' declared Kathleen. 'Dan bought them me only this morning, wouldn't you know. Cheapskate! Gone over already. Phelim found them limp in the vase. Of course, I blamed him and sent him back to bed. Poor boy's not well. Still, he should have known better than to bother me with the flowers.'

'Are you sure they're dead, Kathleen?'

'Sure, can't you see for yourself, Phyllis! They are dead. I suppose you can't expect much in November.'

'They're maybe not dead at all, you know. It'll be the eclipse, didn't you see it? The buds will have closed because of the dark, and they'll have drooped a bit. Still, now you've bent them and binned them, it'll be too late. Never mind. Will you take these for me?'

The woman handed the bottles of beer to the other and reached into her string bag for the eggs.

'Ach, you're good! Will you have a wee tea with me? I have one wet.' Every week, Kathleen said the same, so she didn't wait for an answer. The two friends (for they were that too) sat opposite each other at the small kitchen table and shared a pot of tea.

'You say Phelim's not well?'

'No, *he* says he's not well. I think he fancied another day off school after yesterday's Holy Day of Obligation.'

'Maybe he wants to visit his father's grave. Is he good that way?'

'He is. He says he'll go up later. I could have taken those flowers and all if I'd thought. Shaun wouldn't have minded if they were a bit droopy!'

The two women laughed at the blasphemy. They had finished their tea, and a short silence descended between them.

At length, the visitor set about preparing the meal she would take to Dan. She unwrapped the vegetables from the newspaper they had been sold in, and peeled each carrot and each potato, careful not to take too much away. She popped the lot in a pot of boiling water. She melted a generous knob of butter found in Kathleen's fridge, and fried the whole onion with it in a pan. Her cabbage was poking some

FINDING DAN

leaves out of its bag. There's no harm in it, she thought, as she ripped off some cabbage, shredded it, and fried it up with the onion.

'Oh, a feast!' cried Kathleen. 'And beer too. Phyllis, you spoil that man for the rest of us!'

'It'll keep him going, not a lot more,' the woman said, but she knew she was being modest. She then produced the meat with a triumphant flourish. 'What do you think?'

'He'll never eat all that,' declared Kathleen, impressed.

'Do you think not?'

'Here, give it here, and I'll heat it up for him. I have a way.' Kathleen removed the fried cabbage and onion from the hot pan, and slipped the meat in in their place, but off the heat. 'It gives it a flavour and all,' she concluded.

Both women were satisfied by their effort in the kitchen. Kathleen put the meal on a plate with a lid, and swaddled the lot in a tea towel for easier carriage. Whereas before she was unhurried, now the woman set about the rest of her mission with some haste. She wanted Dan to enjoy the warmth of the dinner, especially on a dark day such as this. Once she had sat with him for a while (she would not have to stay long), she would walk back down Ardmore Road and wait for the bus back. Every Thursday was the same. It had become her habit. On warmer days, she didn't mind it so much. She might delay a while in town, pick up some wool, or call in on Winnie. Once she had had her hair done, shampoo and set, but Dan had made such a fuss she was too ashamed ever to do it again. At least he had noticed: that had surprised her! But when the weather turned, the day was never long enough to dwell about, so she would do much as she did today. She expected this to go on every Thursday from now on, though she never conceived of it this way in her own head. When she got home, she would start cooking the dinner for her own family. Tonight, it would be cabbage.

'It's like I'm bearing gifts,' she thought to herself with a smile, as she started up Ardmore Road with the plate and the tea towel held in front. She liked the neat wee gardens in front of these houses, some had flowers, and she noticed how these had recovered from the eclipse. If anything, the sky was brighter now than it had been earlier. She couldn't see them, but she could hear the birds singing again. Maybe she would sit out with Dan this time after he'd had his dinner. He might invite her to share his beer.

She kept his door key in her coat pocket. She balanced the plate in one hand and reached for the key with the other. She turned it in the lock, and let herself in.

'Dan, it's me!' she called.

oooOOOOOOooo

Dan kept his door key in his jacket pocket. In all his life, he had never possessed what people would call a proper coat, and he hardly saw the need for one now. He held the ginger cake he had bought in one hand and pulled out the key with the other. He was out of breath. Whose idea was it to build Ardmore Road on a hill, and put his house on the top of it? Someone's idea of a joke. He turned the key in the lock and let himself in.

He sat down on the armchair in the living room, and immediately regretted not putting the kettle on the ring first. He had overexerted himself a bit perhaps. He had taken his bicycle into town when he should have walked instead—he could build in more rests when walking. But with his leg giving him gyp again, he thought the bike would be better. Not so: that bloody hill was a bugger to get back up. Now he was out of puff.

Kathleen had warned him in as many words earlier. 'You should know better at your age, Dan O'Rourke,' she had said. 'Riding about on a bicycle like one of those teenagers.' Despite the cold, he had arrived at her door short of breath and with a fringe of sweat about his head. Then with a toothless grin, he produced a bunch of flowers for her from behind his back.

'Oh, Dan! Whose grave did you rob these from?' chided his sister, already reaching for the vase she kept on the table in the window.

'Why must you always think the worst of me?' Dan feigned offence. 'Where's that boy of yours? I thought he'd be here.'

FINDING DAN

'Now, why would you have that idea, seeing as Phelim should be at school right now? He says he's not well, but then perhaps you knew that already, Dan?'

'Can't think what you could be thinking of, Kate. No, just tell him if he's feeling up to it later on, that I'll be at home all afternoon, and his old uncle would be glad of his company. I'm off!'

'You not stopping for a cup of tea?' Kathleen called after Dan, but he was gone already.

Dan picked up the bike outside the electrical shop, and freewheeled it down Main Street as far as O'Hara's bakery.

'Hello, Dan. Have you got change today?' Biddy O'Hara was a good businesswoman. Dan ran a tab at the bakery, at two of the town's pubs, and also at the turf accountant's. He prided himself that he could keep his debts in check.

'I think Kathleen will be in shortly after me. She's expecting company.'

'Are you expecting company, Dan?' Biddy was a good businesswoman also because she was a good gossip.

'The very reason I am here!' Dan theatrically licked his fingers and drew them through his hair. 'And I would like to impress. Now, I know the lady in question has a weakness for ginger cake. And I know there are none finer than your own, Mrs O'Hara.' Exaggerated civility always goes down well, he thought.

'You know I shouldn't, Dan. I do have a business to run here.' But Biddy O'Hara was already wrapping the ginger cake in grease proof. 'I'll put it on your tab,' she added forlornly, knowing she would gain nothing from this exchange.

Dan tossed the cake into the basket at the front of his bike. He cycled past Girvin's and the Central Bar, puffing out short breaths like smoke signal warnings. He was expecting Phyllis later, so he wouldn't drink at least until after she had left. He'd rather not upset her, seeing as how she was helping him out. She and Patsy had helped set him up in this house. He didn't really know how, but suspected it had to be through the council. They would have lied to him if he had asked, as they knew he would object on principle.

So he never asked. He couldn't very well say no. It's the only decent thing I ever done for those people, he thought to himself, seated in his armchair. Getting out of their way. He had a sitting room, a bedroom (two bedrooms really, if you included the box room), an indoor bathroom and loo, a kitchen plumbed for gas and electric. He had no need for the half of it. He hadn't the furniture to fill it. It took him an age to get up the stairs to the bathroom. It was so far away. Minutes can take hours in a place this size, he thought. He couldn't remember how long he had lived there. It felt like years.

Phyllis fitted curtains when he first moved in. 'You don't want strangers peering in,' she had said. 'And there will be less echo.' Dan had never experienced indoor echo before now. He was used all his life to walls he could touch; now, he had walls that answered back. Phyllis also brought round linen to fit the bed he now had.

'I'll get lost in a bed this big, Phyllis.' He noticed that she blushed.

'Well, you had better keep your boots on then,' she replied. She knew it was nonsense, but she had to say something.

Dan had laughed at that. It was the sort of rubbish she and Patsy would say to each other and laugh at together. That Phyllis was a good wife to Patsy. Dan knew it. She had her head screwed on about things he hadn't. He was always making grand plans for the sawmill, and she was always wisely setting his plans to one side until he had forgotten about them. She was a good mother too. Maybe Dan could say just that to her? He had been harsh about her, saying things he shouldn't. Maybe he could tell her now he was sorry he had said that? The trouble was he had already been forgiven. Everyone knew he was that way—it was expected of him. That's just Dan! He'll never change! Phyllis wouldn't know what to do with an apology from him. That's a charmed life I have, he thought. Doing what I like, sticking to my guns, apologising to no man. He set down three fingers, as if totting up his life's achievements. He saw a lad out the window, but it wasn't Phelim or someone he knew.

I'll have that tea, he decided. In the kitchen, he filled his kettle and put it on the gas ring. Then he put a tea bag in his teapot. He listened to the gas burning and the water simmering and was

FINDING DAN

calmer. There are still young boys who come up in the bar and look for advice on their technique, and there are old boys yet who remember the glory days of the Fianna. Dan O'Rourke is not a forgotten name by a long way. In his head, Dan handpassed the ball into the box for Stack to score. In his head, a tackle came crunching in on his left leg, putting him out of the game. The ref's whistle blew. In his head, prison warders kicked him to the ground, paralysing his left side. The siren blasted. In his head, he could recall almost nothing of the previous forty years. The kettle whistled and screamed for attention until he took it off the heat and wet his tea. He sat down on the kitchen chair, the only one there. When a man ends up with so little, has it been a life worthy of such respect after all? Maybe he should have moved away when he had the chance. He hadn't always thought he would see his days out here. There was a time, in the years after he was let out of gaol, and he was still playing football, when he could have settled anywhere in Ireland. He had plenty of offers. He travelled far and wide with Old Joe and the timber wagon, and there were those summers he spent in Rostrevor.

Dan was never much of a scenery man. Not for him were long walks in the country and views as far as the eye could see. But he liked the Mourne Mountains; he appreciated those. Kathleen, his sweetheart, sometimes took him up there. She would point out the long stretch of Carlingford Lough and the wee villages that were strung along it: Warrenpoint, Rostrevor, Greencastle, with the Irish Sea beyond. He never went up there alone, and it had occurred to him that he could only properly cope with a prospect as huge as that if he had Kathleen with him. And Kathleen could not be with him; he could not be with her. He let his tea go cold and drank it black.

He must have drunk it too quickly because it set his heart racing again. A noise at the front of the house drew him back into his living room. He moved carefully, holding the walls for support. He could see a group of girls through his window. Even in this weather, they were wearing miniskirts and laughing like there was no tomorrow. They lingered by his gate, so Dan suspected they were laughing at him. What had they been told? An old man living on his own needn't imply anything at all other than what it was. Dan still had it in him to show them a piece of his mind. He was at his window now, peering past Phyllis' net curtains. What father in his right mind would let a daughter out looking like that—legs all the way up to their arses and not so much as a coat between them! They were giggling still, but not apparently at him. There were two boys the other side of the street. They had skinny suits and floppy hair, so you couldn't see their eyes. They were probably up to no good, but Dan decided to give them the benefit of the doubt. Dan checked again to make sure Phelim was not amongst them. He'd better'd not be. He would think twice about giving Phelim that old Irish coin he had set aside for him. Satisfied, he turned away from his window, but too quickly. He felt a sharp pain in his bad knee and in his chest at the same time. You can limp with a gammy leg, but you've just got to hold on when the pain is in your chest. Dan rested his hand on the mantelpiece to steady himself, knocking something to the floor. He dropped into his armchair, not bothering to moderate his fall.

'Bloody birthday card!' he said out loud, the words bouncing back off the wall with spite. 'Sorry,' he spoke again, quieter this time. He had bought the card himself, and written out the message, *For my Darling little Sister*, and even had the stamp for it. But he had suddenly doubted it would reach New York by 1 October, and he lost the will to send it. Will or courage. He had resolved to keep it until next year, but now that he saw it lying on his living room floor, he loathed it and loathed himself for not sending it anyway. What a stupid, hateful, pathetic man you are, Dan O'Rourke! And a coward, don't forget that! There is Molly, out in the big world from no age at all, and there's me. It was only a frigging card. She might have appreciated it coming from him. She loved and respected him still despite all his faults, and despite all she knew. Of course, she had invited him out to stay with her in Yonkers even recently. He had been tempted for sure. Those negroes seemed to know how to protest for what was rightfully theirs. Dan didn't know the details well—he wasn't a great reader of the newspapers—but he had a dim awareness of boycotts and sit-ins and marches across bridges, and he thought

FINDING DAN

we could do with a bit of that here. Not bloody likely but. Even so, the Irish in America could be relied on to lend a hand, and dole out the cash, if a crisis could be arranged. Molly had been fit to share that with him. Good old Molly, true and angry as ever. I'd love to come over, Molly, but my leg. . . Truth was, he hadn't the money. Molly would have seen to the ticket, but he couldn't put his hand out to her for everything. Besides, they are snappy dressers in America, high rollers, go-getters. They respect a man who is light on his feet and knows where he is going. Forty years ago, Dan thought, that could have been me. You couldn't knock me back then. I had what it took then. But Dan was old and poor now, and New York was no place for the old and poor. Jim had gone instead. Molly sent the ticket and Jim took it. Maybe Jim had something then that Dan lacked, maybe Jim had more courage. Nobody would have said it, but now Dan was here and Jim was in the States still and that must stand for something.

Dan felt his heart ache. He gripped at the stabbing in his chest, and sat forward in his armchair to breathe more easily. A tear raced down one cheek. He wiped it away, shocked and embarrassed by it. He wanted to scream his pain out loud, but did not want the shame of it repeating from the walls. He had so much to say, but couldn't say any of it even to himself. He had had all the time in the world, and he had had not a soul in the world. He had told his story a thousand times, and not at all. His heart ached, he was in pain. 'Molly!' he managed to say, and he heard her name in his ears. This brought a new smile, or a grimace, to his face.

He was lying back in the armchair again, collapsed. He had told Molly all there was then. He had found all the truth there was to tell, and all the words there were to tell it, and he had shared it with Molly. He had bound her to it. She had wanted to tell others (she had especially wanted to talk to Old Joe), but she wouldn't because he had sworn her not to. He would go to his grave and she would go to hers and that would be an end to it. But what he wanted to tell her now was not this. If he could find all the truth there was now, it would not be the same. There might be words for it, but Dan was sure that he could not tell them. And worst of all, Molly was not there. Dan sensed that if his sister were only there now, he would not need words, it would be enough that he was not alone.

Dan's heart ached. It ached in its atria and ventricles. The ache was pulmonary, arterial and massive. It brought tears to his eyes again. He was bereft. His room was massive with its two doors, one window, two chairs and four walls, and him. It had capacity for many more, but it had only him, and so it would be. Youngsters flirted and played outside, and now and then, their playful laughter penetrated into his room. He had pulled his curtains against it.

Then the darkness rushed in, sweeping past the curtains, and shutting down the room. It blacked out the girls and the boys and their laughing and all other living sound. A coldness followed, in the wake of the dark, and bit at his fingers. The sun had been eclipsed, had been replaced.

Dan, collapsed in his armchair, hoped his visitor would come.

oooOOOOOOooo

The woman wrapped herself in her long serge coat and knitted scarf and hat, and grabbed her string bag from the hook in the kitchen. She said goodbye to the empty house before pulling the kitchen door shut, and walking down the long lane towards the main road, where she knew she could catch the bus into Dungannon.

She felt the hardness of the seats on her backside, and the bumps in the road and the fuel-filled air made her nauseous. She knew some of the other ladies and could tell from their chatter that they were looking forward to a day's haggling at the market. She held the empty string bag in both hands, twisting her fingers in and out of the holes, tying knots and releasing them again.

She would not say she was all that familiar with Dungannon itself, but she knew the way well enough. Through Edendork, past the dance hall, the crystal works, up and down, up the Oaks Road, round the White City. There was a bus stop at the top, and she felt safer walking from there. She didn't want to get so far into the town

FINDING DAN

that she wouldn't be able to get out again. Soon, she was among older, grander buildings, Georgian, from a time when Dungannon meant something more than it did now. She would be able to complete all her business here today.

She loosened her string bag and entered the cobbler's. There was just enough room to stand in front of the counter on which there was a new display of polishes and laces. From the workshop behind, she could hear the dull thuds and rapid spinning of the cobbler at work. There was no bell on the counter, so she stood and waited. She was in no hurry. She turned to look instead through the glass door. A woman with a child (who should have been at school); two old men on their way from or to a pub; a woman—a girl really—hurrying to her job, working in a shop; all these people, she thought, will be dead too one day.

The cobbler knocked the top of the counter to tell her he was there. He was dumb, his tongue out either because he was trying, or because he had given up trying. He licked one finger and pulled a slip of paper from his breast pocket to tell her she needed hers. She produced the docket from her coat pocket, and with this, the cobbler darted back into his workshop. Soon he re-emerged holding five fingers up, the minutes she would need to wait. He seemed to expect her to leave, come back later, but she was staying. She knew she would not want to hang around after her next job. She was happier where she was. Jim, her son, would never trust his work boots to any other cobbler. Her husband had been the same, claiming he had only ever bought one pair in his life: he had replaced the uppers a few times and the soles countless times, but to him, he had only ever worn the same boots. Jim was turning out the same.

She had the coins ready for the man when he came back out. He dropped the boots in her string bag, and thanked her with a bow. The bag now sagged alarmingly (she thought of ferrets in a sack). She wondered now whether it would not have been better if she had come back for the boots, given that where she was going was a rather formal sort of a place. But the man had already struck through her docket with a pencil stub, so it was too late.

There were women, she knew it, who would go into Dungannon for a cake and a cup of tea. Rather than sit at home, they would sit in a tearoom, often with a friend. The woman really wanted to do that right now even though she had never done it in her life before. She would have had to go in alone, but that was all right; and she did have the money on her, so that wasn't a problem. But to go to the tearoom she had in mind would involve going past the town hall, and it was the town hall she needed for her final errand. She would have her tea and ginger cake next time.

She had checked already with her husband where exactly she had to go. He would have come himself, only he was busy—in Tandragee or some such place—and this other business really couldn't be put off any longer. So it was down to her. It seemed only right, seeing as it was her who found him. It was the decent thing to do.

There were steps to climb into the town hall, rounded and bevelled. The revolving door spat her into a lobby whose carpet was too deep and too swept for her shabby shoes.

'Yes?' a voice found her from behind a deep mahogany desk.

'I'm here to register a death.' The woman had practised this line, and it served her well enough in this instance.

'Well, you've come to the right place, dear!' the voice came back, too jauntily. Reconsidering her tone, the receptionist concluded, 'Fill in this card for me, dear, and the registrar will be with you in . . . ' (she checked a wall-mounted clock, and then her own watch) ". . .in five minutes. Is that all right?'

The woman sat alone in a waiting area in the middle chair of five. A large corkboard covered the opposite wall with a few scanty notices. Something about the Housing Executive, someone's marriage banns.

'Hello, can I help you?'

'I'm here to register a death,' the woman said.

'Of course you are,' said the registrar, not unkindly. 'Won't you come in and take a seat.'

The woman took the seat opposite the registrar's desk. My husband would be impressed by the turn of these legs, she thought

FINDING DAN

to herself. *I like the leather top, a nice shade of green.* She had placed her bag of boots at her feet, but moved them now to one side out of the way. They kicked the wooden table leg, leaving a scuff.

'I can see you are a little nervous, which is natural. Were you close to the deceased?'

The woman blushed, embarrassed by the directness of the question. *What does he mean by close?* 'I was his sister-in-law. Is that close enough?'

'For our purposes, absolutely!' The registrar opened the ancient ledger. *I bet that could contain the history of just about everything,* the woman guessed. *Every person who died would go into that book. On the open shelves behind the official were other big books. All the births would go into those, and all the marriages too.* The woman was distracted by this for a moment, wondering if everyone in her family had found their way into those books or would do in the end. *What would it say about them?* 'Now, what was the name of the deceased?'

'Daniel O'Rourke.'

'Is that with a U and ending in E?'

'O'Rourke, yes!' The woman had never known another spelling of the name.

'And when did Daniel pass away?'

'Last Thursday.'

The registrar checked a desk calendar. 'Died, second November, nineteen hundred and sixty-seven. Yes? Was Daniel married ever, or was he widowed?' After the woman paused, apparently offended, the registrar pressed again. 'I'm sorry, these are standard questions.'

'Dan never married.'

'Fine, we'll say "Bachelor". And how old did you say he was?'

She hadn't said how old Dan was. She didn't really know how old he was. She tried to recall a birthday for him, but gave up. However, she didn't want to seem even more foolish in front of the official.

'He was sixty-six. He lived at 6 Ardmore Road, Coalisland.'

'Thank you, that's helpful. What did the deceased do for a living?'

The woman laughed because she thought the registrar had told a joke. Realising her mistake, she realised also that there was no true answer to the question.

'I suppose you would have to say Dan was retired. He did use to work for his father, but that was more than twenty years ago. And he'd help out my husband from time to time, you could say.'

'That's as a...?'

'Timber merchant.'

'Good. We'll say "Retired Timber Merchant". Almost there! Now, would you have anything on you from the doctor, giving cause of death? As that would be a great help. Oh, you do, that's great.'

The woman had found a folded note in her coat pocket. Checking it wasn't the docket from the cobbler, she passed it over.

'It says here 'Coronary Thrombosis. Was that right?'

'It looked that way to me.' The woman was unused to being asked her medical opinion. From the way Dan was slumped in his armchair, a heart attack looked the most likely thing.

The registrar carefully recorded this last in the ledger to avoid looking at the woman. 'Right, we are there! Now, could I ask you to sign and print your name here, please?' He pushed the book across the table towards the woman who also took hold of the fountain pen she was proffered. She signed quickly, and then more deliberately, printed her name, announcing each part: 'Phyllis. O'Rourke.'

'Is that all?'

'Yes, Mrs O'Rourke. We're finished. Thank you for coming in. Enjoy the rest of your day.'

Phyllis picked up her bag of boots and went to the door, where she paused. The registrar was already focused on his next chore, opening and closing the doors of a tall metal cupboard. Phyllis suddenly wanted to say more.

'I had to wait, you know, for the doctor to arrive, after I found him. I couldn't do anything, so I tidied up a bit and waited. His dinner was wasted, I had to throw it out.' The registrar, standing at the cupboard with an open file in his hand, said nothing. 'After a while, a wee lad from next door came in. Never seen him before in

FINDING DAN

my life, but he knew Dan sure enough. "Please, could I have Dan's cup, the one he made his penny chews in?" He stood there staring at Dan, as if he were asking him himself. I found a cup, any old cup, in the kitchen, and I found a ginger cake too, and I gave the lot to the boy. It was no good to Dan anymore, was it?'

'I suppose not, Mrs O'Rourke. That was a nice thing you did.'

Phyllis realised the registrar had spoken the last word. She reversed out the door, kicking the doorframe with the boots on her way. She passed the same woman on reception as before who looked again at the clock on the wall, satisfying herself that Phyllis had not taken up too much of the registrar's time. She smiled at Phyllis efficiently and professionally, and that saw her out of the building.

She was halfway to the bus stop before she remembered about the tea and cake. She could have treated herself, and no one would have been any the wiser. But she was on her way now, so she might as well carry on. The bus that picked her up was empty. She worried for a moment that it might not take her all the way, that it might instead be headed for the depot. She kept her eyes on the road, looking out for wrong turnings-off until eventually, she accepted she was indeed on the correct bus. As the bus accelerated and slowed, the boots in her string bag swung forwards and backwards, and it reminded her of when she was a little girl, and she would swing her school satchel way out in front and way out behind. It was a happy memory, and as there was no one else around, she didn't feel silly smiling about it now. She manoeuvred the bag out to the aisle between the seats to allow them a freer go, and she allowed herself a little laugh. Shame about the tea and cake, she thought, but all in all not a bad day. She let the driver know where to drop her off. As the bus drove on towards Coalisland, pulling along its cloud of black exhaust, she waved after it. She took a deep breath, pulled her scarf tightly around her neck for warmth, and started the long walk up the lane to Creenagh.